SLAVES ON HORSEBACK

ALLAN W CHAPMAN

AC WRITINGS
SOLANA BEACH, CA

Printed in the United States of America

FIRST EDITION

LCCN 2007904837

ISBN 978-0-9796780-1-1

We are all on a spiritual path. I thank God for opening my heart and the eyes of my soul as I have journeyed.
I pray you, dear reader, catch a glimpse of enlightenment as you engage in this journey.

"I have seen under the sun another evil, like a mistake that proceeds from the ruler. A fool put in lofty position while the rich sit in lowly places. I have seen slaves on horseback while princes walked on the ground like slaves."

Ecclesiastes 10: 5-7

SLAVES
ON
HORSEBACK

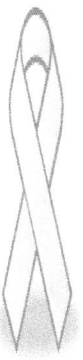

CHAPTER ONE

As the white stretch limousine swung off the main highway onto a barely paved road illuminated only by the car's headlights, I felt a wisp of fear creep over me like a slowly swirling fog. The fear became a stab as a huge pothole jarred the limousine to its frame. "Where are you taking me?" I demanded.

"To Las Palmas, as arranged." The driver spoke in a soothing tone. "But here in Puerto Rico, the main roads, only they get fixed. And after the rainy season..." Shrugging his shoulders, he left the sentence unfinished. Moments later the long limousine shuddered again as it smashed through another crater.

We bumped and rocked our way for two miles until we finally reached smooth new blacktop and the Las Palmas guardhouse. Four men suddenly materialized, all squinting in the blaze of the headlights. "Who are they?" I asked, my voice rising in panic.

"The tall one, the one with the mustache, is Inspector Lopez. He's FBI.

"The short, fat one," the driver continued, chuckling, "he is Lieutenant Carvajal of the local police here in Humacao. The other two work for the lieutenant. Don't worry. They're just checking identification and looking for bombs." He chuckled again. "I'll just lower your window."

"Hold it, not so fast" I ordered, regaining my composure. "I'll do it. When I'm good and ready."

Lopez strode up my side of the limo, and then shined his flashlight through the window, illuminating my face. Lopez produced his badge from his sports jacket side pocket, and then held it under the flashlight beam. I felt my stomach relax, and then I sighed and pushed the electric button to lower the window. A rush of warm, jasmine-scented air filled my air-conditioned sanctuary, a sharp contrast to the sub-freezing temperature of Manhattan I had left only five hours before.

"Good evening, sir," Lopez said, speaking slowly, in perfect American English, with no trace of an accent. "Your name, please."

"Nick Shepherd," I replied, my voice catching slightly.

"May I see your identification, please, sir?"

I was still amazed at the Inspector's perfect American as I withdrew my thick passport from my inside coat pocket. Lopez opened it and studied my photo. "It's you, all right, red hair and all. Looks as though you've picked up a little gray since the photo," he chuckled. Then he flipped through the accordion of pages, closed it, and passed it back through the window. "Thank you, Mr. Shepherd. I see you're a world traveler, so I'm sure you understand our need to take every precaution, particularly with you oil industry people. Get out of the car, please."

"No problem," I said as I opened the door, swung my long legs out, and stepped onto the new blacktop of the access road. "I'm certainly glad you're being so cautious," I added as I rose and stood eye to eye with the Inspector.

One of Lieutenant Carvajal's men strode up with a bomb detector and passed it over me. The driver opened the trunk, removed the luggage, and placed it on the macadam. The policeman passed the detector over the driver and then the luggage. He nodded to Lopez who smiled and said, "Thank you for your patience, Mr. Shepherd. The rest of your associates are already here."

"Thank you. I figured they would be." And I knew Melville and the others, some of whom I hadn't met yet, would be in the bar.

My winged-tip shoes clacked on the marble floor as I strode across the lobby to the reception desk. The scent of jasmine and the croaks of tree frogs permeated the air. Potted palms and hanging bromeliads added

2

to the sense of outdoors brought indoors. I checked in, tipped the bellman, and headed straight for the bar at the opposite end of the lobby.

I climbed three marble steps, and then turned right into the jammed, smoke filled room. I scanned the crowd a few moments, and then spotted an arm waving at the far end of the bar. I recognized Melville who shouted something, but I couldn't make it out above the din. He beckoned to me, and I squeezed my way through the throng. Melville grinned as I approached shouting, "Nick! You made it! I was beginning to wonder."

I returned the smile. "Not even two feet of snow could keep me away from a good party, Walt."

He laughed. "You were lucky you got out. Why didn't you fly down with me this morning?"

"Couldn't. I had a luncheon presentation to our domestic distributors. You remember our distributors."

"How could I forget?" he said, throwing up his hands. "As you know, our international distributors are a whole lot more grateful."

He waved the bartender over. "What are you drinking today, Stoly or Dewars?"

"Stoly," I told the bartender as he arrived. "Make it a double. It's a long ride from the airport."

"You can bring me another double Tanqueray," Melville added.

Then he turned to the short, overweight man standing to his right. "Harry, I want you to meet Calderone's replacement, Nick Shepherd. Nick, shake hands with Harry Hendricks of Rocky Mountain Oil."

"Welcome to the club, Nick," Harry said, extending his hand.

I shook his hand, saying, "Nice to meet you, Harry. You work for a first-rate company."

"Thank you. We're small, but powerful." I wondered if he was talking about himself as well.

"Yes, you are. When I was at International, I knew Barry Winslow well. You have very aggressive expansion plans overseas. Of course, we have to be careful what we discuss here in Domestic."

"Of course," Harry agreed.

During the next hour and several rounds of drinks, Melville introduced me to more oil company compatriots, most of them from the western states. "Well," he said, clapping me on the shoulder, "I'm turning in. Early to bed, you know. See you in the morning."

"See you then," I said. A few minutes later, I finished my drink, and then headed for my room.

My wristwatch alarm beeped at six the next morning. I slid into my running clothes, donned my running shoes, and then stepped out into the dawn light. I peered down the long stone stairway next to the front door and spied a macadam road, which appeared to run along the beach. I started bounding down the stone steps.

Halfway down, I heard a familiar voice behind me call, "Wait up, Nick!"

I turned my head to see the tall, muscular figure of Walter Melville speeding down the steps after me, his blond hair flopping up and down on his head. I paused, jogging in place until Melville caught up. "I didn't know you were a runner," Melville said as we descended the rest of the steps together.

"I ran in school," I said, "but I'm just now getting started again." I patted my stomach. "I've got to get rid of this banquet belly."

"There's no better way," Melville agreed. "I've been running ever since I was in the school myself. And believe me, it keeps up that competitive spirit." He grinned. "But I was just planning an easy day today. Do you want to run together?"

I shrugged. "Why not?"

"That was quite a crowd last night," Melville said as we headed out the beach road. "Our competitors and lawyers were at the bar. It was perfectly legal. I'll introduce you to some more of them at breakfast. But I'm leaving right after breakfast. Sullivan never attends these things anymore, so he wants me to meet him in Rotterdam tomorrow morning "

" I'll be getting to know everyone soon enough."

"You won't have to go it alone. You know Ed Shepherd from Legal is also here to represent the Company. Anyway, ... Say, I hope there's no ill will about my taking over International. We never really talked about it."

"No problem. I was getting tired of all that travel." I felt the bitterness welling within, but managed to smile and continue, "Besides, I like running Domestic better anyway."

An ephemeral look of surprise flashed across Melville's face. "You do?"

"Oh I know International has the high visibility, but I think Domestic Retailing is the challenge. Your old boss, Calderone, did a decent job when he was ... there ..." I was now beginning to pant, "but he ... was slipping. I think ... more ... can be done."

This time Melville smiled. "Well I'm glad you haven't lost your competitive spirit, Nick. And rest assured I'll be aiming to improve your performance."

I acknowledged the thrown gauntlet with a nod, and we ran without further conversation for a while. I finally broke out with a chuckle. My breathing was labored, but I no longer was gasping. "Actually, I thought you might be the one with hard feelings ... because I got Calderone's job instead of you."

Melville laughed without mirth. "Nope. No hard feelings ... How's Susan?"

"She's fine. She's at a writer's conference in San Francisco, looking for new talent."

Melville nodded, and we ran the rest of the way in silence.

At breakfast Melville led the way to a table already occupied by two others. "Nick Shepherd, say hello to Grady Benson of Southwestern and Jerry Wagner of Paramount. Nick is our new Vice-President of Domestic Sales and Marketing."

Benson shot me a conspiratorial look as we shook hands. "Welcome to the family, Nick. We've worked very well with Walt here, together with that old codger of a boss of yours. What's Sullivan's excuse for not coming this time, a bad case of the D.T.'s?"

"No, some problem in Rotterdam," Melville answered, chuckling. "And I'm on my way over there to fix it for him." We all laughed.

Wagner extended his hand to me. "I'm glad to see you again, Nick. We met in Riyadh, what, five years ago?"

"Five years ago, it was," I said, shaking Wagner's hand warmly. "It's good to see you, too."

"Sullivan's absent, but never mind," Wagner said. "We do all the work, anyway. Just ask Walt; he was number three, below Calderone, and he was the one who made things happen. All the corner office boys do is have delusions of grandeur."

After breakfast, Melville rose, shook hands all around, then turned to me saying, "Walk me to the door." When we were out of earshot, he continued, "It's good you know Jerry already. Stay close to him; he'll show you the ropes. He's right, you know; we did do all the work. Did Ed Shepherd talk to you before you left?"

5

"No."

"Never mind, he will. Remember, the whole program is based on the legally accepted practice of commodity exchanges."

I stared at Melville and my jaw dropped. "I don't believe it. It's still going on?"

"Got to run; the limo will be waiting. Remember, stay close to Jerry."

Chairman Yarhi Mamoodi, CEO of Trans-Arabian Oil Company, convened the U.S. Oil Institute meeting at 9 a.m. Mamoodi was an Arab running the only U.S. Company with private operations in the Middle East, and I had had several dealings with him. After a brief welcoming statement, he introduced Governor Rodriguez of Puerto Rico.

"It is indeed a pleasure," the Governor began, "to personally welcome you to Puerto Rico. We offer all the advantages of being part of the United States but have the lowest tax structure of any state or territory. I will explain this in greater detail, but first I have a few slides of our Island I would like to share with you."

He reached for the light control switch on the podium. Nothing happened. He pressed it again. Still, the lights remained on. He smiled, and then joked, "This must be an import. Would someone please turn off the lights?"

I sat in the rear, closest to the light switch. I rose, walked over to the far wall, and flipped the switch. Explosion and fire engulfed the room, hurtling me against the wall and into darkness.

CHAPTER TWO

As I drifted back into consciousness, I became aware of a dazzling light. My eyes were closed, and I wondered if I were dead. I slowly opened my eyes to the brilliance and at once, squeezed them shut. It was the sun, blazing straight into my face. I opened my eyes again, and then blinked repeatedly, trying to adjust to the glare. Finally, I turned my head away, and a searing pain shot across the base of my skull.

"Awake at last," said a diminutive, rotund man in the white guayabera standing at the foot of the bed. I squinted, but I couldn't make out the man's features. "Señor, you are one very, very lucky hombre."

The word that echoed in the confusion enveloping my mind was "lucky." I repeated the word aloud, questioning.

"Si, Señor Shepherd," responded the man. I recognized him as the Humacao police lieutenant, Caravajal. "*Unbelievably* lucky. Our beloved governor, and the rest of those people died, Señor. Except for you."

"Died?" I echoed, staring at Carvajal.

"Si, died. At Las Palmas." He spoke rapidly, his tone impatient.

I just blinked, feeling bewildered. I couldn't think. The pain in my head was excruciating. Finally, I managed to mumble, "I don't understand."

"Están muertos! Dead!" Carvajal shouted. "They were murdered! In the explosion!"

Suddenly the memory of the flash and the blast of the explosion erupted into my mind. "Oh my God I remember," I half-whispered. "What happened?" I asked.

"Come now, Shepherd," Carvajal said, his voice now replete with sarcasm. "You don't know what happened? They were your friends, weren't they?"

I nodded slowly.

"And you don't know who blew up your friends? Give me a break."

Images of body parts arose in my mind's eye. I closed my eyes as though to blank out the vision.

"Well, Señor Shepherd," Carvajal pressed on. "You were the only one not at the table."

My eyelids sprang open. "What the hell do you mean?" I bellowed.

"You know what I mean," Carvajal spat. "Exactamente."

Rage roared in my head, then swept through me like a typhoon. I struggled upright, but pain shot up my spine. I clutched my chest and fell back into the pillow, panic replacing the rage. Carvajal hesitated, studying me suspiciously, then finally grabbed the call button at the head of the bed and barked into it, "El Medico, pronto."

Seconds later the door flew open, banging against the wall, and a doctor and two nurses rushed over to the bed. "I can't move," I gasped.

The doctor pried my hands from my chest, jammed his stethoscope into his ears and slapped the cold monitor against my skin. As he listened, my panic rose even further. After a while, the doctor grunted, turned to Carvajal, and then spoke rapidly in Spanish. The lieutenant listened, then looked down at me derisively. "A good try, Señor, but your delaying tactics won't work. Your heart is okay."

"You son of a bitch!" I roared. "It's not my heart! I can't move my legs!" I grimaced as I struggled against the invisible force of paralysis.

Carvajal turned back to the doctor spoke in Spanish at blistering speed. Then the lieutenant faced me once again, saying, "The doctor examined you completely when they brought you in, and he found nothing wrong. He does not know why you cannot move. He thinks you may be suffering from…" He paused, then continued, "Como se dice…he called it traumatic shock."

"Perhaps the good doctor would explain what that means?" I growled.

Carvajal looked at the doctor, raising his eyebrows. The doctor turned his gaze to me, saying in perfect American, "I believe your mind has locked your legs. It's the shock of the explosion. You should recover in the next few days. I'm not certain, so I'll do some tests tomorrow. All you need is rest."

"Then get the lieutenant to leave me alone. I already told him I know nothing about what happened. No more questions." I closed my eyes.

"No more for now," Carvajal agreed. "You can be sure, Señor, I will return with more questions. And I strongly suggest you have the right answers." He left the room, followed by the doctor and nurses. I lay with my eyes closed for a few minutes, feeling exhausted. Then I dropped off to a deep sleep.

Later, the flash and crash of a lightning bolt jolted me from sleep. I awoke bewildered, not knowing where I was. I noticed the black of the window beyond the foot of my bed and the darkness of night beyond. Another flash of lightning split the sky and lit up the darkened room. Then I tried to move, and my lifeless legs catapulted the day's memories into my consciousness. "This did not happen," I said aloud, as though saying the words would erase the reality. But it did happen. I began to sift through the events of the day in search of clues.

Carvajal had said everyone died in the explosion, except for me. Was it a bomb? Probably. Someone had thrown it. No ... no... I concluded. The FBI, local police, and Las Palmas security officers had surrounded the conference room. The bomb was planted in the room.

But where? Why hadn't there been any ticking. Bombs were supposed to tick, weren't they?

I remembered the light switch. Had that detonated the bomb? My memory was sketchy. It had gone off a second after I had flipped the switch ...

A single knock interrupted my reverie. The door swung open, and Bruce Sullivan, President and CEO of Universal Natural Resources Company, strode in. "Hello, Nick," he said in an imperious tone. He stood right over me. I looked up at his ruddy face, complete with tiny broken blood vessels in his bulbous nose.

"Bruce," I said. "What ... what are you doing here?"

"I wanted to personally assess the situation. I happen to have had the Company plane with me, so when I heard about it this afternoon in Rotterdam, I headed straight here." He glanced down at his watch. "And in less than 10 hours.

"In any event," Sullivan continued, "I want to find the underlying cause of this. Right now. The police say you're a suspect."

"That's outrageous!" I exploded. "I know absolutely nothing about it!" I finished as though it were the final word on the subject.

Sullivan stared down at me long and hard. "If you are innocent," he said finally, "I'll get you out of here. After all—"

"What do you mean, if I'm innocent!" I interrupted.

Sullivan's stared at my face, as though hunting for a sign of guilt or innocence. "I want to know the truth."

"I already told you, Bruce, I don't know the first thing about it," I insisted.

The expression on Sullivan's face remained doubting. "Damn it, Bruce!"

Sullivan looked away. "I can't take that chance. UNRC is in the public eye. This can't appear to be a cover up. The slightest appearance of impropriety would torpedo our stock, and I simply can't afford to have that happen in this corporate takeover environment. I'll call for a full independent investigation."

He paused, and then continued, "In spite of the way I feel personally, I'll have to suspend you until the investigation is complete. If you are exonerated—"

"Bruce! That's liable to take months! I was not involved! Why would I want to kill them? I had friends in that room."

"I know people who don't let even friends stop them from getting what they want."

He turned to leave. "By the way, how do you feel?"

"Fine, except I can't move my legs."

"Don't worry, I'm sure you'll be up and around before you know it. And about that suspension, don't take it personally."

The next morning, I awoke to Carvajal and another Latino, who looked familiar, standing at the foot of my bed. "I have brought Inspector Lopez, of the FBI," Carvajal said, his tone sullen.

"Good morning, Mr. Shepherd," Lopez greeted me. "I'm glad to see you again. I hope you are feeling better."

I recognized the perfect American English accent as belonging to the Agent who had questioned me the night I arrived at Las Palmas. The previous night's medication had dissipated. I wasn't in any mood questions. I said nothing.

"Inspector Lopez has a few questions for you," said Carvajal, glowering at me. "Maybe you will answer the FBI."

I struggled to lift my head from the bed, saying in exasperation, "I'm tired of all these damn questions." I lowered my head back down.

"Relax, Mr. Shepherd," Lopez reassured. "You don't have to answer any questions you don't want to. Besides, we have a lead which removes suspicion from you."

Now that piqued my interest. I raised my head. "You have a confession."

Lopez nodded, and then said, "In a way, I suppose we do. The P.P.I.P. Have you heard of it?"

"What's that, some new government agency?"

Lopez laughed. "Hardly. Although I do admit we have our renegade agencies No. The P.P.I.P., translated into English, stands for the Popular Political Independence Party."

"No, I don't think I ever heard of it. What is it?"

"It's a new terrorist group," Lopez began "It operates here on the Island and in other major cities on the Mainland. They're committed to forcing Puerto Rican Independence. Until now, they've limited their activities to bank robberies and kidnapping to raise money."

"Until now?" I asked, pushing the bed control button, and raising my head further.

"Yesterday," Lopez began, raising his index finger, then pointing it at me, "fifteen minutes before the bomb exploded, a man identifying himself as being from the P.P.I.P. telephoned the *San Juan Star*." Lopez was jabbing his finger toward me with every word. "He warned that the heart of Yankee Imperialism would be cut out of the United States cadaver at 10 a.m. And then, fifteen minutes later ...boom!"

I shuddered as the image of the blast swept into my mind. Carvajal strode from the end of the bed over to me and hovered. "How much did they pay you?" he shouted. His dark face was now even darker with rage.

Inspector Lopez scrambled to Carvajal's side and took him by the arm, pulling him back. "Easy, Benito," he soothed. "I know how close you were to Governor Rodriguez." His gaze shifted to me, studying my

11

face. Then he nodded as he said, "I think Mr. Shepherd was just another victim."

Relief surged through my body, and I closed my eyes, took a deep breath, and then exhaled through my mouth. I liked Lopez. A few seconds later, I opened my eyes to see the Inspector nodding his head again.

"Yes," Lopez said, " I really do believe he was just another intended victim. Besides, Benito, how do we know that 'the heart of Yankee Imperialism' meant the Governor? The oil industry pumps a lot of life into us as well."

Carvajal had relaxed and was straightening himself up. "Perhaps you are right, Ricardo. You usually are right with your hunches."

Lopez extended his hand to me, and I shook it. "I'll be in touch," he said. He and Carvajal then turned and left.

I had just finished slurping my lunch of chicken noodle soup when the door swung open. "Hi, Nick," my wife said, smiling as she strode over to the bed and kissed me lightly on the lips.

"Hello, Susan," I responded. "Thanks for coming. I know how important that conference was for your career."

Susan drew back her head, and then shook it back and forth. "My God! You were practically killed, and you're talking as though I'm squeezing you into my appointment schedule! My job, no job, is that important! We're talking life and death here!"

"Don't be so melodramatic. And that conference was important to you. You've had two successive flops, and I know how that boss of yours, Harris, is. You must discover a new Robert Sand. Don't you care about that?"

"Maybe I don't. It's just a job. There are more important things. Let's stop talking about our business lives for once and tell me how you are."

"Stop mothering me," I said with a wave of my hand. "I'll be all right. I must get back to the office." I felt myself wincing as I strained to move my legs.

"Nick, what's wrong?" Susan asked, alarm in her voice, and her hand reaching out to touch my shoulder.

"Don't touch me! I said I'd be all right. I just have some temporary paralysis."

"What!" Susan asked, looking astounded.

I plopped my torso back on the bed, my stomach muscles weak from my struggle to move, and feeling like a small boy despite myself. "Yea," I murmured. "They said something about shock to the Third C in my neck when I hit the wall."

"You hit the wall? You must have been terrified."

"I thought I was dead," I admitted, feeling strangely exposed.

"It is a miracle you're alive."

I cleared my throat as I regained my composure. "I'm sure I'll be back in the office in a couple of days. There's nothing organically wrong. Don't worry about me; if you want to worry about something, try worrying about keeping your job." I turned my head away and gazed out the window. Immediately, I regretted my words.

"When are you going to stop?" Susan exploded. "You want nothing but work for us. What happened to the us we were in school?"

"That was then," I said, suddenly feeling sad. "Now is now."

"And now all that matters to you is getting Sullivan's job when he retires. You're worried Walter Melville has the inside track, now that he has your old job in International, even though your Domestic Division is far larger. And you've been studying finance so that you can be as qualified as Casey who is, by your own admission, the best chief financial officer in the oil industry. You want to know the law like Stockton and science like Hudson. Shall I go on?"

"No," I murmured." I get your point."

"No," Susan countered, "I really don't think you do. Business fills all your time. The only hobby you have is golf and, except when you play with your doctor friend, Dick Jameson, that's all business too. You've been promising for years to teach me how to play, but you haven't made the time. And bridge—we used to play all the time in school. We haven't played since."

Susan suddenly shivered. She shook her head. "Something's wrong with this picture," she said.

I turned my head back towards Susan. "With yours, but not with mine. I'm perfectly fine with my life. Business is my life. I thought it was yours, too ... But ... go learn golf. Join the bridge club, if that will make you happy."

Susan sighed. "What's the use? It's like talking to a deaf person. If you need me, I'll be at the hotel. I'll be back later this afternoon."

"Don't do me any favors," I muttered. "You'd just pick a fight, anyway. Just leave me alone."

Susan stared at me in anger, then wheeled around and stormed off toward the door. When she reached it, she stopped, and then turned back. "Someday you're going to push me too far."

At 6 o'clock that evening, I awoke to the sound of footsteps on the linoleum floor. I blinked my eyes open to see Susan standing next the bed. "You came back," I mumbled sleepily.

"Are you any less grumpy?" Susan asked.

Anger snapped me fully awake. "See!" I bellowed. "There you go again! Picking a fight! Just like always!"

"Well, you've answered my question," Susan said sarcastically.

"Then you can leave," I said.

Susan shrugged her shoulders, and then turned. "Wait," I said. "Don't go. I guess I am a little grumpy."

Susan turned back towards me. "Are you okay?"

"I feel fine, but the orthopedic surgeon wants me to stay here so he can run a battery of tests just in case there is something organically wrong. In case! It can't be in my head. I want to get on my feet. Now that the FBI has cleared me, Sullivan wants me back. I've got to get back on my feet—fast! But I want to go home to Greenwich, to a real doctor!"

"Nick. Please. Relax. Puerto Rico is part of the U.S., you know. And this hospital has an excellent reputation."

I shrugged my shoulders and looked up at the ceiling. "I'm getting out of here," I said simply. "Watch me."

"I am, too. Tomorrow. I called Harris from the hotel, and he made it really clear he wanted me in the back in the office at once, if not sooner."

"I agree with Harris," I said, but I felt vaguely sad once again. "The job comes first. I'm glad you came to your senses and are going back."

"Well," Susan said, smiling, "I'm not sure I did come to my senses. Immediately after I hung up the phone with Harris, I went out and took a golf lesson. I really enjoyed it, and the pro said I had a great natural swing."

CHAPTER THREE

Three days later, I was on my way to the San Juan Airport in an ambulance. After clearing security, we swung onto the tarmac and moments later pulled up near the UNRC corporate jet. The two attendants emerged, opened the rear door, and then lifted me from the gurney into the waiting wheelchair. "It's great to see a familiar face, Ron," I said to the co-pilot who stood behind the wheelchair, steadying it.

"I'm glad to see you as well, Mr. Shepherd," Ron said, as he began to push the wheelchair towards the aircraft.

"Is Hap in the left seat, as usual?" I asked.

"Of course. You're his best customer."

"And is Inspector Lopez here yet?"

"Yes, he's waiting inside, out of this sun. Personally, I'm enjoying this heat, particularly after what we left behind in White Plains."

"Oh? Cold?"

"And snow. Lots of it. The snowplows were barely able to keep up with it. We were lucky to get out."

When we reached the bottom of the aircraft stairway, Ron and the two attendants lifted me out of the chair and struggled up the narrow stairway, into the low ceiling cabin, and finally into the seat next to Inspector Lopez.

"Good morning, Mr. Shepherd. I want to thank you for arranging our little meeting here—I've been up to my eyeballs in our San Juan office and haven't been able to get away."

I nodded. "No problem. I'm interested in hearing about your progress; you mentioned on the phone you had a breakthrough on the P.P.I.P."

The Inspector smiled. "Not exactly a breakthrough. The *San Juan Star* reporter had the presence of mind to tape the P.P.I.P caller's voice. Yesterday one of our voice experts in Washington identified the caller as being a Puerto Rican from Spanish Harlem in New York. It's not much of a lead, but it is a start. I'll be flying back tomorrow to follow it up."

"Back? Are you from New York?"

"Born and raised. I've only been on temporary assignment down here, working on this terrorism case. I'll be returning to my Manhattan base."

The Inspector reached inside his guayabera shirt pocket and withdrew a card. "If you remember anything, and I mean anything, give me a call, day or night. My wife doesn't like it, but my home number is on the card."

He rose, shook hands with me, and headed for the cabin door, hunching forward as his head just cleared the low cabin ceiling. Then he disappeared.

Ron closed the door and then Hap fired up the two engines. We taxied to the end of the runway, then, after receiving takeoff clearance from the tower, the compact powerful jet sped down the blacktop and rocketed into the rich blue cloudless sky.

Forty-five minutes later, Hap emerged from the cockpit. "Sorry I couldn't get back here sooner, but it's been pretty busy up there."

"So I imagined. Ron was telling me about the severe weather up East."

Hap pointed towards the window. "You can see the southern edge of the cold front just coming into view. We're off the coast of Florida—500 miles off, but it's due west. The citrus growers will lose most of their crop."

I looked out the tiny porthole down to the blue-green ocean far below. Along the edge of the horizon, as far in either direction as I could see, a white cloud cover appeared to be rushing towards us. "I guess we're in for a bumpy ride," I said.

"We'll be above it for most of the way, but when we come down, it'll be interesting,' Hap responded in his typical understatement.

"Is it still snowing at White Plains airport?" I asked.

"It stopped about an hour ago, but the satellite photos show a bit more snow on the way. The runway is clear now, so they should stay ahead of the new snow." He paused. "We've got some sandwiches on board and, of course, a fully stocked bar. May I ask Ron to bring you something?"

"I don't feel much like eating, but I sure could use a drink if we're in for an 'interesting' a ride as I think we are."

"Scotch, I presume?"

"You presume correctly. Stoly's only for the summer."

Two hours and four scotches later, I dozed off. I slept fitfully, dreaming off and on of sand trucks and ambulances.

A violent jolt thrust me into full consciousness. I whipped my head towards the window, and saw nothing but thick, impenetrable whiteness. The plane was buffeted sharply twice more, then suddenly the whiteness cleared and the sun flashed into my eyes. "Sorry about that," Hap said over the intercom. "I had a little trouble finding this pocket. We'll be all right for a few minutes, but then we'll run into a few more squalls before we touch down."

As Hap had predicted, it was calm for a short while, but then, once again over the intercom, Hap's voice warned, "Hang on!"

Moments later we fell precipitously for several seconds, and I clutched instinctively to the armrests. Then suddenly we were thrust upwards, sucked by the storm's updraft. The violent wind hurtled the snow past the window vertically.

The tiny jet bucked and fishtailed through the impenetrable whiteness for several more minutes. Then we finally broke through the clouds, and the black strip of runway stretched immediately before us, hewn out of the plowed mountains of snow on either side of it. Ten seconds later the jet slammed onto the runway, bounced three times, then fishtailed until Hap slowed it enough to bring it under control. As we taxied towards the terminal and ambulance that was waiting, I called out in the crispest tone I could muster, "Nicely done, Hap."

Fifteen minutes later one of the Greenwich Hospital ambulance attendants finished tucking the blankets around me on the gurney, then called up to the driver, "We're all set back here, Bart."

"Right you are, Jerry," Bart responded.

As Bart pulled out, Jerry continued, "It's a real mess on the roads, Mr. Shepherd. The snow has stopped, but gale winds have whipped up, and the temperature's dropped to 16 degrees. The snow is drifting from the banks back onto the roads and the salt isn't doing much good at this temperature. Those roads are like glass. But don't worry. We made it up here just fine, and we'll make it back. This here buggy holds the road like a tank."

As we moved slowly along, I spotted several cars off the road through the rear windows of the ambulance. In some cases, a car was by itself; in others the accident looked like a demolition derby. "I've *never* seen anything like this," I said, incredulous.

After slowly picking our way around the plethora of cars stalled, crashed, or abandoned on the road, we reached the big hill on Lake Avenue. Bart downshifted, and then began the descent. As the ambulance began to gather speed, Bart started pumping the brakes, but we continued to accelerate. We swerved to the left, and Bart whipped the steering wheel to the left as well to correct the skid, shouting, "We've lost our brakes!"

The ambulance slid to the right gaining even more speed, and seconds later, we smashed into the side of an abandoned car, spun around 360 degrees, and then continued rushing down the hill.

Bart swung the steering wheel once again to the left to correct for our left swerve, then quickly to the right as we spun towards the right ditch. We continued to hurtle down the hill.

Bart flipped the steering wheel back and forth in quick succession, but our speed had become so great, he could no longer control our skids, and we began spinning wildly. The ambulance flew off the edge of the road, flipped over, and landed on its roof in the ditch below. The gurney sailed into the air inside the ambulance, smashing my head against the roof and into unconsciousness.

When I opened my eyes, Susan was standing by the side of my bed. My head pounded painfully with my every heartbeat. I looked around the room without moving my head. "Greenwich Hospital?" I guessed.

"Yes," Susan confirmed, as she reached over and pressed the nurse's call button. "And Doctor Jameson wanted to know right away when you regained consciousness. I was really worried about you. You've been unconscious a long time."

Slowly I moved my head to the left, looking for a window. As it came into view, I saw nothing but darkness beyond it. "It looks like midnight," I said, amazed. "What time is it?"

Susan glanced down at her watch. "You're not far off-it's 10:35."

"My God! The last thing I remember it was around 1:30, and we were screaming down Lake Avenue. With all this snow, I'm surprised we're not still in that ditch. How did anybody find us? We had to have been out of sight from the road."

"Actually," Susan said in a profoundly serious tone, "You're all very lucky to be alive. Dr. Jameson said you would have been killed on impact if it hadn't been for all that snow in the ditch to cushion the crash. The two ambulance men were unconscious several hours also. If the man on the snowplow hadn't seen your accident happen and radioed for help, you would have frozen to death. The temperature's dropped to 2 below zero."

I shivered. "That *was* lucky. And Jerry and Bart, the other guys in the ambulance, are all right?"

"Well, Dr. Jameson believes you all received concussions, and the driver has a broken arm, but," Susan smiled, "now that you're awake, nothing really serious happened."

Just then, the door swung open and Dick Jameson strode in. "Ah," he breathed, "the patient is awake. How are you feeling, Nick?" he asked, as we shook hands. "You must have one terrific headache."

"You've always had a firm grasp of the obvious, Dick."

"Oh, well. You must be on the mend. Your tongue is as sharp as ever. And the next thing I'll know, you'll be wanting to try your hand again at besting me on the golf course."

I lifted my head from the pillow and craned it forward. "Not in this weather. And not with these legs. I still can't feel them."

He reached down and patted my leg, smiling. "Don't worry, Nick, we'll get them moving. We'll start the tests tomorrow. It's either organic or psychological, and we'll simply find out which. Then we can go from there."

"Dick, I'm telling you; it's got to be organic. I'd know if it were in my head."

A serious expression spread across my friend's face. "I've seen the mind do the most amazing things, both positive and negative. I've seen iron will overcome the deadliest of organic afflictions, and I've also seen a negative will destroy the healthiest of bodies. I just ask you to keep an open mind."

"All right all right," I said with a wave of my hand, my words belying my true feelings.

I was sure Dick knew I was just putting him off, but he didn't challenge me. He simply said, "See you in the morning."

"Listen to what he said," Susan said after Dick left. "Try to move your legs," she urged.

"I just got through saying I couldn't feel them," I snapped. "Don't you listen to anything I say?"

"Yes, Nick," Susan said with a sigh, "I do listen to you. I just thought that with this accident..., something might have happened–"

"You mean," I interrupted, putting my hand to my head, "this little bump on the head may have brought me to my senses. This paralysis is all in my head, right?" Without waiting for an answer, I plunged on. "Let me tell you something. I can't walk because something happened to my body, and these fool doctors can't find it."

Susan touched me on the shoulder. "Remember what that specialist in Puerto Rico said—"

I pushed her hand away. "That quack? Damn Neo-Freudian."

Susan replaced her hand. "Now come on," she said, an edge of exasperation in her voice. "All he suggested was that your paralysis is caused by something you've repressed and you're unwilling to face. We all hide from unpleasant things. It's only natural."

I glanced down at Susan's hand, then back to her face. "Well," I said, "I still think it's organic."

Susan patted my shoulder. "Perhaps. If it is, I'm sure your friend, Doctor Dick, will find it."

Two evenings later I awoke from a nap to see not only Susan by the bedside, but also Inspector Lopez. They were talking in whispers. "How long have you been here?" I asked, my voice still groggy with sleep.

The Inspector turned his head towards me and grinned. "Ah, Mr. Shepherd. Good evening. I'm glad to see you. I've only just arrived here.

Susan's been telling me about the tests they've been conducting—they haven't found anything either."

"They wil....What are you doing here? Arresting Mad Dog Shepherd?"

"Mad Dog Shepherd," Lopez laughed. "That does have a certain ring to it." Then his expression became serious. "No. On the contrary. I've come to ask for your help. As I told you in Puerto Rico, I'm convinced you were a victim, just like everyone else in that room when the bomb went off."

I shuddered. "I still can't believe the whole thing happened."

"Believe it. And I need your help to find the people behind it. You're the key. Somebody wanted you dead. Just you. And they murdered a roomful of people to get to you."

"Me?" I said, exasperated. "That's ridiculous. I thought the P.P.I.P. claimed responsibility. Didn't they want to rip out the heart of Yankee Imperialism?"

Lopez picked up the file from his lap, saying, "I've been studying everything we have on them which depicts a pretty small, crude organization. That bomb was simply too sophisticated for them. In fact, it's highly unlikely they even knew of the existence of this new explosive—I'm even having a tough time finding out about it."

"Then, Inspector, how did they know about the bombing before it happened?"

"Call me Ricardo. We may as well use first names, since we'll be working closely together, for a long time. Anyway, Nick, that is part of the mystery. I've been looking for a clue in this file that would show they could have had access to the explosive, but they have neither the money nor the organization. It's just implausible for them to have gotten their hands on it. My working theory is that some person or persons knew your schedule, knew when to plant the explosive in your briefcase, and blew everyone up to disguise that he was after you."

I rolled my eyes up and looked at the ceiling. "Come off it, Ricardo! My briefcase? That's preposterous!"

"Not so preposterous. Especially if you consider your ambulance was no accident."

"What?" both Susan and I echoed.

"You both heard me correctly. I believe the brakes on that ambulance had been tampered with. And a very neat job, too. I can't tell for sure. There's a hole in the brake fluid line that could have been natural, or it could have been induced. The fluid had leaked out completely when you got to the hilly section of Greenwich. If I hadn't called in the local Bureau branch to check it out, it would have gone unnoticed."

"I can't believe it," I said, raising my head back off the bed.

"I can't either," Susan said. "Who in the world would want to kill you?"

"I can't imagine. Oh, sure, I've had a few personality conflicts, particularly overseas, but I never wanted to kill anyone, nor do I think anyone was mad enough to want to kill me."

I shifted my gaze back to Ricardo. "No," I said, shaking my head, "I think you're mistaken." I plopped my head back onto the bed.

"Well, we've got to find the underlying cause of this. Fast. If I'm right, these people won't stop at anything—blowing up this hospital, or even your whole office building. You've got to help me, and you can't do that lying here flat on your back."

"But...but...I'm paralyzed." I struggled to fight the rising panic as I realized Ricardo was right.

"Look, Nick, I'm no doctor, but I've talked to enough of them in your case, plus my experience in other cases, to believe that the key to your walking again is in your head."

I glowered at him but said nothing.

"I don't know what you're afraid of," Ricardo continued. "Maybe you just wanted to remove yourself from the competition for a while. What matters is that you're a stationary target confined to this bed. If I were you, I'd stop playing sitting duck, make up your mind to get on your feet, and find the son-of-a-bitch who's trying to kill you."

"I know you can do it," Susan chimed in. "You've never taken anything lying down."

Susan was right; Ricardo was too. I began contracting my stomach muscles and slowly raised my torso until finally I could support it with my elbows. I felt light-headed from the struggle.

"Way to go, Nick," Ricardo said. "Get back in the game!"

Suddenly my legs began tingling. "I can feel them!" I shouted.

"Come on, Nick" Ricardo urged, as he and Susan pulled down the blankets and sheet. "Let's go get him!"

I strained my right leg and was rewarded with a slight movement. "That's it!" Ricardo cried. "You can do it!"

Then I pushed off with my elbows and swung both legs over the side of the bed. Ricardo grabbed my left arm and Susan my right, as I slowly pushed with my legs until I was standing.

"Come on." I said, taking a tentative step with my right leg. "Let's get the bugger before he gets me.".

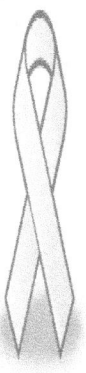

CHAPTER FOUR

The following Monday morning, I caught the 7:06 express train to Manhattan. By 7:55 I was spinning my way through the revolving door into my office building on Park Avenue at 46th Street. I took the express elevator to the 39th floor. As usual my secretary was already at her desk, sipping her coffee. She rose slowly as I approached and extended her hand. "Why Mr. Shepherd, what a pleasant surprise! I heard you wouldn't be back for a while."

I shook her hand once, and then released it. "There's much work to be done, Liz."

I glanced down at my Rolex, which read exactly 8 o'clock. "Is Elliot in yet?"

Liz blushed slightly. I suspected she and Elliot had more than a professional relationship. "Why yes. Mr. Elliot is in his office."

"Call him and tell him I shall attend the staff meeting this morning. Is it in the Board Room?"

"Yes. At 10 o'clock as usual. But Mr. Shepherd, you have a mountain of mail and enough phone calls to return to fill the Manhattan directory. Mr. Elliot is fully prepared, and he can represent you very well."

I glared at her and wished that Pat were still my secretary, not my administrative assistant. "Call Elliot," I ordered.

She hesitated momentarily, and then responded, "Yes sir."

"I presume Pat isn't in yet..."

"I've never seen her here before 9," was the snide reply.

"As soon as she gets in, tell her I want to see her right away."

I strode into my office, pulled out my chair from underneath the desk, sat down, and then rolled forward. I flipped open the bulging "Priority" file and leafed through the sheets of paper until I came to the Inventory/Sales Report. I first studied the Company figures, reported by region, and then turned to the industry statistics. Finally, I scanned the International Numbers, to watch my former area of responsibility, to understand the complete picture. Separately and totally, they all read the same—oil and oil products had reached all-time high inventory levels. And the glut was accelerating.

There was a firm knock on the door. "Come in," I called.

The door opened, and I glanced up as Pat walked in. I scarcely ever noticed her, because there's always so much to do. But this morning I looked at her as though I was seeing her for the first time. She had rich, auburn hair, which cascaded around her freckled face, accentuated with high cheekbones and full lips.

"You're back, Nick!" she chortled. "Am I ever glad to see you! That fool Elliot was driving me nuts!"

"I'm back, " I said, "and we've got a monumental task ahead of us. Is that suit new?"

"No. I've had it a couple of months. I bought this and two others on sale at Brooks."

I shrugged. "I haven't noticed—I've been really preoccupied.... Anyway, we are swimming in excess oil, and we've got to find ways to move it."

"Yes, I've been noticing those inventory figures."

"Well, the first thing we're going to do is cut the price and drive for market share. And as a corollary, I want to re-institute promotions."

"Promotions?"

"You know, free football glasses, Disney tickets, that sort of thing. As I recall, Melville ran a few several years ago, so get with Liz and see if you can find the files."

I noticed a slight color rise in Pat's face as I continued, "And see what Liz can find on Research and Development expenditures."

"R and D will be no problem, but the Promotion files will take a few days. They would be in the Archives, in Pennsylvania."

"Damn! That rotten Records Retention System! You can never get anything when you want it!"

At 9:55 I pulled opened the solid oak door to the boardroom. Sullivan was seated at the far end of the long, mirror finished mahogany table, hunching forward in conversation with Walter Melville who was seated to his right. He rose as I closed the door behind me. "There he is," Sullivan boomed. "I heard you were back. It's good to see you."

I walked across the room to where Sullivan was standing, my feet sinking into the thick pile carpet. "It's good to see you, too, Bruce," I echoed, shaking Sullivan's hand. "It's great to be back on my feet." I turned to Melville, shaking his hand as well. "How are you, Walter?"

"Just fine, Nick. You're looking quite fit. I heard you were in bad shape—paralysis, wasn't it?"

"Just temporary. I feel quite fit now, thank you, Walter."

"Well, it's good to have you back," Sullivan said. "There's lots of work to be done. I'm glad the FBI cleared your name. They think is was some terrorist group, huh?"

"Yes," I lied, heeding Ricardo's warning not to trust anyone. "They figured they'd call attention to their cause."

The door opened, and three more members of the Executive Staff filed in, all coming over to welcome me back. At precisely 10 o'clock all the members were present and were seated in the overstuffed swivel chairs.

"I see we're all here," Sullivan began, "so let's get started. It no secret, gentlemen, that we've got a hell of an oversupply situation facing us. OPEC is involved in an internecine fight, and no one is cutting back production. To make matters worse, consumers are continuing to conserve at record rates, to say nothing of this year's car models and their more efficient engines. Prices and profits are in a free-fall. It's no wonder nobody wants our goddamn stock. What are we going to do? Nick, what about the Domestic U.S. side?"

I had fully expected the question. I knew Sullivan. All business. No excuses. He demanded all his people be completely up to date always, regardless of travel schedules, systems breakdowns, or even terrorist bombings. It was always business as usual.

"I've been reviewing the numbers this morning, Bruce," I began, "and I find striking similarities between now and ten years ago."

"How so?' Sullivan asked. I knew that Sullivan could have answered his own question, but I played his game.

"Both then and now we have a recessionary environment. We have record oil production. We have new discoveries on an upward trend line. We have price wars."

"I know all this," Sullivan interrupted. "Tell me something I don't know."

"You may not know that in both periods the industry has spent less money on Research and Development than the prior year." I felt beads of perspiration forming in my armpits.

Sullivan raised his eyebrows as he asked, "Is that a fact?"

"Yes, Bruce. And the parallels don't end there. Ten years ago, Zenith Oil launched their mileage extender, Petroblend, and their market share doubled in twelve months. As you know, we've been working on our premium formulation which we believe will increase a car's mileage by 20 per cent."

"We want more gasoline consumption, not less!" Sullivan bellowed.

I steeled myself further against my rising temper. I felt the perspiration starting to run down both sides of my body. "Bruce—" I stopped, as anger edged into my voice. "We need," I resumed, my voice now back to normal, "to go for market share. We'll be going for a patent and thereby excluding our competitors. It is true we'll be reducing total consumption, but we'll be able to increase sales at the expense of our competitors. And, more importantly, we'll be able to charge a premium price and increase our margins."

Sullivan nodded, and then leaned forward in his chair. "When can we be ready to roll it out?"

"Well, Bruce, Hudson tells me there are still a few bugs to work out to bring it into compliance with EPA regulations. And then there's the Patent process—"

"I don't want excuses," interrupted Sullivan. "I want to know when we can go to the market with it."

"Minimum of six months."

"You may not be here that long. I want to know what you're going to do right now to regain our lost market share."

"I'm going to introduce promotional programs throughout our entire marketing channel, from the independent distributors to our direct consumers."

"Promotions!" roared Sullivan. "Are you crazy? That bomb must have affected your brain! You're supposed to slash costs, not run them up." He turned to his right, saying, "Walter, why don't you tell us what you're doing in International. I think Mr. Shepherd here could learn something."

"Offshore," Melville began, addressing the room at large, "we've got the same market forces at play as we do here. We all know price is determined by the relationship between supply and demand, and, since we've been unsuccessful in stimulating demand, the only way we have left is to control supply."

"Remember what OPEC did," interrupted Sullivan.

Melville looked over at me. "For those of you who weren't here then, OPEC reduced supply during the Arab Oil embargo, and they were able to manipulate price."

He turned back to the room at large. "I've been running my division for less than six months, but one of the first things I noticed was that the world still fears shortages. I began ordering delays in shipments, as well as circuitous tanker routings. These late deliveries have created the illusion of tightening supply. The net result is that most of our brokers and refiners offshore are buying at our higher contract price rather than buying at the lower spot levels offered by our competitors. They don't want to cut us off now, because they know we won't sell to them if the tight market returns and they're not on the active customer books."

He paused, and then looked back at me. The son of a bitch was positively gloating. "I'll concede that our Offshore brokers and refiners are fewer and more easily influenced that our Domestic ones. But I know those guys well. I believe the threat to cut them off when tight supply returns will be as effective here as it has been internationally. If you like, I'll give you a hand with them."

"That won't be necessary," I said quickly. "I know just how to do it. I'll start with a couple of the independent refiners with the biggest mouths, say Eagle and Pueblo. I'll tell them production capacity is being retired and if they don't resume buying now, we'll refuse to sell them next year. That word will spread like wildfire."

"That's the Nick I remember," Sullivan approved.

"At the same time," I continued, "I'd suggest a discount beverage promotion in two bellwether test markets, say California and Connecticut to see if the increased sales offset the promotion costs. If successful, we'll go national."

Sullivan looked over at Casey, the Chief Financial Officer and asked, "What do you think, Ted?"

"Well, the cost of that sort of promotion would be minimal, particularly if we could swap our products for the beverages from the producing companies on a national scale."

"O.K., Nick. Run it for a quarter, and then let's review it. And by that time, I want to launch the new fuel."

I felt my anger stir once again. "That would be premature, Bruce. It won't be ready for at least six months, to say nothing of the patent process!"

"We will get the patent later," Sullivan responded, speaking slowly, and emphasizing every word. "I want to roll that product out in 90 days. And I don't care what you have to do to achieve that."

I felt my face flush. Finally, I said, "As you say, Bruce. We'll get on it 24 hours a day."

"See that you do. Or I'll get someone who can."

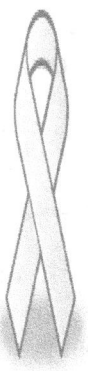

CHAPTER FIVE

     I caught the 4:40 from Grand Central Station to Greenwich. The days were getting longer with the approach of spring, and it was still light as the train left the Bronx. Inexplicably my mind wandered from R and D status report in my hands, and I found I was peering through the grimy window as we gained speed. Early spring buds were bursting through their green covers on the cherry trees. Crocuses had pierced the earth in search of the warming sun. Patches of new green grass dotted the winter brown of the city park.

     As the landscape swept by, I suddenly remembered my first ride on this train as a boy of nine. I was riding with my mother, going up from New York to Greenwich to visit my father's sister, Aunt Doris. "We're going to buy a new home," my mother had said, "and you and I are going to pick it out, all by ourselves. Daddy's going to be away in Europe for a month." My father was in the oil business and was always gone. And then he had had that heart attack, but still didn't slow down. And then he had the second, fatal one....

     I wrenched my thoughts back to the present. Sullivan. The ruthless son of a bitch. I felt my blood stir as I remembered the morning's altercation with him. He was always on someone's case. Someday he may push too far and have a palace revolt on his hands.

As I drove out the freshly resurfaced and relined North Street, I lowered all four windows my black Jaguar, letting in the fresh spring air, which was still warm.

I stopped for the mail at the bottom of the driveway, discovering the latest issue of *Golf Digest*. I had been renewing the subscription for years, but I couldn't remember the last time I'd read it. I had to get back out on the course. I vowed to call Dick Jameson and set up a game on Saturday.

I looked up the driveway at the massive French Colonial reproduction, now silhouetted by the setting sun. Susan and I had been in a comfortable clapboard ranch less than a mile away, but I really wanted more space. "Why do we need six bedrooms?" Susan had asked me when we were designing the plans. "You don't want any children."

"Overseas guests," I had said. "In my new job running the International Division, I'll be hosting foreign visitors constantly."

I opened the glove compartment, withdrew the garage door opener, and pressed the button. As I headed the car up the driveway, the door on the second bay of the four-car garage began slowly rising. I remembered with a chuckle that Susan had won the garage battle. When we were discussing the garage design, I had said, "We really ought to have more than a four-car garage. When the foreign delegations visit, they'll be bringing a whole fleet of cars."

"That's outrageous!" Susan had fumed. "It will be bigger than the house!"

I had wavered, and then finally backed down. "All right," I had said, "we'll extend the driveway behind the garage for the extra cars."

I switched off the engine, gathered the mail off the front seat, and went into the breezeway that connected the garage with the house. At the kitchen door, I tossed the junk mail into the recycle bin. Then I opened the door, went inside, deposited Susan's *Publisher's Weekly* and other mail in the basket hanging on the wall and continued into the den with my mail. I paused by the coffee table, laid the magazines on the table, then went over to the wet bar built into the wall behind the door. I mixed a pitcher of martinis, poured myself one, then shuffled carefully across the newly waxed hardwood floors so as not to spill the rim-filled drink. I settled into my leather chair and began reading *Golf Digest*.

I was on my second pitcher of martinis when Susan entered the den. She strode over to me, bent down, and kissed me on the cheek.

31

"Where the hell have you been?" I demanded, smelling scotch on her breath.

"I don't have to work anymore," she said in a clear, steady tone that belied her inebriated condition. She poured herself a martini, and then took a large swallow.

"What?" I said, scowling.

"You heard me correctly," she smiled. It was her crooked smile that came just before a lie. "I no longer have a job." She took another large swallow of her martini.

"What in the hell are you talking about?" I challenged.

"I'm through at Harvest Books." She smiled again.

"Well, you don't have to look so happy about it," I said, then took a big gulp of my martini, draining it. Susan eased herself down onto the matching leather couch next to my chair.

"What in the world happened?" I asked.

"Harris told me my performance had slipped," she said. "And he also said I would be happier at a slower paced House." She lifted her glass again and drank.

"Don't worry," I reassured her. "You're the best. You'll find another job easily."

"Not after three bombs, I won't."

"Three bombs?" I echoed, unable to conceal my surprise.

"*Golden Light* is the worst in the House's history. Three strikes and you're out in this league." Tears welled up in Susan's eyes. "Oh, Nick," she said, her chin quivering as she spoke.

"You'll simply find another job, that's all," I said. I rose, went over to the bar, and poured myself a martini from the pitcher. "What about Pembroke Publishing?" I asked, carefully walking back towards her, carrying both the pitcher and my glass. "They were trying to pirate you last year."

"That was two years ago. Before I flopped. I couldn't get a job as a go-fer now."

"What about Mitcham?"

"No," she said with a wave of her right hand, "they've been cutting back for the past six months."

"Well then," I persisted, "how about one of the paperback houses? You said they were doing more original titles."

"Oh Nick, will you stop! I'm not going to find another job!" She swallowed the last of her martini, and then unsteadily replaced the glass down on the silent butler coffee table in front of her. "You know," she continued, I've been doing a lot of thinking this afternoon, and I'm beginning to think this may actually turn out for the best."

"Oh?" I questioned.

"Yes," she plunged on. "I believe the Fates are telling us it's time to have a baby."

"Forget it," I said. I reached for the martini pitcher and topped off my glass.

"But now is the perfect time!" she protested. "My cycle is back to normal, and I now will have the time. God knows we have the money."

"Look," I said with a raised finger for emphasis, "we have talked about this so many times it makes me ill. We agreed when we were married, we wouldn't have children."

"You have the sensitivity of a stone," Susan spat.

"Thank you," I said, smiling despite myself. Stones are impervious.

"You said you've changed your mind! You said you wouldn't mind having a child!"

"Susan," I said, holding up my hand like a policeman stopping traffic, "calm down. I know I said that, but I'm just not ready yet."

"But the child will be my responsibility. And we can't wait much longer. My clock is racing, and if we delay much longer, I'd be afraid of birth defects."

I pointed my finger at Susan's empty glass. "That doesn't help either." Then I folded my arms across my chest. "Forget it," I said. "No way."

"What you're really saying is you never really do want to have a baby."

"No! I'm not saying that! I am open to having a baby. Someday. But not now."

"Come on! Admit it! You don't want one!"

"No! Someday! It's just that you're saying it's now or never."

Susan slouched forward, putting her elbows on her knees and her chin in her hands. "I don't know what I'm saying. I don't know what you're saying either. Okay. I hear you saying you're 'open' to having a baby, but you really don't want one. Want one as I do. And just talking about this now makes me want one even more. But," she sighed, "it's not a right time for you," she said, shaking her head. "I really don't think it will ever be the right time for you. And I'm afraid if you don't give me what I want...."

"What," I said sharply.

"Nothing, Nick. Nothing. I'm just upset...."

"Why don't you tell what really happened today," I said.

Susan stared at me. "What do you mean?"

"You didn't really get fired today, did you?"

Susan shrugged her shoulders. "Well, no, not exactly. But Harris really blasted me. I just saved him the trouble of firing me."

"You just walked out when he turned the heat up a little bit."

"You weren't there! Harris was a monster! He was so...so vicious. He told me I had lost control of my writers and my staff. He really yelled at me!"

I took a small sip of my martini. "Was this before or after lunch?"

"After," she said, avoiding my gaze, and refilling her martini glass.

"And you had had a few pops with one of your writers."

"Yes. Robert Sand," she admitted. "And I lost it with Harris. He just doesn't understand how difficult the writers and my staff are. You don't know how bad a person can be!"

"Oh, yes I do."

A small smile spread across her lips as she nodded. "Of course," she said. "Sullivan. What did he do today?"

"Same old, same old. I can't let it get to me. And you can't let anyone get to you either."

Susan refilled her glass and took a large swallow. "You're right, Nick. I shouldn't let this stuff bother me." She giggled. "I can't very well go back to Harvest Books after the things I said to Harris, but I'll start networking tomorrow to find another job tomorrow."

CHAPTER SIX

Susan spent the next three weeks developing her resume. She called headhunters and publishers, but it seemed to me her heart wasn't in it. Then she told me that one of her new friends at bridge club suggested that she free-lance and helped her build a website. To date, nothing legitimate had materialized. Sullivan had been riding me hard on the new gasoline formulation and product introduction, so I had ceased harassing her about a job. Finally, her new young writer, Robert Sand, abrogated his contract with Harvest Books and wanted her to handle his new book.

On the Friday afternoon of the third week, Susan and I headed down to Southampton for a weekend party at Josie Clark's, who had been her roommate at Stanford. The three-day weather forecast predicted unseasonably warm temperatures, and the Route 27 Expressway was jammed with early spring visitors.

We arrived at 6 o'clock—one hour late. Josie opened the great rounded oak door and greeted us with, "There you are! The martinis are so warm they're positively undrinkable." She laughed, then threw her arms around Susan and hugged her. She turned to me, raising her cheek so I could kiss it. "But I forgive you. I'm sure the traffic was unbearable."

Josie glanced to the right, then to the left, and asked, "Where in the world is Robert Sand? I want to congratulate him on *Golden Light* making it to number 1 on the Times book list. Three weeks ago, that book wasn't even on the charts!"

Susan flung her arm out in a dismissive way. "He'll be along in his own time. He is a free spirit, you know. He may not be here until Bloody Mary's on Sunday."

"Well you certainly showed your ex-boss," Josie said, with a maternal air, sliding her arm around her shoulder and leading her into the spacious, slate-floored foyer. "I want to hear all about your new plans. Just leave your suitcases here—I'll have Charles take them up to your room. Follow me."

She led the way through the foyer, stepped down onto the long, thick pile Oriental rug covering the oak-floored hallway, crossed it, and then entered the Florida room on the other side. The far wall of the huge room was totally glass, through which we gazed at the sand dunes, the crashing breakers, and the massive expanse of the ocean beyond.

"I love the ocean," Susan murmured, reverently.

"The view is better than ever," I observed.

"That ocean still dazzles me too," Josie said.

The setting sun filled the room with mid-summer temperatures. The men had removed their sports jackets and the women had shorn the sweaters, piling everything on an alcove seat in the corner. I watched Susan glance around the room, then spot her older sister, Katherine, and her husband, Warren. They were standing next to a love seat, talking to an athletic-looking, blond-haired man whose back was to us.

As we approached, the man turned and smiled broadly. It was Melville. Katherine shrieked, "Susie! You're here!" As they embraced, she continued, "I'm glad you decided to come. We have lots to catch up on."

"Well I have lots of news."

Warren kissed Susan on the lips a bit too long. Then he asked, "How have you been? We've missed you"

"Quite well, thank you," was her response as she pulled away from the clutches of Warren's arms.

"Susan," Katherine said in her formal voice. "May I present Walter Melville. Walter, my sister, Susan Shepherd and her husband, Nick."

Susan extended her hand. "We've met. Hello, Walter," she said. "When was it? The Company Christmas party?"

"Three years ago," Melville said, taking Susan's outstretched hand, then releasing it. "You're more beautiful than ever."

"Thank you," Susan said.

Melville turned to me, and he said as we shook hands, "You're one lucky man, Nick."

"Luckier than you," I laughed. "Have you reached Henry the Eighth status yet?'

"No," he chuckled. "I'm only between wives number 3 and 4."

"Walter," Katherine complained, "you were holding out on us. Oh, you mentioned something about being in Corporate America, but I didn't know you were with number one."

She turned to Josie. "Did you know that?" she asked accusingly.

"Well of course, Katherine. Walter is one of Ted's best customers. Ted says if he trades any more often, Walter will qualify as a stock trader himself. Speaking of my darling husband, I see I must rescue him from that gorgeous overdeveloped teenager. Oh, and Katherine and Warren, come along; the owner of North Forty Vineyards has just joined them—you know, that wonderful chardonnay we had last weekend. You said you wanted to meet him."

"Oh, yes," Katherine bubbled. "I would simply love to add his lines to our wine distribution here on the East End." She faced Susan. "We'll catch up later."

They drifted away, leaving Susan, Walter, and me at a momentary loss for words.

"Have you tried any of the North Forty wines, Walt?" I asked.

"I had their '92 Cab a couple of weeks ago. Chateau Margaux it's not, but I believe someday it could be. But as you know, I really prefer the juniper berry. Stirred not shaken," he chuckled. He turned to Susan. "How's the publishing business?"

"You don't want to hear about it."

He glanced at me, then back at Susan. "I'd rather hear about the power of the pen than talk fossil fuel with Nick here."

Susan smiled. "Well I don't think my business is all that different than yours. It's incredibly competitive, mergers are rampant, and you're on call twenty-four seven."

"Sullivan calls Nick nights and weekends too," Melville said as though stating a fact and as though I weren't there.

"Just as my ex-boss did," Susan agreed.

"Ex-boss?" Melville questioned.

"I left Harvest last month. I'm free-lancing now."

"Free-lancing," Melville exclaimed. "That's great! Congratulations! I'm sure you'll do very well."

"Susan is already doing very well," I interjected. "Robert Sand terminated his contract with Harvest to sign on with Susan."

"Robert Sand," Melville mused. "Isn't he that new writer?"

"Yes," I confirmed. "He wrote *Golden Light* which just hit the top of the *Times* book list."

"Speak of the devil," Susan said, as a tall, gangly man strode across the room toward us. He had long, obsidian black hair, and his youthful face sported a bushy mustache. He was dressed in gray slacks, white turtleneck, and a tweed blazer.

"There you are," Susan greeted him. "You managed to sneak in without our hostess seeing you. Josie is just dying to meet you."

She introduced Melville and me, then said, "How about a drink, everyone. The sun is well past the yardarm."

"A perfect idea," Melville said, "And speaking of perfect, John makes the most perfect stingers."

"Oh, yes," agreed Susan, starting towards the bar. "I remember them from last summer; they kept me up all night. Remember, Nick?"

"Vaguely," I chortled. "It seems to me I passed out after the first dozen."

The massive oak bar extended all the way from the entrance doorway, along the entire wall, and ended in the corner. As we reached it, Susan asked Melville, "Did you know that Josie bought this from a hotel they were closing in Sag Harbor?"

"I didn't." He looked down the full length and breadth of the bar. "How in the world did she get it in here?"

Susan chuckled, pointing to the wall of windows. "Leave it to Josie. Those windows used to be the louvered type you normally see in a Florida Room, but she claimed she never liked them. So, she had them pulled out, moved the bar in through the empty space, and had the sliding glass doors you see now installed."

Melville rubbed his hand back and forth along the brilliant finish of the bar. "Well, I like it," he said. "It reminds me of better times."

"Yes," Susan agreed. "The times of flappers and Stein and Fitzgerald and Hemingway."

"And Rockefeller," Melville added.

The bartender finished serving the couple sitting next to Susan, and then sidestepped over to her. "Why, Mrs. Shepherd, what a pleasant surprise. I haven't seen you since last summer. And Mr. Shepherd. And Mr. Melville."

"Hello, John," she said, extending her hand. "It's good to see you."

John shook Susan's hand, asking, "The usual?"

"How can I resist?"

"I'll have a perfect stinger also," Robert Sand added.

"I'll join you as well," Melville said.

"I'll have a large Stoly," I said.

"Coming right up," John said. He reached for a shaker, added ice, and poured a generous amount of Cordon Noir Cognac into it. He added a dash of white crème de menthe, shook it, and poured the liquid into 3 glasses, straight up. He placed napkins in front of us, and served the stingers to Susan, Melville, and Sand. Then he placed a few ice cubes into a large tumbler and filled it with the vodka.

"There you are," he said as he placed the drink on my napkin, and then he moved back down the bar.

Sand lifted the long stem glass and, looking squarely into Susan's eyes, said, "Here's to a very memorable evening."

"Arriba," Susan said, raising her glass, and looking out at the ocean.

"El bajo," I picked up Susan's Mexican toast.

"El centro," Sand said, joining in.

"Adentró," Susan, Sand and I said in unison, and then laughed. We all took long swallows of our drinks.

"Wherever did you learn that toast, Robert?" Susan asked, with a youthful sparkle in her eyes.

"I picked it up many years ago in Mexico City," Sand responded. "I spent a summer there when I was in school."

"At the Jacaranda?" she asked, her voice excited.

"At El Señorial."

"Did you ever go to the Jacaranda?" she asked.

"The Jacaranda," Sand mused. "Boy that sounds familiar."

"It's in the Zona Rosa. There's a big Jacaranda tree in the middle of the club. Nick and I used to go there when I was at Stanford-In-Mexico."

"Big Jacaranda tree...Oh, yeah. I know the place. I met a girl who lived there."

"Lived there?" Susan asked, looking astonished.

"Yeah, it's an apartment building now, but I remember her saying it used to be a nightclub. The Jacaranda tree is in the lobby."

"Oh," Susan said, taking another long swallow of her drink. "How sad." She turned her gaze to me. "We had a lot of good times there, didn't we, Nick."

"Times change," I said. I drained my Stoly.

Susan scowled. "You're such a party-pooper, Nick."

An alert John was there and refilled my tumbler with ice and Stoly. "The party is now, Susan," I said. "You can't relive the past."

"But the past is part of our experience together. It affects the present."

"That may be, but you can't mourn what isn't there anymore."

Susan shrugged and then finished her stinger. John was ready with another batch and was pouring them when Katherine arrived, empty glass in hand. "Make one more, would you please, John?" Katherine asked.

She turned to Susan, saying, "O.K., little sister, introduce me to your new young man."

Susan made the introductions, and then Katherine said, "I was enthralled so with *Golden Light*. You have so much insight into women for such a young man. I can't wait for your next book. What are you working on?"

"Well, I haven't given it much thought," Sand responded. Then he smiled. "Perhaps I'll set it in Mexico. I spent a summer there when I was a student. Write what you know, right, Susan?" I was beginning to take a great dislike for this Lochinvar.

I looked across at Katherine and said, "Speaking of students, how are the kids?"

She stared at me as though it was the last thing she expected me to say, which it was. "Why, do you want any?" she said coldly.

"You never know."

"Yea, right." But the hook had been set, and Katherine was off and running. She carried on for two more rounds of stingers about her kids, all the neighbors, the gossip at the club, and the politics of Southampton. By the time dinner was announced, she was starting to repeat herself.

In the main dining room, there were place settings for twelve, but, fully extended, the long, rectangular oak table could have seated twice as many. The table was curved at the ends and was covered with a damask cloth. The Italian armchairs were hand carved with red velvet seats. Each place was set with a magnificent Flora Danica porcelain plate, with its individual flower design. Three five-branch candlesticks brightened the dimly lit room. "Ted must have had one helluva bonus last year," Katherine murmured.

"There is a nametag at each place," Josie announced. "I apologize for it not being boy-girl. Too many men—and not enough time," she laughed, and then finished her stinger.

I settled in next to Ted who sat at the head of the table. Katherine was to my right, flanked by three of Ted's male clients to her right, with Josie at the far end of the table. Melville sat opposite me, with Susan next to him. Sand was on Susan's other side, followed by a female client of Ted's, and finally Warren finished the far side of the table. The acoustics of the great, high ceiling room were so good that conversation was easy.

John came around for drink orders. "Another Stoly," I said. "And keep them coming."

The first course was baby lobster with mustard sauce, served with a Grgich Hills Chardonnay.

"Are you back to running, Nick?" Melville asked.

"I sure am, Walt. I'm really enjoying my running. Are you still at it?"

"Are you a runner, Walt?" Susan slurred. The stingers must have really started to hit her small body.

Melville chuckled. "After this debauchery, I'm going to run twenty miles tomorrow."

"Do you really run that far?" Susan asked, taking a large swallow of her stinger.

"Well," Melville admitted, "sometimes I exaggerate. I used to run that far in training when I was in school. Not anymore. But," he added quickly, "I really used to. Hell, I won the NCAA mile when I was a senior in college, and I kept running during my hitch in the Service."

"How far do you run now?"

"Well," Melville said, smiling, "after the work and the wine, there's not much time for much else. But I do average five miles a day."

"Five miles." Susan looked over at me. "Now there's a worthy goal, Nick. You're doing what now, three miles a day, three times a week?"

I glared at her as I finished my Stoly. Some people just shouldn't drink. John appeared, cleared my empty glass, and replaced it with a fresh drink.

"I'm doing just fine," I said. "I'll increase my mileage gradually."

"Nick's right," Melville said. "Increase too fast and you might injure yourself."

Susan finished her stinger, and then turned to her untouched Chardonnay. She took a swallow, then asked, "Where were you in school, Walt?"

"Villanova. And, was that ever competitive. There were three of us under four minutes in the mile. But I think that competition really helped. I found myself being competitive in class as well, and I did very well. I was in ROTC at Villanova, after graduation I spent four years in the Service. After that I got my MBA at Stanford."

"You were at Stanford?" Susan asked, and then took another large swallow of her Chardonnay. "So was I."

"I'm sure it was well after I was there. What did you study?"

"English. I wanted to go into publishing."

"Isn't California great? The weather's the best, everyone's outdoors all the time, and anything you want to do is within easy reach—skiing, surfing, wine tasting—you name it. And the parties—well, only Josie has better ones."

"But," Susan said, "I've always had the feeling everything was so temporary out there. I grew up here in the East, and, to me, Californians have no roots."

"Listen," Melville said, raising his glass for emphasis, "a person's roots are always with him, wherever he is." He spilled some of his drink as he emphasized every word with a shake of his glass. Melville could handle his liquor well, but the stingers appeared to be affecting even him.

"My roots," he continued, "are what I make them. They're here, right now, in this dining room. I came into this world alone, and I'm leaving it alone, so to say there's anything permanent in between is just illusion."

Melville hesitated, and then he smiled. "I'm sorry. This is one of my hot buttons, particularly right now. A lady who shall remain nameless wanted to get married, settle down, and, she said, 'establish roots.' She gave me an ultimatum and, well, I just couldn't go through with it. I've done the marriage thing."

"Anyone I know, Walt?" I asked.

"Yes, you know her, Nick. But as I said, she shall remain nameless."

"What was your last wife like?" Susan asked.

"Why is it that you women always want to know about other women?" I demanded.

Susan glowered at me, then turned back to Melville.

"My ex-wife was a lawyer," he said.

"You sound bitter."

"I am bitter. She hired the top divorce lawyer in New York, took me to the financial cleaners, and then ran off with a Mercedes dealer who was twice her age. You didn't meet Tiffany at the Christmas party 3 years ago?"

"No, I didn't."

"Well, she's twelve years younger than I am, and I'm forty-six now, so...she was thirty-one at the time, but she looked twenty-one. Anyway, the affair with the Mercedes man lasted a month; he was just the first of many. Now she's living with a twenty-three-year-old computer salesman; hell, he's more than ten years younger than she is! Well, enough of this. I should know better than to talk about it; I can feel my blood pressure shooting up."

The entrée was Tournedos with Béarnaise sauce and a Chateau Margaux Cabernet Sauvignon. Dessert was Baked Alaska, accompanied by Dom Perignon Champagne. Ted had listened quietly to our conversation during dinner with only an occasional question or incisive observation. This was why he was so successful.

When everyone had finished, Josie rose and announced, "Coffee and cordials will be served in the library." She pushed back her chair and led the way across the v-inlaid oak floor, down the hallway and into the library. As I rose to follow, I felt dizzy and had to grab the chair for support. I also felt extreme fatigue. I needed a stinger to wake up.

The English walnut paneling in the library created a rich, warm feeling. The shelves were floor to ceiling, loaded with books, reflecting Ted's voracious and eclectic reading. John had started a fire in the massive black marble fireplace along the wall by the door to take the chill out of the damp night air.

John had also set up a portable bar in the corner, and one of the maids, Peggy, was poised with a tray of snifters of Cognac and glasses of port and stingers. Another maid, Sarah, stood by the elaborate carved table upon which sat a sterling silver coffee pot and Flora Danica porcelain cups and saucers.

"Make yourselves comfortable," Josie announced. "Peggy and Sarah will serve you." Susan, Melville, and Sand sat in leather winged-back chairs by the bar, and each of them took a stinger when Peggy held the tray down for them. I started to sit down in the fourth chair, and then decided against it. I grabbed a stinger from the tray and said, "I'm going to warm up by the fire."

The fire was warm, and the dancing flames captured my gaze. As I stared, I felt my eyelids grow heavy. I thought I'd just close my eyes for a minute…

I don't know how long I was passed out. I remember coming to the first time hearing Susan's voice. "Oh, Katherine, he's not on my back. He's just preoccupied."

"Susie. Dear. When are you going to wake up? All he cares about is that silly job. He doesn't want kids, now or ever. And take my word for it—kids are wonderful—most of the time. Get rid of Nick and get on with your life. It took me two tries to find Warren here—and if I were still with Chuck, I wouldn't have my little ones."

"Katherine, please leave me alone with this. I'll deal with it in my own way…."

I slipped back into my sleeping stupor.

When I awoke the next time, I heard different voices.

"And now that we've told you our secrets," Sand was saying, "You've got to tell us yours."

"I have no secrets."

"Not even one?" The voice was Melville's. "An unfulfilled desire?"

"I want children," Susan blurted out.

During the ensuing silence, I almost opened my eyes. "Then have children," Melville said finally. "Forget the publishing business and have children. Children are meant for those who want them."

" I agree, but..." her voice trailed off, "It's not so simple."

"Ah," Melville said, as though making a discovery, "tricky Nicky doesn't want children."

"Yes, but…" Susan said, "I agreed not to have children when we were married. Nick didn't want children and, that time, I thought I would never want any either. I can't blame him because I've changed my mind. Besides, Nick does say now that he wants children someday."

"You're running out of time," Melville warned

"I know that…" I slipped back into unconsciousness.

When I awoke again, my temples were pounding in pain and my mouth was desert dry. I opened my eyes and saw that the roaring fire had become nothing more than a bed of embers. I turned my head to the left and saw Warren standing there. "Where is everybody?" I managed to mumble.

"Gone up – ages ago. All except Katherine – she just left."

I stood up, and then stumbled. Warren grabbed me by the arm and saved me from falling. "Thanks, Warren. You are a good brother-in-law."

"Yea, well, Nick, let me offer you some brotherly advice. Take care of Susan."

"What do you mean?"

"She's got that wandering look in her eye. I know," he chuckled. "I'm an expert in spotting it. And watch out for that Sand character. I can recognize a fellow hunter."

"Warren, I take it back. You're a lousy brother-in-law. Mind your own damn business."

He let go of my arm, and then held his hands up. "All right. Fine. But just don't say I didn't warn you."

I made my way up the granite staircase and into the first bedroom on the left. The light was on in the bathroom and Susan was curled up with her back towards me. I took four aspirin with a large glass of water, crawled into bed, and passed out for the final time that night.

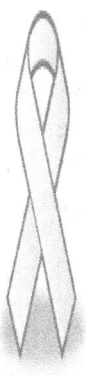

CHAPTER SEVEN

The following Tuesday morning, my intercom beeped, and Liz's voice announced, "An Inspector Lopez is on your private line."

I pushed the flashing white light on my telephone console, picked up the receiver, and said, "Good morning, Ricardo. How are you?"

"I'm excited, Nick. We've got a lead, and I'd like to talk to you about it. Are you free for lunch?"

"Sorry, Ricardo, I really can't. Our Research V.P. from Houston is here with me, and we'll be working through lunch. How about after work?"

"You know… that's probably better anyway. It will give us more time to be sure of what we've got. Come on over when you're ready. I'll be here."

I took a cab downtown and arrived at FBI Headquarters at six o'clock. Ricardo had a visitor badge waiting for me with the guard in the lobby, and I took the elevator to the ninth floor where another guard telephoned the Inspector. A few minutes later, Ricardo appeared through a heavy metal door. As we shook hands, Ricardo said, "You look as though you could use some good news."

"I sure could. We've just had another setback on an R and D project."

Ricardo tapped me on the shoulder, saying, "Well, come on, then. We've identified something particularly important with a little R and D of our own. I've had you cleared to go into the lab. Follow me."

We crossed the deserted reception area and Ricardo opened another heavy metal door on the opposite side. He led the way through the open doorway and down the hall. The linoleum floor clacked under our shoes as we strode down the hallway to yet another heavy metal door at the end. Ricardo opened this one as well, and we entered a large room, filled with all shapes and sizes of scientific equipment. A white-coated man looked up from an electron microscope. "Ah, great timing, Ricardo. I've got them both lined up perfectly now. Look."

Ricardo introduced me to Leo, then leaned over the instrument and peered through the eyepieces. He grunted, and then motioned to me. "Take a look."

I lowered my head to the microscope and saw two clumps of what looked like beads. I looked back and forth at each of them, then said, "They both look the same. What am I supposed to be seeing?"

"Just that," Ricardo said. "Identical molecules of explosive. The ones on the left are a new, top-secret plastic developed for the Navy. We just gained access to this sample. The explosive on the right is a remnant from the conference room at Las Palmas."

"A plastic explosive?" I asked, looking back into the microscope, as though it would help me to understand.

"Yes. The most concentrated form I've ever seen. We figure the bomb was no bigger than a twenty-five-cent piece."

I continued to peer into the microscope. "They sure do look identical," I said finally. I looked up. "What in the blazes does this all mean? The U.S. Navy blew up that room?"

"We don't know," Ricardo said slowly, as though pondering the options as he spoke. "This new explosive is top secret, and even we had a challenging time making this match. But there are many potential leaks, ranging from the producer, the distribution network, and even the Navy itself. If anyone with enough money or power really wanted it, they could get it—terrorists, foreign governments... or even individuals."

"What do you mean?" I asked, fearing accusation.

"That explosive residual was found on what was left of your briefcase."

"What?" I challenged, not believing what I had just heard.

"That bomb was in your briefcase," Ricardo reiterated, "at least the business end of it was. Somehow, sometime, somebody slipped that little medallion of explosive into your briefcase."

I stared at Ricardo in silence. Then I said finally, "How do you know I didn't do it?"

Ricardo grinned. "I don't. But," he continued, "My hunch is that you had nothing to do with it. If you had done it, you would have known enough about that explosive to have been miles from that room. And besides, what about the ambulance incident? In both cases, you would have been running a real risk of getting killed. No. As I told you in the Greenwich Hospital, I think you were the target."

I shook my head back and forth. "That is still so hard for me to believe...Getting back to the bomb, did you find out how it was set off?"

Ricardo nodded as he said, "Electronically. We found the remains of a device connected to the light switch which, when the light switch was thrown, sent an electronic signal to the detonator embedded in the explosive."

"But couldn't the bombing and the ambulance have been the work of P.P.I.P.?"

"No, I really don't think so," Ricardo mused. "As I mentioned at the Hospital, P.P.I.P. is too crude. They don't have either the money or the power to get their hands on the explosive—and I doubt they have the network to have gained access to your movements."

He paused, and then continued, "What about your business enemies? You used to deal a lot with a lot of foreign people and governments. What about the Arab countries? Some of them have both the money and the power to have pulled this off."

Memories of turbulent meetings, replete with implied threats, rushed into my mind. I shivered. "I didn't think much about it at the time, but I did have some pretty emotional confrontations with some OPEC members."

"Anyone in particular?" Ricardo asked.

My laugh was short and nervous. "Everyone in particular. They had all thrown us out of their countries, so they could control production, raise the price, and keep all the profits for themselves. This had been before my time, but we still controlled the technology. They thought they could steamroll the young kid that I was into giving them the latest developments." The same anger I had felt all those years ago flared once again.

"And," I continued, "it wasn't only the Arabs. Actually, I think that Latin Americans were worse."

Ricardo bristled slightly. "What do you mean?"

"Well, not all of them, actually. I had problems with just a few. In fact, just one."

"Was he mad enough to want to kill you?" Ricardo asked quietly.

"Well he threatened me...but that was ten years ago. And the Arabs threatened me too. But no. I really don't think any of them were mad enough to want to kill me, especially after ten years."

"Why were they all so mad?"

I felt uncomfortable. I really didn't want to go into this. I simply said, "I told you. They wanted our latest technology."

The Inspector looked at me in silence.

"All right. They didn't like my tactics. But they were trying to stick it to me first. Like the Latino I mentioned was holding back on our royalty payments. I shipped him some of our old equipment. He blew up, but I told him he wouldn't get anything until he paid what was due. He finally resumed the royalties, but I wanted to teach him a lesson, so I sent him more old equipment. Anyway, the President of the Oil Monopoly in his country heard about it and launched an investigation. It turned out this guy had been skimming profits. Even though he was the President's first cousin, he fled the country. Without a doubt he would have been killed. He called from wherever it was he was hiding to tell me I had cheated him, so he was going to kill me. But I'm sure it was just said in anger—the guy was a real parasite."

"What's become of him?" Ricardo asked.

My frown transformed to wide-eyed revelation. "My God," I said slowly. "Now that you mention it, I had heard he used some of his old connections to sign on as a runner for the drug cartel. I still don't believe Guillermo is the violent type, but..." he grimaced, "maybe he is."

"O.K. We'll check this guy out. Get me his last known address. And get me the same information on the Arabs you used to deal with." Ricardo paused. 'Have you made any enemies in this country?"

I thought back over the recent past. The independent retailers weren't happy because they felt I was squeezing their profits, but...that was just business. My competitors must be livid because I had been extremely aggressive, trying to gain market share, but I couldn't imagine that anyone could have been mad enough to want to kill me. "No," I said finally, "I don't have any lethal business enemies here."

The Inspector persisted. "What about jealous husbands?"

I laughed. "I don't know any, myself included."

"You've never..." the Ricardo began.

"No," I said with conviction. "I don't fool around. Business is my life." I laughed mirthlessly. "Just ask Susan."

"O.K.," the Inspector pronounced in his official tone. "It's your business life, then. We'll have to curry-comb it to find the killer."

I shrugged my shoulders. "I still don't believe anyone's really trying to kill me."

CHAPTER EIGHT

I arrived home at eight-fifteen to find Susan in the den, stirring a batch of martinis. "Who kept you?" she charged, glowering. "Miss Patty Watty?"

I was so surprised by her accusation that all I could do was shake my head and respond with my own question," What did you say?"

"You heard me. Your 'Administrative Assistant.' The one who's always dressed as though she's ready to party."

The image of Pat, dressed in her conservative business suit, popped into my mind. "Susan, will you stop this? You've only seen Pat once in your life—at that Christmas Party three years ago. And may I remind you that you haven't been to one since."

Susan poured herself a martini. "Seeing her once is all I need. That girl is so obvious you'd have to be blind not to see it."

I reached under the bar and withdrew a martini stem glass. "Susan," I said as I filled the glass from the shaker, "this is so unlike you. I rarely even notice what Pat is wearing. We have a professional relationship, and that's the end of it."

"You never notice what anyone is wearing, including me," Susan said. She turned, and then tripped on the edge of the Oriental rug, spilling half of her drink on it.

I scowled. "How many of those martinis have you had?"

Susan continued towards her chair, not looking back. She shrugged her shoulders and said, "Who's counting? And how many did you have on the bar car?" Then she sat down.

I strode over to her chair. I stood over her and pointed my index finger at her. She ignored me, looking out the bay window to the darkened woods beyond. "Something is bothering you. What is it?" I demanded. "Are you still hung up on this silly baby issue?"

Susan sipped her martini and kept staring out into the darkness.

" Did you work on Sand's book at all today?"

No answer.

"No? I'll bet you just sat around here all day long, drinking and feeling sorry for yourself. Get yourself a real job! Then you won't even think about a baby!"

Susan finally turned her head and looked at me. "I have a real job," she spat. "And a helluva lot better job than you have. At least I don't have some asshole boss telling me what to do. Now just leave me alone!"

In the silence that followed, my thoughts drifted back to the early days of knowing Susan when I was in my final MBA year at Stanford and she was a sophomore. I remembered my rush at the beginning; the 50-yard line tickets, off-campus parties in the hills of Los Altos, and the black-tie dinners in San Francisco. I wanted to impress her, a scion of New York Society. Images came up of sharing pizza and beer, long walks under the tall, aromatic eucalyptus trees, and torrid lovemaking among the Pacific sand dunes. And Mexico...

When Susan had decided she would take her fall and winter quarters in Mexico, I had applied to the Master's Program in International Relations at the University of Mexico, even though I had just gotten my MBA. And that time in Mexico was the happiest period of my life. I felt the joy would last forever.

My thoughts moved on to the following year. I joined UNRC in New York, and Susan finished her senior year at Stanford. At first the phone calls were frequent and lengthy. I even arranged a business trip to

San Francisco during the fall for the Big Game against Cal, and Susan went home to New York over Christmas break.

But during the Christmas holiday I felt something had changed. We didn't seem to laugh as much anymore. I often stayed late at the office. I talked about business and Susan talked about the past.

During the winter quarter the phone calls were less frequent. I talked about business and I couldn't remember what Susan talked about. Susan made all the wedding arrangements, which was to be in New York in June, even though I was right there. "I'm too busy," I had said. "That's your mother's job anyway." Susan had protested that her mother didn't know her taste as well as I did, but to no avail.

But then after the wedding, she began working and became extremely busy as well. The publishing business was exciting, and she found her career had become especially important to her. We became close again, both committed to our careers.

Then those bittersweet memories faded, and my thoughts jumped to the jagged-edge realities of today. Something has happened. It isn't just this kid thing. I really wouldn't mind having children someday. It's the drinking. I like a drink just as much as the next person, but Susan is way beyond. She seems so distant. Maybe she's lost her confidence.

Susan did have a point about an asshole boss. I tensed as I remembered Sullivan's words of that afternoon, "Goddamnit, Nick, I don't want to hear about any more R and D failures. Either you have that new product on the market by the end of the quarter, or you're gone—both you and Hudson—and you tell Hudson that, too!"

Then I remembered the evening's revelations with Ricardo. Not only was my career in jeopardy, but also some maniac with enough clout to penetrate the U S. Navy was stalking me. I had not been totally open with the Inspector—there had been those payoffs to foreign government officials I had welshed on for fear of discovery during those investigations. Oh, Sullivan, had recommended it—no, strongly urged me to not make payment—but I was the one on the firing line. Firing line may indeed be the correct description—one of those zealots may be angry and volatile enough to be gunning for me.

Susan's loud sob broke the silence. She sobbed repeatedly.

"What's wrong?" I asked finally.

"Oh, Nick," she wept. "Nick," she sobbed again. Then she broke into another succession of wails.

Gradually her sobbing subsided, and then stopped. Finally, she took a quick breath through her gaping mouth and exhaled, "Let's have an affair. You and me." She took a deep breath and let out a long sigh. "Nick," she said, "Let's go down to the Homestead right now."

"The Homestead!" I exploded. "That's ridiculous! What's wrong with right here?"

"It's not romantic," Susan answered. "I want to be pursued. I've told you that before."

"Oh, Susan, will you grow up? I'm too tired to chase you. The pressure of work is just too much for me. And I've told you that before."

Susan sighed. "I'm just a convenience. You could be married to anyone, as long as she didn't give you trouble."

"Susan, I love you. I don't want anyone else."

"Oh, Nick. I... I love you too, but I need more than words."

It was my turn to sigh. "You just don't understand, Susan. When you get a real job again, perhaps you'll understand better then."

"No, Nick, it's you who doesn't understand, and you probably never will."

CHAPTER NINE

Susan went to visit Josie for the weekend, and I entertained Mark Kemp, a Stanford classmate, who was now with Pueblo Refining. We played golf both Saturday and Sunday.

The following Monday morning, Sullivan opened the staff meeting promptly at ten a.m. with, "Profits are continuing to slide, and none, I repeat, none of you seem capable of staunching the blood. If I don't see any progress by a week from today, I'll get people in here who can. Walter Melville. Where are you?"

"Down here, Bruce," Walter responded from the far end of the table. The table always filled up in the order of arrival, so the latecomers were always at the far end. "Hiding, eh, Walter? Or did you have a big weekend? Okay, both. Well, tell me about International."

Walter cleared his throat. "Well," he said briskly, "I see a glimmer of hope. Orders received last week declined only two per cent last week, versus the previous week's loss of three percent."

"You call that improvement?" Sullivan roared. "We need gains in backlogs, not declines of declines. What happened to your intimidation program?"

Walter picked up a piece of paper from the stack in front of him, and proudly held it up. "I received this fax from Rotterdam just fifteen minutes ago. An order for one million barrels from Hollandia."

"What was the price?" shot Sullivan.

"Well," Walter said in a matter-of-fact tone, "it was lower than contract."

"How much lower?" Sullivan asked, ominously.

Walter hesitated, very much out of character. "Three," he said finally.

Sullivan exploded. "Three dollars under the contract price? No wonder we're losing our ass! You fire them back and tell them contract price, or no deal!"

"But nobody's paying contract price," Walter protested.

"Don't you think it's about time somebody did? Send the fax, now. No. Wait. Nick and I had a little heart to heart last week. I do trust we have a better Domestic scenario, don't we, Nick?"

I smiled, saying, "Let the facts speak for themselves. First, weekly retail gallonage is up two percent versus the prior week. Our market research report attributes this to our beverage promotion. But more importantly, we were able to implement a penny a gallon price increase. This also is the result of the promotion."

Sullivan nodded his head, saying, "Not bad, Nick, not bad. What about your crude sales to the independent refiners?"

"No change. But I have an idea about how to gain market share in the independent sector."

Sullivan leaned forward. "How?"

"As you know, our largest independent customer, Pueblo, has been dramatically expanding its refining capacity over the past three years. With gasoline consumption declining as it is, they are under severe cash flow pressure. I played golf with their CFO over the weekend, and he tells me they would be interested in a friendly takeover bid."

"Are you mad?" roared Sullivan. "We have cash flow problems of our own!"

"That's the beauty of this little scheme," I responded. "My friend tells me the acquisition would take very little cash; the major ingredient would be our stock." I looked over at Ned Casey, our CFO, "Correct me if I am wrong, Ned, but I believe we have sufficient stock in the treasury to fund a billion-dollar acquisition."

Before Casey got a chance to respond, Sullivan interrupted, "I don't want my stock diluted any further, particularly in a declining market! Nick. Look. I don't want you wasting your time on long-term projects such as this Pueblo deal. We need short- term improvement. Where does your higher mpg project stand?"

"Well," I began, "the fact is that we haven't had a breakthrough yet. I thought we had something last week, but the formulation clogged the fuel line."

Sullivan's Irish Whiskey reddened face flushed even deeper. "How many times do I have to tell you? I don't want excuses! We need that product now, and I don't care what we have to do to get it!"

"But, Bruce," I objected, "trial and error takes time. We may stumble onto the right combination tomorrow, or it may take us several months."

Sullivan stared at me in stony silence. "Nick," he said, with the finality of the single largest stockholder of UNRC, "the most important thing in your life is this product. Forget the promotions. Forget the acquisitions. I want 100 percent of your time devoted to Golden Green. Do you understand me?"

I stared back at Sullivan, feeling my own face burning. "Completely." Then I looked away.

Sullivan looked away as well. "Walter, are you still here? Ah, there you are, still hiding. How's Bradshaw doing on getting us out from under those OPEC buy contracts?"

"Bradshaw is still hung up in the State Department. State is worried that if they support us on this, OPEC will disintegrate, member countries will produce all out to generate quick profits, and then the oil price will plummet. Economic disaster will result in the Middle East, with the only possible outcome being intra-Arab war, with the Israelis fanning the flames. No. Bradshaw says State is absolutely committed to maintaining OPEC stability."

"Yeah," Sullivan said in disgust, "and watch us go right down the tubes. Those Arab bastards cut our prices at the refiners yet hold us up at the contract price. I'm all for letting them kill themselves off to the very last one. Tell Bradshaw to push through the idea of expanding the U.S. Strategic Oil Reserve, through us, with a big OPEC purchase at a low spot price. That may trigger something."

"Yeah but, Bruce," Walter objected, "if OPEC falls, then our crude prices will fall as well."

"I really wouldn't mind that," Sullivan countered. "At least we'd then be on a level playing field. The world feedstock cost would be the same, so we could win big with our efficient refineries and derivative plants."

Sullivan turned back to me. "Upon reflection, I now think your acquisition idea might not be a bad one. Have Bradshaw get a reading from Anti-Trust on whether or not they would fight our takeover of Pueblo."

The meeting lasted another half an hour while Sullivan sought updates on financial, legal, exploration, and operations issues. After adjournment, I found Melville waiting for me in the carpeted hallway. "Let's commiserate," he chuckled. "He was pretty rough on you in there."

I smiled. "He wasn't exactly overwhelming you with compliments, either. I know how tough that International market is."

"I know you know," Walter said. "But you also know International has it rewards. I picked up something that may help you with Golden Green Octane."

"Oh really?" I asked, raising my eyebrows, both in doubt and suspicion.

"Yes, really. Why don't we discuss it over lunch?"

"All right," I said slowly. "How about twelve-thirty? We've both got some work to do."

"Perfect. I'll stop by your office; it's closer to the elevator than mine. We'll go from there. Is Sel et Poivre all right?"

"Fine with me."

"Good. I'll have Sheila book us a table. See you later; I've got something to discuss with Sullivan."

Resentment welled up in me as I strolled back down the hallway. Both Melville's and my office were corner suites, but his had been mine when I had run International and I preferred it because of its view of the East River. My current office overlooked mid-town Manhattan. Although UNRC generated most of its revenues domestically, I considered the number two job at the Company to be Vice-President of International. Sullivan had told me when he moved me to Domestic that the change was necessary for me to gain more seasoning, since I had had only limited Domestic experience when I joined the Company. Sullivan would be sixty-five a year from June, but he had given no sign of retiring, and the Company had no mandatory retirement age. "Damn," I thought as I watched Melville disappear into Sullivan's office, "that red-faced bastard is always trying to throw us off balance. I swear he gets off on it!"

Melville and I walked at a fast pace the fifteen blocks to Sel et Poivre. The spring weather was still unseasonably warm, and beads of perspiration flecked our faces as we entered the air-conditioned coolness of the restaurant. "Ah, Mr. Melville," the maître d' greeted them. "And Mr. Shepherd. Nice to see you. I have your table waiting." He led us to a large table in the rear.

After three rounds of straight-up martinis, accompanied by discussions of the latest in golf and tennis developments and happenings, Melville leaned forward across the table towards me, "Do you remember Don Stanley?"

"Don Stanley?" I echoed. "In Iraq?"

"He's the one."

"Sure. I remember Don. He had stayed on after his tour in Baghdad. Married to a local—they disowned her—the whole nine yards. Is he still there?"

"He escaped just before Saddam was overthrown. I have a friend who helped him, and his family get out. So... he owed me a favor." He reached into his inside coat pocket, withdrew a sheath of papers, folded lengthwise, and handed them to me. "Here. Take a good look at this."

I unfolded the papers and studied the pages of formulae. Finally, I let out a short whistle. "I only minored in Chemistry in school, but if this is what I think it is, Golden Green Octane One is fait accompli."

"It is what you think it is. Stanley discovered it years ago, but the Iraqis have been sitting on it ever since."

I nodded my head. "For obvious reasons. Oil and gasoline consumption were falling enough as it was. And I can understand why he never told me; his family were de facto hostages. But, then again, why didn't he sell it to the highest bidder and buy his way out long ago?"

"Until recently, he was happy where he was, and he didn't need the money. But his kids now are taking a lot of abuse for being half American, so he simply wanted to get them out. And his wife figured they'd all have a better chance somewhere else."

"Where are they now?"

Melville smiled. "I can't tell you. Suffice to say the Iraqis will never find them."

I leafed through the papers once again, shook my head, and then let out a sigh. "Good God. We have been working in a totally different area. It would have taken Hudson and his boys forever to stumble onto this. Thanks, Walter. I owe you."

Melville cleared his throat. "Well, as a matter of fact, you can help me out."

"How?" I asked, surprised.

Walter leaned even closer to me. "I believe you can help me break our OPEC contract price for our resales to the European refiners. You know these Europeans can virtually name their own price on direct deals with OPEC. On every resale we make we're paying OPEC price and having to resell it at whatever distressed price we can get.

"Bradshaw might," Melville continued, his voice doubtful, "be able to pull something off, but that's liable to take time, and we both know Sullivan isn't giving us any of that precious commodity. Anyway, you mentioned last year when I took over International that if I ever needed a favor in Venezuela, you could arrange it."

"I did," I responded.

"Venezuela desperately needs cash, and they have lots of oil. I've only been able to make low level contacts, but I sense they might be interested in a secret deal at spot prices if we kept it quiet. Do you think you could arrange it?"

I thought of that fine South American gentleman who had treated me like a brother, one of the few people I could call a faithful friend. Now I regretted having told Melville about him. But then again, my friend was looking to make a quiet deal, and Melville would never find Carib on his own. And I did owe Melville...

"I'll make a call," I said finally.

"Thanks, Nick. I really appreciate it.... How's Susan?"

"I don't really know, Walt. As you know, she's out on her own now, and I'm not sure she can handle it. She has only one client so far and for her the sun seems to be dipping below the yardarm at noon every day."

Melville pointed to his empty martini stem glass. "She's not alone, you know," he chuckled.

"That's different. We stop and go back to work. But she must keep on all afternoon because she's wasted when I get home."

Melville flipped his hand dismissively. "Don't worry about it, Nick. She'll find other clients. She's just going through a period of adjustment."

"Maybe you're right," I said. "Look, I enjoy a drink just as well as anybody, but I think she's overdoing it... Anyway, I'll tell her you were asking about her."

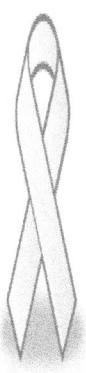

CHAPTER TEN

One week later, my intercom beeped just as I was dashing out of my office.

"Oh!" blurted Liz, startled, seeing me standing in the doorway. "It's…it's Inspector Lopez."

I hesitated, since I was running late, but then I strode back to my desk and picked up the receiver. "Hi, Ricardo. What's up?"

"Nick! Nick! We've got a breakthrough on the briefcase!"

"Briefcase?"

"Yes. Briefcase. Your briefcase. Remember? The one that blew up?"

I laughed, embarrassed. "That briefcase. I'm sorry, Ricardo. My mind is on other things. What have you found?"

"Not over the phone. Are you free for lunch?"

"I'm sorry, Ricardo. I can't make it. I've got an appointment with an old friend from Venezuela. But I can be at your office by...say...two-thirty."

"No, not here. Let's see...How about your house?"

"My house it is. You know where it is. See you there at six."

I spied my friend standing at the bar as I entered the dining room of Sel et Poivre. "Carib!" I called and waved.

"Nicholas!" Carib cried, smiling broadly as he rushed forward to meet me. His even white teeth were a flashing contrast to his rich brown face. Pure Indian blood, untouched by the Conquistadors, flowed through his tall, lean body. In a government dominated by Spanish descendants he would be the last person an outsider would suspect to be the second most powerful man in Venezuela. That power came from the President who had brought him to Caracas from the hacienda where they had grown up together. As we embraced, I said, "It's great to see you, my friend. Thank you for coming all this way."

"And I am happy to see you, my friend," Carib said in his Oxford educated English. "You have lost weight."

"Ten pounds. I've been jogging. And you look as lean and mean as ever."

Carib smiled, as though about to make an embarrassing confession. "I have been jogging as well."

I roared with laughter. "You? Jogging? I don't believe it! You once said you would die first!"

"Only one of many foolish things I once said," Carib chuckled.

I noticed a bottle of Kaliber sitting on the bar. "Still on the wagon, Carib?" I asked.

"Not even a Polar," he replied. "But I still savor the taste of beer and Kaliber is the king of the non-alcoholics. Are you still imbibing?"

The bartender appeared. "Stoly on the rocks," was my answer.

"You'll learn," he predicted.

We stood at the bar, sipping our drinks, and catching up on each other's news. He had, of course, heard about the Las Palmas bombing and I filled him in on the ambulance attempt.

We finished our drinks, and then I asked the hostess to seat us. She led us to the same rear corner table at which Melville and I had sat the previous week. We ordered another round of drinks, and then I glanced at Carib's face, which could be hard and impenetrable, but now was relaxed and open. "Carib, my friend, I... we...need a favor."

"Anything that is within my power. You are a loyal friend. I shant forget what you did for me on those technology developments—that brought our production costs down twenty-five per cent and increased production output fifteen per cent."

"I'm glad I could help. But still, I feel uncomfortable asking you for a favor because I feel I am taking advantage of our friendship."

"Sometimes that's what friends are for. Tell me. What do you need?"

I came straight out with it. "I want to make a sub-rosa deal with you for 100,000 barrels a day at five dollars under the OPEC price."

Carib rolled his head back and roared with peals of laughter. "What's so bloody funny?" I demanded.

The waiter returned with drinks, served them, and then left as Carib was regaining his composure. Then he answered my question, "It really is rather droll." He chuckled, just once this time. "What is so humorous is that your request of me is precisely what I was going to propose to you. About ten days ago Cesaré, Presidente Balboa, asked me to find a quiet home for 100,000 barrels a day. He also asked me what I thought the discount needed to be, and I replied five dollars a barrel!"

This time we both erupted in laughter. When Carib caught his breath, he reached inside his suit jacket and withdrew a neatly folded packet of papers. "Well, " he chuckled again as he reached inside his jacket once more for his Waterford pen, "I just happen to have signed contracts with me. I'll fill in the amount of 100,000 barrels a day, and then you can sign them under Arturo's signature. It appears as though we have a deal."

"We do," I agreed. "After lunch, let's go back to the office and work out the details with Melville..." I paused as I noticed the frown on my friend's face. "Ah. I had forgotten how much you cherish your anonymity. Whom should I have Melville contact?"

Carib smiled. "My obscurity keeps me free of pressure and preserves my objectivity—and that is my true value to Cesaré ... Anyway, just give the contract to Mr. Melville and have him sign it and return it to Arturo who will be his contact. The contract is a standard one, so Mr. Melville shouldn't have any questions, but if he does, have him call Arturo."

The waiter appeared and took our lunch order. "Now that the business is completed," Carib said when the waiter had left, "let's get back to this murder plot. *The Oil News* reported you were paralyzed, and some terrorist group claimed responsibility."

I smiled, feeling embarrassed. "I didn't thank you for your 'get well' card. I thank you now; it meant a lot to me, because things looked bleak then.... Anyway, I don't know who is responsible. The FBI is working on it. In fact, I'm meeting the local FBI Inspector tonight; he says he's got some sort of breakthrough."

"About the terrorists?"

"He doesn't think it was terrorists. He thinks someone was after me alone; some enemy of mine. It's possibly someone at OPEC. Or maybe even Guillermo."

"I presume you have Guillermo Mendez from Colombia in mind."
I nodded.

"I would not put it past him, now. When you knew him, he was just another greedy hanger-on. Today he's into the drug cartel in a major way. He's not a man to be trifled with. But I cannot believe that someone in OPEC is responsible"

"Neither do I, but there is some evidence—and I did make quite a few enemies amongst you OPEC guys."

Carib scowled. "Not in Venezuela, you didn't. But..." he paused, "some of those fellows in those other countries were fairly upset when you withheld that equipment technology, particularly Mundi and Amani. On the other hand, they did have it coming to them."

"Mundi. Yeah. He always seemed very ruthless to me."

"That he is. And there's always been a rumor that he is CIA connected."

I nodded somberly. "Yes. I had heard that as well."

"Well, my friend, I will find out what I can about those two..."

After lunch, we said our farewells, and I returned to the office with the contract in hand. Melville stared at it wide-eyed, stammering, "Where ... where in hell did you get this? I couldn't even get close to Arturo Ramirez—he runs the whole damn Oil Company. Is ... is he your contact?"

"Don't worry about it, Walter. Just call him if you have any questions."

It was just past six p.m. when I drove up my circular driveway. Ricardo's restored 1964 white mustang was parked in front of the main entrance to the house. I swung my Jaguar in behind the little convertible. I opened the door, extracted myself from the seat, planting my feet onto the driveway and walked over to the Inspector's car. The top was down and there was no sign of Ricardo.

I shrugged my shoulders, wondering if Ricardo had gone inside to visit with Susan. As I turned the front door handle, finding it locked, I remembered Susan was at dance class and wouldn't be home until eight o'clock.

I circled the house entirely, but still couldn't find Ricardo. I decided he must be somewhere out on the grounds, so I'd wait inside the house for him to return. As I unlocked the front door, a bullet whizzed past my left ear, through the open doorway and crashed into the far wall of the foyer. I instinctively dove behind the front door as a second bullet raced over my head. I kicked the door shut with my foot, then reached up and shoved the bolt home.

I carefully raised my head to peer through one of the small bull's eye glass panes that surrounded the doorway. I saw nothing. I was crouched, ready to dash for the stairway and my gun in the bedroom when I heard someone running along the side of the house. The footfalls then moved along the front of the house towards the front door. I froze.

I heard the muffled report of a silencer coming from the woods in front of the house, then the instantaneous sound of the bullet ricocheting off the brick house. I sprang over to the corner and flattened myself against the wall. This was followed at once by three loud shots right by the front door. Then I heard, "Nick, Nick," being shouted right outside. It was Ricardo's voice.

"In here," I shouted as I rushed to the door, yanked the bolt back and flung open the door. Ricardo lowered his gun as soon as he saw me, then hurried through the open doorway, glancing back over his shoulder as he did so.

As I closed and bolted the door, Ricardo fumed, "I knew I heard that snake!"

"What is happening?" I asked, bewildered.

Ricardo looked at me. "Good God, you're as white as a sheet. Come on, you'd better sit down." He took me by the arm.

"No, no, Ricardo," I said, pulling my arm free. "I'm okay. Let me go get my gun and let's go get him."

"You know how to handle a gun?"

"My Great-Grandfather taught me. I don't particularly like them, but yes, I'm good with a gun."

"Well, our man is probably long gone by now, but we can take a look, if you like."

"No, you're probably right—he's long gone. Just tell me what happened."

"Well I arrived here about a quarter of six and parked by the front door. I had the top down for the drive up, so I could enjoy the scenery. I was sitting in the car, waiting for you to arrive when I thought I heard a noise in the woods. I wasn't sure—I'm not used to country sounds—I thought it might have been just the wind in the trees...

"But I went into the woods by the side of the house anyway. I searched carefully, but I didn't see or hear anything. The bugger must have risked going out to the road and come back through the woods in front of the house.

"I was on my way back when I heard what sounded like a silencer—I really wondered if I was starting to hear things. But when I heard the second report, I came running."

I looked over at the two bullet holes in the wall and shivered. Then my entire body began to quiver. I tried to speak, but I couldn't open my mouth. Gradually the shaking subsided, stopped, and then I felt strangely calm. "Come on," I said quietly, then led the way through the foyer and into the den beyond. "Have a seat," I said, motioning towards the flower print chair. I eased myself down onto the couch. "I get it now," I said finally, "they really have been trying to kill me. Just me. Bombs and ambulance accidents are one thing, but bullets flying at my head brings it home."

Ricardo nodded his head. "First at Las Palmas, next in the ambulance, and again now."

"Somehow I just didn't believe it. I guess I felt I was such a great guy that no one would really want to kill me. I kept telling myself they were after someone else at Las Palmas and that the ambulance really was an accident. And it's been such a long time since then. But now...now I see that I'm not such a great guy, and that I'm mortal. They really *are* after me."

"They're after *you* all right. And somehow the bloody CIA is involved."

"No way." Then I thought of Guillermo. "The CIA? I thought they were on our side."

"They are!" Ricardo exploded. "But one fact is indisputable. The briefcase that blew up at Las Palmas was one of theirs."

I felt more than a hint of skepticism. Yes, it was true that the CIA had overstepped its bounds in the past, but mass murder? And Ricardo himself had hinted at inter-agency rivalry that day in the FBI lab. Now he was carrying that rivalry a bit too far. "Ricardo," I began, as though talking to a small child who wasn't getting the point, "there are thousands of briefcases just like mine. What in the world makes you think the substitute came from the CIA?"

Ricardo bristled, detecting my attitude. "Because, my friend, that briefcase was equipped with a hidden compartment which is impervious to the probes of Airport x-ray machines. The CIA ordered 100 briefcases from Atlas, who made yours, and added that little modification."

"They can really do that—I mean get explosives through airport security?"

"Yes. They've developed a new alloy that makes the space look empty to the x-ray machine. So, somebody duplicates your briefcase, right down to your initials, loads it with explosive, gets through all kinds of security, and then switches yours with it, probably when it was in your room while you were at breakfast. Someone dressed as a maid or maintenance man wouldn't arouse suspicion going in or out of a room at that time of the day. After breakfast, you go to your meeting, put the booby-trapped briefcase next to your chair, and, when Governor Rodriguez presses the light control which connects to the wall switch, you're expected to be history."

My mind shot back to that morning. The control switch at the podium hadn't worked, and I had been the closest one to the light switch, so I had gotten up and had flipped it manually. "If it hadn't been for that faulty light control at the podium," I murmured, "I wouldn't be here."
I paused. "Why didn't he just put the explosive in the light switch, with the trigger mechanism?"

"I think it was because he wanted to be sure to get you. He didn't know where you would be sitting, and the light switch may have been too far away from you."

I nodded. "That makes sense."

Ricardo's eyes focused squarely on mine. "Why does the goddamn CIA want you fucking dead?" he asked in a penetrating tone.

I recoiled at Lopez's uncharacteristic cursing and then shifted my eyes away from the piercing stare.

"Lord knows," I grimaced, "I don't."

"What the hell aren't you telling me?" Ricardo persisted. "What happened when you were running your goddamn International Division? How involved were you with those freaking foreign governments?"

I felt my blood pressure rise. "I was incredibly involved; many of them were our partners. But what the hell does that have to do with the CIA?"

"Plenty, if you're supporting a goddamn government they're trying to overthrow. And it's even worse if you're involved in a coup attempt against a government they support. What the hell was in it for you?" Ricardo pushed, unrelenting.

I remembered Mundi. We had been friends in the beginning, until Mundi had tried to jam me, and I had retaliated with the equipment swap. And there was the rumor of his CIA connection. "A long time ago..." I began, "I had this friend in Iraq—" I paused and frowned. "But I still don't see—"

"You let me be the freaking judge," Ricardo interrupted. "The goddamn CIA never forgets. Tell me what the hell happened."

I blinked in disbelief at the Inspector's cursing barrage. "Well, as I was saying," I said curtly, "I used to have this friend, Al Mundi, in Iraq who worked in the Oil Ministry. Then he started running with a Marxist crowd, and he began to feel that Saddam and his cronies, himself included, had plenty of petrodollars to spread around, and that the government wasn't doing enough to help the poor. So... he wanted to change the government—in a hurry."

Ricardo nodded his understanding. "He planned a coup," Ricardo said, making a statement, rather than asking a question.

"Yes. He asked me to fund the takeover, promising a 49 per cent share in the oil monopoly in return. I didn't share his politics, but I had seen how cold-blooded and ruthless Saddam had been, so I told him I would present it to New York. Sullivan waffled quite a while, and Mundi kept pressing me. To add to the pressure, he started delaying crude deliveries to us. Sullivan finally relented and wired initial funds.

"Then," I continued, "Sullivan changed his mind, and refused to send additional money. I covered for Sullivan, telling Mundi I stopped the deal because I had heard Saddam learned of the plot. This may have actually been true because several of his friends had disappeared."

"Knowing what we do about Saddam, it probably was true."

"Regardless, Mundi blew up. He cut off our oil supply, and I cut off his equipment. Then he told me he was going to approach the CIA for funding."

"Aha! "Ricardo exclaimed. "That's what I've been pushing you for! He's the CIA connection!"

"Oh, come on, Ricardo. You're really reaching. O.K., Mundi was upset with me, but I don't think he was mad enough to want to kill me."

"Maybe he was, or maybe he wasn't. Or maybe it's the Agency itself. Maybe he told them of your initial involvement, and they don't want to be connected to any assassination—heads would roll. And you could connect them."

My mouth popped open as my jaw dropped. But I was dumb with disbelief. I closed my mouth, licked my lips, and then managed to say, "What about Guillermo?"

"We're still trying to find him. And we will. In any event, I'm going to find out the truth," Ricardo vowed.

My brain was fried. I needed time to think. Think about my tenuous life. About Susan. About my career. "Please, Ricardo. I... I'm done in. I'd like to go upstairs and lie down for a while." I felt strange, admitting my weakness.

"Sure, Nick," Ricardo said, patting me on the shoulder. "You've had another close call. Talk to you tomorrow. I'll contact the Greenwich police and have them keep an eye on the house until I can get my own men tomorrow. And that gun of yours— I presume you have a permit."

"Of course."

"You'd better start carrying. And I'll get you a special permit to clear airport security."

My knees were still weak as I struggled up the carpeted stairway to the master bedroom. I shed my clothes down to my T-shirt and boxer shorts and lay down on the king-size bed. I clasped my hands behind my head and propped myself against the satin headboard and gazed out the bay window onto Long Island Sound. The evening breeze had cleared away the haze, and I could make out the first lights of Oyster Bay in the fading daylight.

Gradually I became aware of the slight rise of my stomach under my T-shirt. "Nuts!" I said aloud. "I've got to get rid of this. Right now!"

I leaped from the bed and strode over to the closet where I kept my running gear. I dressed quickly, and then rummaged around the bottom of the closet until I found my running shoes. As I pulled them on, my newfound energy surged through me. My whole body tingled. I bounded down the stairs two at a time.

I flung open the front door, but then froze in the open doorway. I leaped back, dodging the imagined assassin's bullet. My unbridled energy had made me reckless. I needed to bring myself back to ground.

I heard a car coming up the gravel driveway. I peered through one of the bull's eye glass windows and spotted a police car emerging from the woods that lined the uphill driveway. It rounded the grassy, Belgian block lined circle at the top of the driveway and pulled up in front of the open doorway. Two uniformed Greenwich policemen jumped out, the gravel crunching under their feet as they converged on the open door. I stepped out from my hiding place. "That was fast," I said. "Ricardo said he would arrange for local protection, but I didn't expect you so soon."

"We were in the neighborhood," said one of the officers whose nametag identified him as Bardini.

"Yea..." said the other officer, named Kelly, speaking slowly, as though musing. 'We had a complaint of a prowler next door at the Johnson's. Could have been your man."

"Any description?" I asked quickly, hoping for details I could identify.

"No, Mrs. Johnson just saw a figure in the woods."

"Damn," I said, disappointed. "I could really use a break."

I looked up at fading light in the sky. "Well, I really appreciate your being here. I was about ready to go for a fast run on the roads but didn't because I thought he might still be out there."

"It's unlikely," said Officer Kelly, "but just in case, we'll follow you." The officer patted his protruding stomach, continuing, "From the patrol car."

My mind was blank for the first five minutes of the run. Suddenly I saw myself running on the beach. Now I was playing on the beach. Playing tag with my friends. I was nine years old, and we were all laughing as we dodged and weaved.

This image dissolved into another image of running. Now I was playing football, and I was running after Susan who had the ball. She had just caught a wobbly pass and was shrieking with laughter as she was trying to elude me. She stopped short and sidestepped my onrush. I tried

71

to change direction in full stride but tripped over myself and fell in a heap of laughter.

Now, as I ran, I smiled, and tears filled the corners of my eyes. Then my chin started to quiver, and the tears rolled down my face as I realized that day so many years ago was the last time I really laughed

.

CHAPTER ELEVEN

At the Monday morning staff meeting two months later, Sullivan was jubilant. "Good morning, gentlemen, and lady," he began. "Before we start, I have an announcement which gives me great personal pleasure. Effective today, Miss Pat Campbell will assume the duties of the newly created position of Vice President of Administration, reporting to Nick Shepherd."

"It's about goddamn time," Melville mumbled to me as the room erupted into applause. We were seated together at the far end of the boardroom table.

"It seems I have nothing but good news this morning," he continued, looking down at the computer printout in front of him, as though surprised. "Last week's figures are straight off the computer, and I'm enormously proud of them. Thanks to Golden Green, our Domestic market share is up three full percentage points. And thanks to our private deal with Venezuela, International is buying crude below even the spot price. The bottom line, gentlemen, is that our earnings are up sixty-two per cent!"

The room erupted into applause once again. Sullivan grinned, then held up his hands for silence. "Thank you, gentlemen—and lady. We can all share in this moment."

"Thanks a lot, you son-of-a bitch," Walter murmured to me.

Sullivan paused, then added, "I am also pleased to report that I have completed negotiations with Pueblo and, because of this acquisition, our earnings—"

He paused, looking down at his notes through his half-moon glasses and continued, "will be.... even higher." Sullivan grinned again, his actor-perfect teeth gleaming.

After the meeting, I returned to my office and called Susan. "What are you doing for lunch?"

"What?" came the surprised reply.

"Can you meet me here in town for lunch? I'm a little tired of conversation with FBI agents. Besides, I want to talk with you, and all we do in the evenings is fight."

"Well..." Susan hesitated, "I have a bridge game planned at the Club."

"Oh, come on," I persisted. "They can find another fourth. We haven't had lunch since— "

I paused, struggling to remember the last time. "Well, for a long time."

"Too long," Susan said quietly.

After a few moments of silence, I ventured, "Well, how about it?"

"I won't make any guarantees," she said finally, "but I'll see if I can find an alternate."

I was on my second drink at Le Lavandou. I had signaled the waiter, ready to order my lunch, when I saw Susan descending the steps. "I was about to give up on you," I said as she sat down.

"And I you," she countered, her voice heavy with double meaning. I raised my head up and back slightly, feeling indignant. "Just what do you mean?"

The waiter arrived before she could answer, and Susan ordered a double martini on the rocks, with a twist.

"Just what did you mean," I repeated.

"Oh, nothing," she said breezily. "I just had a tough time rearranging my busy schedule."

"Oh, come on, Susie. What did you mean?"

Susan stared at me. "You haven't called me Susie since we were in school. Oh, you make me so mad! I had about given you up for lost. To business. We—"

I didn't give her a chance to finish, knowing what she was going to say. "Susie, Susie," I said, exasperated, "you know how difficult business has been lately. But now things are improving. I can breathe a little easier. That's why I wanted to have lunch with you today. I wanted to share my success with you, and to spend more time with you."

"Nick," Susan said, impatiently, as though speaking to an errant child, "I've heard all this before. Remember when we were first married— that time when we were going to spend our anniversary in Mexico? And you had been working late every night on some innovative marketing project. And then some other new critical project came up at the last minute, so you decided it would be best to postpone our trip. Do you remember all that?"

Without waiting for an answer, she plunged on. "Well, I do. Sullivan was running your life even then... Anyway, I'm still waiting for my trip to Mexico."

"Well, you were busy, too," I said defensively.

Susan sighed. "I suppose I was. But now...now I don't care if I ever work again. There are other, more important things."

"Let's not start that child thing again."

The waiter returned and served Susan her martini. Then noticing my empty glass, he asked in his strong French accent, "May I bring you another aperitif, sir?"

"Yes, please. A double martini on the rocks with a twist."

"With pleasure, Sir," the waiter said, then left.

"All I said," I resumed, "was that things are improving at the office. I'm not ready to give up my career—we need to pay the mortgage, you know. I just want to enjoy life occasionally now." I shifted my gaze to the FBI Agent sitting at the table by the stairway. "I have a constant reminder of how short life can be.

"Look," I went on. "Why don't we take that long delayed trip? Our Anniversary is next month, you know."

"No, Nick," was Susan's sarcastic reply. "I had completely forgotten all about it.

"I am so sorry," she continued in mock contrition, "but I have been so busy."

The waiter returned with my drink, served it with a flourish, and then glided away.

"Susie, listen to me. I deserve what you just said, but I'm changing. Haven't you noticed it in the last couple of months? I've been laughing more."

"Nick, you can't change the last fifteen years in two months. And besides, I can't honestly say I see a change. As you aptly pointed out on the telephone, we fight in the evenings, even though it may start out with a few laughs. No, Nick, your business is still your whole life."

"Well, maybe you don't see a change," I conceded, "but I sure feel differently. Come on. Let's give Mexico a try."

Susan shook her head. "No. I don't want to go with you. We'd be there two days, and then you'd go crazy. You'd be on the phone to the office to remind both them and you how indispensable you are."

"Susie, give me a chance!"

She looked down at her martini, then back at me. Finally, she murmured, "I'll give you a chance...

"But I'm not going to Mexico with you," she continued, her voice firmer. "Somehow...somehow that would be like running away. You've got to show me in other ways."

"What other ways!" I demanded. My voice choked with frustration.

"I don't know how other men do it," Susan said. "Their lives seem more balanced. I guess...I guess you'll have to figure that out for yourself. I can't help you." She looked back down at her martini, picked it up, and then took a long swallow. "Damn," she said, "I can't even help myself."

I stared at Susan. She never swore. I felt as though I was sitting across from someone I didn't know. I studied her, as though looking at her for the first time. Lines around her eyes and white wisps in her black hair had matured her former youthful attractiveness into full beauty. I felt my heart stir.

Susan's head was bowed slightly, her gaze now transfixed on the white tablecloth. Suddenly she looked up, her big, chestnut brown eyes filling with tears. It had been so long since I had looked into her eyes, I had forgotten how beautiful they were. My heart fluttered once more.

"You make me so mad," she said again, this time hissing the words.

I stared at her again, this time wide-eyed. Finally, I managed to ask, "What...what's wrong?"

"You pretend you can wipe away the last fifteen years by running back to Mexico. That will fix everything. Just feed Susie a few old memories, and then back to business. That might have worked a while back, but no more. Listen, Goddamnit, you're going to have to do better than that!"

"Now wait a minute!" I was surprised at the viciousness of my voice. I paused to regain control of myself. "When we got married," I resumed, "you wanted your career as much as I wanted mine. I was happy with my job, and I thought you were happy with yours."

"Come on! You've done nothing but complain about your job for the last—I don't know how many years!" Susan's tears had stopped, and her face was angry red.

The harsh bitterness of her words cut through my defenses. I really did like my job, but I had kept all that satisfaction to myself. All that I had shared with Susan were my disappointments. But I was angry now, and I wasn't about to admit the truth. "Make up your mind," I said venomously. "First you say my job is my life, and the next minute you say I hate it! What's it going to be?"

"I don't know! You never tell me how you really feel about anything!"

"Not so loud," I said in a stage whisper. "People are looking at us."

"Let them look. And I go back to what I said in the first place; your job is your life." Anger filled every one of Susan's words.

The waiter appeared and took our lunch order, together with an order for another round of drinks.

When we were alone again, I said, "Well, you know, Susie, until recently, your career has been your life too. I've always been second to it."

"But the publishing business wasn't my *whole* life. I played bridge. I worked at the blood bank. I had friends over. You didn't want to be a part of any of that."

"You never asked me if I wanted to be! I like bridge!"

"Now you're yelling," Susan said in the same stage whisper way I had.

I took a deep breath, and then sighed. "Well you never even suggested we play bridge together."

"Neither did you," Susan countered. "And you never asked me if I wanted to play golf with you."

"The only time I play personally is Saturday morning. Women aren't allowed on the course until one o'clock."

"We could have played then. Or on Sunday. Face it. You just didn't want to play with me."

"We always visited your parents on Sundays."

Rage flashed across Susan's face, ignited by the fire of my words. "You make me so mad I could—" She stopped.

"Kill me," I finished Susan's sentence quietly. I shivered with the enormity that it could be true.

"I'm sorry," Susan said. "I really am. You don't need to be reminded."

I nodded, accepting her apology. "That's all right—we were both getting pretty steamed. I don't think much about it. It's as though all that happened to someone else. If it weren't for my FBI shadow and the police patrols by the house, I'd be able to put it out of my mind."

My hands were resting on the white tablecloth, palms down. Susan reached over and covered them with hers. She smiled and said, "Thank you for this lunch idea—it really was very sweet."

I turned my hands over and clasped her hands in mine. "Your welcome," I said simply.

Susan' smile faded, and she bit her lips. She blinked several times, fighting back tears again. "You...you don't know how really...really sorry I am," she stammered.

I squeezed Susan's hands, "It's all right," I reassured her. "Forget it."

"I want to have an affair with you," Susan blurted, her voice sounding desperate. "Let's forget Mexico. Let's forget the killer. Hell let's forget lunch and go find a hotel room."

I withdrew my hands from Susan's. "What in the world are you talking about? We are married, you know. What's wrong with tonight? At home?"

"But that's so staged—it's not spontaneous." Susan emphasized her words with expansive gesticulations. "Besides, at home, you're tired, I'm tired; we really don't feel like it."

I scowled, shaking my head back and forth. "Let me get this straight. You want me to take a couple of hours off for a—" I hesitated, looking for the right word, "a nooner? Because you're tired at night?"

"Forget it,' Susan spat. "I knew you wouldn't understand. You're never going to get rid of the rod rammed up your rear."

"Susan!" I exclaimed, feeling totally bewildered. "What is wrong with you? You never used to talk like this. You're like a stranger."

"That so-called 'stranger' you see is the real me. Swearing is real—it expresses emotion.

"Look," she continued, "I've been here all along, but I've been buried by you, by my job, and," she leaned forward, looking me straight in the eye, "there is something else. I really want to have a child—now. And I'm afraid that if you don't want to have one with me, I'm going to find someone who does."

I cocked my head to the right, as though trying to see a new perspective. "I can't believe you. You're actually threatening me."

"No, Nick. I'm not trying to threaten you. I'm just afraid that if you don't change your mind soon—"

"Oh, Susie," I said, my voice fraught with frustration, "I just can't agree yet. Soon. Please just give me a little while longer."

"I can't promise anything," she said. "I feel as though I've wasted the last 15 years, and I don't know if I can wait any longer."

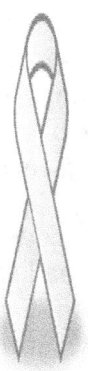

CHAPTER TWELVE

As I walked down the hall towards my office the next morning, I thought I heard my telephone ringing. I quickened my pace, rounded the corner to Liz's desk, and reached over it to pick up the receiver.

"Nick Shepherd," I answered.

"I figured you'd be in," said the voice on the other end that I recognized as Jim Hudson's, R and D Director.

"It's an hour earlier in Houston," I responded. "What are you doing there?"

"I've been here all night," Jim said. "We've got big problems."

"I don't like the sound of that. Hold on while I go into my office." I pushed the hold button and went into my office, closing the door behind me. I eased myself into my chair, my legs stiff from the increased running distance of five miles per day. I picked up the receiver as I pushed the flashing line on the console. "What happened, Jim?" I asked.

"I'm afraid I neglected to consider one thing with that Golden Green formula you gave me," Jim answered, his voice apologetic, "and that was the combustion temperature of the formulation."

Sudden understanding struck me like a demolition ball. "Oh, no," I half whispered. "Engine life. Shortened engine life! We rushed through testing so quickly, I didn't even consider it!"

"I'm the one who should have thought of it. But I guess with all that pressure from Sullivan to come up with the right formula, when I saw yours, I looked at with my blind spot. I thought it was the miracle I was hoping for."

"Yea. We were both looking for a miracle." I paused momentarily, and then asked, "Well what sort of damage are we looking at?"

"I don't expect anything like blown engines or cracked blocks. But there will be a loss of compression over the life of the car, at an accelerated rate."

"How accelerated?" I demanded.

"Well...it's a little hard to tell yet...I'm not trying to be evasive, but I just don't know."

"What's your best estimate?" I pursued, unrelenting.

"Fifty percent," Jim said finally.

"Fifty percent!" I bellowed. "No way! You've got to be out of your mind!"

"Nick, take it easy. It's me, Jim."

I suddenly realized I had been sounding exactly like Sullivan. "I'm sorry, Jim. I just lost it."

"No problem. I know you're under a lot of pressure up there. We can solve this temperature thing, but it's going to take some time."

"How much time? Realistically."

"Well, theoretically, all we have to do is lower the ignition temperature of the formulation, but that change may affect other characteristics. If we're lucky...we'll have a new formulation in about thirty days. If we're not, the trial and error process could take...oh, probably ninety days."

"Ninety days," I echoed slowly. "Good Lord, Jim, I don't know what to do. I don't want to hide it." I felt my armpits flooding with perspiration in the moments of silence that followed. "Well," I said finally, "someone is going to get fired over this, so it might as well be me."

"No, Nick," Jim protested, "this is my responsibility; I should have caught it. Besides, I can get a new job with just one phone call; SoCal has been after me for years. Finding jobs at your level is where it's tough."

"Look, Jim. I've been thinking about changing jobs anyway. All this hassle just isn't worth it. My personal life is suffering."

"I know what you mean, Nick, but don't do anything rash. We've all been under a lot of pressure with this Golden Green Octane project, but we will solve the problem eventually. Then you can bring your personal life back into balance."

"Yes, but after Golden Green, there will be something else. Jim, I don't have a personal life, and haven't for the past fifteen years. My life has been working for this Company. Not that I haven't enjoyed it—I have. It's just that now...well, it's just not fun anymore."

"Nick, I hear you. I've been through what you're describing. It's difficult, and you must decide what you want. And, yes, you may wind up changing your life dramatically. But...Nick, we've been buddies a long time. Take your time with this one. You may find, as I have, that you can have a balanced personal and business life without shooting anything."

I had let down my guard and was now afraid of the consequences. "Jim, please. Forget I said anything. I trust you, but something just might slip. I wouldn't want this to get back to Sullivan.

"You were right before," I continued, "it will pass. And on second thought I don't think either one of us will be sacrificed. Sullivan really wants Golden Green, and, because of his paranoia, you and I are the only ones who have been intimately involved. He couldn't get rid of us."

"Well, do whatever you want; I'm not going to worry about it. Let me know what you decide. So long, Nick."

"Talk to you later," I said, and then hung up.

I sighed as I swung my swivel chair toward the window. I stared down at Midtown Manhattan, mulling over the alternatives. Finally, I picked up the telephone and dialed Sullivan's number. Hazel, Sullivan's secretary, answered and, after a brief wait, Sullivan came on the line. "Good morning, Nick," he said enthusiastically. "How's the Golden Green star?"

"Good morning, Bruce. In fact, it is Golden Green that I need to discuss with you. May I come down?"

"Sure, I can spare a few minutes this early."

I strode down the hallway, turned right into the next hallway, and, by the time I reached Sullivan's office in the far corner, opposite the board room, the stiffness in my legs had vanished. I knocked on the closed door, and then entered.

Sullivan smiled, showing his broad, square teeth. "There's my Golden Green man. You're looking good. How are you doing?"

"Not so plus this morning, Bruce." I knew I looked glum and was surprised Sullivan hadn't noticed it.

"You're not bringing me some problem, I trust. You know I only like solutions." Sullivan was still smiling broadly.

"Oh, I have the solution, all right," I responded, knowing I was sounding flip. "We're going to withdraw Golden Green from the market."

Disbelief spread quickly across Sullivan's face. "What in the hell are you talking about?"

I took a very deep breath through my nose, and then blew it out through my mouth. "Well it's this way, Bruce," I said in a surprisingly calm manner, given I was feeling like a Greek messenger bearing unwelcome news just before his tongue was cut out. "We have discovered that Golden Green accelerates engine wear, so I'm recommending we remove it from the market while we reformulate."

Sullivan was now scowling. "There is no way I'm going to stop selling the most successful product in the Company's history. Golden Green is the rage of everyone, from the Environmentalists to Wall Street. Hell, it's brought us back to life! Without it, we may as well close our doors!"

"But the withdrawal would only be short term. Hudson tells me we would be back on the market in ninety days or less. And our honesty would bring us immeasurable good will from the groups you just mentioned—to say nothing of our customers. I am positive the public would buy our regular products while we develop Golden Green Octane Two."

"No. No way would that happen. We'd lose market share overnight. And Good Will doesn't help the bottom line."

"Bruce," I said, tension raising the pitch in my voice, "the product is accelerating engine wear. Think of it your way—what do you think will happen to the bottom line if someone discovers the problem and announces it to the world, particularly if they learn we knew about it?"

"That's up to you and Hudson to be sure no one does discover it. Look. You tell me Hudson can reformulate in a quarter or less. We can switch to the new formula at that time, and no one will be the wiser."

"Bruce, I still don't believe it's the right choice. And besides, someday, somebody is going to find out about it."

"Listen, Nick. I'm not worried about someday. I'm worried about the here and now and keeping the price of my stock up."

Sullivan paused. "You know, this reminds me of that time in—where was it—Iraq? Yea, Iraq. You had some noble plan to bring down Saddam's government. Forget the altruism; it doesn't work.

"What does work," he continued, "is keeping your eye on the bottom line. I don't mind telling you that I'm going to step down in the next couple of years, and with my control of the Company's stock, I will pick my successor. I also don't mind telling you now that you're the leading candidate to be that man. You've got the brains and the guts to do the job, so don't let that youthful idealism creep back into your head."

"Yea, I was really naive in those Iraqi days," I said as I looked past Sullivan out the window and down at the East River. Sullivan had just told me that the goal that I had been working towards for the past fifteen years was within my grasp, but I didn't feel anything. What was wrong with me?

"Are you all right, Nick?" Sullivan asked. "Have you had your annual check-up?"

I looked back at Sullivan. "I'm fine," I answered. "In fact, the doctor told me I'm in the best shape I've been in the last fifteen years. I guess I'm a little preoccupied, but it will pass... We'll stay the course with Golden Green, work twenty-four hours a day to reformulate, and then just slip the new product in when it's ready. And nobody will be the wiser."

"That's the spirit. Just stay focused.... Say, is everything all right between you and Susan?"

I looked down at the floor. "I don't know, Bruce. I guess we're both going through mid-life crises. Her losing her job—"

"Well don't worry about her; she'll get another one. And I've just told you that you've got the inside track on the top job here."

"Thanks, Bruce. I really appreciate it."

"And on the personal side, you'll get through it. If there's anything I can do, please don't hesitate to ask. You've got to excuse me now; I've got a meeting with Bradshaw." He smiled like a patronizing parent, saying, "And we're clear on Golden Green. Steady as she goes, right?"

"Right, Chief," I echoed as I rose.

Sullivan looked at me, frowning. "And keep me posted on your progress."

"Will do." I turned and left.

As I approached my office, Liz looked up from her computer. "Ah, there you are. A Mr. Carib Conibo is on the line."

I entered my office, shutting the door behind me. I picked up the phone on my desk. "Good morning, Carib. Where are you?"

"I'm here in New York. Cesaré has asked me to buy a bank. You know, employ those petrodollars to expand the world economy."

"I thought you guys in OPEC were trying to shrink the world economy with unconscionably high oil prices."

"Touché," Carib laughed. "What is it you Americans say? Whatever. That's it. I have unearthed some information on Mendez. Can we meet?"

"Sure. How about lunch? "

"Great, my friend."

"How about Fonda La Paloma at twelve-fifteen? And I could use a friend."

"I'll be there."

On the way to the restaurant, I was swept up with the wave of the festival feeling that surges along the sidewalks of New York at mid-day. I usually fought the crowds, dodging and weaving, bumping, and shoving. But now I savored the wide-eyed awe of the summer tourists and the dreamy-eyed pleasure of young office workers passing a joint. And I saw for the first time the anguish on the faces of people such as myself, dodging, weaving, bumping, and shoving.

I arrived at the restaurant ten minutes late, but still had to wait five more minutes until Carib sauntered in. "I'm glad to see you, my friend," Carib greeted me as we embraced.

"It's good to see you too, my friend," I said.

"Beautiful day, isn't it?"

"One of the year's ten best."

The maître d' showed us to our table, and Carib ordered a Kaliber beer. I had planned to order my customary martini but ordered a Kaliber for a change.

"I used to be a beer drinker," I said, "when Susan and I were studying in Mexico. Those sure were good times … But that's a whole different story."

"I believe you will really enjoy this beer for change of pace," Carib suggested. "And you will have a clear head afterwards.

"You said you needed a friend," he continued. A smile crept up the edges of his mouth. "Tell me about you and Susan."

"How did you know? ... "

"Elementary," Carib laughed. "You were just talking about her—and the good times together."

"That's exactly the problem!" I exclaimed. "I don't know what happened to the good times."

"Tell me what you mean."

"Well," I began, grimacing, "we just don't seem to have the same idea of what's fun anymore. I do admit I haven't thought about 'good times' for years, but now I want to take a second honeymoon to Mexico, and she doesn't want to go. She's doing aerobic dancing now but doesn't want to go dancing with me. Again, I admit I never liked to dance, because I wasn't good at it, but now I'd like to learn how to do it well."

The waiter returned with our beers, took our lunch orders for Special Combination Platters, then left. "Is there anything you both like to do?" Carib asked. "Or used?"

I thought for a moment, then responded, "We both used to like to play bridge in school, but now she plays all the time without me, and... somehow...somehow I resent it. I just don't like to play anymore." I thought for another moment. "No," I said, "I can't honestly think of anything we can share together. Now how can that be?" My voice was now tight with frustration.

Carib reached over and patted me on the left arm. "Well, my friend," he began, "you must bring your lives back together. Children. Do you both want children?"

"Susan does, and I do—eventually. But I don't think having children will fix our problems."

"Maybe yes, maybe no. The joys and power of children can make most of these problems seem unimportant. In fact, they may force us to solve the important ones. That's the way it is in my family."

"I just don't know..." I said, gazing at the wall, drifting off in thought for a few moments. "I'm not sure Susan even loves me anymore."

Carib looked me straight in the eye. "Do you love her?"

"Yes," I answered quickly, averting Carib's gaze. I sighed, and then looked back at him. "Well actually, I don't know. She's been so different lately. So bitter. It's hard to love her through all that anger. And

I find now that I'm getting angry with her." I looked down at my hands on the table and found that my fists were clenched.

"It seems to me," Carib observed, "that you're both off course. I think that's what happens when things are not right in our lives. I don't know how you and Susan can bring your lives back into balance; it is up to you two, jointly and separately. You both need to discover what you really want."

The waiter strolled up and served our lunch platters. Carib ordered a diet soda, and I found myself doing the same. When the waiter had left, I cleared my throat, and then said, "There's something else on my mind."

"At the office?" Carib asked, smiling again.

"How did—" I started. Then I smiled. "Oh, elementary. What else is there in my life?"

"Why is business so important to you?"

I pursed my lips. "For my parents, careers came first. They believed business obligations had to be met first, before taking care of their personal lives."

"We have never talked about your parents before. Are they still alive?"

"My father died several years back," I responded. "My mother lives in Los Angeles."

"That's quite a distance away from you," Carib said.

"That's where her career took her. I suppose that's part of why my parents split. "

"Why don't you ask her how she feels about the importance of her career now," Carib suggested.

"I will when I see her," I said with a shrug. "But right now, I have a serious business dilemma. May I trust you not to repeat any of this to anybody?"

"You know you can trust me," Carib said solemnly.

"Not even Cesaré."

"I will tell no one, my friend."

"I probably shouldn't even burden you with this, but, well, you really have a vision."

"I have the gifts of a shaman," Carib said.

"A shaman?"

"A medicine man is the term you are probably familiar with. I am able to see beyond the horizon."

"That is a gift. I trust only what I see in front of my face.

"Well, anyway," I continued, "I think we're making a strategic mistake, but Sullivan doesn't see it that way. Do I do what I think is right, or do I do what the boss says?"

Carib's response was immediate. "If you genuinely believe you're right, go for it. Get facts. Bring Sullivan around to your point of view."

"But he won't change his point of view. I understand what he is saying, but he's wrong. And once he takes a position, it takes wild horses to change it. We'd wind up in major confrontation, which I don't want to happen. Sullivan told me today, I'll be his successor."

Carib extended his hand. "Well, congratulations," he said as we shook. "But that shouldn't change anything. He obviously has faith in you, so he should listen to the facts, which he expects you to provide. But, in the end, if he is still resolute, accept the fact that he is still the boss, unless you want to leave the Company."

"No, I don't want to leave; I've put too much into it...anyway thanks for the advice....

"Well," I continued in a crisp tone, "you mentioned on the phone you had a line on Mendez."

"Yes, he has surfaced in Puerto Rico."

"Puerto Rico?" I echoed.

"Yes, he is channeling Colombian cocaine to Arkansas through Ponce. And my visions have revealed he is involved in this plot against you."

"Visions?" I asked. "As I said, I believe only what I can see in front of my face. Real things. Not visions."

Carib's quick grin revealed his flashing white teeth, contrasting with his smooth bronze face. "I don't blame you for being skeptical, my friend. Yours is the way of ordinary reality. My way integrates what we can see with our eyes with what we can see with our hearts and souls. Some call it non-ordinary reality."

I felt myself squirming. "Sounds like religion to me," I said with a dismissive wave of my hand.

"Not exactly. It is more like a methodology. A way of reaching an altered state at which time you can see beyond what is in front of your face. Anyone can do it, even you."

"Not in this lifetime," I said, taking the last bite of my lunch.

"We shall see, my friend," Carib responded, his eyes twinkling. Then I noticed his eyes shifting up and to my right.

"May I join you?" I heard a familiar voice behind me.

I turned my head to see Ricardo standing there. I rose and extended my hand. "Of course. You're just in time for fried ice cream. Ricardo, I'd like you to meet my very good friend, Carib Conibo, from Venezuela. Ricardo is with the FBI. The fellow sitting by the door is with the FBI also. My bodyguard."

As they shook hands, Carib said, "You have some news about our friend Mundi." It was a statement.

Ricardo stared at him, wide-eyed. "How in the world did you know that?"

"We were just talking about Mendez. Mundi was next."

There may be something to this non-ordinary reality, I thought. But all I said was, "Let's hear what you've got, Ricardo."

Ricardo lowered himself into a chair. "I've had it confirmed that Mundi is, in fact, with the CIA. And it is true they recruited him shortly after his deal fell apart with you, but they cut him off at the knees on his coup plans. My bet is that he is still carrying a grudge around against you. And you know those Middle-East characters are; they get revenge, no matter how long it takes." He smiled. "Reminds me of us Latinos."

"Reminds me of everybody," I countered. "But I just don't think he'd want to kill me over that."

"Maybe yes, or maybe no. But my friend in the Records Section at the Agency informed me Mundi was in Puerto Rico at the time of the bombing. And in New York at the time of the ambulance attempt, and in New York again during the shooting incident. He's back in Iraq now."

"I still can't believe it. We were actually friends at one time."

"Well, time and anger change people... Look, I'm willing to concede he may not actually be the one behind the conspiracy against you, but he certainly appears to be the executioner."

"But what is this conspiracy? Who wants me dead? I don't know—maybe it is just Mundi."

"That's what we have to find out before Mundi—or someone else—get lucky."

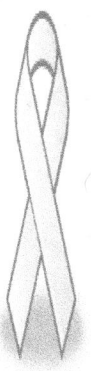

CHAPTER THIRTEEN

On Friday night, Susan and I went out for dinner at Fonda La Paloma in Greenwich. When I told her of my "leading contender" status for Sullivan's job, she congratulated me coldly and announced she was going out to visit Josie first thing in the morning. I asked her to wait until after my golf game, so I could go with her, but she responded that she wanted to get a jump on the traffic, and that she was through waiting for me. We fought the rest of the evening.

We fought again when she returned Sunday night, and I felt relieved as I boarded the flight for San Francisco the next morning. I arrived at UNRC's Western Regional Offices at one-thirty and opened the quarterly Performance Review at two p.m.

I congratulated the team at lunch on Tuesday, citing that the Western Region was the most profitable segment in the Company. I also informed them we were considering expansion in downstream exploration and refining, as well as upstream retail stations. After lunch, I decided to head my rental car down the Peninsula towards Stanford for once, instead of taking the "red-eye" flight back to New York as I usually did.

A steady afternoon onshore breeze had blown away the smog, and the sky was a rich blue, dotted by a few wisps of cirrus clouds. I felt as though I were driving on top of the world as I sped down Interstate 280, which snaked its way through the golden-brown foothills of the Santa Cruz Mountains.

I parked in the Student Union lot and, as I emerged from the car, I decided to go in for a marshmallow sundae. I hesitated in front of the building, wondering if they still even served marshmallow sundaes, but then I bounded up the two steps and strode across the patio to the door. I pushed and held it open for a red-haired woman coming out. Recognition flashed in my memory, and my jaw dropped as I stared at her retreating figure. "Marilyn," I said aloud.

The red-haired figure scurried on across the patio, down the steps, and turned right towards the parking lot. "Marilyn," I called after her. "Wait!"

I caught her by the oak tree. "Marilyn, it's me, Nick!"

Marilyn surged on towards the parking lot without looking at me. "Get lost!" she hissed.

I stopped, dumbfounded, as she hurried off. When she reached the curb and stepped down onto the parking lot, I sprinted after her. I rushed past, and then wheeled around, holding up both hands. "Wait, Marilyn! What is wrong?"

"Get out of my way!" she said adamantly, looking straight into my eyes. We both stood motionless several moments, and then Marilyn's hard gaze softened. She shifted her gaze down to the asphalt. "Please get out of my way."

"Are you still that mad at me?" I asked, my voice filled with incredulity.

"I don't want to see you," she murmured, her eyes still downcast.

"Marilyn," I said softly. "All that was so long ago…. Come on— let's go for a walk."

She slowly lifted her gaze. "Where?"

"Around Campus. I haven't been here since graduation."

The expression on her face remained doubtful. "Please," I said. "Everything has changed. They even moved Mayfield Drive," I chuckled.

"All right," Marilyn finally relented, shrugging her shoulders. "I'll give you the nickel tour."

We strolled in tandem back towards the Union. "What are you doing here?" I asked.

"I could ask you the same thing," she said smiling. "But since you asked me first, I'll tell you that I teach Computer Science here at Stanford now. After John died, I left Corporate America. I think I can make a bigger difference here."

"I read about John in the Alumnae News. I'm sorry." I shook my head. "I should have called you."

"I just would have hung up on you," she said, smiling again. We passed the Union, and then turned right towards two Spanish stucco buildings with red tile roofs. "The post office and bookstore look the same," I commented.

"They're different inside," Marilyn explained. "They've expanded the bookstore to 3 levels."

We moved on a bit further towards a massive building behind the old library.

"That must be the new library."

"It is, and we now have over 8 million books on Campus."

A few minutes later we were at the base of Hoover Tower, rising 285 feet above us, crowned with red tile as well. "That's still the tallest building around here," I said. "Somehow that's reassuring."

We moved on down to Angell Field and its running track. I stared at the red composition oval. "What…what happened to the dirt track?" I stammered.

"Paved over," Marilyn said.

"We both sweated a lot of bullets around that oval," I remembered. "Why did they have to change it?"

"Faster times. High tech. They hold the meets here now rather than in the Stadium."

We cut back around Frost Amphitheater, where the graduation ceremonies were held, crossed Serra Street that was now closed to cars, mounted the steps, then finally entered the Quad through the archway. The gold mosaic on the facade of Memorial Church was as brilliant as ever. "You said you wanted to get married there," I said.

"I never did," Marilyn said, wistfully. Then she laughed, "John and I got drunk one weekend in Las Vegas and got married there. Maybe next time."

Unaccountably I felt a pang of jealousy. "Are you seeing anybody?" I asked.

"I've been dating one guy for about a year," she said guardedly. "Are you still married to Susan?"

"Yes," I said.

"But?" she asked.

"Well, we're going through a difficult period."

"I'm sorry to hear that," she said, her face reflecting concern. "I hope you can work things out."

"What's his name?" I asked, changing the subject.

"Who?" she asked, a smile playing on her lips.

I failed to see the humor. "The guy you're seeing."

"Oh, him. Wiley. Wiley Ferguson." As though reading my mind, she continued, "You don't know him. He went to Cal. He's now with Corporate Bank. Don't look around, but I think we're being followed."

I whirled around, shouting, "Where?" Then I burst out laughing.

"What's so funny?" Marilyn asked, her voice a blend of alarm and curiosity.

"It's only the FBI," I chuckled again.

"What are you talking about?"

"Actually, I'm serious. I'm under FBI protection. Come on, I'll explain as we go."

We wandered on across the Quad, past the Stanford Daily office, by the firehouse, then up towards Lake Lagunita. By the time we reached the Lake's edge, I had explained the attempts on my life. "And now," I said, "If it's not too painful, would you tell me how John died?"

Pain wracked her face momentarily, and then her features relaxed. "Yes, I'll tell you," she said quietly. "I've got to tell somebody. I feel responsible for his death. He had two things raging inside him—his first girlfriend and you."

"Me?"

"Please, Nick. This is hard enough."

"Sorry. Go on."

"John was from Dallas, and all freshman year he said he was going to marry his high school sweetheart."

"I remember."

"Then, that summer after freshman year, his girlfriend dumped him and married the heir to Lone Star Oil. Then the spring of sophomore year, John and I started dating. That summer is when we met and then that fall, you dumped me and went back to Susan."

"I remember."

"Anyway, he never got over 'Dallas', and he swore I never got over you—maybe it was true. In retrospect, we were both on the rebound, and we never should have gotten married, at least not when we did. We had to get over being dumped. Sober, I would have seen it. Now, I do."

"But what does that have to do with John's death?"

"I should have seen the signals—done something. First there were the hang-ups. Then there were the Dallas calls on the bill. I hardly ever looked at the telephone bill; John always paid it. For some reason I looked at the bill that one time and noticed the calls, but I didn't give it a second thought. Now that I do think about it, I believe 'Dallas' wanted him back, and he wanted to go back, but he didn't know how to leave me. He used to play around, but it was never serious. Anyhow, if I had seen all this and left him, the accident never would have happened."

The summer-dried oak leaves crackled under our feet as we walked along the edge of the dried lakebed. "The accident?" I asked.

"Yes," Marilyn sighed, "I was working late on a Friday night, and he called me from a friend's house to say they were having a party and to ask me to come over. He sounded higher than an archangel and, sure enough, when I arrived, they were doing cocaine. Then he switched to schooners of scotch and, try as I might, I couldn't get him to come home. All he kept saying was 'just one more drink'. Well, I finally got mad and left.

"About half an hour later, he started to drive home. He got to a turn out there on Alpine Road, didn't make it, and smashed head-on into a tree. The police said there were no skid marks, guessing he must have fallen asleep at the wheel, and the coroner ruled it was an accidental death. But I don't think so. I think he just didn't want to make that turn." She took a sharp breath as tears formed in the corners of her eyes.

We found ourselves at Roble Hall, where we had waited on tables as "hashers" together. "Shall we continue?" I suggested. "For old times' sake?"

Marilyn looked nervous. "I'd rather not, Nick. Too many memories."

"Ah, what memories," I said, smiling, and looking across the parched, cracked lakebed in the direction of the corner hidden by the broad oaks and tall eucalyptus. "We used to think we were so clever, sneaking around the corner after serving lunch and making out." I chuckled once. Then again. My laughter grew until I was roaring, and my side hurt. When I finally caught my breath, I gasped, "What a riot!"

"What's so funny?" Marilyn said, looking stern. "I was a freshman and you were a grad student. You were dating Susan and I was going out with... I'll never forget old-what's-his-name. What we were doing was pretty serious."

"It was," I agreed, trying to look serious. "But," I chuckled again, "do you really think we were fooling anybody? I mean don't you remember the comments when we got back? 'How was your...er...walk?' And 'Did you enjoy dessert today?'."

Marilyn smiled, and her face began to tinge red. "You know," she said, "I believe you're right." Then she giggled, "I guess the only ones we fooled were ourselves. I feel so embarrassed now."

We continued along the path that ran atop the raised edge of the dry lakebed. We strolled in silence until I finally said, "Getting back to the accident, the way I see it, John is solely responsible for it. I remember him; he made his own hell. Oh, he was brilliant, all right, right down to the photographic memory, but he tried to please everybody. He tried to be perfect—it can't be done!"

I took a deep breath and blew it out through my mouth. "I can imagine how he must have felt—trapped—no way out. No matter what he did, he was going to fail, either with 'Dallas' or you. His death was self-inflicted; you couldn't have done anything to prevent it."

Marilyn shook her head, her long, red hair cascading around her shoulders. "But I still feel as though I should have done something," she said, her voice trailing off. "I should have insisted on driving him home. I knew he was in no condition to drive."

"It was not your fault, Marilyn. If it weren't the accident, it would have been something else—a drug overdose. He was on the path of self-destruction, and the only one who could have changed that course was John. As I said, I can imagine how he must have felt, because I know what it means to try to be perfect. It just doesn't work, and I have to learn that repeatedly."

"Thank you," Marilyn said softly. "Thank you for making me feel better. I never really thought of it that way before."

"Actually," I admitted, "until just now I didn't think of either John or myself as compulsive perfectionists either."

We had made the turn on the sharp bend in the lake bank and were now heading into the obscured corner. We stopped under a huge live oak tree, and I looked up into the vast spread of low hanging branches, reaching out like arms of protection. "Remember this?" I asked.

"One of my life's ten best memories," Marilyn murmured.

I extended my arm in invitation. Marilyn hesitated for a moment, and then took my hand. We picked our way through the low hanging branches to the trunk of the tree. Then we faced each other and gradually, inexorably, edged towards one another, still holding hands. We slid our arms around each other and hugged. Our lips found each other, and we kissed, gently first, then with heightening passion. We broke the kiss and I gasped in Marilyn's ear, "I can't believe this. It was never like this. I... I feel as though I'm soaring...It's like...I'm somebody else, somewhere else."

Marilyn pulled back slightly and looked into my surrendering, soft brown eyes.

"It still seems as though it were yesterday," she said, in a whisper. "I used to feel exactly the way you do now—under this tree, with you."

I looked up into the thick branches and shook my head. "Oh my God. What I missed."

I looked back at Marilyn's flushed face. "I mean," I continued, "don't get me wrong. Those days were great—but somehow—just not quite as intense as this."

Marilyn unclasped her hands from behind my back and let them fall to her side. "Come on," she said, looking down at the ground. "You're married, and this is getting too serious. Let's head back"

Slowly she lifted her gaze from the ground, and then looked up into my eyes once again. She began to blink as tears flowed into her eyes. Suddenly she flung her arms around me and squeezed her head into my chest. "Oh, Nick, Nick," she sobbed. "It's...it is just like yesterday."

I drew my arms around her, and then I hugged her. She was shaking. I started to quiver as well, and my knees felt as though they were going to give way. Tears filled my eyes and began rolling down my cheeks. I placed my fingers under her chin and gently lifted her head. I gazed into her deep emerald-green eyes. Then I winked at her and smiled. "Just like yesterday," I said.

She smiled and winked back. "Just like yesterday," she echoed. Then we hugged each other again.

"I can't believe I found you," I whispered. "And I didn't even know I was looking."

Suddenly I was aware of my FBI guardian whose legs I could see through the branches, jolting me back to reality. Reluctantly I released Marilyn, saying, "But you're right. We both have other commitments. We'd better head back."

We strolled back to the Student Union parking lot without touching each other, but we shared several longing looks. We also shared our common conservative political views. When we reached Marilyn's car, a blue Mercedes convertible, I said, "Say, are you free tonight? I'm not any better than I used to be, but would you like to go dancing?"

"Oh, Nick, I'd love to, but...but I... I really don't think we should. Our commitments remember?"

"Come dancing with me anyway."

"No, Nick. I really can't. Thanks anyway." She looked back towards her blue Mercedes. "I really have to get going."

"Do they still have dancing at Caesar's Palace?" I asked softly.

"It's not Caesar's Palace anymore—it's back to the original name, The Cabana."

"Do they still have dancing?" I persisted. "As they used to?"

"I don't know; Wiley doesn't like to dance very much."

"Will you come with me to find out?"

Her tension was visible in her face. Finally, she sighed and said, "Well maybe for a little while. Wiley's in Hawaii and won't be calling me until about ten tonight."

"I'll go home and change, and," she paused as she looked down at her Rolex wrist watch, "it's now five o'clock, so I can meet you at Caesar's— ah—The Cabana, that is, at ...6:30. You should be able to get a room there, if you want—if not, try Ricky's-nope, that's gone. There is a nice Sheraton Inn next to the Town and Country Shopping Center."

"Or," I chuckled, "there's always the Currier Motel," referring to our undergraduate love nest.

Marilyn flushed. Then she smiled and said, "You're bad."

During dinner I talked clinically about my career, and Marilyn brought me up to date on Stanford's politically correct tenor. She then switched to Wiley, his successful career, and deep involvement in California State politics. Then, as we sipped the last of our champagne after dessert, I said, "I haven't told you about Susan...I don't know why...I guess I thought you wouldn't want to hear about her. I still feel badly about you and me and her."

Marilyn reached across and touched my hand. "Oh, Nick, you were perfectly—well, almost perfectly—honest with me. After we broke up my freshman year, and you went back to Susan, we didn't see each other for what—a quarter?"

"Yes, a whole entire quarter. When Susan and I were in Mexico."

"And then, well, when you returned, we started taking those walks around the Lake again, and then one thing led to another. You didn't say anything about Susan, and I wanted to believe she was out of your life. And then when you did tell me you felt committed to marry Susan, I was devastated and wouldn't see you. Remember?"

"I remember," I echoed, sadly.

"But we just couldn't stay away from each other." She chuckled. "Maybe I thought I could get you to change your mind."

"But Marilyn," I protested, "I never should have let it start up again. I never should have let you...me...us get hooked again. I feel as though...I used you."

Marilyn smiled. "I wouldn't have missed being in love with you for anything. You were the first man who made love to me, and I've never felt love like that since. She sighed wistfully, "Oh I was so in love with you."

I nodded. "I remember. And I remember that scared the hell out of me. I didn't want that sort of emotional complication; I just wanted my career. I was so selfish then! All I did was take and gave nothing in return."

I paused, thoughtful, then continued excited, feeling my eyes come alive, "That's got to be why I married Susan! She was the same way! Career, no children—no real commitment." I hit my forehead with my palm and groaned. "What a waste," I moaned.

"No, Nick. If you and I had gotten married—that would have been a waste because it wouldn't have lasted. As you said, you were focused on your career, but I wanted to waste a few more years having fun. It was you and Susan who were in the same place then, as you just said. Marrying each other was the best thing for both of you."

The tablecloth and pad muted the sound of my hand hitting the tabletop. "We're sure not in the same place now! I don't know what she wants!" I paused, took a deep breath, and blew it out. "But then again," I admitted, "I really don't know what's important anymore to me either. We just seem to be going in different directions."

98

"Don't be so critical!" Marilyn chided, then laughed, at herself for being critical. "What I'm saying is we need to accept that people are different. You can't expect Susan to always want the same things, nor can she expect the same of you. You must minimize the differences and find the common ground. Wiley and I are working on our differences all the time, starting with politics on through to children."

I grimaced. "That may be, but Susan and I have a huge problem that I just don't know how we're going to resolve. When we decided to get married, we agreed never to have children. Now she wants a child, and I'm just not ready. And to boot, she's threatening to find someone who is ready if I don't come around—and fast!"

Marilyn smiled, as though hearing a familiar, shared secret again. "I know how you feel. Wiley wants children, but I still don't. I don't feel ready; I somehow don't feel balanced yet. Oh, I know my biological clock is running out, but I feel that I can't be a good parent until I get myself together. That may be next year, or it may be never. But I think the point for you here is that men can change their minds about having children. If Wiley has, anyone can. And the message for me is that if career-or-nothing Susan can change her mind, so can I. Who knows, maybe both you and I will wind up with kids."

I picked up the napkin from my lap and tossed it onto the tabletop. "The man wants to dance," Marilyn said.

"You got that right," I responded. "You always could read what I wanted."

Marilyn chuckled. "Most of the time it didn't take a lot of imagination." We held each other's gaze for a few moments, and then Marilyn appeared uncomfortable and looked away.

We both rose, and then strolled out of the dining room, down the hall, then into the nightclub. The band was playing a Latin beat, and Marilyn and I broke into the cha-cha. This was followed by a rock and roll number, and by the end of the set, we were gasping.

The band took a break, and a disc jockey grabbed the microphone, announcing a change of pace. He began with John Lennon's "Woman," and Marilyn and I danced a respectable distance apart. But as the succeeding song, Dionne Warwick's "Heartbreaker" got under way, our arms slid around each other, and we clung to one another.

"This is incredible," I whispered.

"Absolute madness," Marilyn whispered back.

We finished the song in silence, bodies pressed tightly against each other, listening to the words, and barely moving. The song ended, and I said hoarsely, "Let's get out of here."

"Things are getting out of control," Marilyn warned.

"They are out of control. Let's go for a walk. I'll go tell our FBI friend."

The agent smiled when I told him we were going to stretch our legs, then Marilyn would be leaving, and I would be going up to bed. We walked up the ramp to the door and into the deserted hallway, then slid our arms around each other's waist. "I hope there isn't anybody in there that I know," Marilyn chuckled, "and I hope that FBI agent is discreet. That was shameless."

We came to the elevators and stopped. "Let's go talk about this," I suggested.

Marilyn looked warily at me, "But only for a moment—I've got to get home."

The FBI agent followed us as we entered the elevator. We took it up to the seventh floor, our arms still around each other's waist. I unlocked the door to my room, crossed it, and slid open the door to the balcony. We sat down in the chairs next to the railing.

"I have a confession," Marilyn began. "I've already spoken to Wiley tonight. He called while I was home getting changed for dinner to say he was going to be out late with clients and didn't want to wake me up later." She grimaced. "You can guess what that means."

I nodded somberly. "Yes, I can. Is that why you're here?"

"I don't know," she moaned. "But," she continued, nodding her head, "The point is that I am here. And I want to be here with you."

"I want to be here with you as well," I said softly.

We both looked out at the lights that sprinkled across the darkness of the Santa Cruz Mountains. "I'm going to have to tell Susan," I said rashly.

"And I'm going to have to tell Wiley. Not that he'll care. If he has a woman, he doesn't care which one it is."

My rational self regained control. "Wait a minute. What are we doing here? How do you know Wiley doesn't care? How do you know he's with another woman tonight?"

"Trust me. Women know these things.

"But you're right," she continued. "We shouldn't go off half-cocked here. We're both vulnerable. You and Susan are having troubles, and I'm grieving and guilty." She smiled and touched my arm. "Let's just chalk today up to one of life's pleasant moments and remember it in our old age."

"I want to grow old with you," I blurted out.

Marilyn's dumbfounded expression spoke volumes. "Nick. Dearest Nick. That's the sweetest thing anyone has ever said to me. And I'm sure at this moment, you really mean it. But I won't hold you to it."

"I've lost you twice, and I don't want to lose you again," I insisted.

"We're both vulnerable," she reminded me. "And I couldn't stand to lose you again."

My reason regained control once again. "Of course," I said. "That was really thoughtless of me."

"It wasn't, Nick. We just need to take this one step at a time."

"First things first," I agreed. "I am still going to have that talk with Susan."

"Don't push it," Marilyn said. "Easy does it. When the time is right, you'll find the right words." She took my hand in hers. "And right now, I just like to sit here and be quiet with you."

My mind was racing in all directions. Part of me wanted to call Susan that instant and tell her it was over. But that wasn't being fair to Susan. And it wasn't fair to Marilyn. I had already hurt her twice. And what about my career? Sullivan was an old-fashioned Catholic who didn't believe in divorce.... Gradually my mind slowed. I began to savor the memories of the day as though partaking in gourmet delights. The past was forgotten and the future too distant. This day had become the epicenter of my entire life, and I wanted each day to be as alive as this had been. I didn't want it to end. I began to slide into twilight sleep.

A hint of smoke snapped me into full awareness. Marilyn stirred as I withdrew my hand from hers. Flames were shooting out of the window in the FBI agent's room next door. "Marilyn!" I shouted. "Fire!"

I rushed into the room and across to the door, feeling it. "It hot!" I shouted, "but it's the only way out! The stairway is down the hall to the left."

I eased the door open a crack. "God! The flames are only a few feet away! We can't stay here! Come on!"

101

I grabbed Marilyn's hand, flung open the door, and we sprinted hand in hand down the hall. When we reached the exit, I grabbed the handle, twisted it, and pushed against the door. It wouldn't budge.

The hall was a tunnel of flames raging towards us. I shoved against the door with my shoulder, feeling it give slightly. "Come on, Marilyn! Help me push!"

We both leaned back, as though we were cocking a trigger. "Ready?" I asked laconically.

Marilyn nodded quickly, and we both slammed into the door, breaking it free. We scampered through the doorway and down the steps. The air cooled rapidly as we descended, but we didn't slacken our pace until we burst through the ground floor emergency exit into the parking lot. I turned to Marilyn and hugged her. "Are you okay?" I asked, breathless.

"I... I'm fine," she gasped. "But...but I can't...can't...believe that door. Having it blocked...is against the law."

Suddenly her eyes widened, and her mouth dropped open as she looked up at the leaping flames. "It's only on the seventh floor!"

Then she looked back down at me. We stared at each other as the same thought formed in our minds. "They tried again," I said, grimacing. We slid our arms around each other and hugged for a long time, watching the people streaming out of the emergency exits. Fire engine and police car sirens screamed from the distance, and then roared into the parking lot. Finally, I looked around at the crowd, and then shook my head, saying, "Our FBI agent. They must have killed him."

We squeezed each other. "Why do they want you dead?" Marilyn wailed, tears rolling down her distraught face.

"When I find that out, I may discover who. The FBI thinks it's a man I used to know in Iraq, bent on revenge, but that doesn't make sense...I just don't know...

"And I just don't know about...well, what happened between you and me."

"I..."Marilyn started, "I don't know either. All I do know is that it has been a wonderful day."

I smiled. "That it has," I agreed.

"Look," I continued, "I'll be out here again next month. Let's see how we feel then."

Marilyn reached up and touched my face. "Be careful," she said softly.

"I will," I nodded. "I'll be back. I'll call you."

Marilyn chuckled. "I've heard that before."

"What do you mean?"

"You see, it goes like this: What a woman hears is, 'I'll call you in the morning.' What a man means is, 'I'll call you someday before I die, maybe.'"

We both laughed. It felt wonderful to find levity in the face of death.

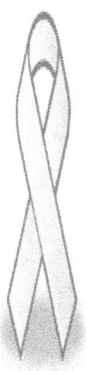

CHAPTER FOURTEEN

My travel agent had booked me on the 8 A.M. flight back to New York the next morning. I checked in at 6:45, and then called Marilyn. "You called," she laughed when she heard my voice.

"I'm the exception that proves the rule," I said.

"You're going to spoil me," she cooed.

"I hope so," I responded.

We chatted for several minutes and just before I hung up, I said, "I'll call you." We both laughed.

Then I phoned Ricardo. His secretary told me the Inspector was on his way to Washington, and she expected to hear from him about noon. I said I would call back. Then I called Jim Hudson in Houston. "How's it going, Jimbo?" I asked.

"Nick!" Jim responded, recognizing my voice. "Where are you?"

"I'm still on the West Coast, heading back to New York."

"Well you'd better change your plans," Jim urged. "I need a brainstorming session—fast—and I can't go to anyone here. We need to figure out what in the blazes to do."

"Why? What's the problem? I thought you were making headway."

"I am, but on the other side," Jim paused as he lowered his voice to a whisper, "the most recent tests predict engine breakdown with the current formulation at an even faster rate than I thought before. We need to discuss this."

"All right, Jim. I'll be there this afternoon."

I switched to the 7:45 flight to Houston but ran into trouble trying to clear my gun through security. After an interminable wait, I was fuming. When they finally cleared me, I sprinted all the way to the gate, arriving just as they were closing the door.

When I disembarked in Houston, I headed for a deserted bank of telephone booths in an alcove off the concourse. I wanted to let my office know of my change in plans and using my cell phone on the concourse was tantamount to public broadcasting. As I entered the alcove, I heard the muffled sound of a familiar voice coming from a man standing in the last booth, with his back to me. I stopped, trying to place the voice. "What do you mean he didn't get on the flight?" the muffled voice demanded. "He was booked on it."

The man rocked from side to side as he listened to the voice on the other end of the line, then he shouted, "I don't want any more of your excuses, Mundi!"

I froze. "Bradshaw," I whispered. It was Bradshaw's voice! Then I leaped back around the corner as though a chasm had suddenly opened before me. Bradshaw started to turn his head in my direction. I was certain Bradshaw hadn't heard my whisper, nor had he seen me. But the guy must have a sixth sense, I thought.

The enormity of my discovery was staggering. Bradshaw! I couldn't believe it It made no sense. Why would the Company's lobbyist want me dead?

I turned and ran back down the concourse, stopping only when I saw an empty gate holding area, right next to security. I scampered around the telephone partition behind the check-in counter and leaned against it, panting.

Bradshaw, I thought once again. Bradshaw's behind this. Now I had discovered who, but I still didn't know why. Bradshaw and I had always worked well together. I liked Bradshaw, and I thought Bradshaw liked me. What in the blazes was this all about?

Then another thought struck me. The CIA. There had been scuttlebutt at the Company he was CIA connected. And he had been talking to Mundi on the phone. Mundi wasn't in Iraq—he was in San Francisco! And Ricardo had said the CIA was involved.

Ricardo! I had to talk with Ricardo. I picked up the telephone and dialed his New York number. Ricardo's secretary said she still hadn't heard from the Inspector. She asked if she could give him a message or have him return the call. I was about to tell her that the FBI agent had perished in the fire, but stopped, not trusting her. No message I said, and she responded that Inspector Lopez could be reached at the Watergate Hotel that evening.

I stood there for several minutes, paralyzed with indecision. I felt I couldn't trust anybody. Nothing made sense. I knew I had to resume my normal life while I sorted things out, but I didn't know what normal was any more. Finally, I decided to call my office.

"Mr. Shepherd's office," Liz answered.

"Good afternoon, Liz."

"Mr. Shepherd. Good afternoon. Are you on the plane?"

"No, I'm still on the ground. I've decided to take the next three days off. Do you have anything urgent?"

"Yes. Mr. Sullivan wants to talk to you; in fact, he just hung up. He wanted me to find you and get a message to you to meet him for dinner tonight."

"Sullivan just called, himself? Not Hazel?"

"Mr. Sullivan himself."

"I can't believe it. What does he want?"

"He didn't say."

"Why didn't you find out?"

The response was sullen silence. "Sorry Liz," I said, breaking the silence. "I'm not quite myself."

"That's all right," Liz said, her voice barely audible, taken aback by my apology.

I cleared my throat. "Well then, please switch me to Mr. Sullivan."

"Where can I reach you the rest of the week? In case of emergency?"

I hesitated. Then I said, "I'll get back to you."

Sullivan's secretary, Hazel, put me right through. "That was fast, Nick," Sullivan said. "Where are you?"

I avoided the question. "I'm taking a couple of days off, Bruce. There was a fire in the hotel last night, and I'm pretty shook up."

"Were you at the Cabana? I saw it on the news this morning."

"Yea, it was the Cabana."

"My God. Four people were killed. You were lucky."

"You don't know how lucky. The fire started in the room next to mine."

"Look, Nick. I know how you must feel, but I think getting back to work will take your mind off it. And you have a lot of work to do."

"Well, actually I'm in Houston right now. Hudson wanted to go discuss his progress. Then I was thinking of going down to Acapulco on Thursday and returning Sunday."

Sullivan was silent for a moment. "All right, Nick. Go ahead. Why don't you stay at El Mirador? It's built right into the cliffs, you know, and has spectacular views."

Cliffs! I thought. I knew the cliffs at El Mirador and the cliff divers. It was one-hundred-and-thirty-eight feet down to the water below... Bradshaw spent a lot of time in Sullivan's office. Bradshaw took orders from Sullivan. Was Sullivan behind it all?

"Are you there, Nick?" Sullivan was asking.

"Yea, Bruce. I'm here. El Mirador sounds good... Liz mentioned you wanted to have a dinner meeting tonight. What's on your mind?"

"Well...I had a couple of marketing ideas, but...they can keep. Just let Hazel know where you're going to be. See you Monday."

"Okay, Bruce. I'll let her know if I can get into El Mirador."

As I hung up the phone, I saw my hand was trembling. Was Sullivan behind it all? He had never tried to track me down when I was out of town. Maybe Bradshaw had reported to Sullivan that I had escaped the fire but hadn't been on the New York flight. No, I couldn't trust Sullivan. I wouldn't go to the El Mirador cliffs. I had to reach Ricardo. I could trust Ricardo... Or could I? Ricardo had been there right after the shooting at my house. Maybe he had done the shooting himself. No, no. Ricardo had fended off the shooter's second attack. "Damn," I said aloud. "I'm getting paranoid."

I carefully retraced my way back up the concourse, keeping close to the wall and watching for Bradshaw. I reached the telephone alcove and stopped, listening for Bradshaw's voice. I exhaled in relief when I heard nothing but unfamiliar voices. I turned and studied the flight information monitor on the opposite wall. I noticed the Washington flight was boarding at the next gate. I moved stealthily towards it, and then past it. I moved onward, all the way to the last gate at the far end of the concourse, where the flight to New York was boarding. There was still no sign of Bradshaw.

Suddenly I was angry. I had a gun. Maybe Bradshaw didn't. I would find him and confront him. I bolted back down the concourse, checking each gate. When I reached the Washington flight, I spotted Bradshaw disappearing down the Jetway, followed by the gate agent who closed the door. I still felt angry, but then I began to feel a strange sense of satisfaction. I had taken a step towards action. I felt a new sense of urgency. I ran the rest of the way down the concourse, past security, to the escalator, descending three steps at a time, then rushed through the automatic doors that opened only the instant before I would have crashed into them. I jumped into a cab and, between gasps of breath, gave the cabbie the UNRC Research Center address. "Somebody after you?" the cabbie quipped.

"You got that right," I laughed

Twenty minutes later, the cabbie extricated us from the choke of traffic and swung onto the broad drive leading to the massive curved white UNRC R & D Center. I rode the elevator to the top floor, and then strode down the hall into Jim Hudson's office. The R & D Director arose, and then skirted his cluttered desk to greet me with a handshake. "Thanks for coming, Nick," he said.

"I'm really glad to be here," I chuckled, "believe me."

"Bad trip?"

"Close call, but never mind. Let's get down to our problem here."

"Okay," Jim said, heading for the door. "I'll show you what we're up against down in the lab."

A twinge of fear snuck up on me as the Las Palmas bomb imploded in my mind once again, but this time it was against the backdrop of the R & D lab. I shook my head back and forth. I couldn't trust even my long-time friend, Jim Hudson. I sat down in one of the low modern wooden chairs in front of Jim's desk. "I'd just as soon do our brainstorming here," I said.

"But I can better show you what's happening down in the lab," Jim objected.

"Look, Jim, I'm a little spooked right now, and accidents can happen in that lab."

Jim shrugged his shoulders, saying, "As you wish," then returned to the low-back swivel chair behind his desk and sat down. He took a deep breath, then exhaled, saying, "What I would have shown you in the lab is a nightmare."

He paused, and then continued, "Golden Green Octane One is causing engine wear in geometric proportions, rather than straight linear. That's the trouble with any new formulation—you just don't know how the pistons and cylinders are going to interact."

"Is there any way to salvage Golden Green Octane One?" I asked.

"That's precisely one of the options I wanted to toss around with you. I believe we can combine some of the additives I was working on before you came up with the Iraqi formulation with the Golden Green Octane One."

"Then why not do it?"

"It's unproven. I just started the trials last weekend. It looks promising, but the results are not yet statistically significant."

"How long will it take to complete the testing program?"

"Fifteen-hundred hours—about 60 days."

"Hum," I mused. "And you have other options?"

"One other good one. And this one is proven; I tested it in tandem with the Iraqi formulation."

"Well," I began, gesticulating with my hands, "then what's the problem?"

"The expense. At today's pump market price, we'd be at break-even."

"What about the cost of your unproven formulation?"

"It's low. In fact, it's lower than the current Golden Green formulation. But I must stress that we could be dealing with a worse disaster than we have now because we don't know the side effects of the unproven formulation."

I rose and began pacing back and forth on the carpeted floor. "One thing is for sure—we must replace the current formula as rapidly as possible. If I were solely making the decision, I'd go for the proven, high-cost option and push for continued market share gains while we test your new, low cost one. Then, sixty days from now, if it were to prove out, we would simply substitute the new one. If not, we'd have the market share and added good environmental press to be able to raise the price." I stopped pacing and looked at Jim inquiringly.

"Sounds good to me," Jim agreed.

"But," I said, resuming my pacing, "I don't believe Bruce is going to see it that way. He will have to agree we must take action now because of the geometric engine destruction, but I think he'll want to go with the low-cost choice."

"That's a mighty substantial risk..." Jim warned, his voice trailing off.

"The only risk he sees is one that jeopardizes the short-term bottom line profit. No. That's why the proven, prohibitive cost way is out. He'll go with the low-cost choice and let the chips fall where they may."

"It may work," Jim suggested. "I mean I do believe in it."

"Yea, but it may also start blowing engines."

"Okay, then, let's just tell him about the proven one," Jim said, looking devilish. "Do you think you could raise the price now?"

"Well, actually I believe I could. But talk about risks—not telling Sullivan would be about the biggest one I could think of. And besides," I paused, stopping my pacing and gazing out the window, "I'm tired of being devious."

I looked back at Jim. "I'm going to lay it out as it is."

Just before I boarded 3:50 flight to Washington, I phoned my office. "Any calls, Liz?"

"Just one. A Mr. Carib Conibo called. He said he was in Washington and that it was urgent. He's at the Venezuelan Embassy."

"Thanks, Liz. I'll be in touch."

I reached Carib at the Embassy. "What's up?" I asked, a bit too brusquely.

"We need to talk, my friend.... I sense you are in trouble. Don't worry, this line is secure."

"Yea, well it seems as though I'm in a swamp and the alligators are gaining."

"I have a line on Guillermo Mendez. Can we meet?"

"Yes, but I'll have to call you later. Probably breakfast tomorrow there in Washington." I hung up, and then I worried that I couldn't trust even Carib.

I called Ricardo as soon as I left the Jetway at Regan Airport and reached him at the Watergate Hotel. "I've got to see you, Ricardo," I said, my voice tight with tension.

"I heard about Caruthers in the Cabana fire. Are you okay?"

"Totally paranoid."

"Where are you?"

"Not over the phone. But I know who."

"What?" Ricardo asked, his voice rising in surprise. "Who?"

"Meet me," was my laconic reply. "Remember where you taught me to walk?"

"I remember."

"There's one near you."

"Yes. I know where it is."

"I'll meet you there in thirty minutes."

Ricardo was waiting in the main lobby of the hospital when I walked through the automatic glass doors. "Were you followed?" I asked as we shook hands.

Surprise registered on Ricardo's face as he answered, "Why, yes, but I lost them."

I raised my eyebrows and grimaced. "I knew it. They are following you, too. I'm not so paranoid. Where can we go to talk? Where is it safe? I know. A hotel. I'll book a hotel. A small one. Out of the way." I reached for my cell phone.

"Hold on, my friend. Slow down. We'll go to headquarters. It's safe."

"Headquarters! They'll be all over that place like sharks in a blood bath!"

Ricardo smiled. "I have a private entrance. Come on."

We flagged down a cab and sped off down the deserted streets until Ricardo directed the cabbie into a narrow alley. We went in the rear entrance of a low, grime covered brick building, through a security checkpoint, then down to the basement. We came to a door at the far end, and Ricardo placed his hand on an ID screen. The door swung open, and Ricardo entered, saying, "We're going under the street now."

We emerged from the door at the far end of the long hallway, passed another security checkpoint, and then took an elevator from the basement to the fourth floor. "We'll use the Conference Room—it's soundproof and bug-free."

Ricardo placed his hand on the ID screen, then led the way through the opening door. He motioned to the plush beige chair at the head of the long, rectangular beige table, saying, "Have a seat."

I settled down into the overstuffed chair, and Ricardo slid into the one next to me. "Now tell me all about it," Ricardo said.

I related all the events of the past two days, and when I finished, I said, "I'm so rattled that I'm wondering if my bumping into Marilyn was staged. And for a while there I suspected even you."

Ricardo nodded. "That's completely understandable after all that you've been through." He paused. "This confirms one of my theories—Mundi has a compatriot, but it puts my revenge theory in serious doubt."

"Why?"

"Because Bradshaw is also with the CIA, and he was giving orders to Mundi, not the other way around."

"So, the rumors about Bradshaw and the CIA are true."

"Yes. And it sure looks as though the CIA is somehow behind this."

I slumped back in my chair. "I can't believe this. What does the CIA want with me?"

Ricardo leaned forward in his chair. "I still don't know, but this Bradshaw connection is a huge lead. I'll move on it right away. I'll get a full run-down on him in the morning from my buddy at the Agency."

"Speaking of moving," I said, changing the subject, "how do I move out of Bradshaw's way? And how do I still keep doing my job?"

Ricardo scratched his chin between his right thumb and index finger as he thought.

"Hum...One thing is for sure. You've got to set up someplace, like one of our safe houses. Or your house in Greenwich. No, on second thought, your place would be too difficult to protect; we'd need a whole army of Agents. Do you know of any else that's defensible?"

I snapped my fingers. "Yes," I said with conviction. "I know the perfect spot, complete with moat. It's on the California coast—my Great-Grandfather bought it from a Scottish Thane. It was a castle on the moor, and he brought it over stone by stone and reassembled it on a cliff overlooking the Pacific."

"Sounds ideal," Ricardo agreed. "Now, go get yourself some sleep. Sid and Pete here will take you down to the hotel and set up a post in the room next to yours."

They took me to the Quality Inn down the block from FBI Headquarters, and we checked in. I called Carib from my room, and he invited me to breakfast at the Embassy at 8 o'clock the next morning. Then I rang Marilyn to tell her where I was. "I was hoping you'd call," she said. "I've been worried about you all day."

"It's great to hear your voice," I said, smiling, and I then gave her the highlights of the day. At the end of our conversation, I said, "Look, I won't be able to call for a few days, but don't worry. I will call you as soon as I can."

"Be careful," she whispered.

A while later, I slid my gun under my pillow and climbed into bed. I slept very well.

I awoke in the morning to a sliver of sunlight sneaking through a tiny gap in the curtains. I moved over to the window, and then pulled open the curtains. The sun shimmered on the white marble of the Washington Monument, and hope sprang to life in my heart. I spotted two joggers appearing from the far side of the Monument, and for several moments I wavered between the joyous urge to run and fear of the assassins that were out there somewhere. Discretion is the better part of valor, I remembered.

At 7:45 A.M. I arrived at the Venezuelan Embassy on 30th Street. It was a 4-story red brick building, with dormers jutting out of its steeply pitched roof. A large tree rose as a sentinel at the corner, with smaller trees lining the front of the building. I rang the bell, and the door opened widely, revealing the tall, lean, and bronze-faced figure of Carib. He smiled broadly, and we embraced Latin American style, first one side then the other. "Nicholas, my friend. Please come in and relax. You're safe here, but," he motioned towards Sid, "you can invite your shadow in as well. I would, however, like our conversation to be private."

He led the way down a long center hallway, and then opened the door to a small, sunny room at the end. Sid posted himself at the door, which Carib then shut. "I hope you like a full English breakfast," he said, motioning towards the herring, bangers, toast, marmalade, Eggs Benedict, cereals, and fruit that lay spread out on the sideboard. "It's a habit I acquired when I went up to Oxford."

"It certainly beats my normal steel-cut oatmeal and dry toast regimen," I said, my mouth watering.

We served ourselves, and then sat down at a small mahogany table set for two. "As I mentioned on the phone, my friend," Carib began, "I have discovered a great deal about Mendez. He has been a busy man."

"More than just running drugs through Puerto Rico?" I asked.

"More. Much more. You may not be aware of it, but Mendez is a Muslim."

"No, I wasn't aware of that. But what difference does that make?"

"We think he's a member of a worldwide Muslim terrorist group. He's organized a cell in Puerto Rico, calling it the P.P.I.P whose ostensible goal is Puerto Rican independence. But there is some speculation that they are raising funds for more terrorist attacks on the U.S. Mainland."

"And the P.P.I.P. is the group that claimed responsibility for the Las Palmas bombing. But I still don't understand why they would want to kill everyone in the room. If Mendez wanted to get me, why didn't he target just me on the way into Puerto Rico or the way out?"

"Perhaps he really did want to kill everyone else as well," Carib responded, smiling enigmatically as though he knew something more.

"Because—" I encouraged him.

"Because perhaps UNRC wants to expand its domination over the worldwide oil industry. With the key executives of your competitors killed, their stock prices plummeted, and your company picked up large shares of your keenest competitors."

"I presume you know what you're talking about, my friend," I said, my mind struggling with the enormity of his charge.

"Yes, I do," Carib nodded. "We have traced these stock transactions back to one of your people by the name of Bradshaw."

Bradshaw again! I had severely underestimated this man. Mundi must be part of this terrorist organization as well. What was their true goal?

"Are you all right, Nick?" Carib was asking.

"I can't believe Bradshaw is part of a Muslim terrorist group. He's CIA."

"Our people aren't sure either, for the very reason he is CIA. But we do know he has had contact with Mendez."

Inexplicably, I thought about Marilyn and smiled. "Ah, a pleasant thought in the face of all this treachery," Carib observed.

I hesitated. Carib was one of my oldest friends. I wanted to tell him, and I knew I could trust him. I started with running into Marilyn two days ago, on to overhearing Bradshaw's conversation at Houston Airport, and finishing with my plan to set up operations in California.

"I see…." Carib mused. Then he said, "What are you going to do about Marilyn?"

I shook my head. "I just don't know, Carib. She…she still scares me. She's so…" I didn't know how to put it into words.

"Full of life?" Carib suggested.

"Yea. Full of life says it. Somehow that scares me."

"Life is scary sometimes. But there's a whole lot of joy too."

"I don't see much of that—not like two days ago."

"Probably because you've got your brakes on most of the time. Let yourself go more often."

I dismissed the suggestion with a wave of my hand. "No. I don't have the time for it."

"You did the day before yesterday. With Marilyn. You know, it's a lot easier than you might think. But, before you jump off the deep end with Marilyn, you might want to work things out with Susan. You may be surprised."

I frowned. "I don't know, Carib. I feel so distant from Susan."

"Give it some time. The rush you're feeling now for Marilyn may fade. And maybe you can build some sort of bridge back to Susan."

I shrugged my shoulders. "Maybe. But Susan's got to meet me halfway."

"You'll never know until you start moving towards her.

"And," he continued, "The Castle might be a good place for you and Susan to have some time together to work things out."

"Maybe," I said, but I was thinking of Marilyn being close to the Castle.

"And go to your Church," Carib urged.

After breakfast, Sid and I returned to the Quality Inn, and I went up to my room to wait for Ricardo's call. I read the *Washington Times* from cover to cover, and then turned back to the crossword puzzle. Every few minutes I glanced at my watch, but time just crept by. I thought about calling the office, but finally decided to risk Sullivan's wrath because I was sure now more than ever that the Company's line was tapped, and the CIA would be able to trace it. And Sullivan himself may be in on the conspiracy as well. I would call him the next day from the safety of the Castle.

My luggage had escaped the Cabana fire because I had left it in the trunk of my rental car. I extracted my running clothes, dressed, and then did my warmup exercises in the room. I strapped on my gun under my sweatshirt and opened the door slowly. I found the hall empty except for Sid, and I moved over to him to explain my plan. I jogged down to the end of the hall, through the exit door, and onto the stairs. I ran up and down the deserted stairways for thirty minutes.

When I finished, I went through the lobby door and bought a deck of cards in the gift shop. Several people stared at me in my running clothes as I re-crossed the lobby. I scrambled back up the stairs two at a time, then scampered into my room, nodding at Sid as I passed. I showered, dressed, and then sat down to play solitaire.

At first, I tried to play without cheating, but I was making so little progress that I began peeking at the unexposed stacks of cards, working the one that had cards I needed. That, too, ended in failure. Finally, I resorted to full scale cheating by withdrawing the cards I needed from the stacks and won. A hollow victory, I thought, sadly. I decided to try again.

I dealt myself another hand, intent on winning fairly. As I matched the cards in sequence, my winning conviction began to mount. I played quickly, yet I didn't feel I was hurrying. My moves became easier as I progressed. I reached the point that I knew I would win. Sixty seconds later, I placed the final king on the final stack, took a deep breath, and sighed with satisfaction.

Then the phone rang. I rose, walked over to the nightstand next to the bed, and picked up the receiver. I listened without speaking. "Nick?" Ricardo asked at the other end of the line. "Are you there?"

"I'm here, Ricardo. I wanted to make sure it was you."

"Look. My buddy was a gigabyte of information. Let's talk about it. Sid will be bringing you here. Are you ready?"

"Are you kidding? I've been ready for hours."

A scant five minutes later, I heard a knock at the door. I picked up the gun from the table and moved stealthily to the wall next to the door and flattened myself against it. "Who is it?"

"California Sid," was the reply.

I laughed, pulled open the door, and then followed Sid out of the hotel to his car in the parking lot. A short while later we pulled into the lot under FBI headquarters.

Ricardo was waiting for us in the conference room. A flip chart stood in the corner behind him. He rose as I approached, and we shook hands. "Have a seat," he then gestured. "Let's get right into it."

Then he motioned to Sid, "Thanks a lot. Please close the door on your way out."

I sat in the same chair I had the night before. "On the phone you sounded as though you got lucky."

"Well, I've gotten a pretty good profile on your man Bradshaw."

"Don't call him my man," I laughed mirthlessly.

"Sorry. Just a figure of speech...Anyway, my man at the CIA is an exceptionally good friend. Mike and I were partners on the New York Police Department before he was seriously wounded and had to take medical retirement. He's now Records Chief at the CIA, and he says Bradshaw had the reputation of being a rogue. Mike suspects he freelances on the side as well."

"Is that how Bradshaw and I are connected—through his 'extra-curricular' activities?" I asked.

"It's a possibility, but there are connections with his assigned activities to you—or UNRC at least."

"Well Bradshaw is our lobbyist, and maybe we've done a few unethical things, but nothing illegal."

"Don't be so sure...Let's follow his activities and see what connections there might be...

"First," Ricardo continued, "He's worked undercover in the Baghdad Connection drug operation."

"Baghdad?"

"Yes, Baghdad functioned as a funnel from Turkey to the West. That's how he met Mundi.

"He was also involved," Ricardo went on, "in arms deals through Israel to groups we wanted to aid but couldn't because of political fallout. And he's organized several foreign political assassinations. Then there's the operation to support world oil prices. Finally, he's organized stock manipulations and takeovers. Oh, and there's even rumors of his being involved with the Mafia."

"This guy s a real winner," I said sarcastically.

"I know this probably sounds silly, but is it possible that any of those activities could involve you?"

"Well, drugs and political assassinations are a little out of my line, but world oil prices and stock manipulations could have involved me. What was Bradshaw doing?"

"He was learning from his CIA mentor, Bob Bentley. You know, of course, about the forming of OPEC back in the fifties."

"Yes, that was before my time, but I know the details. What does that have to do with Bradshaw?"

"Nothing directly," Ricardo answered, clearing his throat, "OPEC was formed in the fifties, but wasn't a powerful force until the Arab Oil Embargo. Bradshaw's mentor, Bob Bentley was behind that."

"What?" I said, incredulous.

"Well, actually it was at the behest of the State Department; Bentley was just the modus operandi. State was worried about the stability of the Middle East, particularly Saudi Arabia. They figured that if the oil price were to rise, Arab economies would boom, and potential unfriendly political factions wouldn't stand a chance to take over. And that is still State's operating philosophy to this day. They call it 'Operation Horseback.'"

"Are you sure?"

"Straight from the files. And Bob Bentley taught Bradshaw all the dirty tricks he knew."

"And we thought we were being so clever, promoting high OPEC pricing behind the scenes so we could increase our gasoline and other by-product pricing and increase our profit margins. Of course, now it's backfired because the Arabs have gone into conversion as well, and our margins are being squeezed.... So, the CIA and the State Department are trying to save OPEC?"

"Yes."

"So Golden Green threatens that goal, since less gasoline and less crude will be consumed," I reasoned. "So, they bump me off, sabotage the formula, and OPEC is saved. Right?"

Ricardo chuckled. "I hadn't thought of that one, but anything's possible in the name of National Security. No, I was thinking more of the 55 mile-per-hour conspiracy. Since you didn't know the real reason behind the Oil Embargo, you may not know about this one either, particularly since it happened before your time."

118

I bristled at the thought of not knowing what was going on at my own company. "Well tell me about it. Better late than never," I said sarcastically.

"Shortly after the success of the Arab Oil Embargo," Ricardo began, "they saw another way to increase profits by removing lead from gasoline which had risen drastically in cost and was projected to spiral even higher. But Detroit was dead set against it because without the lead, the gas wouldn't have enough octane to power cars up a hill at 70 miles per hour without knocking. But a car could make it at 55."

I saw where Ricardo was leading. "So that's why Congress passed the 55 miles-per-hour speed limit! I always wondered about that!"

"And friend Bentley spearheaded the Oil Lobby legislation thrust. He made enough illegal 'political campaign contributions' to buy a small country.... So now that you know about it, what are you going to do?"

"Own up to it. That sort of thing is part of what's wrong with companies in this country, to say nothing of Congress."

A satisfied look crossed Ricardo's face. "We may have ourselves a motive here. Our killer—someone at UNRC— figured that once you moved from International to Domestic, you would eventually discover the plot. He wanted to stop you before you did."

"But if that were true, wouldn't he have tried when I was in International, for fear I would discover the OPEC plot?"

"Not if he wasn't involved. Bradshaw was, but that doesn't necessarily mean that our mystery man was.

"Following this line," Ricardo continued, "who at UNRC deals with Bradshaw?"

"We all do. There's always something legal...environmental... financial... I can't think of one part of our Company that doesn't have something to do with him. But if I had to pick anyone, I'd say Sullivan, simply because he's involved in everything."

"Okay, then, would Sullivan be the likely one to work with Bradshaw on international stock manipulation and corporate takeovers?"

I shrugged my shoulders. "It's possible, but he really only seems interested in his own stock. But speaking of stock manipulation, our competitors' prices plummeted right after the Las Palmas bombing, and huge blocks traded. Someone could be planning takeovers through shell companies."

"And that could be the reason for the bombing—everyone in that room was the target. You just got lucky. Sullivan and Melville were the really lucky ones—they were planning to be there."

"And now Bradshaw is after me to make it appear I was the sole target," I postulated.

"Anything's possible in the name of National Security."

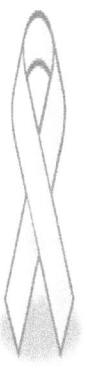

CHAPTER FIFTEEN

When I walked into the den at six p.m. that evening, Susan was seated on the sofa, martini in hand. "Who kept you?" she asked, "some bimbo?"

I grimaced. "No, Susan. Not this time. I was with Ricardo in Washington. As I told you on the phone yesterday, I couldn't tell you where I was."

Susan laughed without mirth. "I know—because the line might be tapped. That makes an exceptional story. I'll have to use it sometime."

Her cutting tongue helped me feel a little less guilty about Marilyn. "Look, Susan, I wanted to talk with you, but not when you have a load on. Come see me when you sober up." I turned to leave.

"But I want to talk with you!" she screamed in a drunken shrill.

I kept walking towards the door. "Come back here!" she shrieked.

I shrugged my shoulders, and the guilt vaporized. I turned back towards her, walked to the winged back chair next to the sofa and sat down. "I'm going to California—to the Castle—for a while. Are you coming?"

"How can I resist an invitation so eloquently tendered?" Susan said sarcastically.

"Susan, if you're going to be this way, I don't want to talk with you."

Susan covered her mouth with her hand. "Well, shut my mouth," she drawled in her best Southern accent. "I'll be a good little girl and listen to Big Daddy."

Again, I resisted the temptation to walk out. "Look," I said, "this is serious. The killer just tried again, and he knows my every move, so I need nothing short of a fortress. The Castle is perfect."

The silly grin disappeared from Susan's mouth, and she blinked rapidly as though trying to clear her vision. "What...what did you say?"

"The killer tried to torch me at the Cabana two night ago. He got the FBI Agent in the next room and would have incinerated me as well if I hadn't smelled the smoke."

Susan looked ashamed. "Oh, Nick, I'm so sorry. It's just...I'm so unhappy..."

Her face brightened slightly. "Sure, I'll go with you to the Castle. When are we leaving?"

"Tonight. We're booked on the nine-fifteen flight. Two FBI Agents are waiting outside."

Susan glanced at her watch. "I'll go pack a bag and be ready in twenty minutes." She stumbled only once as she went up the stairs.

We arrived at the check-in counter at Kennedy Airport at eight-fifteen. Susan showed her ID to the agent, and then turned to me. "I have to go to the Ladies Room," she said. "And then I'm going to pick up some magazines. I'll meet you at security." I completed the check-in process, and then headed past the counter, down the hall to the security check point. I waited. I finally spotted Susan emerging from a phone booth. Suspicion leaped into my mind. "Whom did you call?" I demanded as she arrived.

I thought I saw a shadow of guilt pass across her face. "Why... Josie," she answered. "She was expecting me this weekend."

"You could have called her tomorrow," I challenged.

"But I told her I'd call her tonight."

I stared at her. Something was off — I didn't believe her. Whom did she call? Reluctantly, I said nothing more. I was going to give this a chance. I headed through security and waited for Susan to clear. We headed towards the gate in silence. My thoughts raced back through recent memories. Susan had been acting very differently. She had loved her career—now she'd quit and only had one client, Robert Sand. Before, she hadn't wanted children—now having them was an obsession. Josie had been her friend she would see once a year—now she was in Southampton all the time.

I shivered as I connected her changes with the time of the bombing. Then I shook my head at the preposterous idea. Why would she want me dead? Divorce would have been a whole lot simpler. Or would it?

The gate agent at the doorway smiled at me as I handed the boarding passes to her. "Seats 1A and 1C are up front on your right. Enjoy your flight."

The 2 FBI agents, Sid and Tom, settled into seats 2C and 1D.

I had two martinis, then reclined my seat and dropped off into a fitful sleep. When I awoke five hours later, Susan was still sitting upright, sipping another martini, and lost in the world of her personal CD player. I turned my head, looked out of the window, and saw the lights of the Golden Gate Bridge rising out of the blanket of night fog. I shivered at the excitement of being back in the Bay Area. Then the plane banked sharply to the left for the final approach.

Two more FBI Agents were waiting for us as the front door of the aircraft opened. They led the way down the steps of the Jetway, onto the tarmac, and to a waiting car. "Tom and I will wait for your luggage," said Sid. "Let me have your claim checks. John and Judd will drive you straight to the Castle."

Three minutes later we rounded the flyover entrance to the southbound Bayshore Freeway. I glanced at the luminous dial on my watch. It read 12:30 AM. I figured with the sparse traffic at this hour, we would make the normal one-hour trip in under forty-five minutes. And it would be none too soon; I was still exhausted, despite my nap.

We sped down the open Freeway until we reached Route 92 West. We veered onto the off-ramp, and then swung onto 92. "Car following us," the driver, John, said.

I whipped my head around to see a lone pair of headlights behind us, just swinging onto 92. We crossed El Camino Real and began the climb up the foothills of the Santa Cruz Mountains. The road curved gradually at first, then turned more sharply as we ascended. The other car trailed us at a distance. "What do you think, John?" Judd asked.

"If they are following us, they're good. I'll take the next exit and see what happens."

John swung the car down the off-ramp and along the access road. I looked back to see the lights of the other car shoot down the off-ramp after us. "Get back on the Freeway," Judd ordered.

John whipped the car up the entrance ramp and back onto the Freeway. The other car followed. "No doubt about it," Judd said grimly.

Both cars raced up the mountain. The houses by the side of the road became sparser and soon there was no sign of life, except for our two cars. "They're gaining on us," Judd barked.

"I've got it all the way to the floor."

"Damn motor pool dogs," Judd hissed.

Suddenly the whine of the straining engine was interrupted by machinegun fire and smashing glass as the bullets burst through the rear window. Susan screamed, and Judd shouted, "Get down!"

Susan and I hit the floor. "They're really trying to kill us!" Susan screamed. More gunfire blasted as Judd shot back with his revolver.

The machinegun fire erupted again, and bullets whizzed through the glassless rear window and into the heads of Judd and John. The car decelerated. Without hesitation, I sprang into the front seat between them, grabbed the steering wheel with my right hand and shoved John's limp body against the door with my left. I jammed the accelerator down with my left foot and the car leaped forward. I glanced back and saw the lights of the other car right behind us.

I leaned forward and to the left to get in front of John and swung the steering wheel hard to the left with both hands, just as more machinegun fire rocketed towards us. The bullets missed their mark and the tires screeched as the car spun around in the opposite direction onto the grass, bounded off the metal center divider and back onto the Freeway, going the wrong way. I floored the accelerator, and the car lurched forward back down the mountain.

I crooked my head to the side to watch the other car in the rear-view mirror in the bright moonlight. It slid to a fishtailing halt on the right shoulder, stood motionless momentarily, then spun around and sped off after Susan and me. In the interim, I had gained about two hundred yards and was still accelerating down the mountain.

But we were hurtling the wrong way down the Freeway, and I knew we couldn't outrun them. We had to hide. We had to reach El Camino Real where we could disappear in the myriad of side streets.

Suddenly oncoming headlights blinded me as I rounded the turn. I swerved onto the grass to avoid collision, and the other car swung to the right, then slowed to a stop. I whipped the car back onto the Freeway. Our pursuers rushed past the stopped car which then spun around and joined the chase. "My God, Susan!" I shouted. "There are two of them after us now and they're gaining on us! Get Judd's gun! We're going to have to shoot it out!"

"What.... What?" Susan stammered.

"Snap out of it, Susan! Take Judd's gun out of his hand!"

Susan leaned over the front seat and pried the gun from Judd's rigid fingers. As she scrambled back onto the back seat, more machinegun fire burst out, but the bullets fell short. I shot a glance in the rear-view mirror again and spotted the flash of gunfire from the car behind our pursuers. Suddenly our pursuers' car swerved to the left, across the other lane, flew over the guardrail, and disappeared over the edge. A few seconds later an explosion rocketed skyward.

"My God," I said. "The other car is on our side." I put my left foot on the brake pedal and slowed to a stop on the grassy shoulder. The other car stopped behind us, and two men jumped out. As they strode up, I reached over John's body to roll down the window. Then I recognized them as the FBI agents, Sid and Tom. Sid peered in the window and asked, "Are you all right?"

"We're okay," I murmured, "but they got Judd and John."

"We'll check on the other car," Sid said, then turned and headed back with Tom to where the car had disappeared.

"Are you all right, Susan?" I asked.

"Oh, Nick," she sobbed. "I was so scared. I...I couldn't believe it was really happening."

I reached over and patted her on the head, saying, "It's all right. It's all over now."

Susan pulled away. "It's not over," she said. "They keep finding out where you are. How do they do it?"

"It's the CIA," I blurted. "They can find out anything they really want to."

"The CIA? Are you sure?"

"Yes. Inspector Lopez discovered that. And I found out Bradshaw is involved."

"Bradshaw? Your lobbyist?"

"Yes. He's also with the CIA."

"What the hell do they want with you?"

"I don't know, Susan. I really don't."

Susan dropped Judd's gun to the floor. "They won't stop until they get you. I don't know if I can handle this."

"It's okay, Susan. I understand. This is terrifying. Go ahead and take the plane back home tomorrow."

We sat in stony silence until the Agents returned. "They're burned to a crisp," Tom said. "We'll go down in the morning to see if we can get a make on the car."

The distant scream of sirens penetrated the late-night stillness. Sid turned to Tom. "I'll take them to the Castle. You finish up here."

CHAPTER SIXTEEN

I awoke the next morning to see Susan coming through the door dressed in her robe. "Good morning," she said.

I rubbed my eyes, then sat up in bed. "Good morning, Susan. How are you?"

She chuckled. "Well outside of a horrible hangover, I'm ready to tackle the world." Then she sighed. "Look, Nick. About last night. I didn't mean what I said. I guess with the alcohol and being scared—"

"No," I interrupted. "I think you meant exactly what you said. And besides, there's no sense in risking your life as well as mine. I was selfish to ask you to come."

"But a wife should stand by her husband. For better or for worse, you know."

"Yea, but you never bargained for a 'worse' such as this. You should stay only if you want to, not out of some antiquated sense of duty. And you made it real clear last night that you didn't want to be here."

"Now I do," she said solemnly.

"Look," I said, fighting to keep my temper, "right now you think you should be here, or maybe you may even want to be here, but deep down you really don't want to be here."

"How in the hell do you know what I want?"

"Oh, Susan, let's not start. Yesterday I thought being here together might give us a chance to work things out, but now I see this danger adds to the stress between us. And I really believe there is too much anger and not enough balance between us. You want children to the exclusion of all else, and I shut you out because of my single focus on my career. Now..." I paused. "Now I think now is as good a time as any to make a break, so we can both get on with our lives."

Susan took a step forward towards me, and then stopped. She stood frozen and silent. Finally, she asked, "Is there someone else? Someone who shares your single focus?"

"No...." I said, knowing I sounded tentative.

"Well, yes," I amended. "But not really. She's not really into careers."

"Who is it?"

"I don't want to tell you. Let's just say she's somebody I knew a long time ago. I ran into her a little while ago, and I thought I might be able to reach back into the past. But I know I can't do it, just as you and I can't go back."

"But I don't want to go back! I want to go forward! I want to be a woman! I want children!"

"I'm not ready! I may..." I softened my voice. "I may never be ready," I admitted. "Maybe if the world were a better place..."

"Well that does it!" Susan spat. "I've found someone, too! At least he likes children!"

I stared at her in silence, suddenly remembering my brother-in-law's warning that Susan had a wandering eye. "Who is it, Ted?"

"No," she scoffed. "Ted's happily married to Josie."

"Robert Sand, then."

"Robert?" she laughed. "He's more of a narcissist than Caligula."

"Do I know him?" I asked, my voice rising in disbelief.

"I don't want to tell you. Look. A moment ago, you suggested that we get on with our lives. Well let's just go ahead and do it."

Susan left right after breakfast. I stood in the open doorway as Tom drove her away, my nine-millimeter gun tucked into my coat pocket. I felt surprised at the pain that wrenched my heart and the tightness that gripped my throat. Nonetheless, I smiled slightly, glad that I was beginning to feel.

I scanned the expansive grounds, and then decided to reacquaint myself with the Castle surroundings. As I stepped out onto the Belgian block driveway, I smiled again as I remembered my Great-Grandfather who had found the crumbling castle on the Scottish moor. Stone by stone he had the castle moved to the cliffs overlooking Half Moon Bay and restored it. "You can hold off the world from here," Great-Grandfather had said on my eighth Christmas, the one I had found out about Santa Claus. "Yep," he had said. "It's a tough world out there—don't have any illusions about that."

And the world got tougher four Christmases later, the one my Mother told me she and my father were getting divorced. I felt that somehow, I was to blame.

I came to the brick path leading from the driveway to the Formal Gardens my Mother planned and had installed. Moss filled the gaps between the bricks and cushioned my feet as I strolled along. The hedges had gotten taller and fuller, and the large, rectangular fishpond lay beyond. I looked over at the twelve-foot high stone wall, then back at the Castle. Two of the San Francisco FBI Agents were following me at a distance, scanning all directions for potential danger. I looked back at the stone wall and wondered how secure it was. I turned back towards the Castle again. It was a bright, cloudless California day, but the Castle looked gray and lifeless, its walls rising fifty feet to the turrets on top. I saw the four FBI Agents posted up there.

I circumscribed the Castle along the rectangular outer wall, occasionally looking up at the small windows, squinting out of the huge blocks of granite that made up the Castle wall. When I returned to the entrance, I looked back up the sheer walls to the turrets. "Well at least I'll be safe here," I said aloud.

I went inside and called my office. "Mr. Shepherd's office," Pat answered.

"Good morning, Pat—or good afternoon back there."

"Nick! How are you?"

"Doing fine. I take it Liz must be out to lunch."

"Yes, she just left. She said she'd be back in half an hour...Nick, are you all right? Liz said something had come up, and you were taking some time off."

"That's right, Pat. I called to tell you that yesterday, but you were out. Did Liz give you the number?"

"Yes, but she said to call you only in the event of an extreme emergency, and to give it out only if Sullivan calls personally."

She repeated the question, "Are you all right?"

"I'm fine. I'm working on something big, and it may take me a while."

"Do you need help? That's what I'm here for."

I laughed. Pat successfully combined professionalism with youthful enthusiasm. "No thanks, Pat. Everything's under control... I'll be calling in three times a day. And you know where to reach me if you have to."

"This is about the bombing, isn't it," Pat said.

I hesitated as doubt about her rose in my mind. I usually told her everything—I had to, so we could both do our jobs. It occurred to me that I knew almost nothing about her. But then again, I had worked with Pat for years. Finally, I said, "Yes, as a matter of fact, it is."

"I thought so—it's not like you to not confide in me."

"Sorry, but the FBI doesn't want me to confide in anybody."

"I understand, Nick. We'll keep things running smoothly for you."

"Thanks, Pat. I'll be in touch. Bye for now." Then I hung up.

I spent the weekend in the library, digging through my Great-Grandfather's books and doing crossword puzzles. I felt secure in my mind, but uneasiness tugged at me.

On Sunday I made the 30-minute drive over the hill to Los Altos to attend the 10 o'clock Church Service. "Go to your Church," Carib had urged me. His suggestion had rung true for me; I hadn't been in years, and I knew it was time to return. My Great-Grandfather had liked the Reverend Miller at First Church in Los Altos, and I had gone with him during the summers of my youth. The minister had retired and now his son had assumed the mantle. His resemblance to his father was striking; I felt as though I had gone back in time, and this was his father. Reverend Miller, the Younger, preached on the power of the Holy Spirit and the need for us to be sensitive to God's will. I felt a serenity come over me, which stayed with me during the ride back over the hills and for the rest of the day.

I awoke Monday morning at five A.M. feeling very restless once again. I called the office. "Pat Campbell's office," Liz answered.

"Good morning, Liz."

"Oh, good morning, Mr. Shepherd."

"I take it Pat's not in."

"She's in," Liz said, sounding quite surprised. "But she's down the hall in a meeting with Mr. Melville."

"Is there anything hot?"

"Mr. Carib Conibo called and said it was important. He said you could reach him at the Venezuelan Embassy in Los Angeles." She gave me the number.

"Anyone else?"

"Well, I don't know how important it is, but I neglected to give you one of your messages last Friday."

"Oh? Who called?"

"A Mrs. Boone. Would you like her number?"

For a moment I drew a blank. Then I remembered Marilyn's married name had been Boone. "Yea. Okay," I said slowly, concealing my excitement.

"Her number is 650-555-9047."

I said, "Thanks. Talk to you later." I hung up the phone.

I called Carib but was informed he was out. I left the number at the Castle.

I began pacing back and forth across the room, gazing at the floor-to-ceiling books as though searching them for clues to answer the questions rolling around in my head. After my parents had split, I had spent much of my youth here, in my Great-Grandfather's library, reading, looking for answers and discussing more questions and more answers with my Great-Grandfather. But had those answers been right? Until recently, I hadn't questioned them. My life had been working.

But now I didn't know. Oh, yes, I was in line to achieve the most important goal in my life—CEO of UNRC. But that was the only thing that was working, and at what price? Someone was trying to kill me, my marriage was doomed, and I was foolishly trying to push the clock back twenty years to recapture a lost love. Marilyn. Another question. What was I going to do about Marilyn?

One of the original reasons I had chosen my Great-Grandfather's Castle as sanctuary was to be close to Marilyn. But after talking to Carib, I had decided against seeing her. I had wanted to work things out with Susan, but now Susan had found someone who would give her what she wanted. Which left me free. But Marilyn was in a long-term relationship. And she might want children. And you can't go back twenty years.

And I couldn't very well go see her and put her at risk. Mundi was out there somewhere, I knew. I had to stay put to give Ricardo and Carib more time to find the answers.

But what could Ricardo find out that he hadn't already? How would he get to the person behind Bradshaw? Ricardo could get lucky and lead the way. Not likely though. I reached into my coat pocket and felt the cold steel of my gun. I knew I wouldn't find the answer sitting in my Great-Grandfather's Castle.

I strode back to the great rectangular oak table in the middle of the library, picked up the telephone, and dialed Marilyn's number. "Hello Marilyn."

"Nick! You called back! I... I was afraid you wouldn't. You said it would be a few days..." She left the sentence unfinished.

"I've been fighting against calling you."

"I know. I have too. But I couldn't stand it any longer. I wanted to know how you are. I wanted to hear your voice. I wanted to...to know when you were coming out again. I know it's reckless and impractical. You're married, I'm involved and we're on opposite coasts...but I want to see you."

"I know. I want to see you again, too. How about tonight?"

"Tonight?" Marilyn asked, sounding bewildered.

"I'm at the Castle."

"Your Great-Grandfather's?"

"Yes, but don't come here—it's too dangerous. I'll meet you somewhere."

"Oh, Nick, I can't meet you tonight. Wiley is here for the first part of the week. I'm sorry."

"No problem. I understand. As you said, you're involved. And you love Wiley, despite his transgressions."

"Yes, but...but I love you too. I always have."

"That was then, Marilyn. Twenty years ago. Now is now. We can't go back."

"Yes, but we can go forward."

"To where? Where can we go?"

Marilyn laughed. "You always did have to have a goal."

I chuckled as well. "Yes, I guess maybe you're right. I don't like uncertainty."

"Nick, I don't know where all this is going to lead. All I know is that I want to see you."

"Good. When?"

"Wiley leaves for L.A. Thursday morning for two days. And I'll come over there—it makes no sense to make yourself a target outside the Castle."

"It's too dangerous. I'm sure they know I'm here."

"And you've got protection?"

"You could say that. I've got half the FBI here."

"I'll come there. At least they'll have to get into the Castle and past the FBI to get to us. I'll see you at 5 o'clock on Thursday." She left no doubt the discussion was over. There was no uncertainty.

As I hung up, I looked down at my once-again burgeoning belly. I wondered if three days could make a difference in shrinking it. I strode out into the foyer where I found Sid. "I'm going running," I announced, as though offering a challenge. Sid took it in stride, laughing, "We'll follow you in the car."

I bounded up the stairs two at a time, changed into my running gear, strapped on my gun, and then bounded back down the stairs and out the front door. Sid and Mac, one of the San Francisco agents, were waiting in the car, engine running, and its white exhaust billowing into the cool morning air.

I eased into a jog as the drawbridge began to lower, clanking loudly with each jerky movement, finally settling into place over the moat with a loud wooden groan. I strode through the gateway, across the drawbridge, and down the winding drive to the Pacific Highway. I shot a glance up to the right at the cliffs that hugged the Highway, then turned left, where the road was bordered by gentle rolling dunes and cliffs that dropped to the ocean.

I loped along the left edge of the blacktop, occasionally moving over to the sandy shoulder to give a wide berth to an oncoming car. The sun was bright in a cloudless sky and, even in the cool morning, sweat began to bead on my forehead and arms, and my breathing became short and shallow. This was my only awareness; this was my only consciousness.

Suddenly the image of typed words on a white page, with a familiar scribbled signature on the bottom, flashed into my mind. Then it was gone. I stopped running as though it would bring back the image. I closed my eyes, straining to conjure up the image, but nothing came. I felt as though a lid were covering my mind, bottling up the image. I knew it was important, but still my mind's eye was blank. "Damn," I said aloud as I stomped my foot on the macadam as I ran.

Sid drew the car up alongside and rolled down the window. "Are you all right?"

I grimaced. "I caught a snatch of something important in my mind, but now it's vanished. Some sort of document...I don't know..."

"Well just forget about it for now. Take your mind off it. It will come back when you least expect it—at least that what works for me."

I nodded. "Thanks. Thanks for reminding me. That does work." I turned and started running back towards the Castle.

After I showered and dressed, I called Jim Hudson who reported the tests were normal for his new Golden Green formulation. Then I called Sullivan's office. Hazel answered and explained he was still in Europe and would be going to Japan on Wednesday. I asked her to have Sullivan call me right away.

I ate breakfast and, just as I was finishing, Sullivan called. I explained the two Golden Green options, and, as I had expected, Sullivan opted for the unproven, low cost formulation. I went on to say that I hadn't gone to Mexico, I was still in California, and wouldn't be returning until the following week. Sullivan seemed preoccupied and simply said that if the job got done, he didn't care where I was. And I had meant I would be returning the following week. That was all the time I was willing to stay cooped up in the Castle.

I spent all my waking hours the next three days focused on business. I had a printer installed in the library and began to implement my plan to raise the price of Golden Green. On Wednesday afternoon I thought wryly that if Bradshaw hadn't known where I was before, he sure would by now.

When I awoke Thursday morning, I realized I had been dreaming about Marilyn. I smiled, then grinned, and jumped out of bed. I couldn't wait to see her. I felt light and fresh during my run along the Pacific Highway, free of the burden of assassins and business. My focus was joyous anticipation of being with Marilyn.

As I turned and headed back towards the Castle, the image of the white paper leaped into my mind's eye again. This time I recognized the scrawled signature—it was Sullivan's. Then the image was gone.

When I was showering, I suddenly craved a cheese omelet—not just anyone's, but Marilyn's. She had taught me how to prepare a special fluffy one that one summer. I closed my eyes, the shower beating down on my head, and the memory of that warm summer morning floated into my mind's eye. "Separate the eggs," she had said, and then had shown me how. "Now beat the whites until they stand up," again demonstrating. She added 1 teaspoon of baking soda, 1/2 teaspoon of salt and 4 tablespoons of milk to the four yolks and beat them all together. Then she combined the yolks and whites, poured them into a skillet on low heat, and covered it. When the eggs rose and began to get dry around the edges, she added the cheese and vegetables and waited until the cheese melted. Finally, she scored the omelet down the middle, folded one half over the other and lifted it out of the skillet. It was perfect.

The memory seemed like yesterday as I practiced in the kitchen a brief time later. I overcooked the first attempt, but my guinea pig, Sid, was starving and ate the entire omelet. The second one came out well, and I shared with Sid. When Sid finished, he said, "Now that I'm re-energized, I'm going to town. Is there anything you need?"

"As a matter of fact, there is." I scribbled on the notepad by the telephone, tore off the top sheet and handed it to Sid. Then I pulled out my wallet, withdrew a fifty-dollar bill and gave it to Sid as well, saying, "Try the Hobby Shop."

I called the office and found everything was under control. Then I called the Regional Offices—no problems there either. I even called Jim Hudson, but found the tests were running smoothly. I tried reading for a while but couldn't concentrate—Marilyn's face kept popping into my mind's eye. Then I picked up a crossword puzzle book and opened it to an expert one. I struggled with it for a few minutes, but none of the answers came to me, so I flipped to an intermediate one. I filled in two blanks, but then got stumped again. Turning to the easy section, I found one I could do, but quickly grew bored with it.

Finally, I got up and strode over to the chessboard on the table in the corner. I sat down and moved the white queen's pawn 3. Then I got up, walked over to the opposite chair, sat down, and moved the black queen's pawn 2. I spent the rest of the day on the game. Each time I moved, I concentrated only on that side of the board's strategy, blocking from my mind the other side's plan. I also stifled my thoughts of Marilyn.

The game ended in a draw at 4 o'clock. I went upstairs, showered again, shaved, dressed, and was back in the library at five minutes before five. I stood by the window, watched, and waited. And waited.

At five-thirty I panicked. I rushed to the telephone and dialed Marilyn's number. No answer. I ran out into the foyer where Sid was posted. "They've got Marilyn! We've got to find her!" I stepped towards the front door.

Sid grabbed me by the left arm. "Hold it! Let's not go off half-cocked. What's the problem?"

"She said she'd be here by five! I should have gone there! Why did I listen to her? They must have gotten her."

"You're jumping to conclusions. Just think about it. Nobody knew she was coming here."

"They could have tapped the phone."

"It's not tapped—we check it every day."

"Maybe they tapped her phone."

"They don't even know who she is."

I felt my stomach relax. "Yea, you're right. But I'm still worried about her."

"She'll show up."

Marilyn did drive across the drawbridge fifteen minutes later. I pulled open the arch-shaped oak front door for her, and we hugged. I sensed a barrier between us. "I'm sorry I was late," she said, avoiding my eyes, "but Wiley called from L.A. just as I was leaving."

"I was really worried about you. When you didn't arrive, I thought...well I thought something might have happened to you."

Marilyn's face reddened. "Well, I was on the phone with Wiley..."

"Why didn't you call me?"

"Well...well I just didn't. I'm sorry. I'm sorry I made you worry. I should have called."

I smiled and hugged her again. "That's okay. You're here now, safe."

Marilyn hugged me back weakly. I drew her back to arm's length and looked into her eyes. "What's wrong?"

Again, she avoided my gaze. "It's... it's Wiley."

"What happened? Is he all right?"

"Oh, he's fine now," she chuckled. "Look, this is really hard for me to say."

"Just say it. I can handle it."

"That's the problem. I don't think you can."

"Look, Marilyn. I have spent my life avoiding. I'm not going to do it anymore. I want to know."

Marilyn shrugged her shoulders, and then let go of me. "All right," she began, looking down at the slate floor. "When Wiley goes out of town, he calls me and wants me to talk dirty to him."

I scowled. "Talk dirty?" Slowly, I released her.

"Do you see now why I didn't want to tell you?" Marilyn asked softly.

I nodded as I looked up at the ceiling. Then I looked back down at Marilyn's uplifted face. This time she held my gaze. "But I am glad you told me," I said. "My life has been filled with dishonesty, even with you when we were in school. But now is new, and I want you and I to be open and honest with each other."

Marilyn smiled. "Okay on the big stuff. But on the trivial things—like idiosyncrasies of yours that make me mad—I'm going to keep my aggravation to myself."

"Deal," I said. "So will I. Speaking of deal, how about a game of Milborne?"

Marilyn's eyes sparkled with delight. "Good Lord! I haven't played Milborne since we were in school. Where on earth did you find it?"

"Actually, I had to send the FBI to locate it. They finally found it in an antique store."

"Not really!"

I chuckled. "No, not really. Milborne is one of those things they saved from our generation. You can actually buy it in downtown Half Moon Bay."

"Well, I'm glad some things don't change."

And they didn't change—Marilyn won two straight games, just as she had done the many years ago at Stanford. "I thought you were a ruthless businessman. You didn't go for the throat when you should have."

"I lose my killer instinct around you."

Marilyn smiled. "You're such a sweetheart."

I raised my eyebrows. "Oh we'll see about that. Milborne is your game, but chess is mine. I want a chance to get even. But first, some champagne to dull your mind."

I moved over to the ice bucket next to the chess table. I withdrew the bottle, wrapped it in a linen napkin, tilted it, and then began to twist the cork back and forth. I felt the pressure build in the cork, releasing it very slowly until it popped with a quiet whisper.

"You do that well."

"I've had lots of practice." I smiled. 'Too much, I'm sure."

I poured Marilyn a glass, handed it to her, then poured one for myself. Raising my glass, I said, "To modern times."

"To modern times," Marilyn echoed.

As we sipped, we stared into each other's eyes. I felt startled and exposed. "It's as though I'm looking into your soul," I mused.

"You are. It's always been open to you; you just never looked before. What do you see?"

"I see... I see a little girl. Free and spontaneous. I see love. I see caring. I see honesty...And I see hurt."

Tears brimmed in Marilyn's eyes. "My Lord," she whispered. "You really can see."

"I've been blind too long. And I haven't let anyone see into me either. Tell me. What do you see in my soul?"

Marilyn put her glass down on the coaster at edge of the chess table, stepped over to me, slid her arms around my back and looked up into my eyes. "I see...the little boy in you. Joyous and open and.... a little puckish. I see tenderness and vulnerability. And I see fear." Then she smiled, saying, "But above all, I see love."

I laughed nervously as I placed my glass on the other coaster on chess table as well. "You got that right.

"You know," I continued, shaking my head as though in disbelief, "it's as though all those years between Stanford and now have vaporized."

Marilyn nodded in a knowing way. "Wiley doesn't exist, Susan doesn't, the killers don't...All that's real is you and I, here and now."

We hugged, and I closed my eyes. I felt our souls merging into each other's and soaring. Eventually I opened my eyes, and then slid my lips down her neck, nibbling as I went. She shivered. Then she raised her head, tilted it back, and we kissed. We kissed repeatedly in rapid succession. Then we flung our arms around each other and hugged, tightly and for a long time.

In a singsong cadence I said, "We'd better watch it."

"Or we're going to get in trouble," Marilyn echoed.

We both laughed and released each other. "We've waited this long, we can wait a while longer," I said.

"What do you mean?" she asked.

"Susan and I are finished," I answered.

"What happened?" she asked, sitting down on the buttoned mahogany brown leather couch in the center of the expansive room.

"Well," I started, sitting down next to her, "Susan asked me if I had found someone else, and I found myself admitting that I had. She then said she had found someone who wanted children, and she couldn't wait for me any longer."

I went on to fill her in on the details of the latest attempt. "The terror she went through seemed to bring everything to a head," I concluded.

"Oh, Nick, that must have been horrible—for both of you! And I don't blame Susan for running away. I would have too."

"Would you have? You're here now, and you know the danger."

She flashed a quick smile. "Well maybe I'm a little more reckless than Susan…. In any event, I don't think you should be too hasty. You've both been through a huge trauma."

"This isn't hasty, Marilyn. It's been a long time coming. Besides, I believe there's truth in trauma."

Marilyn glanced away. "I see," she said.

"As I said, I can wait. Clearly, you're in love with Wiley. Perhaps it is not our time just yet."

Marilyn whipped her head around to face me, tears glistening in the corners of her eyes. "But I love you too!"

"And I love you," I said, drawing her head to my chest. "And I'm going to try to win you back."

"What am I going to do?" she moaned. "How can I choose?"

"I don't believe you'll have to force it," I said, my heart pounding. "I think it will become clear, and I hope it will be me."

Marilyn smiled slightly. "Perhaps you're right."

"I'd like to improve my chances," I said. "Can you spend the night?"

She looked doubtful.

"In separate rooms, of course."

"Oh, Nick, I'd love to but—"

"I'll barbeque you one of my Harris Ranch steaks," I interrupted. "And I'll throw in a fluffy omelet for breakfast tomorrow," I persisted. "I've been practicing."

"Really?" she asked. "You've been practicing?"

"Really," I said.

"Now that's an offer I cannot refuse," she chuckled. "Steak and eggs. And I'm sure Wiley won't be calling me again tonight. Even if he were to, I wouldn't care. It would be good for him to know he's got some serious competition."

The phone rang. "Now who in the blazes could that be?" I wondered aloud. I rose and strode over to the phone on the desk by the floor-to-ceiling window. I picked up the portable receiver and said, "Hello."

"Hello, my friend," said the voice on the line.

"Carib!" I shouted. "How are you?"

"Just great, Nicholas. I have a new deal for you."

"Don't tell me you would like to sell us more oil," I laughed. The world markets were drenched in oil.

"Let's just say I'd like to find a way we can mutually benefit. I'm at our Embassy in Los Angeles. May I come to see you?"

"Sure. How about tomorrow morning here at the Castle?"

"I'll be there at 9:30," he said. "And I have some more news about Mendez."

"Icing on the cake," I said.

"This is serious about Mendez," Carib warned. "Watch your back."

"Thanks, my friend. I've got lots of backup here. See you tomorrow."

Just as I replaced the receiver, my cell phone rang. I looked down at the digital screen and saw Ricardo's number displayed. I pressed the talk button, held the phone to my head and said, "This had better be good."

"Hello to you too," Ricardo laughed. "It is good."

"A connection?"

"You might even call it a hot line, straight from Bradshaw to your Mr. Sullivan."

"Sullivan?" Part of me believed the charge, simply because Sullivan was the type of man who had the brains and ruthlessness to engineer the conspiracy. But Sullivan had been my mentor, and I was the heir-apparent. Why would Sullivan want me killed? "Are you sure?" I asked.

"I can't prove anything in court yet, but Mike in CIA Records tapped into Bradshaw's e-mail and found a note strongly suggesting Sullivan is in charge. And this note also implies a U.S. OPEC exists."

"A U.S. OPEC? No. No way. I'd know about it." I walked over to the champagne bucket and lifted the bottle. I looked back at Marilyn and raised my eyebrows. She shook her head, and I slid the bottle back into the ice.

"Think about it, Nick," Ricardo was saying. "You've been in Domestic less than a year. And do you really make the pricing and production decisions?"

Images of the Monday morning staff meetings flashed into my mind, with Sullivan running them in his fiery way. I really had to admit that Melville, the rest of the staff, and I only followed Sullivan's orders.

"Okay, Ricardo, you're right. Sullivan really does run the show. Why shouldn't he; he's the largest single stockholder. But I still can't believe there really is a U.S. OPEC. There's too much competition. Just look at Golden Green. He really busted my chops to develop it. And we're killing the competition with it." I grunted as I pushed open the French doors and headed for the grill on the terrace.

"Am I interrupting something?" Ricardo asked.

"In fact, you are. But go ahead. It's 8 o'clock out here, and I was just going to put a steak on."

"I know it 8 o'clock—I'm in San Francisco. Anyway, it seems to me that Golden Green is a disaster. In a few months, someone is going to figure out it's destroying engines, and the Oil Industry can say they tried mileage extenders, but they failed. And consumption and prices will rise again."

"Then why is he pushing me so hard to reformulate before the problem is discovered?"

There was silence on the other end of the line as I pulled the grill top up, turned the gas knob, and pushed the ignition button. Then I added, "Jim Hudson believes he can reformulate successfully. The only question is whether he can do so before the engine compression loss is noticeable."

"Did you ever wonder why Golden Green failed?"

"It failed because we didn't consider the elevated combustion temperature."

"Maybe somebody knew it would fail."

"But I got it from Walter Melville. Oh, we've been competitors, but he wouldn't set me up like that."

"Well maybe he got it from Sullivan."

"No, he said he got it from someone in Iraq."

"Mundi is from Iraq. Mundi is connected to Bradshaw, and Bradshaw is connected to Sullivan."

The possibility that Ricardo's speculation might be true stunned me. He was saying that if A is equal to B and B is equal to C, then A is equal to C. But the formula did not necessarily come from Mundi. I needed more convincing. "Tell me more about the e-mail to Bradshaw."

I heard the rustle of a paper on the other end of the line. "I have a hard copy right here. I quote, 'Contact SLAVES. Crescent Reunion Sunday midnight.' And it's signed, 'BMS.'"

"What in the world does that mean?"

"We don't know for sure, but we can make a good guess. One of my friends over at the Justice Department has been working on this U.S. OPEC theory for some time, and he believes SLAVES to be a code name for a sub-rosa group of the U.S. Oil Institute which functions as the cartel. As I'm sure you know, the next meeting of the USOI is in New Orleans, also known as 'The Crescent City.'"

I whistled sharply. "Maybe you really are onto something."

"I've got some photographs from my friend at Justice which will be the pièce de résistance. I'd like to show them to you tomorrow."

"I'll be here, but I tell you, I don't know for how much longer— I'm getting cabin fever."

"We can talk about that tomorrow morning. I'll see you around 9."

I pressed the end button on my cell phone and slid it into my pocket. "Steak time," I said.

"May I help?" Marilyn asked. "I make a mean salad, especially if you have artichoke hearts."

I smiled as I remembered that Marilyn and I used to eat artichoke hearts straight out of the jar. "We have artichoke hearts. And hearts of palm. Tomatoes, carrots, and cucumbers as well."

"You have everything I need," she said, returning my smile.

I led the way from the terrace, through the library, the dining room, and into the kitchen where Sid and Tom were just finishing their dinner. I wanted to dine out on the terrace, but Sid advised against it. "Let's eat in the library," Marilyn suggested. "I love that room."

"It's my favorite as well," I said. "The dining room is too austere."

Out on the terrace I barbequed the steak and corn-on-the-cob, covered with only a single layer of husk. Sid stood guard, while Marilyn prepared the salad in the kitchen. By the time I had finished cooking and brought the food into the library, Marilyn had put two settings on the chess table, with my Nambé aluminum salad bowl in the middle. I carved the steak into slices, placed the platter next to Marilyn, and then sat down. She helped herself to steak and corn, and I filled my salad plate with her colorful concoction. She passed me the steak and corn, and then she filled her salad plate. I waited until she took her first bite, and then I took a mouthful of lettuce that had a drizzle of brown dressing on it. "This dressing is delicious! What is it?"

Marilyn smiled. "I call it Balsamic Moutard. I invented it a couple of years ago when I was trying to make something else."

I speared an artichoke covered with Balsamic Moutard and slid it into my mouth. "This is really tasty. What's in it—besides balsamic vinegar?"

"How did you guess?" Marilyn laughed. "Six tablespoons.

"I start with one cup of olive oil," she continued. "Then I add the balsamic vinegar, two tablespoons of lemon juice, two cloves of garlic, and three tablespoons of Grey Poupon mustard."

"Ah, French mustard," I said. "Hence the name 'Moutard.' That's French for mustard, you know."

"Duh," she laughed.

We savored our salads in silence for a few moments. "Do you go to Church?" Marilyn asked suddenly.

"Where in the world did that come from?" I asked, avoiding the question.

"I found myself thinking about the day I invented Balsamic Moutard. It was the day I had found my way back to Church."

"Tell me about it," I said.

"Well, it was right after John died. I felt guilty, and I guess I was looking for forgiveness."

She paused. "You didn't answer my question."

I felt myself squirming. "I don't go regularly," I admitted.

"Nick, my sweet," Marilyn laughed. "This isn't the Inquisition."

"Susan and I used to go when we were first married, but then we got into a crowd of heavy Saturday night drinkers and had a tough time getting up Sunday mornings. I went to First Church in Los Altos last Sunday, but the time before that was Easter, probably about 5 years ago."

I sensed an opportunity to enhance my chances with Marilyn. "Does Wiley go with you?"

Marilyn laughed. "Hardly. Sunday is his golf day."

"I'll go with you this Sunday," I said. "Where's the Church?"

"Why, at Stanford. Memorial Church."

"What a question," I said. "Still at ten A.M.?"

"Still at ten."

"I'll be there."

After dinner, I walked over to the unfinished The New York Times Sunday crossword puzzle, which still lay on the table between the two leather winged-back chairs on the left side of the French doors. I held it out to her. "I just started working these things again. Do you do them at all?"

She looked down at the puzzle. "With a passion." She nodded her head. "I remember this one—it's a real bear."

We sat down in the chairs, and with several hints from Marilyn, I finished the puzzle during the next half hour. Then I yawned involuntarily. "I'm sorry," I said. "I still haven't adjusted to the time change."

"Then let's go to bed," Marilyn said, an impish smile on her lips.

I must have looked as shocked as I felt, with my heart pounding in my ears. "I'm sorry, Nick, my love," she said. "That's not fair to you, particularly after you have been so gallant. I was mostly teasing. Separate bedrooms, you said."

"What was I thinking?" I said, chuckling.

"You were thinking for both of us," she said.

We mounted the stairs, arms around each other. We went into my bedroom, and I outfitted her with pajamas and toiletries. Then we went on to her bedroom, stopped outside the door, and hugged. We kissed for several long, delicious moments, and then hugged again. "Sleep well, my love," I whispered.

"Sweet dreams, dearest," she responded. "Wake me when you get up."

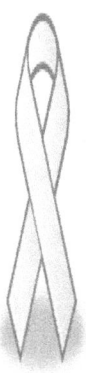

CHAPTER SEVENTEEN

I arose at six A.M., brushed my teeth, donned my robe and slippers, and then tapped on Marilyn's door. A moment later, the door swung open, and she stood dressed and smiling before me. "Good morning, my love," she said, and then kissed me.

"You're dressed," I said, marveling at how well she looked, her red hair cascading over the front of her shoulders. She must have brushed it one hundred times.

"I even showered. Go ahead and take your shower, and I'll get the coffee started."

The front door knocker resounded at eight-fifteen. We were still sitting at the chess table in the library, sipping coffee. Marilyn said, "Your omelet was perfect."

I responded, "Your hashed browns and rye toast were as good as I remember." I lifted my cup. "And this coffee is the best I've ever had."

Sid opened the library door, and Carib walked in. "You're early," I said.

"I caught the six o'clock." He approached the table, looking questioningly at Marilyn. "Marilyn," I began, "may I present my longtime friend, Carib Conibo. Carib, this is my even longer time friend, Marilyn Boone."

"A pleasure to meet you, Mrs. Boone," Carib said, smiling broadly. "Nick told me about your reunion."

"He did?" she asked, looking at me and grimacing.

"Don't worry, Marilyn. I know Carib is completely trustworthy."

Marilyn's face relaxed, and then she smiled. "Actually, it would be easier if Wiley heard about you from someone else." She laughed. "Then I wouldn't have to tell him."

"It won't come from me," Carib said.

"Drat," Marilyn chuckled, "then I guess I will have to tell him."

"Well," she continued, "I was just leaving. It was nice to meet you, and I hope to see you again."

"I'm sure we'll meet again," Carib said in a tone that made me believe it was a certainty.

I followed Marilyn out of the library, down the long hall and to the front door. I opened it, and we stepped out into a thick blanket of fog. We kissed tenderly, and then I said, "You understand I have to get back out there next week."

Marilyn nodded. "Yes, I understand," she said softly.

"I'll see you at Church on Sunday, but I would like to see you again here before I go back."

"Wiley is going to Denver Monday. I'll be here after school."

"Five o'clock?"

Marilyn smiled. "Five o'clock sharp. No delays next time."

"Be careful driving," I said. "That fog is about as bad as it can get."

"I will."

We kissed again, long and hard. Then Marilyn whispered, "Goodbye, my love," and scampered down the stone steps to her blue Mercedes.

Carib had helped himself to a cup of coffee in the kitchen. I poured myself another cup and said, "Come on." I led the way through the dining room and into the library. On clear days, the morning sun rises above the Santa Cruz Mountains and casts its golden rays upon the books, but this day the thick fog blocked the sun. I switched on the lights. "Not as beautiful as when it's bathed in sunlight," Carib observed, "but still a magnificent room. I believe it rivals Thomas Jefferson's at Monticello." "It's funny you should mention that. My Great-Grandfather had Jefferson's library in mind when he designed it." I motioned to the winged back chairs by the French doors. "Have a seat and tell me what's on your mind."

Carib eased his tall frame into the chair. "First, I want to alert you that we have credible evidence Mendez is planning some kind of attack on you here."

"Then what are you doing here," I jibed.

"I'll face even certain death for an oil contract," Carib replied, smiling broadly, and revealing his large white teeth. "But I am serious about Mendez. Our intelligence people are monitoring his cell phone, and he's setting up a rendezvous."

"Out here?"

"I believe so."

"How do you know?

"Mendez was talking about preparing to roll at 1400 Greenwich Mean Time on D-Day. The other fellow asked him what time that was on the West Coast. Mendez exploded and told him to figure it out himself."

I calculated three hours difference between here and New York, plus five hours more to England. "That's 6 A.M.," I said. I glanced down at my watch. Then I looked out at the curtain of fog. "Well, I guess today isn't D-Day."

"Perhaps not. But I wouldn't call off the guard just yet."

I retrieved the walkie-talkie from my belt. "You there, Sid?"

"Still in the kitchen, Nick."

"We may have some unwelcome visitors. Pass the word."

"Roger."

I turned back towards Carib. "Perhaps Mendez was behind the attack when we were on our way here from SFO Airport."

"Perhaps. Tell me about it."

I related the details of the incident, ending with the fiery crash. "Could the FBI identify the men?" Carib asked.

"Two were locals, identified by their driver's licenses. The other two couldn't be traced. Latinos, though."

"Were they locals Muslims?"

"Could be," I mused, trying to remember what Sid has said. "I think one of the names was Abdul." I snapped my fingers. "That's right! You said Mendez was a Muslim!"

"Right you are. This lends ever more credence to the evidence of an attack here."

"We're ready," I said. "But now let's talk about an oil deal. What do you have in mind?"

"How many barrels per day are you buying from Iran?"

"About a million," I replied.

"That's what I thought," he said. "How would you like to buy that million from me rather than Iraq?"

I liked the idea, immensely. I smiled. "What's in it for me?"

"You get to cut The Ayatollah off," he said.

"That's good for openers," I said. "What else?"

"Same deal as we currently have. Five dollars off."

"Five dollars off what?" I asked. I smiled again, knowing that he knew that I knew that the Iran price was already less than the official OPEC level.

"Off Ayatollah's price," he said, his teeth flashing white against his bronze skin as he grinned.

"Deal," I said, extending my hand. "Walt Melville has been asking me if we can do more with Venezuela. This will make his day."

Carib clasped my hand and we shook. "I want to congratulate you," he said.

"This is a win-win deal," I protested. "It's good for both of us."

"I don't mean our deal," he said. "I congratulate you on Marilyn. She's aces."

"Isn't she the best?" I said, smiling involuntarily. "But…but how do you know. You met her for all of one minute."

"That's all I needed. She has a superb aura. Worth fighting for, I'd say. And it is going to be a fight. She's tightly wired to that other fellow."

"You know Wiley?" I'm sure my face betrayed my dumbfounded feeling.

"I don't know him. I just know he's got a good hold of her. But you can win her. Just be open and honest with her, just the way you are with me, only more so. You've got to tell her your feelings."

I felt myself squirming. "It's not easy," I said.

"What are you feeling now?" Carib asked.

I struggled to identify the feeling. "I feel as though I'm a totally helpless worm on the end of a hook," I said finally.

"Perfect. You got in touch with that feeling and expressed it. That's how you'll win Marilyn. Wiley is as closed as a bank vault at midnight."

Ricardo knocked on the library door a few minutes before 9. I opened it and we shook hands. As I led the way to the table behind the sofa, I noticed sunlight streaming through the French doors as the fog was lifting. Ricardo shook hands with Carib, and then swung his Government Issue gray plastic briefcase onto the table. He opened it and withdrew a packet of pictures, which he spread out on the table. "I need your help," Ricardo said. "We can identify most of the people in these photos as either U.S. Industry Oil Executives or low-level OPEC staffers. Look at this one." He slid the first picture towards me.

I studied it. The group was sitting under a tall stand of trees with a swimming pool in the background, and the scene looked familiar. I suddenly realized the picture was taken at Las Palmas!

"My God, you're right! You've got nearly everyone in the Oil Industry right there. Where in the world was I?"

"That was taken in the afternoon, before you got there."

"How did the OPEC guys get past security?"

"I don't know, exactly. They were probably staying in various houses around the Marina, and just took the Jitney over, cleared the weapon scanner, and met at the pool bar."

I looked at Ricardo, puzzled. "Who took the picture?"

"My friend at Justice. And he got a lot more than he expected. Do you recognize everyone?"

I nodded slowly, shaken at seeing the U.S. Representatives so full of life, just before being blown apart. "Yes, I knew them all."

"Including the OPEC people?"

"Well, they're not all OPEC people."

"Oh?" Ricardo sounded surprised.

"No," I answered, pointing to one of the figures in the photo. "That's Geoffrey Hunter. Assistant to the Chairman with Anglo Petrol. At least that's what he does now. I heard he used to be with MI5, got caught with some woman who turned out to be a Russian spy, and left the Service shortly thereafter. Nothing was ever proven, let alone became public, but I heard about it from Carib."

Carib nodded. "Actually, the Brits discovered recently that he had been a double agent, working with the Russians"

I studied the other faces in the picture. I knew some of them better than others; a few I had met just once, that morning of the blast. I saw Jerry Archer of Pueblo, the Company that we were now acquiring.

Next, I came to a familiar, clean-shaven Latin face, with dark, penetrating eyes. "There's Pablo Ortega, of Petro de Mexico—they're not OPEC members either... And come to think of it, he used to be with the Federales...I can't believe it, but it sure looks as though there's a worldwide oil cartel."

"And," Ricardo added, "there's a worldwide Intelligence cartel. These pictures are full of people we know in the Community."

"What do they want?" I shouted, pounding my fist on the table, knocking some of the pictures onto the floor.

"I don't know," Ricardo answered, "but we'd better find out fast, before there's any more damage done."

Suddenly there was a blast on the roof of the Castle that shook the entire structure. Moments later a second explosion erupted in the direction of the drawbridge. Simultaneously Ricardo, Carib and I whipped out our guns and dashed to the French doors which looked out onto the courtyard and the drawbridge beyond. Sid rushed into the room with a gun in one hand and walkie-talkie in the other. "They're coming up from the beach!" a voice crackled over the walkie-talkie. "And they're carrying—" Gunfire erupted, and the voice ceased.

A gaping hole had been blown in the raised drawbridge. Another missile screamed through the air and exploded on the grass, short of its mark, but the impact blew the French doors off their hinges, smashing several glass panes, flung Ricardo, Carib and I onto the floor and pushed Sid back against the wall. The remaining glass panes shattered as the French doors crashed onto the floor. I lay dazed momentarily, but our peril swept away my dizziness, and I scrambled to my feet. Ricardo and Carib were up seconds later, and Sid dashed across the room to join us, walkie-talkie in hand. We peered out into the courtyard to see a stream of men crossing the moat on a wide, wooden plank, automatic weapons at the ready.

Ricardo fired his thirty-eight, the bullet piercing the leader's forehead, killing him instantly and dropping him onto the hard, Belgian block driveway. I aimed my nine-millimeter gun at the second assailant and fired. The blast was deafening, and the recoil rocketed up my arm and shoulder. The deadly bullet slammed into the on-rusher's chest, felling him as well. I stared at the lifeless body in disbelief. Carib and Sid fired simultaneously, killing two more. The others scattered, seeking protection behind the trees that lined the driveway. As they dashed, gunfire erupted from the roof, hitting another two, sending them crashing to the driveway where they lay motionless.

"Looks like more than twenty of them," Ricardo said tersely. "Wonder how many more there are." He pointed his gun in the direction of the mangled drawbridge. "Is that the only way in?"

"Yes," I said, then added quickly, "but there is another way out. A tunnel to a cave down by the beach."

"How do we get to it?"

"Through the wine cellar."

Machinegun fire blazed from behind the trees, the bullets hurtling through the open doorway and slamming into the wooden paneling behind us. Gunfire from the roof followed seconds later. "Let me have that thing, Sid," Ricardo said, pointing to the walkie-talkie. Sid tossed it to him. "This is Lopez. What's the status on the roof?"

Tom's disembodied voice crackled through the black box. "Phil, Larry and I are here. Andy and Rudy bought it when that missile hit."

"Any signs of life at the drawbridge?"

"No, nothing. Those bastards must have gotten them. I don't know how—"

His words were cut off by new bursts of machinegun from the invaders behind the trees. "Return the fire," Ricardo ordered, "then get your butts down to the cellar. We'll meet you there."

Shots erupted from the roof as the FBI trio opened fire simultaneously. Ricardo, Carib. Sid and I fired as well. The others missed, but my shot blew a hole through the head of one of the marauders, dumping him backwards onto the grass. He lay still. "My God!" I croaked. "I've killed another one!" My head was swimming. I leaned back against the library wall for support, my knees weakening under the impact of what was happening. I felt totally out of control.

"Nick!" Ricardo shouted. "Snap out of it! It's them or us!"

"Okay, okay," I said defensively, but I remained frozen against the wall. The firing from the roof had stopped. The invaders had ceased as well. The brief silence gave me the chance to dump the horror of killing and focus on the reality of escape. "Come on!" I shouted. "Let's get out of here!" I dashed across the room, with Ricardo, Carib, and Sid at my heels. I flung open the door, shot down the hallway to the cellar door, and yanked it open. As I flipped on the cellar light, the invaders opened fire once more, their bullets smashing through the sidelight windows surrounding the front door and ricocheting off the foyer walls. "They've seen us!" Ricardo shouted.

I heard footsteps above me, and I looked up to see Tom, Phil, and Larry racing along the landing towards the stairway leading to the foyer. I turned and then hurtled down the cellar steps, with the others rushing down after me. I sprinted across the concrete floor to the wine rack against the far wall. Sliding my gun into its holster, I pressed my fingers against the right side of the wooden rack, halfway up. Nothing happened.

"What is wrong?" I shouted, my voice choked with frustration. Frantically, I pushed repeatedly at a knot in the wood, first higher, then lower. Still nothing happened.

"Are you sure that's the right spot?" Ricardo queried, glancing back over his shoulder at the stairway.

"I'm positive!" I bellowed. "I've done this a hundred times!"

"Try again! It's probably rusty!"

I pounded the knot with my clenched fist, and then heard a faint click. The wine rack swung open, away from the wall, revealing a small opening leading into darkness. I yanked out a flashlight from an outlet in the tunnel wall and flipped it on. I led the way into the opening, the cone of light from the flashlight cutting through the darkness. I waited for the others to scamper through. As I pressed the control to close the opening, I heard the running footfalls of the invaders pounding on the slate foyer floor upstairs. The door closed with a click, shutting out the sounds.

I played the light along the wall, across the ceiling, then back down the other wall, revealing huge, rough-hewn beams supporting the tunnel. My Great-Grandfather had had the tunnel constructed from the cave on the beach to the Castle during Prohibition. He had told me he had built it just to assure his private stock of liquor would be intact, but I suspected my Great-Grandfather had been one of the rumrunners. My Great-Grandfather had always wanted excitement in his one-hundred-and-two-year life, and he had gotten it.

I thrived on excitement as well. My trepidation and shock had now given way to plans of counter-attack. From the bluff we could see everything.

"Do we wait it out?" Sid asked.

"No," Ricardo answered. "We'd be sitting ducks if they got lucky and found this place. I wish I knew how many of them there are, and where they all are."

"I know how to find out," I said.

"How?" Ricardo asked, surprised.

"This tunnel leads down to a cave on the beach. From there it's a short distance to the cliffs. Don't worry; it looks impossible to scale, so they won't be waiting for us. I've climbed it countless times, though, and we can look down on the Castle from up there without being seen."

"Let's go," Ricardo agreed. "But as soon as I can get a signal on my cell phone, I'm calling for back-up."

I led the way, cautiously at first, inspecting the massive beams with my flashlight for signs of decay. Satisfied that they had not weakened, I quickened my pace until the tunnel narrowed and began sloping downward. Here the walls changed from granite to sandstone, crumbled bits of it piled up along both sides of the tunnel. Here, too, the beams were spaced closer together. I turned back to Carib who was now following right behind me. "I was worried about this section, but it appears safe."

"It is," Carib said in his knowing way. "Let's forge ahead."

The tunnel sloped down gradually at first and began to narrow. A shower of sandstone sprayed down on me as the top of my head grazed a crossbeam. "Low bridge," I called back to the others.

"How much further?" Ricardo asked.

"We're almost to the cave," I answered.

I slouched forward as I hurried down the steepening tunnel floor. Then the slope gradually leveled, and the tunnel widened and became granite once again.

We came to the end of the tunnel, faced by a solid granite wall. I drew close to it, playing my flashlight along the right-hand side of the wall. I illuminated a small, black protuberance. "There it is!" I exulted, then turned and handed the flashlight to Carib. "Here, hold this right on the spot."

I turned back to the wall, crouched, and then pushed against the illuminated spot with both hands, grunting with the effort. There was a whirring sound, followed by a grating as a small section the granite wall began sliding to the left. I took the flashlight from Carib and shined it along the base of the wall, revealing two steel tracks along which the granite door was sliding, creating a small opening. "Thank God," I breathed in relief.

I crawled through the opening, into a dimly lit cave, followed by the others. We picked our way around the stalagmites rising from the floor, and then stopped at the small opening at the far end. I dropped into a prone position and eased my head out through the opening. I blinked rapidly as my eyes adjusted to the bright midday sun, and its reflection off the sand and sea, eight feet below the gently sloping cliff wall.

The beach was deserted. I inched out far enough to see the top of our objective, the bluff. As I had suspected, there were no signs of life up there either. "The coast is clear," I called back to the others.

I found hardholds on the face of the cliff and pulled the upper part of my body through, then swung my legs out, into a sitting position on the mouth of the cave. I jumped and plopped into the soft sand below. A few minutes later all seven of us were gathered at the base of the cliff. Ricardo whipped out his cell phone. "Damn!" he said. "There's no signal!"

I pointed to the sheer cliff two hundred yards down the beach, saying, "That's where we're going. Maybe you can pick up a signal there."

"What do you think we are, mountain goats?" Sid groaned, wide-eyed and only half-joking.

"I chiseled out toe-holds. We can make it. It's the safest place around, and we can see the Castle, as well as the road in both directions."

"Lead the way," Ricardo said.

We ran the two hundred yards down the beach to where the gently sloping cliff changed to a sharp rise. I lifted first one foot, then the other, into the toeholds, and then reached up for the next two grooves. I looked down at the others and said, "As you climb, hug the cliff for balance. Believe me, it's easier than it looks."

Fifteen minutes later I pushed myself up from the last niche, scrambled onto the narrow summit, then crawled away from the edge to make room for the others. When we had all made it, Ricardo grabbed his cell phone again and grimaced. "Still no signal."

I shrugged and then said, "Well, let's have a peek," I chuckled at my unintended pun. That broke the tension, and we inched prone over to the far edge.

The Castle turrets lay slightly below our eye line. I stared down on the grounds, unbelieving. Scores of men and vehicles swarmed it. My gaze followed the winding driveway down to Route 1, then to the cliffs beyond, where another cadre of men stood ready with rocket launchers. "So that's how they hit the roof and the drawbridge," Ricardo observed, following my stare.

Route 1 was clear of all traffic, except for a small blue car, pulled over to the side of the road. "My God!" I cried. "That's Marilyn's car! I've got to help her!" I started backing away from the edge.

"Hold it, Nick" Ricardo commanded. "Let's not panic. We can't take them all on just by ourselves. We've got to get some help in here. It looks as though they've blocked off the road from both sides. Broken down trucks, most likely. Is there a house near here, a house with a phone?"

"The closest one's about a half-mile further up the beach," I said, pointing north, beyond the bend in the shoreline and our view. "But nobody will be there—the Thorndikes use it only on weekends. There should be a phone, but I'm not sure."

"We'll have to break in, then, and just hope there's a phone." He turned to Sid. "Nick and I will go. You guys stay here and," he pointed to the walkie-talkie clipped to Sid's belt, "keep us posted on what's going on down there."

"I'm coming with you," Carib said.

I nodded, and then headed back the way we came.

The descent was faster because we didn't have to pull ourselves up, as we did on the ascent. I hit the beach running. Ricardo and Carib caught up with me a few moments later, and we sped along in tandem at the water's edge towards the Thorndikes'. Despite wearing street shoes, our pace was fast on the hard sand. Fear for Marilyn's life drove me to the limits of my speed. Why in the blazes didn't I go to see her, as I wanted to, instead of letting her come to the Castle? Some fortress! Bradshaw, or Mundi, or Sullivan, or whoever had knocked it over as though it had been made of sand. And in broad daylight!

As we approached the Thorndikes, Carib shot into the lead. Instead of heading for the front door on the far side of the house, he made for the stairway leading up to the deck on the ocean side of the house. He slid to a stop at the bottom of the stairway, and then dropped to his knees. He reached under the first step and pulled out a small box. By the time we reached Carib, all three of us were gasping in huge, rasping gulps. My legs were so wobbly that I had to hold onto the stairway to keep from falling. Carib slid open the box and withdrew a key.

"Well…" I gasped, "I'll…. be…"

I led the way around the side of the house to the front door. A numerical security pad was installed to the right of the door, but Carib slid the key into the lock and turned it.

Instantly the high-pitched scream of the burglar alarm cut through the air. "At least…that will bring…the cops," Ricardo gasped.

Carib pushed and as the door swung open, we hurried inside. We rushed down the long front hallway and into the kitchen off to the right. The phone was hanging on the wall by the stove.

Ricardo punched the speakerphone button, and then dialed in a number. "Walt? Ricardo. We're being attacked by about 50 men."

"We figured there was trouble. The back-up team just called in a minute ago. They're stuck in a huge traffic jam about 5 miles north of the Castle. What's the status?"

"We're not in any immediate danger—we escaped, but they have a hostage. They probably have the road blocked from the south also, so we can't bring in the team from San Jose…Okay. Get a hold of Commander Johnson at Moffat and have him send in the Navy Helicopters—with plenty of men. And warn him to expect trouble from the air—my bet is that our attackers will be leaving that way. And tell him about the hostage."

Just then Sid's excited voice blared on the walkie-talkie clipped to Ricardo's belt. "Ricardo are you there?"

"Hold on a minute, Walt," Ricardo said, unclipping the walkie-talkie from his belt. "I'm here, Sid," he spoke into it. "What's up?"

"They're moving! Looks as though they're headed for the beach!"

"The sea," Ricardo said, as though to himself. Then he spoke into the unit, "Any sign of a boat, Sid?"

"No," came the reply. "The horizon is clear."

Ricardo frowned, trying to understand the move. Then he spoke into the walkie-talkie, "Okay, Sid. Navy helicopters are on the way. I'll call in the Coast Guard as well. I'll be in touch."

Ricardo picked up the phone, saying, "Walt, you'd better send the Coast Guard to cut off a possible sea escape."

"Will do. And we've already got Moffat scrambling."

"Thanks. I'll keep you posted."

When Sid had reported the invaders heading for the beach, a plan began to form in my mind. Thorndike had a dune buggy. I had to find the keys! I scanned the room. There! Hanging next to the door leading to the garage. I dashed over to the door, and Ricardo called after me, "Where are you going?"

"Dune buggy in the garage," I answered over my shoulder. "Going after Marilyn." I grabbed the keys and yanked open the door, sending it crashing back against the wall.

Carib and Ricardo raced after me. "We'll need help," Ricardo said. "We can't tackle them alone."

"You can wait. I'm going." I jumped into the dune buggy.

"Wait up," Carib said. "I'll go with you. Two fools may be better than one."

"Make that three fools," Ricardo said.

Carib sprang into the passenger seat and Ricardo jumped into the back as I roared the engine to life. "See if the garage opener is in the glove compartment."

Carib found the little plastic beige box lying on top, grabbed it, and jammed his thumb into the opening device. The electronic signal clicked, then the opener motor whirred, barely audible over the deep roar of the dune buggy's engine. I threw the gearshift into reverse and backed up to the slowly opening door, waiting impatiently for enough clearance. Then I floored the accelerator, and the tires squealed as the buggy shot out into the sunlight. The tires screamed once more as I ground the gears into first and jammed the accelerator down. Seconds later we flew off the end of the driveway and landed with a jolt on the beach below.

We sped along the hard-packed strand at the water's edge, obliterating our footprints from our run to the Thorndikes. "We can't go racing in there with our six-guns blazing," Ricardo shouted above the roar of the engine and whistling of the wind. "Let's see if Sid can spot Marilyn."

Just then we heard Sid's voice through the walkie-talkie, "Ricardo!"

Ricardo retrieved the unit from his belt and spoke into it. "Yea, Sid. What have you got?" He turned the volume up, so he could hear above the din.

"Helicopters! Coming from the west!"

"Too soon for Navy or Coast Guard. Any markings?"

"Too far off. Big ones though...Where are you—what's that racket?"

"In a dune buggy, heading towards you. Do you see Marilyn anywhere?"

For several seconds, the only sounds were the engine and the wind. We were fast approaching the bend in the shoreline that would bring us into view of the bluff. Then Sid's voice broke through, "No sign of her on the beach."

Rage erupted deep inside me. "Those bastards!" I shouted. "They've killed her! I'm going to—"

"Wait!" Sid's voice cut through the rest of my sentence. "The missile group on the other side of the road. Yes. Yes, they've got her."

I reached behind me and grabbed the walkie-talkie from Ricardo with my right hand and continued steering with my left. "Exactly, where are they?" I demanded.

"They just crossed the road, north of the driveway. They're heading cross-country, up towards the Castle. And they're herding Marilyn—she's down! Looks as though she tripped. They're grabbing her, pulling her up. One of them is aiming his gun at her!"

"Do something!" I shouted into the walkie-talkie. My heart was pounding in my throat.

"They're out of range! Wait. They're moving again. They must have just threatened her."

My mind was racing. We had to reach them before they got to the top of the driveway and the steps leading to the beach. Did I dare risk going past the cave and up the hill, within the range of the invaders waiting on the beach? Or should we take the shorter, steeper route north of Lookout Point, which the dune buggy might not make? The sudden appearance of six black specs on the horizon forced my decision. "Hang on," I shouted. "We're going in behind them."

I downshifted into first and swung the steering wheel to the left. Seconds later the buggy mounted the base of the sandstone mountain that rose precipitously between two granite bluff outcroppings. The wheels spun, and the wheels fishtailed, looking for traction in the sand. The whine of the engine slowed until I thought we had stalled. I jammed down the clutch and the accelerator at the same time, preventing the stall, but we started to roll back. I let out the clutch again, and the buggy lurched forward.

We gathered speed as the sand became rutted sandstone. The buggy bounced and swerved wildly over the ruts. Once I thought we would topple, flying into mid-air out of a deep rut at a severe angle, and then landing on the right front and rear tires only. But the buggy righted itself and sped on upward.

We flew over the summit, and then landed squarely on the other side of the mountain, which was less rut-ridden and sloped more gradually down to the road. I floored the accelerator again, and we raced down the mountainside at a traverse angle. When we reached the base, I swung the wheel hard to the right. Seconds later we were speeding past the sheer leeward granite wall of Lookout Point. We rounded the sharp bend at the end of the Point, and the hill rising towards the Castle lay before us. Marilyn and her captors had nearly reached the top.

As the roar of the buggy reached the ears of the fleeing band, they stopped running and turned, startled expressions on their faces. The leader judged the distance between them and the onrushing buggy, and then shot a glance up at the crest of the hill. He waved his men on, and then broke into a sprint. The others leaped after him, two of them pulling Marilyn between them.

The buggy ate up the gap between them and us rapidly but had covered only two thirds of the distance when the marauders disappeared over the top of the hill.

Moments later the buggy careened onto the black macadam driveway, just below the top of the hill. Carib whipped out his gun, and I followed suit, clutching the steering wheel with only my left hand. Without looking I knew Ricardo had his at the ready. We raced upwards along the driveway until we crested the hill.

We were greeted with a blast of gunfire. The windshield shattered, and a bullet tore into my left arm, wrenching my hand from the steering wheel. The buggy sped on, out of control, amid a continuing flurry of bullets. It sailed off the driveway, then landed on the two rear tires, pitched forward onto the front two, and rolled on.

The jolt jarred me back to my senses, and I grabbed the steering wheel with my numb left hand and jammed on the brakes. The buggy skidded, spun around 180 degrees, and then stalled, facing the assailants, 75 yards away. Unhurt, Ricardo and Carib leaped out of the buggy and raced around to the rear, pursued by another hail of bullets. I flung myself across the seats to duck the blast aimed at me. Then I swung my legs onto the floor of the passenger side and rose to peer out of the shattered windshield.

Carib and Ricardo opened fire behind me, downing the leader and two others. I picked off two more, which left only the two that held Marilyn between them. They were retreating across the macadam, scrambling backwards, one of them pulling Marilyn by the neck and the other shielded behind them.

As they left the macadam onto the Belgian Block walkway to the steps that descended to the beach, the one dragging Marilyn stumbled on one of the Blocks. Marilyn let her body go limp, and her dead weight pried loose his grip, and he fell backwards onto the other captor. Marilyn managed to stay on her feet, dashed back across the macadam, and headed towards the buggy.

Just then I heard the whir of helicopters to our left, coming from the direction of the beach. I shot a glance up and saw they were unmarked. I whipped my head back down to see Marilyn racing towards the buggy, and her two captors back on their feet. The guns of Ricardo and Carib roared behind me, and the one on the right hurtled backwards onto the ground. But the other one fired at Marilyn, the bullet slamming into her back, and she crumpled onto the macadam. I aimed through my white rage and fired at the assailant who stiffened with the impact of my bullet, and then pitched forward into a clump of brush.

I jumped back into the driver's bucket seat and whipped the ignition key to the right. As the engine churned, still flooded from the stall, Carib and Ricardo sprang into the dune buggy. Finally, it caught, and I raced the buggy up the hill to where Marilyn lay motionless in a fetal position. "Marilyn!" I cried. "What have I done?" I raged.

I jumped out of the buggy, ran to her, and dropped to my knees. "She's still breathing!" I exclaimed, looking up at Carib who stood next to me.

But her bright red blood was spreading across the back of her white silk blouse like ink on a blotter. The bullet had entered the upper left side of her back. Carib crouched down, feeling her pulse. "She's bad," he pronounced. "We've got to get her to a hospital, fast."

"The traffic!" I spat.

Carib looked up at the buggy, then at my blood covered left arm that hung by my side like a useless appendage. "We'll have to drive cross country. I hate to move her, but we have no choice."

He slid his hands underneath Marilyn. "Now gently roll her over onto my arms," he instructed. "I'll lay her across the back seat."

Marilyn's eyelids were closed, and all color had vanished from her face. I grimaced as excruciating pain shot down my left arm when I eased Marilyn over onto Carib's arms. "She's in shock," he said. "I noticed a beach blanket on the back seat. Ricardo, open it up and spread it out— we've got to keep her warm."

As soon as we lay Marilyn on the seat and covered her, I became aware of the increasing pitch of the whirling helicopters on the beach, and moments later the giant machines rose into view, 200 yards away. They swept west, out over the ocean, except one, which hung in mid-air for an instant, then lurched towards us. "Damn them!" I roared, whipping my gun out of its holster.

The helicopter headed straight for us, but then veered at the last second and shot past us overhead. "That was just an inspection tour," Ricardo shouted above the din, as he unsheathed his gun. "Now they know we're not theirs!"

The helicopter bore down on us, and its door slid back. A swarthy man crouched in the doorway, machine gun poised. "Take cover behind the buggy!" Ricardo shouted.

"I'm not leaving Marilyn!" I vowed, standing up in the buggy and aiming my gun at the dark figure. The machine gun erupted, spraying bullets that whizzed over our heads and ricocheted off the macadam behind us. We all fired but missed the helicopter as it swished past us and went into a tight, right-hand turn for another pass.

The machine gun bullets hit short of the buggy on the next run, slamming into the ground in front of us, flying harmlessly by. Again we fired, and again we missed the hurtling target.

The helicopter rose again, swinging left for another attempt, but then paused in the middle of the turn. I spotted a squadron of Navy Helicopters rushing towards us over the foothills from the east. The enemy helicopter fired a missile at the Squadron leader, but the shot was low, exploding into the side of the bluff. "The Cavalry at last," I breathed.

The attacker then swung into another tight turn and headed west. As the fleeing helicopter shot past the beach cliff out over the ocean, the Navy Squadron Leader fired his missile which tore through the main rotor, splintering it into dozens of pieces. The main body of the helicopter began spinning wildly, as though caught in a whirlpool sent up from the sea. Seconds later it plowed into the water, tail section first, its still whirling rear rotor cutting through the surface, pulling the main body into its ocean grave after it.

I waved my good arm at the Navy Medical helicopter, which then peeled out of formation and landed on the macadam. Three Medics jumped out and sprinted over to us. "Inspector Lopez, FBI," Ricardo identified himself. Then he pointed to Marilyn's motionless form, saying, "Get her to the nearest heart specialist, fast."

"Stanford Medical Center," I said. "It's the closest and the best."

I scanned the western horizon, now deserted except for the Navy helicopters. "The others got away," I murmured, fighting the dizziness I felt.

"Not yet they haven't," Ricardo said. He turned to one of the Medics as the other two were easing Marilyn onto the stretcher, and said, "Get on the radio and advise your Squadron Leader there are five more bandits out there, heading west."

Carib came up and inspected my dangling wounded arm. "Come on," he said. "We'd better get you to that hospital as well."

I looked at Carib. "Well, I've got one less enemy."

"What do you mean?"

"Did you see who was standing in that doorway, shooting at us?"

"No. I really didn't get a good look."

"It was my old Iraqi friend, Mundi."

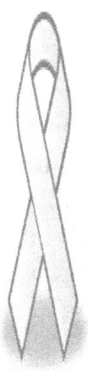

CHAPTER EIGHTEEN

I stared up at the nurse through the grogginess of the anesthesia that still gripped me. "Good morning, Mr. Shepherd," she was saying. Her nametag read Shelia Warren.

"What...what happened," I stammered.

"The bullet shattered your left humerus. Dr. Hadden had to rebuild it. And you lost a lot of blood." She pointed to the hanging glass IV container, with its thin plastic tube leading to my right hand. "The medication will help ease the pain."

My consciousness burst through the drug-induced fog that shrouded my mind. "Forget my arm! Is Marilyn all right?"

"Who?" Nurse Warren asked, her expression blank.

"Marilyn! Marilyn Stroud! No— Marilyn Boone! They brought her in with me! She was shot in the back!"

"Oh, my. Then she must be up in intensive care. I'll find out right away." She turned and scurried out.

Nurse Warren returned ten minutes later. "Mrs. Boone is up there, all right. The bullet was stopped by one of her ribs, next to her heart, but they don't want to operate until she's regained some strength. They anticipate that will be tomorrow morning."

"I must see her," I demanded.

"She's unconscious and in grave danger," was the nurse's solicitous reply. "Doctor Burroughs won't allow any visitors. And besides, I have orders you are to remain in bed."

"I want to see her!" I repeated.

She hesitated. "Well, maybe if you just looked in on her. I'll see what I can do."

As she pulled open the door to leave, Carib was standing in the doorway, fist poised, ready to knock. "I'm a close friend of Mr. Shepherd. May I come in?"

She looked at him dubiously. "He's not supposed to have visitors."

"Dr. Hadden told me I could spend a brief time with him," Carib reassured her.

"Well, all right," she said, stepping back to let him by, "but only a few minutes." She stepped out into the hall and pulled the door closed behind her.

"How are you feeling?" Carib asked as he sat down in the chair by the foot of the bed.

"Grumpy and ugly."

"Oh, a troll," Carib chuckled, his teeth flashing.

"Yea, a troll. But I'm okay. It's Marilyn I'm worried about, and they won't let me see her."

"They wouldn't let Wiley see her either. They want her totally undisturbed. The next 24 hours are critical."

"Wiley is here?" I asked, surprised.

"Yes," Carib answered, nodding. "The police finally reached him at home late last night—he had just returned from L.A. He's been here since."

"What...what does he know?"

"That Marilyn was the innocent victim of a terrorist attack."

"Does he know about me?" I asked, feeling anxious.

"I think he can guess." He shook his head, a look of disdain crossing his face. "I don't know how the media found out, but they plastered you and the Castle and the Stanford Hospital all over the eleven o'clock news last night. Wiley doesn't have to be a computer chip to figure out the connection between you and Marilyn."

I groaned. "Oh *God*! Why did I ever involve her? Why didn't I listen to her at the very beginning? She told me to get lost! Why didn't I listen to her? Now she's got a bullet next to her heart and her relationship with Wiley is ruined!"

"Nick. She's going to make it. She's one strong lady, judging by what she did out there. And Doctor Burroughs gives her better than a 50-50 chance." He shrugged his shoulders. "As far as Wiley is concerned, my bet is that if she wants to work things out with him, she can. On the other hand..."

"She said she loves us both."

"Don't worry about that now. Let her recover first."

"Fair enough," I agreed, my voice crisp as I pushed down my feelings.

There was a sharp rap on the door and Ricardo strode in. As he approached the bed he said, "You look good. The nurse made it sound as though you were at death's door. I had to pull rank to get in."

"I'm going to make it, Ricardo. Thanks for all that you did out there."

"Just doing my job. You were the real hellion. I hear Marilyn's got a good chance."

I nodded my head. "She's going to make it too. Any news about Mundi's helicopter?"

"Only that it was a charter out of LA. And it was Mundi all right—the Navy Frogmen retrieved his body."

"What about the others? Who were they?" I queried, raising my head from the pillow.

"We think most of them were Iraqis. But two of them were Americans—ex Green Berets."

I shook my head, and then lowered it back onto the pillow. "This makes absolutely no sense. Bradshaw, Iraqis, Green Berets—what's the connection?"

"It's got to be the Oil-Intelligence Community conspiracy we talked about yesterday—we just don't know what they want."

I raised my head from the pillow again. "Look. The best way to find out is to be in the thick of things. As soon as I know Marilyn is all right, I'm going back home. Back to my regular routine."

"That's too dangerous," Ricardo disagreed. "The trail has led us to Sullivan. Leave it to us to take it from here."

"Ricardo, I just want to get this over with. If it is Sullivan, the best way to flush him out is for me to be right there with him. If it isn't Sullivan, the fastest way to find that out is to be with him."

Ricardo stroked his chin between his thumb and index finger as he mused. "All right," he agreed finally. "We'll do it your way. But I want you to work overtime on the why behind all this that has been happening."

"It's a deal."

I dozed off several times during the day, but during my waking periods I mulled over the events and years of my career, looking for the why. Sullivan certainly appeared to be running Bradshaw, and Bradshaw had been running Mundi—but why? Why was I a threat to them? I had always been a Company Man—well, almost always. But even when I had done things my own way, I had the Company's best interests at heart. And Sullivan had chosen me to succeed him.

Or had he? I only had Sullivan's word on that. Maybe Sullivan was setting me up for the kill, literally. But why? Or, on the other hand, maybe I was Sullivan's choice and that's why I was the target. If that were true though, why would Sullivan be involved?

I sensed that there was a clue stirring just below the floor of my conscious memory. My doctor had told me that those memory lapses both before and after the bombing indicated I was avoiding something I didn't want to remember. Some unbelievable, overwhelming event that paralyzed me. I knew I had to remember, before it was too late.

Nurse Warren pushed open the door at 10 p.m., a cup of pills in hand. She must have been working a double shift. "Good evening, Mr. Shepherd," she said, smiling. "I have a bit of good news for you. Mrs. Boone's condition has improved, so they are going to proceed with removing the bullet."

"That is good news," I said, a warm feeling of hope pricking my lethargy. "When?"

"Tomorrow morning at eight." She extended the pills towards me. "Now then, you've been asleep much of the evening. I'm going off duty now. Would you like a sedative to help you through the rest of the evening?"

"No thank you," I smiled wanly. "With Marilyn doing better, and after the events of yesterday, I don't think I'll have much trouble. And lose the IV too, please."

She looked at me, her face full of doubt. "Are you sure?"

"I'm sure."

She shrugged her shoulders, shuffled over to my bedside, and removed the IV. She extracted a plastic strip from her pocket and applied it to the IV puncture on the back of my hand. She turned, shuffled back to the door, and pulled it open. She flicked off the light as she pulled the door closed. A minute later, I was asleep.

For the first 3 hours, I slumbered deeply, but awoke when the night nurse looked in on me. My arm ached, and I lay with my eyes closed, letting my consciousness wander to take the focus off my pain. I felt myself shooting down a dark hole, then popping out onto a field of rolling hills. I climbed up the first knoll, down into the vale, then up the next, steeper rise. I looked towards the summit, and I saw a large figure waiting for me. As I approached, I realized the figure was a lion, sitting on his haunches. He remained motionless when I strode up to him, and I reached down and patted his head. I then took hold of his mane and followed him down into the next vale. The vision faded, and I dropped off to sleep.

I dreamed for the first time since the bombing. I stepped off the elevator, strode down the hall to my office, and sat down at my desk. I reached for the stack of papers that had accumulated in my "In" box during a long absence from the office. A manila envelope caught my eye. Through the amorphous details of the dream I strained to bring the writing into focus. Finally, I saw it was addressed to E.B. Shepherd and marked, "Personal and Confidential." I stared at it, realizing it was intended for Ed Shepherd in Legal, not me. Curiosity got the better of me, and I carefully unsealed the envelope, withdrawing the single page within. It read:

To: E.B. Shepherd

From: B.A. Sullivan

Dear Ed:

Something has come up in Rotterdam, so I won't be attending U.S.O.I. I know it's risky but explain the Program to Nick Shepherd. He had been active in it Internationally but is unaware of the Domestic resurrection.

Regards,

It was signed, "Bruce."

I stared at the page, unbelieving. The Program could mean only one thing—competitive conspiracy. It was happening again, Domestically! And I didn't know about it!

My consciousness penetrated my dream. Thank God, I told myself, I've just been dreaming. I opened my eyes and blinked three times, as though to clear away to reality of the dream. At once, I knew the dream was reality.

I reached up and switched on the gooseneck lamp over my bed. My watch read 4:10 A.M. I picked up the phone and dialed Ricardo at the Sheraton Inn. "Hello," Ricardo answered, his voice sounding wide-awake.

"It's Nick. I'm sorry it's so early, but I've got to talk with you."

"I'll be right over. I'm done sleeping anyway."

Fifteen minutes later, Ricardo burst into my room as I was pacing the floor, my cast-covered left arm hanging by my side. I turned at the sound of Ricardo's entrance. "I remembered," I said somberly. "You were right about a U. S. Cartel. And I've actually got a memo from Sullivan that is strongly circumstantial."

I grimaced. "And I can't believe I actually blocked it from my memory!"

"Relax, Nick," Ricardo urged. "Go sit down and tell me about it."

I sat down on the edge of the bed and took a deep breath. "I told you I was a hot shot MBA from Stanford, with a Master's in International Affairs from the University of Mexico to boot. I joined UNRC who put me on the 'fast track.' One of my first assignments was to prepare data for the upcoming U.S. Oil Institute meeting in Baton Rouge. During my research, I found out from the old timers that the U.S.O.I. had been the forum in the old days for the Petroleum Trust."

"You mean similar to the Railroad and Steel Trusts that were outlawed by the Sherman Anti-Trust Act?" Ricardo questioned.

"The same. Except Sherman was 1898, but the Oil Cartel continued to operate sub rosa under the guise of the U.S.O.I. until the 1950's. The major oil companies would meet to fix prices, control production, divide markets, and all that sort of thing."

"No wonder OPEC was so effective," Ricardo concluded. "They had an effective working model."

"Yes, they did. Anyway, when I went to the meeting in Baton Rouge with Sullivan and Melville, who was another 'fast tracker,' I was surprised to see so much discussion with our competitors. Sullivan said it was social, and I accepted that. The Justice Department had been sending people to jail in other industries for Sherman violations, so I didn't think anyone at our meeting would risk jail terms."

"And then you moved over to International," Ricardo remembered. "What was the situation there?"

"Oh, there was a lot of contact between the U.S. companies, but it was all legal, under what's called the Webb-Pomerene Act. We could set Offshore pricing, divide Offshore markets—you know, all those things I said are illegal in the Domestic Market. We disbanded that organization as well, fearing the Justice Department might try to make the case we were discussing Domestic markets."

"Were you?" Ricardo asked, more like an accusation than a question.

"Absolutely not! We even had a lawyer there who would warn us if he thought we were heading in any Domestic direction. And the only attendees were persons with solely International responsibilities. Sullivan never attended one meeting."

"Well, then what happened when you moved back to Domestic?" Ricardo asked, this time his tone more conversational. "How did you find out about the U.S. Cartel?"

"Only by accident," I replied plaintively. "I had no clue. I really did believe the U.S. Industry was very competitive, and we were in a battle for survival. And I still felt the same way I did during the first Baton Rouge meeting—nobody would risk the fines and jail terms."

"So, you couldn't believe it was happening in the first place, and, particularly under your own Domestic nose without you knowing it," Ricardo concluded.

"Yes," I nodded reluctantly. "If I hadn't accidentally received that letter from Sullivan, I don't know when I would have found out."

"And you actually forgot about it?" Ricardo asked, incredulity creeping into his tone.

"I forgot about it!"

"How could you forget about something like that?" asked Ricardo, still sounding like a Dutch Uncle.

I scowled in confusion. "I... I don't know. It saw it the day before the bombing. Maybe...what I wasn't willing to face was that it existed, plus the fact that I hadn't known about it."

Ricardo was silent. Then he finally said, "Well it doesn't really matter. We'll leave that to the doctors. What counts is that you have remembered. Now, just where is this letter and what does it say?"

"I sent it on. But I kept a copy. It's Sullivan's instruction to Ed Shepherd to advise me of the Cartel."

"Do you think Sullivan knows about the error?"

"It's possible. I resealed the envelope, and then sent it over to Ed Shepherd with a note it had been sent to me by mistake. He may have mentioned something to Sullivan."

"Do you think Sullivan is our man?" Ricardo continued the interrogation.

"Why would he want to kill me?" I protested. "Why would he silence me on something he wanted me to know, but hadn't even told me? I mean I know the evidence is mounting against him, but I don't understand the why."

Ricardo had an answer. "To avoid fines and jail. He figured he would bring you in on the conspiracy to head off your finding out for yourself and ratting on him. Then his little secret would remain hidden under the Las Palmas blast."

"Well, I want to find out. As I said before, I'm willing to make myself a target."

"Sometimes it takes a target to find a weapon," Ricardo agreed. "And we'll get you outfitted with a Kevlar vest when we get back East," he added.

Ricardo left shortly thereafter, and I slept soundly until Claire Johnson, the morning nurse, woke me at 6:45 A.M. for breakfast. "Good morning, Mr. Shepherd," she greeted me as she raised the head of my bed and wrapped the gray blood pressure tourniquet around my right arm. She pumped air into the limp sack and continued, "Nurse Warren told me you were interested in Mrs. Boone's condition. I thought you'd like to know she is stable, and they've moved the operation up to 7 A.M."

"Thank you," I responded, nodding my head appreciatively.

Carib stopped by at 8 A.M. "What's wrong, my friend?" I asked. "You look worried."

"I am worried, Nick. Our President, Cesaré, is saying some very strange things. He's talking about nationalizing several industries. I'm leaving for Caracas today to try to talk some sense into him. And if I am unable, I must build a coalition to stop him."

171

"I can't believe that. Cesaré has always been a capitalist. And compared to other OPEC countries, Venezuela gives us private oil companies free reign. Thanks to your influence, I might add."

"I'm concerned my influence may be waning. He has a new advisor who has been warning him he is losing popularity and that the people want the government to take over the big, fat cat companies."

"I'm sure you will prevail. You'll either get him to understand something clearly at last or get others to stop him."

Carib flashed his brilliant smile. "Thank you for your vote of confidence. Enough about my little problems. How are you doing?"

I told him about my waking vision and sleeping dream that unlocked reality.

"This is good news my friend. In my Shaman tradition, your waking vision is called a journey. You have met your power animal, the lion. Someday soon you will meet your spirit guide. In your Christian tradition, you call this your guardian angel."

I lay there silently, trying to mentally absorb what he was saying.

"And perhaps," Carib continued, "your journey released your repressed memory through your dream."

"But how did this all happen?"

"I would say it was involuntary meditation. You had been shot, you were immobilized, and you had nothing better to do. You quieted your conscious mind, your spirit took over, and you embarked on your waking hill and vale journey. You might want to try it again. Perhaps when you're running."

Carib's words rang true for me, although my conscious mind was screaming, "No way!"

"I will," I said without thinking. Then a question popped into my mind. "How did you know the key to the Thorndike's front door was under the deck stairway?"

"Would you believe it came to me in a vision?"

I smiled. "Maybe I would," I said slowly.

"Well," Carib said. "I've given you a lot to assimilate. I'll be in touch." We shook hands, and then he turned and left.

Dr. Hadden arrived at 10 A.M. He glanced at the chart hanging on the foot of the bed, then back up at me. "How are you feeling?"

"Much better today. My arm is still a little sore, but I feel as though I could go home today."

Dr. Hadden flashed a knowing smile, as though reading my arm and seeing the real pain in my heart. "Not quite yet," he said as he began the blood pressure test. "You're in decent shape, so you're recovering quickly, but you did lose quite a bit of blood. I'd like you to stay a couple of more days."

He glanced over at the blood pressure gauge on the wall. "Are you having any dizziness?"

"If you think my blood pressure is low, it's not—I'm a runner."

Dr. Hadden understood. "That does explain it. I expected it yesterday with your loss of blood, but I thought it would be higher today. Keep it up—you'll live to be a hundred."

I chuckled. "Yea, if I don't get murdered first... You've got to have some pull around here; may I go up to see Marilyn...Mrs. Boone, that is...when she comes out of surgery?"

"All right," Dr. Hadden said, smiling, knowing his permission was merely a formality. I would have gone up anyway.

"Could you check on her for me?" I asked, sensing the Doctor's good nature. "She has been in the operating room for over three hours."

"I'd be glad to," Dr. Hadden agreed, reaching for the phone on the nightstand and dialing. "This is Dr. Hadden. Do you have a report on Mrs. Boone?" He nodded as he listened, then asked, "What is her condition?" He nodded again, said, "Thank you," and hung up.

He turned back towards me. "They just brought her out of surgery. Dr. Burroughs removed the bullet, but her left ventricle has been damaged. She's critical, but she's strong—pulse and blood pressure are good. Dr. Burroughs believes she has a good chance."

"When may I see her?" I asked. I knew my voice was anxious.

"That will be up to Dr. Burroughs. Definitely not until tomorrow at the earliest and maybe not even until the day after."

But Marilyn *was* strong and the next morning she was off the critical list. Sid, the FBI Agent, accompanied me in the elevator to the fourth floor, and when we emerged from the elevator into the fourth floor waiting room, a sandy-haired man with horned-rimmed glasses sitting in the corner looked up from *The Wall Street Journal.* He rose and asked, "Are you Nick Shepherd?"

I nodded as the man moved towards us, and Sid tensed, ready for action. "I recognized you from your red hair," the man said. "I'm Wiley Ferguson."

"Marilyn's significant other," I murmured to Sid.

Wiley and I sized each other up, steel eye to steel eye, as we approached each other. "How do you do?" I said, clasping Wiley's extended hand and shaking it firmly.

"I really want to thank you," Wiley gushed, as politicians do, "for saving Marilyn's life. If you hadn't been there..." He left the sentence unfinished.

"I'm glad she's going to be okay."

"You're glad; I don't know what I would do without her. I take it you're going to see her."

"Yes," was my short reply. I fought to quell my anger at this man who had been unfaithful to Marilyn, yet now spewed such deep concern for her.

"Before you do, I'd like to talk with you," Wiley said, motioning towards the far corner of the room, away from Sid.

"Okay," I said, and then followed Wiley back where he had been sitting.

"Look," Wiley began, "you don't have to say anything because the only thing that's important to me is that you saved her life. I don't want to know anything else."

But I wanted to tell the truth. And I wanted to hurt this man who had hurt Marilyn. "Well, Wiley, I feel that you should know what's going on. I've avoided the truth all my life, and the truth is that I am in love with Marilyn. You see, Wiley, I was in love with Marilyn a long time ago, when we were in school together here at Stanford, but I didn't know I was then. And now I found her again, and I'm not going to let her go."

"Well, I'm not going to let her go either!" Wiley fumed. His ruddy face flushed even redder. "I want Marilyn, and I need her. I've been in love with her since John died; before, in fact."

"Is that why you're running around on her?" My voice was cold steel.

"You had your chance, but now you have lost it," Wiley retorted.

"We'll see who has lost his chance," I said.

"Are you going to talk to her about that now?" Wiley sounded as though he were pleading. This guy really was a chameleon.

"Actually, I hadn't been planning to," I said, my voice softening. "I just wanted to see her, to be sure she was all right." I turned and headed towards the double door leading to the patients' rooms. As Sid and I approached the doors, they swung open automatically, revealing the nurses' station beyond. I presented my pass to the nurse, and we moved down the hall to Marilyn's room, the last one on the left. Sid stationed himself outside the door, and I rapped lightly, and then slowly pushed open the door.

Marilyn's eyes were just fluttering open, and she rolled her head in my direction. She looked pale, but her inner radiance beamed. "Nick," she said, smiling, and gazing into my eyes. "I was hoping you would come." Her voice was steady but lacked the usual vigor. She looked down at my arm in the sling and scowled. "They told me you were all right."

I bent down and gently kissed her. "I'm fine. I'm just not ready for a 5-mile run yet. How are you feeling?"

"A little tired still." She smiled faintly. "I guess I'll be taking a little vacation, although this isn't exactly the south of France."

"You look wonderful. I don't mind saying I was really worried about you."

My voice caught. "Anyway, I'm really happy you're all right. I'll let you get some rest."

"Wait. Don't go. I want to talk with you."

I hesitated. "Okay. A couple of minutes more. They didn't want me to stay long."

"Wiley was here a little while ago," she began.

"I know. I ran into him in the Waiting Room."

"You did? What did he say?"

"He wanted to thank me for saving your life. He said he didn't want to know anything more."

"That's what he said when he was here. I tried to tell him about you and me, but he wouldn't listen. He kept saying all that mattered was I was alive, he didn't want to lose me, he loved me, and he didn't want to hear anything more."

"Wiley does know about you and me."

Marilyn raised her eyebrows slightly. "How? Did you tell him?"

"Yes. I told him. I told him I loved you."

Relief spread over Marilyn's face. "I'm glad he knows."

"So am I."

I smiled. "He's really fighting for you. He told me I had lost my chance with you, and I didn't deserve you now. He was right about before; I didn't appreciate you. So maybe I don't deserve you."

"But that was then. Now is now."

"And now you love both of us. That simply will not work. Someone has to make a choice."

"I can't. Not now."

I took a deep breath, and then blew it out. "Well then, it has to be me. I'll head East as soon as I'm able, to flush out the killer. You stay here and regain your health.

"I've had a lot of time to think about mortality," I continued, "so I'm looking at having children in a little different light. And if that's the only issue standing between Susan and me, I suppose I ought to give our relationship a chance."

"You want to go back to Susan?"

I averted Marilyn's penetrating gaze. "With me out of the picture, you may find your choice will be easier."

"Or harder. I know I'm going to miss you." She smiled and raised her right hand. I clasped it with mine, and then squeezed it gently. Still holding her hand, I stooped and kissed her softly for several moments. Then I rose and said, "Wiley's one very lucky man."

"Be careful, my love," Marilyn whispered. "And thank you," she added, smiling in a knowing way.

"For what?" I asked, returning the smile.

"As though you didn't know."

CHAPTER NINETEEN

The following morning Dr. Hadden strode into my room with a broad smile on his face. "Good news," he announced. "The x-rays we took this morning confirm that you are healing miraculously. You can break out of here."

"When? Right now?"

"Any time you like. And that cast can come off next week. I'll send your records to Doctor Jameson in Greenwich. And keep up that running."

I grinned. "I will. And thanks for everything, especially running interference with Mrs. Boone."

"Glad to help a fellow alumnus."

I dressed, discharged myself, and then Sid and I headed for the 10 o'clock services at Stanford Memorial Church. Reverend Renaud announced he would be departing from the regular Lectionary Scripture to read a favorite passage of his. He promised to tie it in to the week's Lectionary theme. "This reading is from Ecclesiastes, Chapter 10, Verses 5-15." He donned his reading glasses, cleared his throat, then began, "I have seen under the sun another evil, like a mistake that proceeds from the ruler: Fools are put in lofty places while the rich sit in lowly places.

I have seen slaves on horseback and princes walking on the ground like slaves.

"He who digs a pit may fall into it, and he who breaks through a wall may be bitten by a serpent.

"He who moves stones may be hurt by them, and he who chops wood is in danger from it. If the iron becomes dull, though at first, he made easy progress, he must increase his efforts; but the craftsman has the advantage of his skill.

"If the serpent bites because it has not been charmed, then there is not advantage for the charmer.

"Words from the wise man's mouth win favor, but the fool's lips consume him.

"The beginning of his words is folly, and the end of his talk is madness; yet the fool multiplies words.

"Man knows not what is to come, for who can tell him what is to come after him?

"When will the fool be weary of his labor, he who knows not the way to the city?"

He paused, and then said, "Skipping over to the Epilogue, Verse 13, I should like to add, 'The last word when all is heard: Fear God and keep all his commandments, for this is man's all; because God will bring to judgment every work, with all its hidden qualities, whether good or bad."

Reverend Renaud stopped, and then flipped his Bible to the next marker. He looked up and said, "Now we return to the Lectionary. This passage is from Luke 6, Verses 20-26:

'Blessed are you who are poor, for the kingdom of God is yours.

'Blessed are you who are hungry, for you will be satisfied.

'Blessed are you who are now weeping, for you will laugh.

'Blessed are you when people hate you, and when they exclude you and insult you, and denounce your name as evil on the account of the Son of Man.

'Rejoice and leap for joy on that day! Behold, your reward will be great in heaven. For their ancestors treated prophets in the same way.

'But woe to you who are rich, for you have received your consolation,

'But woe to you who are filled now, for you will be hungry.

'Woe to you who laugh now, for you will grieve and weep.

"Woe to you when all speak well of you, for their ancestors treated the false prophets this way."

Reverend Renaud looked up again. "In Ecclesiastes we see a world turned upside down with fools running things, and no real answers. But Jesus says that if you believe in him, the world may be upside down for you in this life, but your reward will be everlasting life in heaven. He also says if you follow God's ways in this life, you will achieve serenity."

He reached down, closed the Bible, and then lifted another book. "This is the *Art Of Happiness,* by the Dahlia Lama. He speaks of becoming an enlightened person through compassion, prayer, and meditation in this life so that happiness can be achieved in this life as well as the next. The Dahlia Lama believes that each one of us is fundamentally good, and that we must nurture this goodness every day."

Reverend Renaud lowered the book back onto the lectern, removed his glasses, and then slowly looked around at all of us. "To me," he resumed, "the common theme is that whatever our beliefs, we must practice them every day. You might say to me, 'Oh, that's easy for you to say because you're in the God business. I'm studying or I'm working 24 hours a day, 7 days a week, and I don't have time right now. When this quarter is over or when this project is completed, then I'll get connected.'

"I understand this. Even in the God business, we have deadlines, politics, jealousies, and financial concerns. And the Devil – the word I choose to personify evil – tempts us all to deviate from God's path. We hear both God's and the Devil's words, and sometimes it is hard to know the right path. We have, and we will continue to make mistakes, but the more we try to hear God, the fewer mistakes we will make. But just how do we hear God?"

Again, he looked around at all of us. Sid was squirming in his seat. "Just as there are many paths to God, Allah, Buddha, or Higher Power, there are many ways to hear the Divine Word. For some of us it is on-your-knees prayer, for others it is meditation, and for still others it is quick whispered wish for aid or guidance. The point is it doesn't matter how you do it, but you should do something every day. I believe you will notice over time God's voice will become stronger and easier to differentiate from the devil's. You will feel a certainty of truth. Be patient. It takes time. But strive to be God-like every day, starting today."

I had been seated in the front pew, so at the end of the service, I was the last in line to shake hands with Reverend Renaud, who stood on the top granite step in the Narthex. Sid was waiting at the bottom of the steps. "That was quite a sermon," I said. "You made being God-like sound so universal and so doable."

He beamed as he chuckled. "I'm glad you were listening. Sometimes I get so convoluted I lose everyone.... I don't believe we've met before."

"No, we haven't," I said as we shook hands again. "I'm Nick Shepherd – a friend of Marilyn Boone's. I was going to meet her here today."

"I was wondering where Marilyn was. I figured she was on summer vacation."

"No, I'm afraid she's at Stanford Hospital. She's been shot."
Alarm flashed across the Reverend's face. "How is she?"

"She's okay, but I'm sure she would like to see you."

"What happened?"

"It's a long story. The condensed version is I've been in love with her a long time, and I wanted her back in my life. As a result, she was in the wrong place at the wrong time. She can fill in the details. But she's very confused right now, and I can't help her. That's why I think she needs you."

"Thanks for coming to tell me this. I'll go right over." He smiled as we shook hands yet again. "See how easy being God-like is?"

He turned, scampered down the three granite steps to the archway corridor, and disappeared around the corner of the Church.

I called Susan from the Admiral's Club at noon, just before Ricardo, Sid and I boarded the flight. "I've decided to return to work, so I'm coming back tonight. The flight gets in at 9 o'clock, so I'd like to stop by around 10:30 to pick up some papers."

"10:30!" was Susan's shrill drunken reply. "No way. Not until tomorrow."

I stifled my rising frustration. "All right, then. Tomorrow. I'll catch the 5:05 tomorrow night."

"I hope you know you're not staying here."

"All right, Susan, if that's the way you want it. I did want a chance to talk things over—"

"You said it all at the Castle," Susan spat, then hung up.

180

I called Liz and asked her to book me a room at the Constitution Club.

The limo rounded the circle drive and pulled up at the front door of my house at 6:15 the next evening. As Ricardo, Sid and I mounted the single front step, Susan pulled open the door. She wore a scooped neck, short yellow dress, which revealed her well-shaped legs and the beginning rise of her breasts. Her volcanic black hair glistened. "Nick," she began, her voice slightly unsteady, "I'm really sorry about yesterday. I was having a dreadful day."

Finally finding words, I said, "I owe you the apology. It was presumptuous of me to think I could come that late...You remember Ricardo. And this is his partner, Sid Simpson."

Susan flashed a smile. "How nice to see you again, Inspector Lopez. Inspector Simpson, it's a pleasure to meet you." She shook hands with each of them; even her handshake was sensual.

Susan stepped back, pulling the door open further as she moved. "Please come in. Cocktails are waiting in the den." She led the way through the foyer, into the oversized den, and crossed the random-width hardwood floor to the wet bar behind the far door. Ricardo, Sid, and I all opted for diet soda, but Susan poured herself a martini into a straight-up glass with an olive from a pitcher already prepared. Ricardo and Sid excused themselves to take up sentry positions, and then Susan led the way to the sofa and chairs along the bay window. I stared out at the panorama of Greenwich Harbor and Long Island Sound that spread out beyond the window. "I've never really appreciated this view," I observed.

"You never saw anything but your work," Susan remonstrated.

"I suppose I deserved that," I replied.

As we sat sipping our drinks, I recounted the essence of what had transpired since Susan had left the Castle, including the presence of Marilyn. When I explained I had run into Marilyn on Campus and one thing had led to another, Susan just sat in stony silence. But I didn't mention Mundi; despite my new commitment to truth, I still had a basic trust issue with Susan. I couldn't quite put my finger on it.

When I had finished, Susan simply asked, "Do you sleep with her?"

"No," I answered. "She's in a relationship. And you and I are still married. I'd like to give our relationship one more chance."

"I can't," Susan blurted. "Oh, you may not have slept with her—yet. But you will. I don't think I could ever forgive you. Or...or myself. As I told you in the Castle, I've been sleeping with someone."

I stared at Susan, still finding it hard to believe. "Whom?"

"Never mind'" she said, taking a large sip of her martini. "I'm not proud of it, and I don't want to tell you."

"Do I know him?"

"No," she said, as she gave me her crooked smile. She was lying. "And I just don't want to talk about it," she concluded.

I sat, trying to decide what to do. I rose finally, saying, "Well, if that's the way you want it, I'll get my papers and be on my way."

Susan rose as well, revealing more of her cleavage. "You don't have to go; I didn't mean what I said last night. This house belongs to both of us, and you're welcome any time. Spend the night."

I tried to bring my eyes up to her eyes, but my gaze froze on her breasts. She looked down to the point of my focus, smiled, and then took a long drink of her martini. I shook my head, wrenching my vision to the left, out the bay window.

"Spend the night," she repeated. She took a step towards me. "Stay with me."

I continued to look out the window. I took a deep breath, and then blew it out my mouth. "As tempting as your offer is, Susan, I think it would be a mistake. I'm afraid we've caused a lot of damage to each other. I'm staying at the Club in the City, and we can try to sort things out objectively. I've had some second thoughts about having children."

"You what?" she laughed. "Children? You want children? You make me laugh."

"I'm serious, Susan," I said quietly. "These experiences with death are teaching me the value of life. New life. I might be ready."

"You might!" she shrilled. "You might!" She strode over and pushed me with her left hand, spilling some of the martini that she clutched in her right. I stumbled backwards. "You really make me mad!" she raged on. "If you want children, go have them with your precious Marilyn." She downed the rest of her drink.

I stood with my mouth open, speechless. "Have another drink, Susan."

"You bet I will. And another one after that." She turned, walked over to the bar, and poured herself another martini. "Just get out of here. Go to the City."

"Look," I began, and then stopped, fighting my anger. "I've got to get going," I said instead. "I'll be at the Club."

I stomped out of the den, slamming the door behind me, and then went through the kitchen to my study beyond. I unlocked my desk, found my miscellaneous file, and laid it on top of my desk. Although I knew it was true in the back of my mind, I still stared in disbelief when I found a copy of the letter from Sullivan to Ed Shepherd. I stared at it for a long time, then finally folded it up and slid it into my inside coat pocket. I returned the file, locked my desk, and then strode through the kitchen and dining room to avoid going through the den. As I approached the front door Ricardo looked at me and asked, "Did you find it?"

I withdrew the letter and handed it to him. "I still don't believe it, but it was there." Ricardo studied the letter for a few moments, and then said, "I'll have the lab look at it."

"Why?"

"Just a hunch."

The following morning Ricardo was waiting for me in the reception area at FBI Headquarters at 7:30. "Billings just arrived," Ricardo said.

"Is he the one with the electron microscope?"

"The same. It will be difficult to determine from a copy, but I want him to study Sullivan's signature on that letter."

Billings was hanging up his sports jacket on the coat rack and donning his white coat when Ricardo pushed open the door to the lab. "Sorry I'm late," Billings quipped. "Nothing much happens when you're not around, so I get lazy."

"Oh come on, Ted, you practically live here." He placed his briefcase on the long metal lab table, opened it, and withdrew Sullivan's letter. Handing it to Ted, he said, "Please take a look at this under the scope."

"What am I looking for?"

"I don't want to prejudice you, Ted. Just tell me what you see."

"I don't have to tell you; you can see for yourself. This scope has a screen." Ted sounded like a proud father. He slid the letter into place under the eyepiece, and then flipped 2 switches on the microscope. A screen on the shelf above them lit up, revealing large, black letters, against a white background.

"Well," Ted began, "nothing unusual here. Lightweight bond paper; the black specs means it's recycled. The printing was done on a standard printer; an HP LaserJet, I'd say."

Ricardo turned to me. "Are Sullivan's memos done by his secretary, rather than a communications center?"

"Sometimes, yes. He doesn't entirely trust the Center, so he has Hazel type some things personally."

"On a LaserJet?"

"Why yes, I believe it is."

Ted smiled in a self-congratulatory way as he slid the letter along the base of the microscope until the black letters gave way to the swirl of the signature. "Hum," Ted mused. "That's funny. That looks like a rubber stamp signature. See the way the ink appears spread out along the edge?"

"Does Sullivan or Hazel use a rubber stamp?" Ricardo asked me.

"No, I don't believe so. Sullivan wants to see everything before it goes out. I think he signs everything personally." I scowled. "So you think the letter's a forgery?"

"Entirely possible. But then again, he or Hazel may have a rubber stamp signature and we just don't know it."

"How are we going to find out?" I asked, frustrated, and addressing no one in particular. "Wait. I have an idea. He keeps some of his confidential files in his desk; I've seen him pull out secret memos from his lower right-hand drawer. But I'm sure he keeps it locked." Then I remembered where I was and smiled.

"No problem," Ricardo chuckled. "And I'd like to search the Communications Center files as well."

I felt bewildered. "I don't know the first thing about it."

"No problem," Ricardo repeated. "We'll bring Molly who runs our Communication Center here. We'll meet you at your office at 6."

I walked back to my office, flanked by two of Ricardo's men. The sky was shrouded by haze, and the temperature had already risen to 95 degrees, with humidity to match. The streets were a thick throng of summer tourists, suburban shoppers who had abandoned their malls, and office workers heading for their skyscraper tombs. Even at the slow pace, impeded by crowd and caution, I sweated profusely, and I could feel my shirt clinging to my chest and back. The heat and the crowd stifled me, and I felt a momentary weakness, being so dependent on Ricardo's men. I wanted to fend for myself, as I always had. But knew I could not solve this alone.

As I stepped off the elevator onto the 39th floor with the two Agents, Pat was just coming down the hall with a cup of coffee. "You're early," I observed.

"I made a summer solstice resolution," Pat laughed, "to be here by 8. And I've made it every day for the past 2 weeks."

I studied her as we strolled down the hallway. She was dressed in a summer weight pin striped seersucker skirt with matching jacket and a white button-down blouse, but they couldn't hide her full, pointed breasts, thin waist, and hips, and tanned, muscular legs. Her rich, auburn hair partially covered her pretty face that was accented by high cheekbones and full lips. It was then I realized that Pat reminded me very strongly of Marilyn.

"Is something wrong?" Pat asked.

"No, I was admiring your suit. Is it new?"

"Yes. I bought it last week to reward myself for getting here on time."

One Agent had remained by the elevator, and the other one went into the vacant cubicle across from my office. "Why don't you come in?" I invited Pat. "If you have a minute, that is. You can bring me up to date."

As we entered my office, Pat said, "I'm glad you're back. With you gone, as well as Sullivan and Melville, this place has been positively boring."

"I could do with a little boring," I chuckled, looking down at the cast on my arm. "I've had enough excitement for this month."

Pat shook her head. "Another close call. How may I help?"

Suddenly amusement brightened her face. "You need a hideout? I have a two-bedroom apartment."

I studied Pat's deep coral-blue eyes, looking for meaning. "No, thanks, Pat. My life's complicated enough."

"My place beats the Constitution Club."

I frowned. "How do you know about that?"

"I heard you and Susan were having troubles. And I heard Liz make an indefinite reservation for you."

"Well, thanks for the offer, but I really do have a lot of complications."

Pat nodded. "I understand. But I'll keep the offer open. Is there anything I can do?"

"Well you know, maybe there is," I mused. "Ricardo and a few of his staff are coming up about 6, and I think he could use some more inside help. Would you be able to stay?"

"I'd be glad to, Nick." She stared into my eyes, riveting my gaze. Once again, I was struck with the deep blue of her eyes. I thought I saw the wisp of a thin veil, but then it was gone. Her eyes were clear. Inexplicably, I thought, "Eyes are the mirror of the soul."

Then I asked, "Why do you work here, Pat? I mean with your qualifications, you could get a job in any of the high-tech industries."

"Because I enjoy being here. I want to be a part of basic industry."

"You enjoy being in a ruthless, cutthroat commodity business?" I laughed.

"I enjoy being part of what makes the world work."

"Meaning?"

"Meaning the world revolves around its business center. Business is energy. It creates. And our Company fuels the world economy, quite literally."

"Pat, you're twenty-something–"

"I'll be 30 next month."

Talking quickly to hide my surprise, "Well, I've got more than a few years on you, and I'd say that's pretty naive."

"Why? Because I view business in a positive light, rather than a negative one, the way most of the world does? Business is the reason all the other institutions even exist. I mean without business who would pay for governments?"

I held up my one good arm defensively. "Don't get me wrong. I happen to agree with you; that's why I'm here. All I'm saying is that sometimes this business power is abused. Power needs to be used, not abused."

Pat looked intently at me. "Then it's up to us slaves to see to it that it isn't."

I returned Pat's gaze. Did she know more than she was letting on? Was she Bradshaw's confederate? No... her eyes were clear; not even a hint of treachery. But then betrayal could be shrouded...I decided to take the plunge. "What do you know about this bombing business?"

Pat's expression turned thoughtful. "Nothing really...I just...I just have my suspicions."

"Sullivan?"

Surprise wrinkled Pat's brow. "Why...why, yes. He's always checking on you. He wants to know where you are every minute. Then there's the gossip down the hall. They think Sullivan's trying to cover something up. References in memos such as, 'Proceed with that matter we discussed this morning.' We never get memos such as that."

"What do you know about Bradshaw?"

"Well, not much. Hazel says Sullivan talks to him in Washington several times a week and sends him the type memos I mentioned a minute ago. Walter—" She stopped, her face reddening. "Melville," she continued, "says he's all right, and that we need slippery characters like Bradshaw to deal with the Beltway crowd. But I just don't trust him. On the other hand, I can't think of him as a killer. He seems as though he is a big, but slippery, teddy bear."

"A bear with deadly fangs, Pat. I know he's involved, but he's taking orders from somewhere; probably from here, but it could be from anywhere." I paused. "You mentioned Walter. Do you have any suspicions about him?"

Once again, her face reddened. "I... well...I was seeing Walter for a while, right after his wife left him, and... again this year, but it ended recently. I think he's in love with someone else. Anyway, thank God it's over."

"Do you suspect him of being involved in the murders? Is it possible?"

Pat shrugged her shoulders. "I suppose it's possible. I tend to pick abusive men, but...no, I really don't think so; he just wants to hurt women." She shook her head. "Wow," she breathed. "Was I blind. Twice."

"What about me? Are you suspicious of me?"

Pat stared, wide-eyed. "You? You're the target!"

"Are you sure? How do you know I didn't stage those other attempts just to divert suspicion?"

Pat furrowed her brow and bit her lower lip. "Well, I guess I really don't know. You can't trust anybody."

"Not even you."

Hurt flashed across Pat's face, but she simply said, "I don't blame you. The proof will be in the pudding. And I would like to prove myself to you."

I smiled. "I really do trust you, Pat. And thanks for offering to help Ricardo tonight. You're a real friend."

The 39th floor was deserted, except for Pat, the two FBI Agents, and me when the phone rang at 6 o'clock. "Nick Shepherd," I answered.

"Mr. Shepherd?" asked the voice on the other end of the line. "This is Frank in Security. Inspector Lopez, Mr. Billings, and Ms. Wiggins are here to see you."

"Thanks, Frank. Please send them up and tell them I'll meet them at the elevator."

Sullivan had left for Europe that afternoon with Melville, but I pushed the speed-dial button on my phone for Sullivan's office just to be sure nobody was there. I let it ring until the voice-mail came on, and then hung up. I strode down the hall, and then stopped in front of Pat's open door. Pat looked up. "Come on," I said. "Time for intrigue."

As we approached the elevators, the bell rang, and the doors slid open. Ricardo emerged, followed by Billings, and a young black woman. Ricardo looked at Pat, then over at Nick, with eyebrows raised.

"Ricardo, you remember Pat Campbell, our Vice-President of Administration. She's offered to help; she knows the system around here."

Ricardo introduced Molly Wiggins, and then looked back at Pat, holding her gaze for several moments. Apparently satisfied, he said, "I think you may be able to help. Do you know how to access Sullivan's private files in the Communications Center?"

Pat smiled devilishly at the invitation to conspiracy. "If you can access his secretary's desk, I would be able to. Hazel says Sullivan is so paranoid he makes her change the password every other day, so she must record them in a log to remember. She complains about it all the time; she's afraid she'll forget the keys to her desk, as she did a couple of months ago. Sullivan wanted a copy of a letter he had done the previous day, and since she's not allowed to keep any hard copies, she couldn't get one without the password. She said she had never seen him so mad."

"But I thought Sullivan kept his correspondence copies in his desk," I said, alarmed we wouldn't find the evidence we sought.

"Hazel says he keeps the copies of the work she does on her computer in his desk, but the majority of the documents are maintained in the computer files "

"Well," said Ricardo, "we have three places to look. Sullivan's desk, his private computer file, and the general communications file. Let's get at it. Where's the Communication Center?"

"Down on 38," Pat answered.

We moved down the hallway to Sullivan's office. Ricardo pulled a wad of keys from his briefcase and selected one which opened Hazel's desk. Pat found the codebook, and announced, "Today's password is Guinness." She turned and led Molly toward the elevator. Then, keys in hand, Ricardo moved over to Sullivan's door and, on his third try, opened it. "I'm losing my touch," he chuckled.

I strode over to Sullivan's desk, switched on his computer, and then typed in his password. Eagerly, I scrolled through his document files. Nothing caught my eye. "It's got to be here," I breathed, returning to the beginning, and scrolling through more slowly.

I came to the last file that was labeled, "West Coast."

"Why in the blazes does he have a separate file for the West Coast," I wondered aloud. I clicked on it, and then began scanning the memos. A few moments later I found one that looked promising. I clicked on the print icon, and moments later I withdrew the several pages of hard copy from the printer with a triumphant, "Got it!" Then I handed the packet to Ricardo.

While Ricardo and Ted studied the memo, I returned to the computer to scan the file myself. After a while, I let out a low, long whistle. "This is dynamite. Sullivan and the other Oil CEO's created a mini-cartel on the West Coast. Price fixing, dividing markets, production limits; they went the whole nine yards. I wondered when I returned to the Domestic Division why the West Coast was such a better market than the rest of the country. Now I know."

"And to this day, he hasn't even hinted it to you?" Ricardo asked. "I mean in his memo, he instructed Ed Shepherd to inform you."

"Yes, but Ed was killed, along with everyone else. And in the memo, he alludes to the risk of telling me. With Golden Green he might be figuring he doesn't need the cartel any longer. Anyway, he obviously decided against telling me. And that rat! He gave me more grief about the rest of the country; why couldn't I bring it up to West Coast levels. All along, he had the whole thing rigged."

"But he's chosen you to be his successor," Ricardo reminded me. "Surely he will tell you sometime."

"Not if he doesn't have to. It is illegal. If Golden Green gives us the market dominance he expects, he won't need to."

Suddenly the door flew open and Pat and Molly rushed in. "Molly recovered this!" Pat cried, memo in hand. We have proof! Sullivan is behind it!" She handed the document to me, saying, "Here is the order."

I read these words:

TO: RUB
FROM: BAS
RE: PALMAS

Proceed with the matter we discussed this morning. No survivors.

Regards,

As with the other memo, it was signed "Bruce."

CHAPTER TWENTY

The entire group of us took the memos back to the FBI lab. As Ted was sliding the new one into position and switching on the electron microscope, Ricardo said, "Something is off. This is too easy. Okay, I buy that Sullivan rigged the West Coast, but it's one big giant step from price fixing and dividing markets all the way to mass murder. And why in the blazes would he leave such an incriminating letter in the memory bank?"

"You don't know Sullivan," I responded. "He believes he can do anything and get away with it."

Ricardo smiled. "Somehow I don't believe your point of view is entirely objective. There. Look at that signature," pointing to the blue swirl below the black dots of the text. "Ted, please explain."

"Quite simply," Ted began, "the signature is computer produced. Notice the letters of the text are comprised of scores of tiny dots. That's the way the computer prints."

"And the computer is able to print a signature as well?" I asked, frowning in disbelief.

"Yes," Ted confirmed. "The signature can be programmed into the computer and will print it the same way as the text, with tiny dots of ink. Now let's look at a real signature."

He picked up a blank sheet of paper, took out his pen, scribbled on it, and slid the paper into position on the electron microscope. The screen displayed a solid, irregular blue swirl. "See?" Ted said. "No dots, no squeegee marks. That signature is real."

"So the new memo is a fake," Ricardo concluded.

I slammed my clenched fist against the long metal table, hurting my hand. "Oh come on, Ricardo! The man is guilty! What more proof do you need?"

Ricardo reached over and switched on the lights. "Something less obvious. Why would he first leave a memo such as that in memory and secondly not even sign it personally? No. I think the person we're looking for not only is gunning for you, but he also wants to take Sullivan down with you. Who comes to mind?"

"All right, Ricardo," I agreed, reluctantly. "We'll play your game." I paused, and then chuckled mirthlessly. "I don't know where to start; I don't know anyone who even likes the guy."

"Okay, okay," Ricardo said, his voice impatient. "Start with who has the most to gain. Who wants his job?"

"Well...That's a lengthy list too. Let's see...Outside of me, there's Flannery, the Vice-Chairman, Stockton, Senior Vice-President of Legal, Melville, International Senior Vice-President, and, I suppose Reigel who is Walter's Operations Vice-President. Then there's my Operations Vice-President, Rick Thompson, Casey, our Chief Financial Officer, and Pierpoint, Vice-President of Exploration. All of them could see themselves as Sullivan successors. Oh, and I suppose you should add our R & D Vice-President, Jim Hudson. No, on second thought, Jim would never take the job."

Ricardo withdrew a pen and notebook from his briefcase.

"Okay. Who is ruthless enough to kill for the job? You've already eliminated Hudson."

"Yes, and I can't really picture Tom Pierpoint, either. The greatest excitement for him is a new oil field discovery; he could care less about Company politics.

"I suppose the most ruthless and calculating," I continued, "is Dean Stockton in Legal. He jumped five times in twenty years between the Federal Anti-Trust Department and the private industries he was investigating. You can't do that anymore, so he's stayed with us for the past five years. And with his Fed contacts, he's steamrollered over more than one young lion investigating us. He got them fired. And he's bilking long-term Company Union Employees out of their pensions by laying them off just before they qualify. But Sullivan doesn't like him, probably because they're so much alike, so there is no way he can succeed Sullivan. That's because Sullivan controls the stock and, in that way, controls the Board of Directors."

"What if Sullivan were out of the way?" Ricardo asked.

"Hum," I grunted, scratching my chin thoughtfully. Then I nodded my head. "Sure. He could tie up Sullivan's shares in Probate. And he knows his way around the Board and Stockholder meetings. He could pull it off."

Ricardo scribbled in his notebook. "Who else?"

"Ned Casey, our CFO. All he cares about is the bottom line, and he doesn't care who gets hurt, if he looks good. When I was in International, he was constantly delaying Overseas Payrolls, Agency Commissions, and Complaint Settlements to 'improve' the cash flow and make the profit look better. He is still using 'creative accounting,' particularly when it comes to asset valuation. And he's got the credit controls so tight that we're always losing Independent Dealers, both here and Overseas."

"But is he capable of mass murder? There's an enormous difference between pulling a credit line and pulling a trigger."

I shrugged my shoulders. "I never thought I could pull the trigger against another human being until it was a matter of survival at the Castle. And Casey isn't exactly what I would call a humanist."

Once again Ricardo jotted in his notebook. Then he looked up, asking, "What about the Vice-Chairman—what was his name, Flanagan?"

"Flannery. He's a simple yes man. That's why he's there. Whatever Sullivan wants, he gets." Suddenly I scowled. "Wait a minute! That's why we have had such a tough time finding a trail to Sullivan. We may have been looking in the wrong place! It may lead to Flannery!"

Ricardo chuckled. "You always have to bring the guilt back to Sullivan. Forget that for now. The question is whether or not Flannery is ruthless enough to carry this off by himself."

"No! That's my point! He's spineless enough to carry out orders to the letter, but not ruthless enough to originate them. Sullivan orchestrates everything he does!"

"Relax. I hear you. We'll consider that later. For now, let's keep on track. Who's next?"

I grimaced. "Well we can't forget Walter. I mean we are friendly, but we are competitors as well. He's older than I am, but we joined the Company the same year. He had opted for the Service after graduating from Harvard Business School. We were both were selected for the MBA "fast track" program at the Company. He worked his way up in Domestic and I did the same in International.

"And now we've switched Divisions," I continued. "Until just recently I felt International was the best place to be to have the best shot at Sullivan's job when he retires because it's more prestigious than Domestic. But that's not the way it's turning out."

"How do you think Walter sees it?" Ricardo asked as he continued to make notes.

I shrugged my shoulders again. "I don't know. You do have to be tough in this business; we are dealing with a basic commodity. Customers are always trying to get the best deal, suppliers are always trying to charge us the highest price because we're 'big and rich', and the world's governments are always after us for the same reasons. And Walter must deal with the same political infighting that I do; the people we work with in the Company are jealous of the fast track we're on, fighting us for our jobs. But as far as being heartless enough for mass murder..."

I paused and looked over at Pat with a questioning expression on my face. She smiled, and then chuckled. "Don't ask me," she said, chuckling again. "I was in love with the guy, even though he was no good for me. That was why I was in love with him. But it's still hard for me to conceive of him being a murderer, even though he was very jealous of you, Nick." She shivered slightly.

I nodded, and then looked over at Ricardo. "Walter is tough, but a killer...I don't know."

Ricardo finished writing in his notebook. "Okay. That's everyone except the Domestic Operations guy, Thompson, wasn't it?"

I nodded as I said, "I've known Rick a long time. He is a recovering alcoholic who finally realized he had hit bottom when he guzzled a bottle of 1937 Ramos Pinto Port as though it were soda pop. That was two years ago. I was with him at the time. We were at the Company meeting at Greenbrier, and when the meeting broke the next

194

morning, Rick headed straight for New York Hospital and checked himself into the Rehab Center at the Billy Rose Mansion that very day.

"He spent two months there, becoming a Born-Again Christian in the process, and has been clean ever since. We don't see each other socially anymore, because we used to drink a lot together. But we talk every day, either personally or by phone if we're traveling, and I can tell you that man is at peace with himself. Nothing can anger him. Rick has a compulsive personality, so I suppose he is ruthless in his pursuit of excellence and wouldn't mind having Sullivan's job, but only if it were God's will."

"He wouldn't be the first one to kill in the name of God, or Allah, or whatever the Deity may be," Ricardo rejoined. "Just look at the Christians during the Crusades, right on through to modern times with the Arabs and their Jihad."

"Well, I just don't think that's Rick." I shifted my gaze over to Pat. "You know Rick; he told me you went out a few times after his wife left him. What do you think?"

"I think his wife was crazy," Pat chuckled. "She had stayed with him during all his drunkenness, yet she left him when he straightened out. He's the one good guy I ever went out with. Come to think of it, I dumped him after two dates." She chuckled again as she said, "I must be crazy too!

"But seriously," she continued, still chuckling a bit, "he is a zealot; I mean he fell wildly in love with me. He sent flowers every day, overwhelmed me with extravagant gifts, and he even wrote me love poems. I am quite serious, but I wasn't looking for that kind of relationship. I felt smothered. Anyway, he does go to extremes, but much less so now than before. I suppose he's capable of engineering the entire conspiracy, but I agree with you, Nick. I just don't think that's Rick."

Ricardo looked up again from his notebook. "One more question occurs to me; who could have produced the bogus letter?"

"That someone would had to have known the computer system," Pat offered, "plus had the access code to Sullivan's files. Of course, Hazel complained about Sullivan changing the code to everyone, so it was common knowledge. Another point, too, is that Sullivan's signature has been in the computer system for over a year since he wanted the quarterly letter to the stockholders to appear personally signed."

"So all someone had to do," Ricardo surmised, "was type the letter into the computer, access Sullivan's signature, access Sullivan's files, and park it there. Whom amongst the people we have been discussing could have done that?"

"Probably not one of us," I proffered. "We're all computer illiterate."

"Then the killer has a confederate who is," Ricardo concluded. He made a few final entries into his notebook, then said, "I guess that's it for tonight. Thanks, everybody. Goodnight...Oh, Nick, would you stay for a minute?"

When everyone else had left, Ricardo asked, "Pat knows an awful lot about this. How well do you really know her?"

"Not very well, personally. Why, do you really suspect her? I don't get it."

"I don't either, really. She may know a lot more than she realizes. I'd stay close to her."

"My life's complicated enough without another woman in it!" I railed. "She invited me to stay with her, you know."

"You don't have to sleep with her."

"But I think that's what she wants."

"Look. Nothing will happen if you, truly, don't want it to."

"Ricardo, I can't deal with any of this; Susan, Marilyn, the murders, and now Pat! I want to just go crawl in a hole!"

"I understand, my friend. But she could provide the haven you're looking for. And you could keep an eye on her as well."

"Well we do get along ... Do you really think we could just be friends?"

Ricardo smiled. "You can do anything you want to do."

I grimaced. "All right, I'll talk to her tomorrow."

Sullivan returned two days later, and I spent most of the time in a series of meetings with him. When I passed Pat's office at 5:30, I looked in to see Pat preparing to leave. "Do you have a moment?" I asked.

Pat looked up. "Nick. Certainly." Her voice was warm and expectant.

"I was thinking ..." I began.

"Yes."

"I need a friend ... Is your offer still open?"

"Of course," she gently chided, implying there had been no need to ask. "I was just leaving to pick up fish for dinner. I'm trying a recipe I haven't cooked for a while, so I'll get enough for two." She wrote her address on a buck slip and handed it to me. "Come over when you're ready; I'll tell the doorman to expect you."

At 6:45 I pushed the doorbell at Pat's apartment. The door opened, and Pat greeted me with her bright, wide smile. I marveled at her perfectly straight teeth, wondering if they had been a gift from God, or the flawless artwork of a gifted orthodontist. "Come in. Welcome to the fish house."

As she wrinkled her aquiline nose, I decided her perfect teeth were God's gift; she wouldn't have fixed her teeth without fixing her nose. "I need help opening the window in the kitchen. I love everything about fish, except the smell when it's cooking."

She led the way into the kitchen, and I helped her force open the window with my cne good arm. "Thank you," Pat said. "Now I can put the fish on. But before I do, would you like a drink?"

"A beer would be perfect."

"Coming right up." She glided across the hexagonal red tile floor to the refrigerator and withdrew a green bottle and frosty mug. As she opened the bottle, I observed, "Oh. Pschorr. I haven't had one of those since I was in Germany."

"It's the clcsest I've found to Düsseldorf Ault beer," she explained as she handed the open bottle and mug to me.

"Düsseldorf. Yes. I had forgotten you went to Europe last summer. Where did you have the Ault? The Urigue?"

"Yes, as a matter of fact," she confirmed as she led the way into the living room. "And I can prove it." She picked up an ashtray from the silent butler in front of the sofa and handed it to me.

I studied the German words scribed on the back of the ashtray, then looked up saying, "My German's a little rusty. What does it say?"

"It says, 'Taken by mistake from the Urigue.'"

We both laughed as we settled ourselves into the sofa. We chatted more about Germany, about the Rhine River, its beautiful villages nestled in the rolling hills and contrasting ominous castles. When I finished my beer, Pat said, "I have another challenge. You can open the wine while I cook the fish."

We returned to the kitchen, and Pat opened a drawer and handed the corkscrew to me. "The wine is in the refrigerator."

I found a bottle of Poilly Fuisse and chuckled, "I'm glad the wine isn't German."

I rose to the challenge, as I cradled the bottle with my injured arm and turned the corkscrew with my good hand. "The sole place I imbibe German wine is in the Fatherland. My speculation is that German palate opts for a dulce emphasis, as opposed to a drei wein, which is the aberration. I prefer the dry wine which is precluded from the export market."

Pat smiled at me as though she were indulging the minor infraction of a child. "Loosen your tie, Nick. You said you needed a friend. You're not in the office or at the Club with people you must impress. You're here and nobody knows you're here, except for the FBI. Relax."

I felt my stomach unknot. "Thank you. I guess I needed that." I reached up, unknotted my tie, and pulled it off with one stroke.

A short while later, I took my first bite of fish, my mouth filling with delicious flavor. "Good Lord. This is the best fish I've ever tasted. This even tops Paul Bocuse's in Lyon."

Pat flushed with pleasure. "I'm so glad. It does happen to be my favorite recipe, but I haven't had it in such a long time. I fixed it for Walter—oh it must have been 4 years ago now—and he told me he hated fish. I haven't had it since." I felt a jab of discomfort at the mention of Melville's name.

"I'm sorry," she said reading my expression. "I know you're not the best of friends."

I took another bite of fish, chewing slowly, savoring the flavor as I struggled for words. "I'm sorry for my reaction. It's just that I have a tough time seeing you two together. He's such a ..."

"Bum," she finished. "I know that now, but I didn't see it then. I always pick the wrong man."

I shifted uncomfortably in my seat. "But at least I have good taste in friends," Pat said, smiling warmly at me.

"To friendship," I toasted, raising my wine glass.

"To friendship," Pat echoed, touching her glass to mine.

As I poured the last of the Poilly Fuisse, Pat cleared the dinner dishes. She returned from the kitchen with fruit, cheese, and crackers. "Now I understand how you stay so slim," I observed. "No decadent deserts."

Pat laughed. "Oh, no. Don't get me wrong. I just had a good day today in my battle against the chocolate monster. I think I'm losing the war. For me it's easier to run three miles a day than pass the dessert tray."

"I didn't know you were a runner." I chuckled. "I am, too, when I'm not wounded. How long have you been running?"

"Four years ago, during my first encounter with Walter."

"First encounter? Oh, yes, you mentioned you had broken it off for a while."

Pat's smile was self-effacing. "As I said a little while ago, I keep picking the wrong men. And sometimes more than once. Anyway, after he left the first time, I kept on running. Somehow it eased the pain."

"Do you want to tell me about it? That's what friends are for, you know."

Pat took a deep breath, and then blew it out. "To put it most simply, Walter reminded me of my father. Successful, debonair, handsome, just as Dad was. What I didn't consciously see, which was also true of Dad, was that he was an emotional cripple. He didn't know how to love. Oh, he faked it well, and I bought it twice. I even bought his reason for leaving the first time. He said he wanted some time to think about us. He had gone through one divorce and didn't want to make another mistake.

"In retrospect, I'm sure he was seeing someone else. There were too many times I'd call him at his place in Southampton when I would sense someone was with him. Or I'd call him at his place here in Manhattan in the middle of the night and he wouldn't be there when he said he would be."

She paused and sliced off a slab of Brie. I felt her pain sear through me as though it were my own. "Thank the Lord you finally saw the truth about him."

"Oh being apart helped, the first time he left. I began to see the distance he always put between us. And he was critical and jealous. So when he wanted to get back together again, I had a new perspective. I sensed he was still seeing this other woman, even after I reluctantly agreed to give it another try."

"What happened in the end?"

"I gave him an ultimatum: Get married or get out. He got out."

"Did you really want to marry him? What if he had said yes?"

"I knew he wouldn't say yes. I guess that was my way to run him off."

She paused. "Now I need to be out of love for a while, be just with friends. I need to de-tox. You said you needed a friend; well, so do I. That's why I'm glad you took me up on my offer."

"So you just want to be friends," I confirmed, breathing relief.

"Yes, I've never had a male friend."

I smiled. "So, my friend, what do you want from this friendship?"

"I want to be able to be me; to be where I was when I was a kid. I was happy. I laughed a lot, I didn't worry about my so-called 'image,' and I was very trusting. And I loved the outdoors—skiing, camping, and sailing."

"What happened? How did you lose that?"

"Well," Pat breathed, "the nearest I can figure is that my parents were always criticizing me for being too silly or looking sloppy. And then there was that part about not trusting people too much. So I cleaned up my act and stopped trusting people."

She paused and grimaced. "I guess that's why I picked the men I picked. They all had clean acts and were untrusting, and untrustworthy to boot. And abusive. My parents were always fighting. I thought that was normal behavior."

I laughed, "Well isn't it?"

Pat threw her head back, closed her eyes, and giggled. "Oh, no. I can't even pick good friends!"

"Well, I don't know about that,' I chuckled, "but I hate fighting; I get enough of that doing my job. Susan and I never used to fight—that is until she started drinking heavily. We kept all our feelings sewn up inside. Now I see that extreme doesn't work either. She and I were squelching what we really wanted, until it was too late, and we realized we were strangers to each other."

"There's got to be a happy medium," Pat agreed, catching my eye, and holding the gaze. "Tell me more."

I settled more into the softness of the sofa. "I could go to sleep right now."

"Oh no, you don't," Pat teased. "Not before you tell all. What you need is a spot of Cognac to keep you awake."

I grinned. "Well… all right."

Pat rose and strode over to the dry sink in the corner of the living room. She flipped over two snifters and poured a small amount of Cognac into each one. She returned to me and, handing me a snifter, said, "Cheers," as we clinked glasses and sipped. "Now talk."

"There's not much to tell," I began. "I've had only two serious relationships in my life. The first was Susan."

Both Pat and I took a sip of our Cognacs. "How did you meet Susan?" Pat asked.

"In a graduate finance class. I was working on my MBA and she was just a freshman. She was so level-headed and mature, I couldn't believe she was just a freshman. Anyway, we started dating and, finally at the Spring Fling we got drunk and slept together."

I paused, taking another sip of my Cognac. "Susan went back home to New York for the summer, and that's when I met Marilyn. It was between my first and second year in the Stanford MBA program. I was taking an international marketing course in summer school when I met Marilyn at a party. It was one of those 'your eyes meet, and the rest is history' torrid affairs. She had a casual boyfriend who was wandering around Central America in his International Van and, when he returned for the fall quarter, I thought it was over; just a summer romance. But it wasn't."

"What happened?"

"Well my Great-Grandfather was paying my tuition, and he believed in the work ethic, so I was waiting on tables in a dorm. By chance Marilyn started working at the same dorm, so we started taking walks around Lake Lagunita after lunch. We started holding hands again, and then we couldn't stop it at just those noontime walks. Her boyfriend, John, worked two nights a week at a bar, and Marilyn and I would meet out at the golf course those nights and make love under a low spreading live oak tree."

"Did you feel guilty?" Pat asked as though she had been in similar situations.

"All the time. But I guess the guilt made it okay. I mean as long as I was feeling guilty for cheating, I was punishing myself enough to justify my behavior."

"What finally happened?" Pat asked, taking a sip of her Cognac.

"We got caught. John had gotten suspicious, so one of the nights he was supposed to be working, he followed Marilyn out to the golf course, and while we were kissing, he grabbed her and flung her to the ground. I saw red, tackled him, and started punching. He blew up, shrieked like a maniac, and flung me off him." I shook my head. "We nearly killed each other."

"Was that the end of it?"

"Yes, but it wasn't easy. Marilyn had a wild streak in her—I guess that's what appealed to me—and she tried repeatedly to keep it going. But then I went back to Susan, and Marilyn finally backed off."

"Did you ever tell Susan about Marilyn?"

I resisted the temptation to lie; to simply say yes. But I grimaced and said, "I never had the guts to tell her the whole story. Marilyn said hello to me at a party as she was walking by with John, and Susan got jealous. I told her she was just someone I hashed with. The real story never did get around because, naturally Marilyn didn't want it spread, and John didn't want anyone to find out that Marilyn could possibly run around on him."

I paused again as I took another sip of my Cognac and savored it. "That's about it. I got my MBA the following year, then studied international relations at the University of Mexico while Susan was a junior at Stanford-In-Mexico. Then I went to work for the Company, and Susan and I got married a year later when she graduated."

"Did you ever cheat on Susan?" Pat asked, squinting at me with a sidelong glance.

"Yes," I admitted. "Susan and I were having problems, and I felt drawn back to Marilyn. But then Susan wanted to reconcile. I was really torn, but I finally ended it with Marilyn. I guess I felt obligated to Susan. After that Marilyn didn't want to have anything to do with me."

"What about after you were married?"

I averted her gaze. "Nothing. Nothing, that is, until last month. I ran into Marilyn at Stanford and, before we knew it, the 20 years that had elapsed simply vaporized. Nothing actually happened, but I wanted it to."

"Was that the night of the fire at the Cabana Hotel?"

"Yes. We were at the hotel together."

Pat cast another sidelong glance at me. "Do you think Susan's cheated on you?"

I sipped my Cognac. "Yes, she told me she has, but she won't tell me with whom. She's been very unhappy. The bottom line is that she wanted kids, and I wasn't ready. Now she's always trotting off to those

Southampton parties, and I just don't want to go. And she's drinking all day, every day. We just don't seem to have anything in common anymore."

"So having kids was your major issue?"

"That's the irony," I laughed once, without mirth. "After facing death like this, I'm beginning to feel differently about kids. Life is a gift, and gifts are meant to be given. And I'm able to give life through children. The problem is that I don't want to put it back together with Susan."

"Are you sure?" Pat asked, raising her eyebrows.

"Yes, I'm sure now," I said, nodding my head. "Yesterday I thought Susan and I might be able to reconcile, but now I see there's too much distance, betrayal, and anger between us. All this has simply killed the love we once had."

Pat sat in silence her eyes thoughtful. Then she nodded, "Yes. Yes, I guess that it is too late for you two...But what about Marilyn? That is very much alive."

"I know," I said, my voice tight. "But she's in a long-term relationship, and she still loves the guy."

"Does she love you as well?"

I shrugged. "She says she does. I just had to put some distance between us. We have to get our heads straight."

"Don't you mean your hearts? Your hearts really know. All the while I was in these many destructive relationships, I knew in my heart they were wrong. You and Marilyn trust your hearts; they will see the truth."

I took the last sip of my Cognac. "Thanks for the reminder, my friend," I said, feeling slightly sheepish. "I've only recently rediscovered my heart."

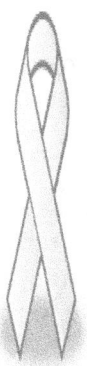

CHAPTER TWENTY-ONE

I had the cast removed from my arm one week later. I returned to the office by mid-morning and began canvassing the regional managers, focusing primarily on routine matters, but also probing for feedback on Golden Green. When I reached Howie Cameron in the Phoenix office, I found what I was looking for. "I got a weird-ass complaint," Howie said in a bewildered tone, with a trace of a southern accent. "I just got this here letter from a traveling salesman who drives 100,000 miles per year covering Arizona, New Mexico and Nevada. He blew an engine valve in the middle of the desert and claims he's been driving with nothing but Golden Green."

"Was there any oil in the engine, Howie?"

"His letter says he guar-damn-tee's it. Just changed it, like he does every three-damn thousand miles. The engine's covered by warranty, but he thinks we ought to take a look-see at Golden Green. Actually, it was a damn nice letter."

"Considering," I muttered.

"Say again, partner?"

"Could have been worse. Look, Howie, would you fax me a copy?"

"Consider it done."

A few minutes later Liz knocked on my closed door, and then entered with Howie's fax in hand. After she had left, closing the door behind her, I dialed Sullivan. Hazel answered, saying Sullivan was in a meeting. "Tell him it's urgent," I said and waited.

Several minutes later Sullivan came on the line. "What is it, Nick? I've got some problems on the West Coast."

"Golden Green is blowing engines."

"What are you talking about?" Sullivan was making no attempt to disguise his irritation.

"I have a letter in my hands from a customer who blew an engine, burning nothing but Golden Green."

"All right, all right. Come on down."

I hurried down the hall towards Sullivan's office at the opposite corner of the floor, followed discretely by the FBI Agent, Sid. Just as I rounded the corner, I caught sight of a familiar figure standing sideways and looking back into Sullivan's office. I froze, and then murmured to Sid. "It's Bradshaw, our lobbyist, the CIA connection, coming out of Sullivan's office. Sullivan's got to be our man."

"Don't be so sure," Sid cautioned. "That's merely guilt by association."

Bradshaw turned as we resumed our way towards Sullivan's office. He smiled in an enigmatic way, nodded, and then headed in the opposite direction, towards the elevators.

"Look," Sid said. "I'll stay close to you. Introduce me to Sullivan's secretary as a consultant, and I'll wait for you in one of those chairs right outside."

We strode the rest of the way down the hall to Hazel; I introduced Sid, and then knocked on Sullivan's closed door. "Come in," Sullivan barked.

I opened the door and stepped into the expansive office. "Was that Bradshaw I saw leaving?" I asked as I marched over to the desk.

"Why yes, it was," Sullivan confirmed, but sounding defensive. "We're having some trouble with the government, but nothing I can't handle." He glanced at the fax in my hand. "Let me see that thing."

He took the paper from my outstretched hand and read it. As he looked up, he said, "Not our problem. It's the goddamn car."

I stared straight into Sullivan's eyes. "We both know that isn't true. We have a responsibility to the public. We've got to maintain our integrity."

"You're not running this company yet. I say our first responsibility is to the stockholders. Integrity be damned!"

I felt myself flush with anger. "Look, Bruce. Regardless of my beliefs, if we don't take Golden Green off the market, we'll be blowing engines all over the country! Then where will the stockholders be?" I remembered Sullivan was the biggest one.

Sullivan put his palms and fingers together and studied them, as though he were looking for a hangnail. I stood, waiting in silence. Finally, Sullivan looked up and said, "Sit down, Nick. Let's discuss this."

I sat in one of the three chairs in front of Sullivan's massive cherry desk. My heart was pounding in my throat, and I was dizzy with tension. I knew I had taken a huge risk confronting Sullivan, but I felt good about it.

"It's a helluva problem," Sullivan began. "If we admit the problem, we'll have a class action suit that will put us clear into Chapter 11; just look at the asbestos cases. If we don't, engines keep blowing, and they prove Golden Green is the culprit, we'll have an even worse problem. Nick, we've got to have the new formula now!"

"Hudson says we're close, but we're not there yet; the ignition temperature is still a bit too high. I told you a while back he had developed a formula that worked but was higher in cost than Golden Green. You wanted to wait until he proved the new, lower cost formula before we made the switch. We need to reconsider that option."

I hesitated as I gathered my thoughts, and then plunged on. "We could announce a recall of Golden Green based on the truth, excessive engine wear, and offer the new formulation as our new premium and sell it at the same price. Customers will get the performance value they have come to expect from Golden Green, so we'll continue to gain market share. Then when we perfect the new, low cost formulation, we'll launch that as Golden Green II, with the appropriate upcharge."

Sullivan smiled. "I like it, Nick. I like it. And you can maintain your precious scruples."

I grimaced. "Well, not exactly. It still ignores the original problem we caused."

"Goddamn it, Nick! What more do you want?"

"To make full restitution. Don't forget, I sourced the formula. That is ... "

I swallowed hard. "I actually got it indirectly from someone who smuggled it out of Iraq."

"It came from the Iraqis?" Sullivan's eyes mirrored surprise.

"From Iraq. An American project engineer developed it years ago, but the Iraqis buried it. Melville arranged to get him out of Iraq in return for the formula."

"Melville did?"

"Yes, and he supplied it to me for a favor in Venezuela. Anyway, the formula does work in older engines, but, as you know, it burns too hot for the new ones. We should have checked it out more thoroughly before bringing it to market. The point is that the new engines will have shortened lives because of our product, and I believe we should make full restitution."

"Now just how do you propose we do that?" was Sullivan's sarcastic response.

"Offer cash compensation to documented users."

"Are you crazy!" Sullivan bellowed. "That would open us up to a class action suit that would put us under!"

"We'd have the suit, all right, but remember only the new engines are affected, so the class would be limited. I don't believe any court would rule against us after we had already made equitable restitution. And I believe the public will increase gallonage with us in response to this honest approach."

Sullivan pressed his palms and fingers together again, as though still seeking the elusive hangnail. Finally, he said, "All right. I'll talk to Stockton about the legal implications, but it might just work. We'd be creating the image of being a responsible corporate citizen, which does count these days." He looked over at me. "Yea. Yea. I like the idea. Hell, we couldn't buy that kind of image with the largest advertising budget. We'll gain 10 per cent market share! That's how to turn a setback into a win," he congratulated himself. As an afterthought he added, "I knew my faith in you was well-placed."

My tension vanished. This was only the second time in my entire career that Sullivan had complimented me. I had gone for broke and emerged intact. O had I? This could be just one more ploy in Sullivan's grand scheme of conspiracy and murder.

I called Ricardo when I returned to my office. "Bradshaw was here with Sullivan."

"I know," Ricardo responded, "I'm having him followed. He just went into the Bull and Bear at the Waldorf.

"I'm glad you called," he continued. "I've had computer profiles developed on the suspects at UNRC we discussed yesterday, and I'd like to go over them with you."

"Okay, how about lunch? Say Sparks at 12:30?"

"Good. See you there."

At 12:15 I left my office, accompanied by Sid and Mickey. Walter Melville was standing by the elevator as we approached. "Hello, Nick," he greeted, glancing at the Agents without comment.

"Hello, Walter," I responded, realizing too late that my reply was curt.

"Are you feeling all right?" Melville asked, cocking his head to one side. "I see your cast is off."

"Just the stress, Walter. We're having some difficulty with Golden Green."

"Oh?" Melville cocked his head to the other side. I suddenly realized Sullivan really must have kept my initial warning of Golden Green problems to himself. "You'll hear about it soon enough." Again, my tone was rude.

"If you like, why don't we discuss it? I'd suggest lunch, but I'm already late for an appointment. And it looks as though you have a lunch as well." He looked at the Agents.

"Okay, Walter. I'll be back by 2. How about then?"

"Let's make it 3; I have to go up to the Waldorf, and it's likely to be a long, difficult negotiation."

Just then Flannery, the Vice-Chairman and Casey, the Chief Financial Officer, strolled up. "Nick, Walter," Flannery greeted us in his soft-spoken, yes-man voice.

"Buy your lunch?" Casey offered. "We're going to the Waldorf to celebrate the latest profit figures."

"I'll share a cab with you," Melville said, "but I already have a lunch appointment."

"No thanks," I declined. "We're headed for Sparks."

Ricardo was waiting for us by the maitre 'd at Sparks. Following Ricardo's instructions, the maitre 'd led the way into the dining room, seating Sid and Mickey by the doorway and Ricardo and me at the far corner table.

While we waited for our diet sodas, Ricardo said, "Nick, this may have nothing to do with our case, but there's a possible connection with the IRA."

"At UNRC?" I asked, my voice rising in surprise.

"It's possible. As I mentioned on the phone, the computer profiles are in, and two of your people have suspected IRA connections."

"Sullivan's got to be one of them," I charged.

"I don't know; his profile is fairly clear, except for his anti-trust law violations, and my friend at Justice is already initiating action. Your document gave him confirmation of what he has suspected for a long time.

"If I didn't know better," Ricardo continued, chuckling, "I'd swear you're after Sullivan's job."

I chuckled as well. "Not this way... Anyway, if it's not Sullivan, who is connected to the IRA?"

"Flannery and Casey."

"What?" I asked, incredulous. "All right, Casey, maybe, but not Milksop Flannery."

"They have been very clever. Separate business trips, but they meet in Belfast along the way—that sort of thing. The expense reports are very revealing. What I want to find out is that if they are IRA connected, are they funneling UNRC funds to the terrorists? If so, we might have a motive for the attacks on you."

"Why? Because I'm Protestant?"

"Very funny. No. It could be because you saw or heard something you shouldn't have, say June 16, last year, in London."

"How did you know?" I asked, and then I realized the answer. "Oh, the expense reports. Yes, I did run into Flannery at Heathrow Airport. He was with two men, and he looked nervous when I asked him where he was headed. He hesitated, then said he was headed to Belfast, back to his roots."

"And you didn't see Casey?"

"No. Just the two strangers he was with. And he didn't introduce me to them."

"Well, he was there somewhere, probably buying cigarettes, or something. They were both on that same flight to Belfast."

"And you think they're afraid I'll put the two of them together and come up with the IRA? I'd believe it if Sullivan were involved."

Ricardo shrugged his shoulders, his palms facing up. "It's a possibility. You do have the reputation of having a straight streak. And I'm not saying Sullivan's not implicated; we just don't have the documentation on him the way we do on Flannery and Casey."

The waiter reappeared with our sodas, and we both ordered red snapper, resisting the waiter's effusive recommendation of the special filet steak in a rich wine sauce.

After the waiter retreated looking offended, Ricardo resumed, "There are a few more interesting things the computer turned up. First, Melville. He's mostly clean, but back when he was in the Service, he was involved in a "Friendly Fire' Inquiry. He killed a guy from his own outfit, but he was cleared of blame. He eventually went on to earn the Medal of Honor."

"And you suspect Walter? Pat said he could be pretty abusive, but he stopped short of murder."

"I don't suspect him any more than anyone else. It's just that he's killed before."

"Yes, but it was an accident. It was war."

"Maybe ... Then there's your friend Hudson, the one you said you couldn't give Sullivan's job to. He came from a moneyed family, was spoiled, got into gambling, lost heavily, and the mob got into him. He's been paying it off, but he still owes them a substantial chunk. The only reason they haven't killed him is that his old man has cancer and when he dies, the son comes into millions from the trust fund. Or maybe they keep him alive to do a little industrial espionage."

"Good Lord," I said, astonished. "Golden Green ... No, I don't believe it. His father works in the oil fields."

"His father owns half the oil fields in West Texas."

"But he never acted as though he were rich," I protested. "Modest home outside Houston, drives an American sedan, 2.3 kids, you know."

Ricardo laughed. "That's the point. He's not rich; he owes the mob. His father owns 17.6 per cent of UNRC stock, which goes to the son also. So it could be the mob is orchestrating a takeover bid with Hudson as the instrument. Or maybe he wants to do it on his own."

My mind flipped into overload. "The mob, arbitrageurs ... who's next, Momar Khadafi?"

Ricardo smiled as I joked in the face of my distress. "I hadn't thought about him," he jested in return. "No, your Exploration V.P., Pierpoint is, and he seems to be acting on his own. Back during price controls, he was found guilty of rigging exploration records so that old wells began showing up as new wells, so that the company could charge the higher, 'new well' price."

"That was before my time, but I heard about it," I confirmed. "It was wrong, but that hardly qualifies him as our man. Besides, the rumor was that Sullivan was really behind the scheme."

"Well Pierpoint could be our man if you consider he may be sitting on billions of barrels of undiscovered oil reserves and isn't telling anyone at UNRC about it. That's my speculation. As you know, Anti-Trust has been after Sullivan, but they've also been keeping an eye on Pierpoint. He's been in contact with several of your competitors, and an informant saying he's discussing massive new reserves with them. I'm just wondering if he's trying to cut the best deal for himself for that location. Or he wants to parlay himself into the number one position at one of those companies. But none of that would be possible if UNRC could prove he made the find while with you. His expense reports reveal he has spent a lot of time in Panama, which has no oil. Did he ever mention anything to you about reserves in Panama?"

The waiter shuffled up to the table, laden with our lunches, which he served in dour silence. I searched my memory for something Pierpoint may have written or said. Where was he coming from? Was he honest or larcenous? He had manipulated "old oil" records, and he was holding back information on reserves, but was he a killer?

My mind flashed back to Panama. "One time," I began, remembering aloud, "Pierpoint and I were having way too many of those Polar beers at the Marriott in Panama City, and he started telling me what a beautiful place Costa Rica was for retirement, and that he had bought some land there. It's right next-door to Panama, and he said he was going up there for the weekend. I said something like, 'Knowing you, there's a billion barrels of oil under your land.' He smiled in a conspiratorial way and said, 'you never know in this business.' I shrugged. "So maybe he does have something going on the side."

"And if he does, he knows you know."

I chuckled. "Only if he's a better drinker than I am. I hadn't remembered it until just this moment."

"Well it didn't matter to you, but it does to him. I'm sure he most definitely remembered it the next morning. That makes him another candidate for wanting to silence you."

I laughed again. "It seems there's one behind every executive desk. Have you got any more?"

"No, no more, but there is another nefarious connection that came up. Sullivan and Melville appear to have been in this West Coast price fixing conspiracy together. Back when he had your job, Melville would travel with Sullivan to those meetings with your competitors."

"This was over and above the legal industry meetings?"

"Yes. This was only to the West Coast. And it could be one of your competitors suspected the Anti-Trust boys were getting too close and wanted to turn States Evidence in exchange for immunity from the massive fine and jail sentence than can be imposed. So Melville and Sullivan had him blown away."

"And they made sure I was with him," I added, "so that I couldn't discover internally what they had been doing."

"They also made sure they weren't there. As I recall, Sullivan was in Rotterdam and Melville was on his way there."

"Yes," I mused, "but you would think they would have been in the same place the whole time if they had been in this together."

"Maybe," was Ricardo's non-committal response.

Just then Sid strode up to the table. "Everything okay, Ricardo?"

"The salmon was great, Sid. What did you have?"

"The steak special, but that's not what I meant. I've got that uneasy feeling."

Ricardo's face tensed. "Check the street; I'll take the kitchen." He motioned to the other agent, Mickey, to come sit with me.

Both men disappeared while Mickey hurried over and took Ricardo's seat. We waited tensely in silence as we both scanned the expansive room, which teemed with the movement of waiters and diners.

A vision rose in my mind's eye. I saw a man jump up and open fire at us. I dove for the floor, and then tucked up into the fetal position, arms folded across my chest. I lay there quivering as more bullets flew, slamming into Mickey who slid to the floor on his side, his lifeless open eyes staring into mine. Then more gunfire and the sounds of breaking dishes, flying utensils and then Ricardo's body crashing to the floor. Still more firing, followed by the sound of Sid's limp body tumbling down the stairway. Finally, I heard the scamper of footfall as the assassin ran from the room, leaving me curled up and shaking, unseen under the table.

The touch of Mickey's hand on my shoulder shook me out of my vision. "Are you okay? You're shaking all over."

I took a deep breath, pursed my lips, and then let the air out slowly. "I've got to get a hold of myself. I'm freaking out! I've got to do something!"

"Relax. That's what we're here for."

"No. This is my battle. It's me they want."

Sid returned, followed seconds later by Ricardo, and they both sat down. "Anything?" Ricardo asked, his tone terse.

"Normal mid-day crush of humanity on the street," Sid responded.

"Nothing unusual in the kitchen, either," Ricardo said. "See anything here, Mickey?"

"I didn't see anything, but something's really bothering Nick."

"I know one of them is in here," I droned, as though in a trance. My eyes lazed around the room. Suddenly my gaze froze on the man I had seen in the vision, who was partially hidden from view in the far corner by the stairway. "Him," I said with certainty.

I called the waiter over and asked loudly, "Where's the men's room?"

"Down the stairway by the bar," the waiter replied, pointing towards the front door.

"What in the blazes are you doing?" Ricardo whispered.

"I'm tired of hiding," I answered, as I pushed my chair back and rose, ramrod straight. "If he follows me, grab him."

I strode quickly towards the stairway, as though the only thing on my mind was to reach the men's room as quickly as possible. Just as I passed the lone man, I whirled and leaped. I flung my right arm around the man's throat, pulling him back, while pinning the man's left arm up and behind with my left. The man inhaled a gasping, pained breath, and then struggled with his right hand to reach the holstered gun on his left side, exposed by his now open coat. "Touch that gun, and I'll break your neck," I growled.

The man froze. I glanced up to see Ricardo racing towards us, gun drawn. Sid and Mickey were backing towards us, covering the rear. Seconds later, Ricardo reached us and yanked the gun from the man's holster. He glared at me. "Are you crazy? You could have gotten yourself killed!"

"I didn't want to turn my back on him," I replied, my voice grim. "Besides, this is my fight."

I tightened my grasp around the man's neck. "Where are the others?" I demanded.

"You're crazy," was the rasping reply. "Let me go!"

I glanced around the room. All conversation had stopped, and people stared at me. Nobody moved. Then I looked over at Ricardo. "What do you think?"

"They're outside. This guy's the back-up."

I yanked the man to his feet. "Okay, pal, you're going to lead us out of here." I released the man's neck, pulling his left arm up beyond his shoulder blade. The man winced with new pain.

"Wait, Nick," Ricardo urged. "We don't know how many are out there. I'll call for back-up."

I tilted my head towards my captive. "This is our back-up. Let's get this over with."

The prisoner whipped his head towards Ricardo. "This man is crazy! Do something!"

Ricardo shrugged his shoulders, and then looked at me. "It's your party; lead on."

The maitre d' came blustering into the bar and accosted them at the top of the stairs. "What's going on here?" he demanded. As Ricardo whipped out his ID, he explained, "FBI. There's going to be trouble. Clear everybody out of here into the rear dining room."

The maitre d' nodded, saying, "Yes, sir," then hurried off.

I continued along the bar, through the doorway, into the foyer, and up to the front door. "They're out there; I know it," I said with conviction.

"I feel it, too," Sid confirmed.

We moved to the left of the front door and peered out the window onto 44th Street. Streams of people and rows of parked cars met our gaze, but nothing appeared abnormal. Ricardo shook his head. "I know they're out there, but I don't know where."

He glanced through the doorway to see that the maitre d' had cleared the bar. Then he cast a sidelong glance at our obese captive whose broad forehead was sprinkled with perspiration and read him his rights. "The next step is up to you. You can save us all a lot of trouble by telling us where they are. Or, I can leave you to my mad friend here who's ready to charge out there like Don Quixote, using you as his lance."

Terror flashed across the man's face. "They'll take me out with you!"

"Not if you tell us where they are," Ricardo growled.

The man shifted his eyes as he weighed the alternatives. "I want to make a deal," he breathed finally. "I'll tell you where they are if you give me full immunity."

"No deals," Ricardo pronounced.

"Come on," I urged. "He's just stalling. Let's go find them ourselves."

"I can tell you who ordered the hit!" the man blurted.

"Who?" I demanded.

"I'm not talking without a deal. I know you guys do it. New identity and plenty of dough. Look, you guys need me. Even if you arrest me, I'll be out in an hour."

"Not if you're dead," I threatened.

"Relax, Nick. I'd much rather solve this without violence."

Ricardo stared into the pig eyes of our captive. "I'll tell you what. Tell us where they are and who is behind it, and you've got yourself a deal." He paused. "Tell me, have you always been a rat-fink?"

The man's voice was ice-cold. "They wouldn't think twice about blowing me away with you. A man's got to survive."

"What's the signal?" Ricardo demanded.

The man glanced down at his right wrist, then back to me. I was still pinning his left arm behind him. "Do you mind, buddy? You're killing my arm."

"Hold him, Nick!" Ricardo commanded, grabbing the man's wrist, and unbuckling the watch on it. He studied it quickly. "Electronic signal. CIA issue."

He looked up at the man. "You have nothing left to bargain with. We already know who is behind this, and all we have to do push this little button and they'll come running." He poised his finger above the button.

"Wait!" the man shrieked. "You don't know who's behind it!"

"Let's hear him out, Ricardo," I agreed. "Besides, you were right to want to settle this with as little violence as possible. If you push that button, we could have a major shoot out, and bystanders are likely to be hurt. We have some time because they won't be expecting us to finish lunch for another 15 minutes. Let's find the car; it's bound to be near here. If we can jump them, we can avoid bloodshed."

Ricardo nodded his approval, and then turned to our prisoner. "All right, I'll still make the deal. I'll need the car's description, its location, and your testimony in court. Then it's on to a new life."

A spark of hope glimmered in the middle-aged face, then vanished. "They'll find me," he murmured.

Ricardo smiled in a reassuring way. "No, they won't; I haven't lost one yet."

"You don't know Bellini." The man's pig eyes filled with fear as they darted to the window.

Surprise flickered across Ricardo's face at the mention of the crime boss, but without missing a beat, he rejoined, "You'd be surprised. A few years back I gave a new life to one of your compatriots that everyone thinks is dead. I can do the same for you."

The man studied Ricardo's face for a long time as though looking for truth. "I could use a new life," he said finally. "You've got yourself a deal."

As they shook hands, Ricardo said, "The back-up team will take you out the back way."

He turned to Mickey. "Call them in and wait with him in the kitchen. And tell the maitre d' it's business as usual."

Ten minutes later, Mickey returned. A group of six diners were preparing to leave, so our cadre emerged onto 44th Street with them. We followed the group over to Second Avenue, then Sid and Mickey headed north, and Ricardo and I turned south. I felt my blood pounding in my ears, and my throat was tight, but I felt ready for battle. "It's a dark blue van," our captive had told us, "with dark, bullet-proof glass all around. It'll be parked on Third Avenue between 43rd and 44th for an easy drive by the restaurant at my signal."

Ricardo and I waited at the corner of 43rd and Second. Minutes dragged by. Finally, Ricardo's walkie-talkie beeped, and Sid reported he had located the van in front of a construction site, jammed a nightstick into the exhaust pipe, and escaped undetected. "Number one danger past," Ricardo murmured, then devised a plan with Sid for the arrest.

He turned to me. "All right. You move into position at the west corner of Third Avenue. I'll go up to 44th and cross over to Third from there. Then we'll converge diagonally on the van from both directions.

As you heard, Sid and Mickey will move in from the construction site." He paused, looking at his watch, "Be in position in three minutes, at 28 past the hour. Then move in on my signal."

43rd Street was still jammed with mid-day pedestrians, cars, and buses. People rushed past me, all focused on reaching their destination as quickly as possible to escape the crush. Yet I felt all alone in this plethora of humanity. The risk was immense, but we could discover the connection between Bellini and the conspiracy. The CIA issue watch of our captive suggested Bradshaw again, but there would be a clue leading beyond him. In any event, if all we got was Bellini off the streets, the risk was still worth it. I felt the surge of renewed purpose.

When I reached Third Avenue, the flashing "Don't Walk" became a steady shining red. I glanced to the right and saw the building under construction rising as an edifice to the "new" New York. The entire eastern side of the block was closed to pedestrian traffic by a blue fence. The lone vehicle parked in front of it was the dark blue van.

I waited while the 'Don't Walk' signal burned a steady red. Finally, the light flashed to a green 'Walk', and I slowly stepped off the curb and sauntered across Third Avenue, with other pedestrians pushing past me. I scanned the figures crossing one block up on 44th Street and caught a glimpse of Ricardo. I reached the west side of the street and waited, while the rest of the crowd swarmed north on Third and further west on 43rd.

The signal was starting to flash red when I saw Ricardo's signal. With my heart pounding wildly, I sprinted diagonally across Third Avenue towards the van, gun drawn. One of the van's rear windows flew open, and gunfire erupted. The bullets ricocheted off the pavement to my right, and then I heard the screeching of brakes from the oncoming traffic behind me. I approached the fence in full stride, reached up, and vaulted over to the sidewalk beyond as bullets slammed into the fence just below my vaulting hand. Seconds later Ricardo leaped the fence as well and landed amid a flurry of bullets.

The van's engine roared to life, and the tires squealed as the driver engaged the clutch. But then the van bucked several times, and the engine seized up and fell silent as Sid's sabotage cut off the engine's vacuum. "Let's move!" Ricardo shouted, and all four of us vaulted back onto the street, with Mickey and I landing south of the van and Ricardo and Sid on the north side.

The gun muzzle reappeared through the rear window, and Mickey and I fired simultaneously. The muzzle disappeared amid the flying bullets, and the van's engine cranked, then caught. But once again, the van bucked, and then the engine died.

Seconds later, all four doors flew open, and four men leaped out. One attacker blasted his machine gun at me, and two bullets slammed into my bulletproof vest, hurtling me backwards. I managed to get off two shots as I stumbled to regain my balance, and my assailant cried out, his gun clattering to the street. As he squatted to retrieve his fallen weapon, I barked, "Don't!"

The man straightened slowly, holding his right sleeve, which was now turning red with blood. A flash of movement behind my captive caught my eye. I fired twice more, hitting another assailant in the upper right thigh, and the man crumpled to the street. Behind him Mickey lay in his own blood, half his head blown away.

Fury raged in me as the second assailant tried to aim the machine gun he still clutched. "Go ahead," I growled, pointing my gun right between his eyes, "Give me a reason."

The captive glared at me with a feral look, then finally released his weapon and slid it across the pavement. I sidestepped to the side of the van, and then peered around to the front. Ricardo stood there, his gun trained on another of the assailants.

"You okay?" I called.

"Yea. I got lucky; this guy's gun jammed. And Sid captured the other one. You okay?"

"Your bullet-proof vest saved me...but Mickey wasn't so lucky."

Ricardo grabbed his captive and pulled him around behind the van where Mickey lay. He quivered as he fought back the tears. "He was the best," he finally managed to say, his voice husky. He looked over at Sid who had come alongside with his prisoner in tow. "Read them their rights." Then he looked up the street at the sound of sirens. Two police cars were wedging their way through the choke of traffic. "Then we'll take them downtown and get some answers."

I nodded, my expression grim. We had accomplished our goal, but had it been worth the price? I decided Mickey would have said the results justified his sacrifice. We had five of the mob members, plus a real shot at putting away Bellini who had slipped through the FBI's fingers for years. I, too, would have paid the price; the pain in my chest reminded me that I nearly did. Somebody had to stand up to this evil.

I would do it again.

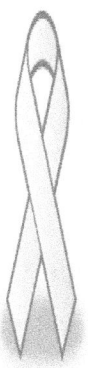

CHAPTER TWENTY-TWO

Accompanied by Sid and Mickey's replacement, Alberto, I met Ricardo at the Constitution Club at 5:30 the next afternoon. The two Agents stationed themselves by the door, and I ascended the marble steps to the Library, where Ricardo was waiting, reading *The Wall Street Journal.* "Learning anything?" I quipped.

"I'll leave this business game to you professionals. I know it all comes down to money, but how you get there is the great mystery. I'll take a nice simple kidnapping or terrorist plot any day."

I chuckled, then led the way across the marble foyer, through the billiard room and into the bar beyond. "What would you like?" I asked my guest.

"A sparkling mineral water with lime," Ricardo responded.

"Two sparkling mineral waters with lime, please, Clarence," I said to the bartender.

"What, no martini?" Ricardo mocked, with an exaggerated rise in his voice.

I gave Ricardo a half-smile. "Well, this morning I made a personal vow. No alcohol until the case is solved."

"That's admirable," Ricardo said, his tone now serious. He offered his hand. "Congratulations."

I nodded as I shook his hand. "Yesterday was mind boggling. I've really got to keep my wits about me."

"Speaking of yesterday, our first captive, DiNapoli, is telling all. He's given us enough names and dates to really nail Bellini this time. The unwelcome news is that, once again, we're coming up with only the Bradshaw link. DiNapoli says Bradshaw has given Bellini several CIA contracts, but Bradshaw is the only contact he knows."

"Maybe Bellini knows whom Bradshaw works for," I suggested as Clarence served our drinks.

"Could be, but Bradshaw is an old buddy of his; they were in the Green Berets together. If he knows anything more, I doubt that he will tell us. He'll be denying everything."

Ricardo paused as he looked around the spacious, high ceiling room. "This is the first time I've been here. I can see it's really steeped in tradition. And it's a veritable fortress."

"You know, I was thinking the same thing. Who knows what Bradshaw and Company are going to try next? I really don't want Pat in the middle of it. And I still think she may want to be more than friends."

"So, you'll move over here?"

"Yes. Tomorrow."

"Good. And it will be easier for Sid and the new man, Alberto, to protect you here."

"Are you Latinos taking over the FBI?" I jested.

"Give us another couple of hundred years," Ricardo laughed, "you know how slow we are.

"Alberto," he continued, "has just transferred back to Manhattan from Washington. He was CIA liaison down there, but before that, he was here for 10 years. He's a good man."

We finished our drinks, and then I headed for Pat's. When she opened the door to my knock, an appetizing aroma wafted out into the hallway. "What is that delicious smell?"

"A new sauce for the chicken," she responded, smiling at my compliment. "Another special recipe."

She led the way into the kitchen. "How are you feeling?" she asked.

"My chest is still sore, but otherwise I feel terrific. I've been thinking a lot about yesterday. I told you last night what happened, but not what really happened. Now I don't feel so powerless. Yesterday I really risked it all, with no escape clause, and, for a few seconds, I thought it was all over when those bullets were flying at me. But by my risking, Ricardo has five of them in custody, and we have a chance at finding out who's really behind it all."

Pat removed the sauce from the burner and began pouring it over the chicken breasts. "But it should be Ricardo and his men who are taking the risk," she protested. "They know what they're doing; you don't. I guess you can handle a gun, but it's not your job. It's the same as Ricardo trying to do your job; he doesn't have the fine-tuned skills."

I placed my hands on my hips. "Sometimes you have to stretch to stand up for what you believe in."

Pat looked at my determined face. "I still think you should leave it to the professionals," she grimaced. "Having said that, I do understand where you're coming from. I'll help you any way I am able."

"Thank you. What we're looking for now is a mob connection."

"The mob? At the company? Which one; Italian, Irish, Black, Latino? I can't believe it."

"Believe it. And it's Bellini."

Pat stared in disbelief. "Slippery Sal?"

"The very same. He's connected to Bradshaw; they were in the Service together. But there may also be a direct link between Bellini and somebody at Head Office."

"Nothing would surprise me at this point. I'll nose around the rumor mill for mob whispers."

Thinking of what Ricardo had said about Flannery and Casey, I said, "See if you hear anything about IRA connections as well."

Pat scowled. "Good God! This is beginning to sound like Zurich in the Thirties; bad guys everywhere."

"We just have to find the right person. And speaking of the right one, he or she must know we're getting close. We're expecting another attack. One of the Agents is in the lobby and the other is down the hall, but this place isn't all that defensible. Tomorrow I'm moving over to the Constitution Club because it is more secure. Besides, I don't want to lose a good friend."

Pat nodded but hurt showed in her eyes. "I agree, but for a different reason. I remembered what Walter told me about his divorce. Connecticut is a no-fault state, but the judges still look at adultery with disdain. We know we're not doing anything, but how would it look in court?"

"I get your point. And that reminds me. I need to sit down with Susan and hammer out the details of the divorce agreement. The whole thing comes down to money. We have no kids, so that makes it simple. We can keep the lawyers out of it. I'll go up early Saturday morning while she's sober and lay it out."

"There you go again trying to do everything yourself. Don't you think you ought to see a lawyer first? Remember, he's the professional."

"Yea," I said sarcastically, "just look at how they professionally handled this country. The number one profession in Congress is law. Look what they've done! God forbid if someone falls in front of your house; you'll be sued for everything you're worth. No, people should settle their problems by talking to each other directly, not through their greedy lawyers."

"Take it easy, Nick. I agree with you. Just get some guidelines. I mentioned Walter's divorce. He consulted a lawyer, but then negotiated the settlement himself, and he was ruthless. He claimed he had glossies of her and another man, and she believed him and admitted she had been having an affair. I can't blame her, the way he runs around. But anyway, she settled for half the house in Greenwich. He got the house in Southampton, the boat, and pays no alimony. Not too many people know that."

"Well, I don't think I should pay alimony either, but I believe we should split everything 50-50. Sell the house, divide the furnishings, and start over."

Pat smiled. "Good luck. I hope it's as simple as that. The only advice I can offer is to treat it like any other business negotiation; deal from strength. She's been having an affair, so call her on it. If there's something in the house she really wants, and you don't care about it, trade it for something you want and then some. Keep your anger and other feelings out of the negotiations."

"How in the blazes do you know so much about this?" I said, amazement filling my voice. "Are you divorced and haven't told me?"

"No," Pat chuckled, "but I have gone out with divorced men. Not one of their divorces was easy, and all said they let their emotions get in the way. Women's emotions are always right on the surface, even in divorce. What really surprises me is that men are in such control of their emotions in business and personal relationships, except when it comes to divorce."

My brow wrinkled as I remembered all the recent fights Susan and I had. She had run circles around me, always faster on her feet. I would get confused and tongue-tied. It was only later that I could think of the retorts. It was no wonder men lost the divorce battles; they were completely outmatched. Why did men lose control of their emotions when it came to divorce?

"I guess it has to do with guilt," I said aloud. "In my own case, we both know our marriage is over, but because Susan said she still wanted to work things out, I feel guilty for not wanting to. And I'm sure if a guy had a child, he'd feel twice as guilty. He wants to make it okay and gets drawn into the emotional battle in which he gets killed."

"Come to think of it, the divorced guys did talk a lot about guilt. The only one who didn't was Walter. He handled it as though it were a business deal, and he's the only one who reached a reasonable settlement."

I nodded. "It sounds as though in his case, the wife was coming from guilt, not Walter.

"Well," I continued, "I'm going for a reasonable settlement as well. I'm putting it all down on paper and keeping my emotions somewhere else. First thing Saturday morning."

After dinner, the phone rang. Pat answered it, then a sad, rejected expression crossed her face, and she handed the phone to me, saying, "It's for you."

"Hello," I spoke into the instrument.

"Nick, it's Marilyn." Her voice was frantic.

"Marilyn. Are you okay? How did you find me?"

"I called the FBI and finally found Ricardo. He told me where you're staying. I didn't know what to do." She now sounded desperate.

"Your wound. Are you having a relapse?"

"No, no. It's been 3 weeks. It's all healed."

"Well then, what's wrong?" I asked, my voice inflicting with worry.

"Wiley knows that man Bradshaw! He's going to meet him!"

"What?" I was incredulous.

"Bradshaw called here a little while ago, looking for Wiley. He left a Washington number. I didn't think too much about it, since Senator Crock was killed, and Wiley said he was running for the open seat."

"I saw his announcement on the news."

"Anyway, when Wiley got home, he said Bradshaw was a buddy of his from the Green Berets, and he was going to meet him in San Francisco for a reunion. I remembered who Bradshaw was. It was all I could do not to run screaming from the house that instant."

"Where are you?"

"The computer lab at Stanford. I told Wiley that I had to complete a program for the fall quarter. I'm afraid to go home!"

"Okay," I reassured her. "Calm down. Just because Wiley knows Bradshaw doesn't mean the worst; it may be simply a reunion. In any event, go home and act naturally. If he is involved, you don't want to raise any of his suspicions"

I paused. "Are you through for the summer quarter?"

"Yes. Just finished. Wiley and I had been planning a cruise, but because of the race he can't go."

"As I recall, your parents live around here, don't they?"

"Yes. They still live in Manhattan."

"Then come visit them. Tomorrow."

"But Wiley wants me to stay here and campaign with him."

"Tell him you're stressed out and need a week off. Which is true."

Marilyn chuckled, then sighed in relief. "Okay. I think it will work. I'll book the flight right now."

The next day I worked on the property settlement draft during lunch, then caught the 3:37 express train to Greenwich. Flanked by Sid and Alberto, I walked from the station to the office of my lawyer, Bart Shatto. At precisely 4:30, I was ushered into Bart's office. As we shook hands, Bart said, "I was sorry to hear about you and Susan. Are you really sure you want to go through with the divorce?"

"Yes," was my emphatic reply.

"Why?" Bart shot back.

I recoiled slightly. "Well," I started, "Well, we fight like demons."

"Everybody fights. It's healthy."

"I don't think it is," I rebutted. "She abusive. And besides, she's cheating on me."

"Who's she fucking?"

I shook my head. "Bart, I don't know. She wouldn't tell me."

"Find out. Connecticut judges are still conservative, so if we can prove she's violating the sacred marriage bed, we can force a great settlement. There are an increasing number of cases in which the judge awards alimony to the wronged husband."

"Hold on, Bart," I said, shoving my arm towards him to emphasize the point. I don't want to break Susan's back; I want a nice, simple divorce."

"There's no such thing. Once you have decided to proceed with divorce, my job is to smash the marriage and get the best deal for you. Divorce is disunion, so it's a messy, complicated business."

"By your definition, but not mine. To me divorce equals money, and I'm willing to be fair."

I handed the draft to Bart, saying, "So I want you to look this over and tell me if you think it will fly."

Bart read through the agreement while I waited in silence. Finally, he looked up and grimaced with disgust. "If I were Susan's lawyer, this would be what I could only hope for in my wet dreams; the opening barrage, as it were. Hell! You're giving her half of everything!"

"I believe that's fair." My tone was level. "I just want to know if you think it will be accepted by the court."

"If you sign it and she signs it, sure it will fly in court. Has Susan seen this yet?"

"No, but she's agreed to review it Saturday morning."

"I think you're making a big mistake," Bart warned. "I know women; she'll want more, no matter what you offer. Hell, you make 100 times what Susan does, so it makes no sense to give her 50 per cent. The major issue of the court is financial provision for any minor children. Goddamn, you've got no kids!"

"But she wants kids in the future. With half the assets, she can make a fresh start, have her kids, and not worry about the future."

"Nick, why don't you let her future husband worry about that? Listen to me! Give her one-third if you insist on being more than fair. Hell, if it were me, I wouldn't give her a goddamn cent if she were out fucking around!"

"You don't have to be crude, Bart."

"The hell I don't! You're not listening to me! I know how these things work; these women are vindictive! No matter what you offer, she's going to want more, just to be a fucking bitch!"

Bart's face was deep red. He took a deep breath, and then continued, "Look, Nick. Just leave it to me. I'll contact her lawyer, and the two of us will work it out"

"Like this?" I chuckled. "Thanks anyway, Bart, but Susan and I will work it out. You've warned me, and, for the record, I have listened to you. But I just don't feel as ruthless as you are, at least with Susan."

Bart took another deep breath, and then sighed. "All right, Nick. Just don't sign anything. Let me know what she says, but I'll bet you a hundred bucks she won't agree to it. Oh, and thanks for that ruthless compliment; I pride myself being that way in my business."

"You're welcome, and you're on for that hundred-dollar bet."

When I returned to my room at the Constitution Club that evening, the phone was ringing. It was Marilyn. "Are you at your parents?" I asked.

"Yes, in my old room. They think I'm calling Wiley."

"Are you all right? I mean your bullet wound; you didn't really say last night."

"I'm fine; I was incredibly lucky. And I only have a little scar," she laughed. "I'll show it to you someday. I should have called you, but I didn't want to interfere."

"It wouldn't have mattered; Susan and I didn't make it. And I didn't want to call you, so you could get you head together."

"I'm sorry to hear about you and Susan. Are you sure it's over?"

"Yes, she's found someone else. What about you and Wiley? I mean forgetting this Bradshaw business for a moment."

"It was coming apart. He's been suspicious of my every move, even in the hospital; he thought I was having an affair with Dr. Burroughs. And when I told him I was going to Mom's and Dad's for a rest, he accused me of coming to see you." She laughed. "He got that right."

"We need to be extremely careful. If Wiley is in Bradshaw's league, he's undoubtedly having you followed. And, of course, I'm being followed all the time."

I paused as a plan began taking shape in my mind. "Look. I'm going to Greenwich early tomorrow morning to review the property settlement with Susan. I should be back in time to make the 12:15 Circle Line sailing to Bear Mountain."

"What a wonderful idea! And I'll pack a picnic lunch. I know a place where my parents used to take me near the landing."

"That sounds great! I'll ask Ricardo to meet you at your parents' place, and I'm sure he can slip you out unnoticed. What are you going to tell your folks?"

Marilyn giggled. "I'll say I'm going for some mountain air."

I took the 8:10 train to Greenwich the next morning. As my FBI companions and I rode in silence in the taxi from the station, sadness welled up in me. The memories of the good times with Susan exacerbated my pain, because I knew they were gone forever and there would be no more with her. I began wondering whether there had been that many troubled times; more than 50 per cent. And had they been that bad? I decided that in the past year the bad had been more than half the time, and it really had been that bad. Yet I stubbornly clung to those good memories.

I remembered the early days in Mexico. Spending an exciting Sunday afternoon at the bullfights, balanced the following Sunday by boating slowly around Xochimilco, the floating gardens. Then there were the vigorous climbs up the steep Teotihuacan Pyramids, followed by a relaxing lunch at the nearby cave restaurant, La Gruta.

I recalled horseback riding in the Grand Tetons during one of our infrequent vacations. How connected to Susan, Nature, and God I had felt then. What had happened?

I suddenly realized that we had stopped doing what little we had in common together. After that they were her vacations. The time we rented the house in Acapulco for two weeks over Christmas, we had gone with her friends and their husbands. None of them wanted to play golf or tennis, saying that it was just too hot. All they wanted to do was drink, eat, lay on the beach and shop. I finally met the owner of Cerveca Fina who invited me to play at Villa Vera. But I played only once, despite repeated invitations from the beer baron because Susan gave me such grief about "deserting everyone."

Then we sold our place in Manhattan and moved up to the little house in Greenwich. And we filled up the house with her things and with her friends from the publishing world. She wanted nothing to do with my friends; "all they ever do is talk about the stock market and golf," she would say. I finally insisted on the big house, so I could entertain my friends, who were mostly from business. Now, I realized I was seeking a refuge.

Then I remembered her BMW. "What's wrong with your Buick?" I had asked.

"I'm worth more," she had said.

The cab driver swung off North Street and accelerated up the driveway, snapping me back into reality. The driver followed the circle at the top of the hill and pulled up at the front door. We emerged from the cab, Alberto went around back, Sid stationed himself at the front door, and I went inside.

Susan was waiting in the kitchen, dressed in flowered shorts and pink shirt. Her face reflected her fatigue, and she was sipping black coffee. I took a deep breath, and then blew it out. "Good morning, Susan. How are you?"

Susan's attack was instantaneous. "What do you care? You never gave a shit about me! All you ever cared about was that goddamn job of yours! And I never wanted this goddamn house! And that Buick! I was embarrassed to drive around in it!"

Anger stirred in me, then rushed to my temples. I opened my mouth to defend myself, then closed it as I remembered my commitment keep my emotions out of it.

"What's the matter, cat caught your tongue?" she taunted. "Or does the truth make you speechless?"

"I'm not going to get into it, Susan. We both want a divorce, and I'm here to give you a settlement."

"Give me a settlement!" she shrieked. "Give me a settlement! I'll take everything you've got! I don't want this divorce! You do! And it will cost you everything to get it!"

"Susan. Listen. You want this divorce as much as I do. You've met someone—"

"I do not!" she interrupted. "You're the one who's giving up! You're the one who doesn't want to work things out! You're the one who doesn't want kids!"

"That's what I was starting to say. You've met someone, so raise the family you want with him."

Susan scowled, probing my eyes with hers. "So, you admit it. You still don't want children."

I was tempted to simply agree. Instead, I said, "I don't want children with you."

Susan's clenched fist flew from my blind side, slamming into my jaw. White light flashed in the front of my eyes and pain seared through my jaw to the top of my head. "You son of a bitch!" she screamed. "You son of a bitch! All these years! All these years you didn't want kids, and now you do, but not with me! You want them with your precious cunt Marilyn!"

"We have no plan."

"You liar!" She drew back her fist, but I grabbed her arm. "You hit me again, and I'll have to flatten you. You have hit me and screamed at me for the last time. I have never hit you back. But, by God, this time I will."

Susan's arm went limp. She burst into tears. "Oh, Nick. I'm so sorry. It's just ... it's just that you get me so angry." Then she started shaking all over as she sobbed uncontrollably.

A wave of pity swept through me. I wondered what I had done to her. I wondered if I were as awful as she said. I agonized over these questions as Susan wept. Then it dawned on me that Susan was throwing every manipulation she knew at me. "No more," I said quietly.

Susan looked up quickly, tears rolling down her cheeks. "What ... what ... do ... do you mean?" she asked between sobs.

"No more histrionics. I don't want to go through this anymore. We both know we should be divorced. We have no future together. We both know that splitting the assets down the middle is more than I must do, but I am willing to do that to give you a fresh start. But I will not pay alimony. Your half will be more than ample to provide a comfortable life for you. Is this agreeable?"

"If you only knew..." she started, and then stopped.

"Knew what?"

The shake of her head was barely perceptible. "Nothing," she said finally.

"Is this agreeable?" I repeated.

This time the nod of her head was barely perceptible. "Yes," she whispered.

"Good. I'll send a draft of the agreement to you Monday."

"So, you're really leaving," she murmured, as a statement rather than a question.

I nodded my head slowly. I turned quickly, and then left, to hide the tears rolling down my cheeks.

CHAPTER TWENTY-THREE

I waited impatiently by the ticket booth on the pier. Flanked once again by Sid and Alberto, I scanned all directions, particularly the north, the direction from which Ricardo and Chet should be bringing Marilyn. Finally, on one of my glances to the south, I spotted the familiar red head bobbing and weaving through the crowd with Ricardo at her side.

When Marilyn spotted me, she broke into a run. I rushed towards her as well and swept her up in my arms. I swung her around in a full circle, and then eased her to the sidewalk. "How I missed you," she breathed.

"And I missed you," I echoed, grinning like a teenager with his first love. "What took you so long?"

"You were right; we were followed. It took us a long time to lose them."

"Well you're here now. Come on. They just announced final call."

We boarded the red and white double-decked boat and mounted the stairs to the upper deck. There were plenty of seats still available, so our little company settled down in the first two rows of chairs in the bright sunlight on the starboard side.

Moments later the boat engines roared to life and the guide announced over the loudspeaker we would depart immediately. One of the crewmen cast off the lines, and the *Lady Jane* glided gently away from her berth onto the mid-summer smoothness of the Hudson River. That tranquility could suddenly erupt into treachery with the violence of a summer thunderstorm, but the forecast was for clear skies the next five days.

Soon we were steaming past the magnificent old pre-war buildings, with water towers still crowning their roofs. A few minutes later the clusters of humanity grew sparser, leaving the stands of ancient tall trees, with deep green leaves, and solid brown trunks and branches. The brilliant sun beat down on us.

"How about a soda from the snack bar?" I suggested.

"Mmmm," Marilyn gurgled. "That sounds great. I went for a run this morning, and after chasing Ricardo around, I have a massive thirst."

I crossed the deck, and then approached the bulkhead. I glanced back to see Ricardo following me, and Marilyn leaning back in her chair, closing her eyes, and basking in the sun. There was no line at the snack bar, and a brief time later I was back on the upper deck, approaching Marilyn. She fluttered her eyes open and looked up at my tension-ridden face. I smiled slightly as I handed her the soda, then she said, "Thank you, Nick," taking a sip. "Now, please sit down and relax. Take a couple of deep breaths. The sun is wonderful; just what the doctor ordered for both of us."

I smiled again, and then eased myself into the deck chair. I took a deep breath, held it, and then blew it out with a groan. I took another deep breath, held it, and then let it out slowly. I felt my tension ebbing, replaced with the flow of relaxation. "Ah," I sighed, looking into Marilyn's peaceful emerald-green eyes. "That's better. I needed that. Thanks."

The mammoth George Washington Bridge loomed above us now, its crossing humanity contrasting with the wilderness. A Boeing 767 streaked across the horizon. "I don't remember seeing planes take off in that direction," Marilyn observed, taking another sip of her soda.

"They usually don't; the wind must have shifted, so they've got to take off to the west."

"How would you know about that?" Marilyn teased. "I thought all you cared about was the oil business, the stock market and fine wines."

"You left out running," I protested.

"All right, running," Marilyn conceded. "But airplanes?"

"They're a secret passion of mine. My Great-Grandfather was a military pilot, and then became a test pilot. He had exceptional stories, and, well, it must be in my blood. I still want to learn to fly."

"Well then learn," Marilyn suggested.

"But—" I started to protest.

Marilyn cut me off with a wave of her hand. "And don't bother with the excuses."

I grinned. "Yes ma'am," I agreed.

The George Washington Bridge was receding in the distance, and both sides of the Hudson were now steep cliffs, covered with thick green foliage. "This reminds me of some parts of the Rhine," I observed.

"But these cliffs are steeper," Marilyn said, pointing to the western bank, and shivering slightly. "The Palisades still scare me. I went hiking there when I was in high school, and one of the girls in the group slipped on the edge of the cliff and fell to her death. I never went back."

"I don't blame you," I commiserated. "How awful."

Marilyn's smile was wan. "Actually, I should go back up there now to deal with that fear. Anyway, let's talk about something more pleasant. Tell me about your running; I remember you were good back in school. Are you still racing?"

"No, not since school, and I was in much better shape then."

"Why aren't you racing?"

I frowned. "No time," I protested.

"That's ridiculous," she chided.

I flushed slightly. "I was afraid of failing," I admitted. "Success has always been important to me. I used to feel that if I couldn't be the best at something, it wasn't worth doing."

Marilyn drained the last of the soda from the can. "Used to?"

"I guess more than my body was shaken up when that bomb went off at Las Palmas. Some of the things I thought were important — well, they don't matter that much anymore. I've realized that in an absolute sense there can be only one victor, but life in the absolute isn't very much fun. Now I believe I can be satisfied with the best that I can be at what I'm doing at a given moment under given circumstances. I feel that's what we should all do; nothing more and nothing less. You know, I will start racing, and it's okay if I don't win now. Maybe by next year, I will, but it doesn't really matter."

Marilyn smiled at me, caught my gaze, and held it. "Now you look as young as you did when we were in school. Your face is relaxed, your eyes are alive, and you don't look so driven anymore."

"Being here with you is the reason. The trick is to stay relaxed all the time. I don't know how."

"It isn't easy. Our jobs alone create tremendous tension. I know what it is for me; Stanford is a very politically correct institution. We can't simply teach what we feel the students should learn. I can just imagine what it's like for you, being bombarded from all sides.

"But," she continued, "I've found a few simple aides. Running helps ease the tension. Eating a balanced diet does as well. And the occasional glass of wine."

Smiling, I shook my head. "We've known each other a very long time, but I never knew any of this about you."

"Well, I wasn't like this when you knew me," she laughed. "I just wanted to have a good time, remember? And the wine was a lot more than occasionally. Truth be known, I have Wiley to thank for the little secrets. He taught me the value of carbohydrates as tension relievers and proteins to enhance clear thinking. He also showed me the article on the French study, which correlated moderate red wine consumption with lower incidence of heart disease. Running really helped too, particularly after Wiley and I had a major fight. I would return from the run with all the hurt, anger and tension gone. Wiley got me into running as well; he's been running all his life, even in the Green Berets—

She interrupted herself, "I want to thank you for sending Reverend Renaud to me when I was in the hospital. I was really confused, and he reminded me that clarity would come through prayer and meditation. He told me not to push the decision, and that the answer would come when I needed it. Boy was he right about that!"

She grimaced. "I still can't believe this about Wiley."

"We don't know for sure," I said in a reassuring tone.

"Ricardo and I were followed!"

"Maybe they were just following Ricardo."

Marilyn sighed. "Well, maybe you're right. To know Bradshaw doesn't have to mean he's in this thing with him. Regardless, I have made my decision. I want to be with you, if you still want me."

I reached across and covered her hand with mine. "I've always wanted to be with you, and I always will." I leaned over and we gently kissed.

I leaned back in my deck chair, took a deep breath, and then blew it out. "Getting back to stress," I said, "the worst has been the competition for Sullivan's job. The toughest direct competitor has been Walter Melville because we were so much alike."

"I remember you mentioned him; he runs International, doesn't he? Your old job."

"And now that Sullivan's supporting me to take over, it somehow doesn't seem as important as it once did. I almost feel as though Melville can have the bloody job."

"Nick," Marilyn said, as though talking to a small child, "the job is never as important as we think it is. It is an important part of life because we spend so much time doing it, but it is only a part. Now, today, tonight, tomorrow, you're not doing it, so forget about Sullivan, Melville and UNRC. Now we're here on this boat, so enjoy the sun, the water, the warm breeze, and me."

I reached across and touched Marilyn's cheek. "Forget the rest; I'm enjoying you." I left my hand on her face for several moments as though to fuse the bond that was soaring between us. Then slowly, reluctantly, I withdrew my hand as I remembered I was still married. Somehow that had become sacred to me once again.

The *Lady Jane* continued her leisurely voyage towards Bear Mountain. On the way the cruise guide cited points of interest, including the Harriman Estate and the Tappan Zee Bridge, the gateway to Washington Irving's Sleepy Hollow country. Gradually our destination rose in the distance, appearing much closer than it was because of the pristine air. As we neared, Marilyn and I, surrounded by our entourage, descended to the main deck.

When we disembarked, we gathered at the end of the pier and scrutinized the few passengers that followed and passed us. Then Alberto turned and headed for the telephone, saying, "I'll check in."

Marilyn handed the picnic basket and blankets to me, saying, "I'll take this opportunity to powder my nose."

Ricardo scanned the sparse crowd once more and found it to be solely comprised of families and couples. "I believe we can give you and

Marilyn a little space. We'll follow you into the woods close enough to keep you in sight, but you might have to strain to see us."

A few minutes later, Marilyn emerged from the snack bar, followed shortly thereafter by Alberto. We set out for the woods, with Marilyn and I in the lead, and the FBI following in the distance. Very quickly the trees closed around us and the brightness of the day dimmed. Under our feet, the forest floor was spongy, a thick mat of pine needles and leaves that had fallen over the years. We picked our way through the maze for several minutes until we came upon a clearing, a huge meadow shimmering with sunlight. Wildflowers sprang up through the green sea of grass, and a wisp of warm air caressed our faces. We paused at its edge, nurturing ourselves with the natural beauty.

Our guardians arrived a few moments later, and Ricardo scanned the panorama with partial admiration and partial strategic evaluation. "This will do," he grunted. "You and Marilyn set up just behind that tiny knoll; that will protect you from this direction. We'll guard your backs and flanks.

Marilyn opened the picnic basket I was carrying and handed out sandwiches to Ricardo, Sid, Chet, and Alberto. Uttering thanks, they spread out to their positions at the forest's edge. Marilyn and I crossed into the meadow, went over the knoll, and settled into the cusp between the knoll and the hummock beyond.

I spread out the blanket on a patch of grass encircled by wildflowers, and we settled in. Opening the basket she had placed behind her, Marilyn reached in and withdrew a sandwich, saying, "Choice of one—turkey."

"My favorite," I chuckled. "You remembered."

"How could I forget? That's all you ever used to eat."

She handed the plastic wrapped sandwich to me, and then reached back into the basket again. "I've also brought you potato salad."

I pulled off the plastic wrap and bit into my sandwich. After I chewed and swallowed, I said, "This is delicious; you even remembered the mustard!"

"Thank you, but I can't really claim the credit. First, food always tastes better at a picnic."

"This is true," I agreed.

"And second," Marilyn continued, "I bought the turkey breast at the deli around the corner from my parents' place. Sol cooks it fresh every day; Lord, he must be a hundred by now!"

Suddenly a huge bumblebee buzzed right at our heads. Instinctively we both dove for the blanket and wound up with our legs entangled, side-by-side. We burst into laughter simultaneously and roared, peal after peal. Finally, Marilyn gasped, "Stop! I can't ... I can't laugh ... anymore ... It hurts!"

"That ... was," I said, struggling to catch my breath, "a buzz bomb!"

We erupted into giggles again, this time tears rolling down our cheeks. "Stop! ... Stop!" Marilyn pleaded again. "Your laughing ... makes me laugh!"

"Okay ... okay," I finally managed, catching my breath. I inhaled deeply, and then exhaled with a groan. "Wow. I really needed that."

"We both did. I can't remember when I last laughed like this."

Our eyes caught each other's gaze, and we each saw our joy mirrored in the other. Impulsively I reached over and gently touched Marilyn's right cheek. Then I began stroking her silky soft skin. Marilyn's face flushed a deep red at once, and she began caressing the back of my hand with her long fingertips. "Ah," she sighed. "I've been wanting you to touch me again for hours."

"Believe me, I've wanted to! But then I remember I'm still married."

"There's no harm in this," Marilyn ventured.

"Oh yes there is," I chuckled. "I don't know about you, but I'm only a silly millimeter away from totally losing it."

"I'm dangling at the edge as well," Marilyn responded, "and I'm still a lot more reckless than you are. So..." her voice inflecting upwards as she patted the back of my hand, "we'd better let this lay, as it were." We both chuckled.

After we finished lunch, Marilyn lay down on the blanket, stretched, and yawned. "You know, I could actually take a nap. I feel safe here."

"Go ahead. It's really relaxing here. I might not be far behind you."

I lay back, clasping my hands behind my head and gazing up into the clear, deep blue sky. We had been avoiding discussing Wiley, and now speculation ran rampant through my mind. Despite my reassuring Marilyn, I was convinced Wiley was part of the plot. Both he and Bradshaw were involved in politics, a dirty game. And I simply didn't like the guy. I wondered for a moment if my judgment was being colored by my love for Marilyn, but then surrendered to my gut feel that Wiley was in it up to his eyeballs.

I closed my eyes and my mind journeyed back to the beginning at Las Palmas, looking for the link. I had a vague feeling there was still a critical clue to be unearthed, but even as I carefully sifted through all that had happened, it remained hidden.

Suddenly an image of a cave floated into my mind's eye, and I felt myself shooting down a dark hole, then popping out onto a field of rolling hills. I climbed up the first knoll, down into the vale, then up the next, steeper rise. I looked up towards the summit, and I saw a large figure waiting for me. This was the same journey I had experienced when I had been at Stanford Hospital.

As I approached the figure, I saw it was that of a boy. The face was familiar, but I couldn't quite place it... He seemed to be from long ago... Then I remembered. It was Hank, my best friend in high school who had died of leukemia in our senior year.

Hank smiled, and we embraced. I knew I had found my guardian angel. Slowly I drifted back to the here and now and opened my eyes.

I rolled over on my side and looked over at Marilyn. Her eyes were closed, and she was breathing the slow, full breaths of deep sleep. Her breasts rose and fell tantalizingly. Quickly I looked away, but just as quickly a patch of the strikingly beautiful wildflowers in the distance arrested my gaze. I rose, glanced around at the horizon, and then sauntered over. The stand was tall and dense, and the wildflowers were pink, yellow, violet, and white, unlike anything I had ever seen. I hesitated as I bent over them, feeling irreverent with my intention to pick the flowers. Then I noticed several other clumps further in the distance, so I went ahead and plucked mine. I carried my find back to the blanket and kneeled at its edge.

Marilyn's eyes fluttered open. "Good morning, Nick," she said, her voice still sluggish with sleep. She blinked a few more times as she focused on the flowers. "Oh, Nick! Thank you! They're beautiful! And, my Lord! They're Alpine Daisies! I've never seen any around here. Only out west; high in the mountains."

"I felt guilty digging them up, but I saw others nearby, just like them. I've never seen so many colors growing out of the same plant ... Then again, I never spent much time looking at flowers. Even when I was outside playing golf or running, I concentrated on what I was doing, not on my surroundings."

Even now, as I spoke, my image of the golf course was my clubs, the ball, and only a vague sense of green. But my images of running were a bit sharper; the bright blue skies, the crunch of my feet on the leaves as I ran through the woods, and the smell of fresh cut grass rose into my consciousness. I was paying more attention now, after being close to death so many times.

Marilyn's voice cut through my daydreaming. "Do you meditate?"

Surprised, I looked at her with a scowl. "Not really. Carib mentioned something about it, but I really don't think it's for me. It may be all right for some people, but I don't see its value. Maybe to relax or something..."

"Or something more." Marilyn stood up and extended her hand. "Come on. I'll give you a start."

I kept my kneeling position. "I don't know..."

"What does that matter? Are you afraid of a West Coast flake? You were one once too. Remember?"

"This is true," I acknowledged and then rose slowly, gently closing my fingers around the back of her extended hand. We ambled through the ankle-high grass towards a large clump of Alpine Daisies. When we reached our destination, I glanced all around and felt reassured as I spotted Ricardo, Chet, Sid, and Alberto just inside the wood's edge. Still, I had a nagging feeling that all was not well. "What's wrong?" Marilyn asked.

"Nothing. I was just making sure everything's all right."

She looked at me quizzically for a moment, then her face relaxed. "Now find a comfortable spot," she instructed, "and lie down."

I know my face reflected the doubt I felt, but nevertheless I eased myself onto an island of moss in the meadow. "I feel silly ... What's next?"

"It's okay to feel silly. That's what meditation is all about; getting in touch with yourself. Letting things flow.

"Now just stretch out and let your arms flop down by your side," she continued her instructions. "Good. Now close your eyes."

I blinked once, and then shut my eyelids. "Okay," Marilyn resumed, "now take a deep breath and hold it ... Good. Now let it out with a loud sigh. Take another deep breath and hold it ... Now let it out slowly between your teeth and release all your tension with it."

I made a hissing sound as I released my breath between my teeth. And strangely, I did imagine my fears and anxieties flowing out of my soul on the stream of air. I swallowed, and then became aware my stomach was relaxed; the usual knot was gone.

"Now imagine yourself stepping into a brilliant beam of white light. You're standing right next to it, and now, go ahead. Step right into the full glare of it ... Let it flow through you, cleansing you and protecting you...

"Now imagine," she continued, "that the white light changes color to a radiant red. And don't worry if you don't see the red; just think red. Let it flow through you ... Okay, now the red fades and becomes orange. Again, let it flow through you ... and the orange fades now and becomes yellow. Let it flow ... Now the yellow fades and the light is now green. Bask in it."

I did. A surge of green light flowed out of my soul's eye and washed over me. A deep, rich forest green filled me instantly.

"Now the green fades and becomes blue ... Okay. The blue disappears, and purple replaces it ... Now the purple is gone and you're standing in violet ... Feel the rich violet flowing through you...

"Now you are centered. Images will be coming up. Just let them come and go."

And the images did come. After a few moments of emptiness, the memory of being lost in Ensenada, Mexico surged into my soul. I was five years old, shopping with my parents, but then I had an urge for ice cream and wandered off in search of it. I couldn't find it anywhere and then couldn't find my way back. I was terrified. Then a policeman spoke to me in a strange language and led me to the jail. Finally, my Dad came charging in shouting. "How could you do this?" My Mother screamed, "You scared us to death!" Fear and guilt knotted in my stomach, but then gradually released their hold. I felt strangely light.

Suddenly the blast of the bomb at Las Palmas flashed into my soul, then darkness. Gradually light penetrated the darkness as I awakened in the hospital, followed at once by the panic of paralysis, but then the fear seemed to burst and scatter like snowflakes.

The specters of the other attempts rose up; the ambulance wreck, the sniper at the house, the hotel fire, finally the mob shootout. Then a prolonged period of emptiness.

Gradually a blue-green image began to take shape. I realized it was a body of water. Then there was another shape; it looked like ... I wasn't sure ... yes, it was a boat. And what was on the stern? A black flag? Then deep down, under the layers of protective covering, I felt a hint of panic. A shiver rushed up my spine and my panic erupted. I flipped my eyelids open as though to deny the reality of my panic, seeking solace in the brilliant blue sky above. But the fear remained. Slowly I raised myself to a sitting position. "Oh my God," I murmured, still seeking to exorcise the fear.

"What did you see?" Marilyn asked quickly.

I described the Mexico and murder attempt images to her. "And then," I continued, "I saw a boat. I don't ever remember seeing it before ... But then again, I used to go out on my Great-Grandfather's boat when I was quite young ... And there's something scary about it. I do remember being scared those first few times out with my Great-Grandfather." The fear lingered. I shook my head as though to rid myself of it.

"How do you feel?" Marilyn asked.

"I feel kind of funny," I responded. "The terror I would feel whenever I thought about being lost in Mexico or being paralyzed in that hospital has all vanished. But that boat..." Shaking my head, I said, "I wish I could remember."

Marilyn smiled. "You will." Then she looked down at her watch and sighed. "I guess we'd better be heading back to the landing."

Ricardo led the way back through the forest, followed by Marilyn and me, then Sid, Chet, and Alberto brought up the rear. The afternoon sun spread its shafts of lights through the trees, and hosts of birds chirped and flitted from branch to branch. I looked across to Marilyn, saying, "You know, it's hard to believe there's evil lurking out there, maybe even behind the next tree."

"Don't imagine the evil. Enjoy the here and now. We'll deal with the evil when it arises."

I patted the gun under my seersucker jacket. "I am enjoying being here, but I am ready for the evil."

A few minutes later we emerged from the woods onto the riverbank. Below us, our boat appeared on the far horizon, slowly cruising towards us. We wended our way down the riverbank trail to the landing. Ricardo led us to the far corner, away from the other passengers. "Wait here," he instructed, and then Sid, Alberto, Chet, and he fanned out in a protective web.

"I've been thinking about this meditation," I began. "When should I do it?"

"Twice a day, morning and night, until you get the hang of it. And if you feel particularly stressed during the day, close your door and take a twenty-minute meditation break."

"At the office?" My voice rose with incredulity.

"I do it all the time."

"But ... but you're—"

"A West Coast flake," Marilyn laughed, finishing my sentence. "I know."

"That's not what I meant," I defended myself. "You're a professor. You can take breaks during the day."

"Oh yea?" Marilyn countered, a little pugnaciously. "My 422 students are always after me. How many people are after you?"

I grinned sheepishly. "I take your point. But why at the office?"

"Because it really will help reduce the stresses of the day. And another thing, you should know. You've been meditating before today. Running is another form of meditation. It helps clear your consciousness of a lot of trivia. A lot of truths come to you when you're running."

I thought for a moment, and then nodded my head. "You know, I believe you're right. Many answers to difficult business problems have come to me when I've been running."

"If you allow yourself," Marilyn suggested, "you might find the answers to many questions. Stick with it. Meditation is like any skill; it takes a while to develop. I started a couple of years ago, but then stopped after a few months. I only resumed earlier this year, and I can tell you, it really has made an enormous difference in my life."

A pained expression crossed her face. "I know we've avoided talking about Wiley all afternoon, but I saw him as a conspirator when I meditated this morning. I saw him standing on a dock with a group of men. A giant whale swam to the side of the dock, his back opened, and Wiley and the others climbed inside. It was like a submarine, complete with periscope. They put out to sea underwater, and eventually an oil tanker appeared in the periscope sights. Someone fired several torpedoes, which missed the tanker. The ship finally started firing back, and the whale turned and swam away."

"Good Lord, how weird!" I exclaimed. "What does it mean?"

"Most of the meditation imagery is weird, filled with symbols. What it suggests to me is that Wiley is in the thick of this conspiracy directed at you, symbolized by the tanker."

I saw Ricardo beckoning us out of the corner of my eye. The *Lady Jane* was approaching the dock, cutting a white foamy wake in the blue water of the Hudson. As Marilyn and I made for the dock, the deep roar of her engines ceased, followed moments later by a high-pitched whine as the captain reversed the power. The vessel slowed as the captain slipped the controls into neutral, and she glided into her berth.

Two hands, one forward and one aft, threw lines compatriots waiting on the dock. When the lines were secured, another hand lowered the gangway onto the dock. Ricardo sprang onto it as soon as it touched down, racing ahead, while Sid, Chet, and Alberto buffered Marilyn and me from the other passengers as we waited. After they climbed up the gangway, Ricardo reappeared at the railing and nodded the all-clear sign. We boarded, and Alberto remained on the lower deck while we mounted the steps to the upper. Sid posted himself in a chair next to the stairway, and Marilyn and I took seats in an empty row along the railing. Ricardo and Chet sat in the empty row behind us. The engines roared, and moments later, the captain began backing away from the dock.

I glanced around at the other passengers. "They look harmless enough," I murmured, "but I have this very uneasy feeling."

"Don't ignore the feeling," Marilyn advised. "Besides, I feel it too."

The *Lady Jane* gathered speed, whipping up a breeze into our faces, breaking the hot stillness of the late afternoon. There were other boaters on the river that waved as they cruised past the *Lady Jane.*

After being in the warmth and the lulling breeze for a while, I began to nod off, despite my uneasy feeling. Part of me felt safe and secure. We were protected by the FBI and away from Manhattan's millions, where death could come from any direction. Yet, I still hadn't been able to shake the sense of foreboding. Marilyn had said to stay with the feeling, but I didn't want to think about it. I felt myself nodding again, and this time I let my chin drop to my chest.

My dream started on my Great-Grandfather's yacht, but he wasn't there, and I was fully-grown. And it wasn't California; I was on the Hudson River, alone, with no captain and no crew. The boat was just drifting...

Then a boat appeared down river, long, sleek, black, and powerful. At first the engines were a distant hum. They gradually grew louder, until they had risen to a roar.

The black boat shot past, then suddenly veered to the left, cut across my wake, then swung back towards my starboard side. Fear sprang into my soul, and I popped open my eyelids. There, 300 yards away, the black boat was hurtling straight towards us. I glanced quickly over at Marilyn whose eyes were closed. I spotted Ricardo two rows back, but he was scanning the other passengers. I shifted my gaze back on the black boat, spotting a rifle equipped with a telescopic lens pointing straight at me. I reached over and grabbed Marilyn, and both of us fell to the deck just as the bullet whizzed over our heads. Milliseconds later the rifle report shattered the air.

Dazed, Marilyn stared at me. "What ... what happened?" Before I could answer, a second bullet ripped through the railing just to our left. "Stay down!" I shouted. "It's the black boat in my vision!"

Another blast erupted, but this was Ricardo's .038. He fired again, then dove for the railing as the assassin swung and fired at him.

Screams and shouts burst all around us as the other passengers scrambled for cover. Ricardo peered over the railing, drawing another assassin's bullet that narrowly missed its mark. Ricardo squeezed off another round at the gunman who was now only 50 yards away. Ricardo's bullet crashed into its target, felling the assassin to the deck. The skipper of the black boat swung hard to the port, crossed back over the *Lady Jane*'s wake, then decelerated.

I was now on my feet with gun in hand and began moving towards the port side just as Alberto reached the top of the steps from the main deck, gun drawn. The Agent aimed at me. Without pausing to wonder why, I dove for the deck once again. Chet fired at Alberto, and the bullet tore through the back of the chair just above him. Ricardo wheeled at the sound and stared in disbelief at the scene, paralyzed. Alberto hesitated also, still training his gun on me. I rose up and fired at him. The bullet ricocheted off the metal railing, then Alberto wheeled, and fled down the stairway, and I raced after him. By the time I reached the top of the stairway, he had reached the far side of the main deck. I fired at him, but missed. He dove into the Hudson and swam to the waiting black boat. He pulled himself in, and the boat roared off, back in the direction of Manhattan. I whispered a quick, "Thanks, Hank," to my guardian angel, and then rushed back to Marilyn who was slowly raising herself to her knees. She smiled at me, and then turned her head towards Ricardo. "I'm not sure I like your choice of friends," she said with a short laugh.

Ricardo shook his head slowly. "I can't believe it. I've known Alberto for years! We used to be partners! What happened?" He scowled in exasperation.

Across the deck, Sid had identified himself to the passengers and was assuring them that everything was now in control.

Ricardo's expression had turned thoughtful. "Let's see," he began, "Alberto transferred to Washington about four years ago; he said he had met a girl down there. A slot had opened up as CIA liaison, so he bid for it and got it."

Ricardo and I looked at each other as the light of discovery dawned. "CIA?" I echoed.

Ricardo nodded. "That's got to be it. Somehow Bradshaw got to him."

Then his eyes widened. "Unless he was already involved! He was in the Green Berets too! And I'm almost certain he was in at the same time Bradshaw was!"

"You know," Marilyn interjected, "I thought there was something familiar about Alberto. Now I remember. I saw him talking to Wiley at one of those political fundraisers last spring. I'm certain of it!"

"That settles it," I pronounced. "You can't go back to Wiley."

Marilyn smiled wanly as she gazed into my eyes. "I had already made my choice."

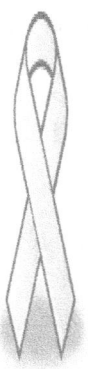

CHAPTER TWENTY-FOUR

The following Monday, Federal Marshals served Sullivan with a subpoena to appear before the San Francisco Grand Jury investigating oil industry price-fixing. Sullivan was furious when he announced it at the staff meeting, accusing everyone in the room of complicity with the Government and staring with his steel gray eyes at Walter Melville as he railed. Then he turned to Stockton. "Dean, I want to delay this as long as you can, and I want you to handle it for me in court."

"I can't and I can't."

"What in the hell are you talking about?"

"I can't delay it, and I can't represent you before the Grand Jury; you have to go in there alone."

Then he glowered at me. "Well, I'm not going to take the fall for this. See me after the meeting, Nick. And Walter, you and I will have lunch."

When Sullivan adjourned the meeting, I followed him down the hall to his office. He closed the door, took the seat behind his desk, and motioned to me to take one of the seats in front. "I've told you my position on your future," he began. "The man who runs this company must anticipate problems before they arise. You didn't give me the first warning of this Grand Jury investigation."

"Did you fix prices on the West Coast?"

"Don't tell me you didn't know about it!" Sullivan exploded. "Why do you think the prices were always so much higher than the rest of the country? You've been around OPEC! You know how it works!"

"I did not know it was going on!" I shouted.

"Never mind!" Sullivan roared. "If I go down, you do down with me! If you want my job, you've got to make sure that doesn't happen!"

After work I met Marilyn and Ricardo who were waiting for me in the deserted library at the Constitution Club. "What's wrong?" she asked, her face worried.

I grimaced "My job's in jeopardy." I explained the events of the day, but when I finished, my face brightened. "Now that I've told you, it doesn't seem that important anymore. Whatever happens, happens. Come on, let's go have a drink."

I led the way into the bar and seated Marilyn at a table next to the railing, away from the window. "What would you like?" I asked her as I sat down.

"A Virgin Mary, please."

I turned to Ricardo. "That sounds good to me."

"Three Virgin Marys, Cosmo," I told the waiter when he arrived.

After Cosmo retreated, I asked, "What did you tell Wiley?"

"I lied to him; I told him my mother had cancer, and I wanted to stay with her until the beginning of the fall quarter."

"What did he say?"

"He had a fit. He said he needed me to campaign with him. But I finally convinced him it would look good politically if I were tending to my sick mother."

I looked over at Ricardo. "Do you think Alberto knows who she is?"

"I didn't tell him. No. I don't think he could have made the connection."

"Maybe not," Marilyn interjected, "but he did accuse me of coming to see Nick, and he is having me followed."

"I just don't want him coming after you," I said, my voice full of concern. "I'm afraid Alberto may describe you to Bradshaw who probably will remember you. Or if he does mention you to Wiley."

"I've got Bradshaw covered all ways," Ricardo reassured us, "with tails, phone taps, and computer monitoring. Alberto hasn't contacted him yet."

"How did you manage to get him covered like that?" I asked.

"Remember my friend in Records that I mentioned at your Castle?"

I nodded.

"He finally broke Bradshaw's personal codes yesterday." He tuned his head to Marilyn. "Alberto didn't contact him, but Wiley sent him a computer message, confirming he had changed his schedule and would be at the reunion a week from Friday. Do you know what that means?"

At first her face was blank. "Oh my God," she whispered finally, dread spreading across her face. "It's their Green Beret Unit reunion."

"Where?" Ricardo asked, his voice urgent.

Marilyn spoke as though she were in a trance. "At the Beach Chalet. In San Francisco. A week from Friday. He'll find out the truth."

"No," I countered. "We'll find out the truth."

The following day Federal marshals came to our office and served subpoenas to twelve more of us, including Pat, Stockton, Melville, and me. Having argued before grand juries during his government tenure, Stockton informed us that Sullivan was the "target" and we were "subjects" which really meant we were targets as well. He led us in preparing our defenses. In front of the others on the subpoena list, he badgered, cajoled, and stroked each of us, inuring us to the certain multifaceted attacks by the San Francisco prosecutors. Sullivan had been right. I understood quickly how the West Coast Cartel worked because I had seen OPEC in action, firsthand. Sullivan and Melville had originally set up the organization, without Melville's boss, Calderone, even knowing about it. Nothing was disseminated in writing outside. The only documents were internal, and Sullivan had kept them all personally. I presumed the other oil company chairmen who were subpoenaed had limited their internal communication as well, so Sullivan maintained the Government couldn't have a documented case. Stockton refuted that contention, citing several anti-trust cases of employees who had kept personal documentation and turned state's evidence for reasons ranging from self-preservation to revenge.

Stockton eventually developed a strategy that we would deny everything, regardless of written documentation. If the government presented any evidence, Sullivan would blame Mark Hamilton, Melville's former assistant who had been killed in an auto accident right after the Las Palmas bombing. He had driven into a tree, without leaving skid marks. I remembered the accident of Marilyn's husband, John. I wondered how accidental both the deaths were.

The following Sunday, all twelve of us flew out to San Francisco on six different flights, following Company procedure of no more than two executives on any one flight. The next day Sullivan testified first, behind the closed doors of the grand jury courtroom. During the first break, Sullivan emerged from the courtroom looking homicidal. "How do they know what they know?" he spat, his face reddening with fury. "Goddamn bastards must have hacked their way into my computer files."

He turned to Stockton. "Isn't there a goddamn law against that?"

"Not if they can show probable cause."

"Never mind!" he exploded. "They're capable of anything! Whatever they can't find, they manufacture! They've got so-called 'evidence' in there I know I didn't write. I know there's a goddamn law against that!" He grabbed Stockton by the arm. "Come on, you've got to help me with my counterattack," he continued, leading him down the hallway.

Melville scowled. "That's a bad sign; Sullivan taking Stockton off alone like that. I know he's going to feed us to the sharks in there, and I'm not going to let him."

I raised my eyebrows. "What do you have in mind?"

"I have a Pearl Harbor file on this whole thing, just in case of a sneak attack like this. Oh, I was involved in it all right, but he planned everything and set up the deals. I was simply the executioner. If I were you, I'd dump my stock"

Melville was called to testify at 2 p.m. that afternoon. During the one hour and forty-five minutes he was sequestered, I operated out of an office down the hall that Ricardo had arranged for me. My cell phone rang constantly, with nothing but problems. It was one of those afternoons. When the bailiff appeared at the door at 3:45, I felt a sense of comic relief.

I followed him down the hall and into the grand jury courtroom. The twenty jurors sat huddled together on the right side of the room. The empty witness chair was in the center, and as I sat down, I felt like a gladiator. A short, young WASPY-looking Federal Prosecutor hovered over me as he swore me in. He drew himself up erect and announced, "I am Assistant U.S. Attorney Mitchell St. Clair. State your name please."

"Nick Shepherd," I replied.

"And who is your employer."

"Universal Natural Resources Company."

"And what is your position?"

"Senior Vice-President of Domestic Operations."

"Do you know why you're here?" St. Clair asked, bending down and hovering over me again,

"To tell the truth," I answered.

"Do you know what the truth is?" was his sarcastic next question.

"Probably better that you do."

The smooth, unlined face reddened, "We'll see," he mused, and then he began pacing back and forth in front of me. Finally, he asked, "In your business, Mr. Shepherd, what really counts?"

"Character counts."

"Oh, come on, Mr. Shepherd, don't you really mean profits count? Remember, Mr. Shepherd, you said you were here to tell the truth."

"I am. At one time, I would have given you the answer you wanted. But not now."

"Ah, now we're getting somewhere. At one time you conspired to fix oil prices to achieve higher profits." This was a statement, not a question.

"No," I replied. "I did not know about the West Coast conspiracy."

"So, you admit there is a conspiracy." Again, it was a statement.

"Not anymore. I just ordered a cut in our West Coast prices."

St. Clair cast his eyes to the ceiling, and then back at me. "Mr. Shepherd, how long have you been with Universal Natural Resources?"

"Fifteen years."

"Do you mean to tell me, Mr. Shepherd, that you have been with your company for more than a decade, you run domestic operations, and you did not know about the West Coast price-fixing conspiracy?"

"The conspiracy was established before my tenure. I only recently discovered its existence."

"And did you discover who set up this conspiracy?"

"Based on the written evidence, it appears that our President and Chairman, Bruce Sullivan met with other oil companies with Western operations to put a pricing mechanism into place."

"And, pray tell, how did you discover this conspiracy?"

"I was part of an FBI investigation."

"And you led the FBI to this written evidence?" St. Clair asked, arching his eyebrows.

"Not... not exactly," I answered, hesitating, sensing where St. Clair was going with this.

"I believed Mr. Sullivan was behind attempts on my life, and I thought there might be evidence in his private files."

"So, you just marched into his office, pulled open his file drawer and, voilà, incriminating evidence."

"No, we had assistance from one of my colleagues."

"Aha. A colleague. And just who is this colleague."

This guy was a real snake. "I'm sure she didn't have anything to do with this," I said.

"You are not the judge here, I am. And these grand jurors," he added with a wave of his hand. "Who assisted you in finding these files?"

"What are you implying?" I asked, feeling my anger mount.

"And I'm the one who asks the questions here. Answer it."

I paused as I remembered Stockton's words, "The Prosecutor will do everything he can to rile you. If you lose it, you're done." I took a deep breath, and then let it out. "Our Vice-President of Administration, Pat Campbell," I answered.

"And just how did she assist you in finding these files?"

"She knew where the passwords to Sullivan's computer files were kept."

"And just how did she know this?"

I didn't like this guy one bit, but I was committed to the truth. "She is a friend of Sullivan's secretary, Hazel Biggins." I explained that Sullivan changed the password every other day, and that Hazel kept them in a notepad in her desk. I went on to describe how Ricardo and I had found the notepad, gotten into Sullivan's computer, and found the files. I concluded with the highlights of the violations of Anti-Trust law committed by Sullivan and the other CEO's.

When I finished, St. Clair sighed. "Mr. Shepherd, that is quite an incredible story. It is so incredible in fact, that I don't believe you. I believe you and Miss Campbell planted those files to get rid of Mr. Sullivan, so you could take over UNRC."

"That's ridiculous!" I snapped.

"If that's so ridiculous, then what about that so-called 'Slaves' file that was planted."

"How did you—" I started. Then I remembered Ricardo had turned the entire file over to the U.S. Attorney's office. "Apparently," I continued, "the 'Slaves' memo was a fake—."

"And the West Coast memos were also," St. Clair interrupted. "Anyone, including you, could have planted them."

"Only if they had access to Sullivan's terminal," I challenged. "The West Coast files were generated on his terminal, and, of course, copies were generated on the mainframe. The 'Slaves' memo was found on the mainframe only, and it was generated outside the system from an unknown computer."

This took the wind out of St. Clair's sails, and his shoulders slumped forward. "But you could have gotten onto his computer," he said weakly.

"I didn't," I said. I looked over at the grand jury members. Their heads were nodding, and I knew they believed me.

Melville had been right. Ricardo called me at our San Francisco Regional Headquarters the next morning. "Two news flashes," he began. "First, my friend over at Justice tells me Sullivan testified that you were behind the whole conspiracy, which was OPEC inspired, and Melville was your confederate."

"Melville thought that might happen. He says he has evidence which proves Sullivan's guilt."

"That's what my friend said. Melville said Sullivan planned the entire conspiracy. The second flash," he continued, "involves Bradshaw and Alberto. Yesterday our team accessed a coded e-mail to Bradshaw from Alberto requesting a meeting at the Air and Space Museum. Bradshaw confirmed for 4:30. We didn't have to tail him since we knew where he was going, so he didn't have a clue we were there. I had a warrant out for Alberto, but when we tried to make the arrest, they both opened fire. One of our guys was killed, but he took out Alberto in the process. Bradshaw escaped, and we've lost him."

"I'm sorry to hear about Alberto," I commiserated. "I know you wanted him alive."

"I wanted him alive to get some answers! And Bradshaw's disappeared!"

"There may be one good thing that may come out of it, though."

"What's that?" Ricardo asked, with an edge of disappointment still in his voice.

"Mr. Big may have to come out."

Marilyn called shortly thereafter, panic penetrating every word. "Wiley's coming in tomorrow for a meeting with some big contributor of his here in Manhattan and wants to see me. What'll I do?"

"Meditate," I quipped.

Marilyn laughed despite herself. "It's not funny. Seriously, I'm scared. What'll I tell him?"

"Check your mother into the intensive care ward at Lennox Hill. I'll get Ricardo to arrange for beds for her, as well as you and your father. He can visit all of you there. Besides, I really don't think he wants to hurt you."

"Thank God you're in my life again," she whispered.

Just before 10 a.m., my phone rang. It was Marilyn. "How was your encounter with Wiley?" I asked.

"It was awful," she answered. "He ranted about my place being at his side, and that his campaign was more important to the country than my old dying mother. We were out in the hall, but Mom and Dad heard him, as well as half the hospital staff. The more I tried to quiet him down, the more enraged he became. Finally, I couldn't take it anymore, so I told him I was leaving him."

"You did?" I asked, incredulous. "What did he do?"

"He just stared at me with black hatred. I know he would have killed me on the spot if he thought he could have gotten away with it. Then he turned and stormed off."

"Look. I want you out of there. He may just come back and try. You can still catch the 5 o'clock flight out here. Call me at the Ritz Carlton when you get in."

"I'm going to go for the 3:45," she said.

She did make the 3:45 and called me from SFO Airport at 7:15. "Have you eaten?" she asked.

"No. I was kind of hoping to have dinner with you."

"Great, I'm starving. The Bistro meal they served on the plane was my lunch."

"I'll book us a table downstairs at the Terrace Room. Ricardo and Carib will stop by later. And I'd like you to stay in the other bedroom in my suite here at hotel the as well."

"See you soon," she said. "And thanks."

I was sitting on a Louis the 14th reproduction chair in the Ritz Carlton lobby, with FBI agents Sid and Chet standing nearby. The doorman pulled open the door, and Marilyn surged past with a grateful nod. I leaped to my feet as she flew across the room into my arms. We hugged each other until I felt my knees quiver. Echoing my experience, she said, "We'd better sit down before we fall down."

"Can you make it to the elevator?" I joked.

"If you hold me up," she replied, smiling.

I asked the bellman to take her luggage up to the room. We shuffled across the marble floor to the elevator, arms around each other. The elevator door was open, and we scampered in, followed closely by Sid and Chet. We were on the fifth floor, and I pushed the down button for the third floor and the restaurant. As we emerged from the elevator, we heard piano music drifting our way from beyond the bar. A gravelly voiced baritone was crooning, "The world will always welcome lovers, as time goes by." We strolled past the bar, still arm-in-arm, and the maitre d' greeted us with a flash of a smile. He granted the request I had made when I booked the table and seated us in the corner. He placed Sid and Chet next to us.

"Were you followed from New York?" I asked after Konrad, our German-accented waiter, took our tonic and lime orders.

"I don't think so. I snuck out the service entrance of my parents' apartment building, and I didn't see any one car following my cab. Traffic was pretty light."

"Good. I want to keep it that way. We've got to keep you out of Wiley's reach. Ricardo's said he would join us for dessert, so let's see if he has any ideas. Carib is going to stop by as well. He says he has some news, and he might have an idea as well."

"It will have to be a good one," Marilyn chuckled. "I'm sure Wiley can figure out I came running to you. And he won't have far to look—he'll be at the Beach Chalet Friday night."

"Along with Bradshaw and who knows who else."

We both ordered the Chef's Special, a baked ling cod with fresh tarragon, "caught and picked fresh this morning," according to Konrad.

As we were finishing our fish, I spied both Ricardo and Carib approaching our table. We all embraced, and then Ricardo and Carib sat in the 2 empty chairs at our table. "We ordered a chocolate soufflé for you, Ricardo, but we weren't sure when you were coming, Carib."

Carib flashed his smile. "It is just as well," he chuckled.

Konrad appeared, to take Carib's order. "Will you be having dessert, sir?" he asked.

"I'll have fresh fruit, please," Carib replied. Konrad nodded, turned, and then left.

"Any sign of Bradshaw?" I asked Ricardo.

"No, but he should show up at the Beach Chalet Friday night for the Green Beret reunion, if it's as important as I think it is."

"Even if he knows you're on to him?"

Ricardo smiled. "Particularly if he knows we're on to him."

"Have you ever heard of Rick Arnold?" he continued, looking around at us.

"Yes," Carib and I answered in unison.

Surprise flashed across Ricardo's face. "You both have?"

"After you," Carib said, nodding his head in my direction.

"Rick was with UNRC when I first signed on 15 years ago. We both worked in the International Division at that time. In fact, he took me under his wing and showed me the ropes. Some years later he got into a major dispute with Sullivan, who was running the Division at the time, and he left. He raised some capital and, with some Arab friends, started up Trans-Arabian Oil, the only private oil company in the Middle East. He's been hugely successful. In fact, he recently approached Sullivan about a merger of equals, but Sullivan turned him down."

I looked across at Carib. "How do you know Rick?"

"I've known him since the early days of his start-up. He wanted some of our heavy crude oil for his first refinery, and we granted him extended payment terms. And from time to time we swapped our heavy for his light crude.

"But," he continued, looking around at all of us, "we've just discovered he's connected to Mendez! I received an intelligence report that he met with Mendez six times over the past two years."

"No way!" I exclaimed. "Rick's a good guy!"

"I'm not sure I believe it either. We always had a good relationship. It is possible that he and Mendez have a legitimate business connection only.

"How do you know Rick?" he asked, looking at Ricardo.

"He sent an e-mail today to Bradshaw, confirming he would be arriving in San Francisco tomorrow."

We all looked at each other. "The reunion," we said in unison.

After we finished our desserts, I put down my spoon in the saucer, saying, "How about us all going for a run in Golden Gate Park tomorrow afternoon?"

"That's a wonderful idea, Nick," Marilyn said. "I haven't run in the Park for years."

"Count me in," Ricardo said. "You're keeping my men in shape, and I'd like some of that."

Carib looked serious. "You might need some help. I'll be there."

The following day the grand jury issued indictments against Sullivan and five other oil company CEO's for violations of the Sherman Anti-Trust Act, carrying a potential fine of $10 million for each company, $1 million for each CEO, as well as five years in jail. All companies' stock plummeted. I had considered unloading my large block the day before and decided against it. I thought about it again, but upon reflection after the big drop, I bought more.

After lunch, I noticed Pat hesitate at my open office door, then start to pass by, her long auburn hair bouncing off her shoulders as she walked. "Hey Pat," I called after her.

Pat stopped, turned, and strode into my office. "Why such a long face?" I asked.

"Oh, I guess this Grand Jury investigation has been more stressful than I thought."

"Now that the investigation is over, are you heading back to New York?"

"No, I thought I would run in the Dipsea on Sunday."

"The Dipsea?"

"It's a 7.1 mile run over in Marin, from Mill Valley to Stinson Beach. Speaking of running, are you still running in Golden Gate Park?"

"Yes."

"Have you run up Strawberry Hill?"

I laughed. "Another hill? No. I just go up Kennedy, across Kezar, and back down Martin Luther King."

"Strawberry Hill is quite nice. You run along Stow Lake, cross a bridge, and up the Hill. There's a magnificent view from the top."

"Do you want to join us today?"

"Us?"

"Yes, Marilyn just arrived, and Ricardo and Carib will be coming along as well."

"Thank you, I would," she said without smiling.

"We're meeting at the Beach Chalet at 5."

"See you there." She turned part way around, and then stopped. She faced me again. "I didn't want to be the one to tell you this," she began, "but I have a good idea whom your wife is seeing."

Despite myself, a pang of jealousy shot through me, as I demanded, "Who is it?"

"I don't know for sure," she hedged, "but I was passing one of Walter's watering holes in New York last week, and he and someone who sure looked like Susan stumbled out onto the street together."

I stared wide-eyed, incredulous. "Susan and Melville? I don't believe it."

"Well, I was pretty far away on the other side of the street, so I'm not really sure it was Susan."

"What does she see in him?"

Pat smiled, a bitter expression on her face. "He's a silver-tongued devil. He can make you believe you're the most beautiful woman in the world, and that you're the only one for him. And he is able to convince you repeatedly!"

I shook my head. "I'm really sorry to hear that. I was hoping she would find someone who would make her happy."

"Oh, he'll make her happy—for a while, until she finds out what a two-timer he is. Oh, what do I see in him!"

I left the office at 4:30 with Sid and Gary, and we drove out Geary, past the Cliff House, and found a parking space halfway down the hill along the Great Highway. The fog was rolling in from the Pacific, and we zippered up our sweat tops that covered our shoulder-holstered guns, as we emerged from the car. In the cool weather we didn't look out of place. We walked down the hill towards the Beach Chalet at a brisk pace to begin our warm-up.

As we reached the corner of Great Highway and Kennedy, I stopped dead in my tracks. Across the street, Susan and Melville were climbing the steps of the Beach Chalet. I blinked, not believing my eyes. Susan turned her head in my direction. It was her. No mistake. So, it was true! What was she doing in San Francisco? Was she that gaga over Melville? Then I remembered the one of the writers' conferences was here.

Moments later Pat came loping up from the south. I was still staring at the Bistro Chalet entrance. "What's wrong?" she asked, with no sign of breathlessness.

"You were right about Susan and Melville."

"I was?" she said, as though not comprehending my words.

"Yea. They just went inside the Chalet."

"What's she doing here?"

"She's here for a Writers Conference."

Pat scowled. "So, it is true."

Just then Marilyn, Ricardo, Carib, and Chet jogged across the street from Kennedy and pulled up in front of us. Only Ricardo's breathing was slightly labored. "Any trouble?" I asked.

"None," Ricardo breathed, "except for my lack of conditioning. The jackals weren't anywhere in sight."

"We didn't have any trouble either," I said. I looked back at Pat. "Are you ready?"

Pat hesitated, and then nodded wordlessly. "Lead on," I said, and she eased into a slow jog, leading the way across Great Highway, onto Kennedy, and past the Beach Chalet. I glanced up, as though looking for final confirmation that it really was Susan. Before my still unbelieving eyes, Susan was sitting down at a window table. She looked out but didn't appear to see us. Sid had fallen in behind me, followed by Marilyn, Ricardo, Carib, and Gary, with Chet bringing up the rear.

Pat led the way through the throng of runners who jammed the trail in both directions along the road. The fog thickened rapidly as we began the slow climb up Kennedy. We passed the Dutch Windmill and then reached the edge of the Golden Gate Park Golf Course. The fog was becoming even denser, and we could barely make out the golfers on the course.

At the juncture of Kennedy and South Drives, Pat took the left fork, staying on Kennedy. The trail began to rise more steeply as we passed the stables and the riding academy. A group of riders on their horses rushed past us on our right at a gallop. Pat was beginning to draw away from me. I looked back and saw that Marilyn was right behind me, but the rest of our group was dropping behind. I eased my pace, and shortly thereafter, Pat looked back, and then she slowed perceptibly. By the time we reached the baseball diamond, we were back in a tightly bunched cluster. A few minutes later we reached the intersection of Kennedy Drive and Crossover Drive.

Pat veered to the right at a forty-five-degree angle, onto a steep trail. Logs were dug into the dirt, and tall trees arched over the path. We reached the summit in less than a minute, and Pat slowed to a walk. "Let's take a break," she called back to us.

Picnic tables and barbeque pits spread out across the grassy knoll. Ahead lay the boathouse, a low wooden structure with wooden beams forming the siding, built on a cinderblock foundation. We rounded the building, revealing Stow Lake, with Strawberry Hill rising from the center of it. Pigeons, gulls, and brewer's blackbirds hopped along the path, and mud hens swam by with their heads bobbing with each stroke of their webbed feet.

When we reached the stone bridge, Pat began to run again, crossing to Strawberry Hill beyond. We followed and caught up to her as she began to ascend another steep trail. Railroad ties flanked the macadam path on the right side. By the time we reached the stone steps near the summit, I was gasping. "Close it up!" I heard Ricardo shout from right behind me. I looked back to see Sid, Gary, and Chet had fallen behind. The image of cattle being led to slaughter flashed into my mind. I looked across at Marilyn, and she caught my gaze. "I feel it too," she breathed.

We reached the top of the stone steps, and the terrain leveled out. We were all gasping for air, and Pat stopped, mercifully I thought for the moment. The rest of us stopped as well. "Let's ...rest a minute," Pat panted. A reservoir lay to the right of us, and a waterfall cascading over huge rocks was off to our left. Three workmen dressed in Golden Gate Staff garb leaned over their rakes as they made piles of what looked like dead leaves and branches. One of them looked up as we approached. "Wiley!" Marilyn gasped.

Suddenly Pat charged, screaming, "I can't do it!" Startled, Wiley stepped back, then reached inside his golden overalls and withdrew his gun, just as Pat hurtled headlong into him, both crashing to the ground. At the same time, the two other workmen had produced guns, and 2 more gunmen leaped up from behind the rocks on the far side of the waterfall. Pat's diversion had given the rest of our troupe time to reach our guns as well. As the bullets flew, I recognized Bradshaw and Mendez who, after the first volley, dashed for cover behind the rocks.

Pat and Wiley were struggling on the ground for his gun. A shot burst from the gun and Pat grabbed at her chest. Wiley flung her off him and struggled to his feet, aiming his gun at Marilyn. But Marilyn had recovered from her shock and was rushing towards him. She leaped into the air with a karate cry and slammed her right foot into his neck, snapping his head back. He fell back onto the lifeless body of one of the conspirators, who had fallen in the flurry of bullets, and lay still.

I glanced to the rear and spotted Ricardo collapsed on the steps we had just run up. Marilyn rushed over and pulled him to safety behind a large pine tree. In fury, I rushed toward the waterfall. Carib, Sid, and Chet were right at my heels, and we all dove for the protection of the rocks on the near side of the waterfall as a flurry of bullets flew at us. I peered over the rock and caught a glimpse of Mendez, his black eyes blazing with hatred. We both fired simultaneously, and his bullet whizzed past my ear. I heard a yelp, the clatter of Mendez's gun on the rock, and then a splash as it plunged into the pool of water just below the waterfall. I edged up again and saw Mendez grabbing his shoulder as he ducked down. Bradshaw fired at me, and the bullet ricocheted off the rock right next to my head, flinging dust into my eyes. Blindly I fired twice, and I heard Carib's, Sid's and Chet's guns shooting several rounds. I ducked behind the rock, blinking, and rubbing my eyes with my arm. Then there was silence.

"Are you all right?" Carib called after a few moments.

My vision cleared, and I nodded. I poked my head above the edge once again. Bradshaw was leaning against the far-side rock, and then he slid slowly down to the ground in a sitting position. His gun lay in front of him and he was smiling. A dark red blot was forming on the front of his uniform.

I leaped up from behind the rock and rushed over to him. Moments later, Marilyn and Carib were at my side. Sid and Chet ran on and grabbed Mendez who was trying to escape down the other side of the waterfall. I glared at Bradshaw and demanded, "Who is it?"

Bradshaw's smile widened, then he coughed, erasing his smile. "Who is it?" I roared.

Bradshaw smiled again. "What's long—" Another cough racked his body. "And slimy—" He coughed again. "And drags on the ocean floor?" Then a fit of coughs overcame him, his pupils rolled back in his head, and his torso slid along the side of the rock, down to the ground.

"How strange," Marilyn murmured, her eyes wide with wonder. "It seems to me I heard that riddle ages ago."

"What in the blazes does it mean?" I wondered, looking down at the lifeless body of Bradshaw, my voice tight with frustration.

Carib straightened up, and then dashed over to Pat who lay motionless in the dirt. He kneeled and felt her pulse. "She's alive!" Carib shouted as Marilyn and I approached. "I'll call 911," he continued, as he withdrew his cell phone from the pocket of his sweats and dialed.

Wiley was beginning to stir. He raised his head and looked around, his eyes darting like those of a trapped feral animal. I lowered my gun, aiming straight between his eyes. "Give me a reason," I growled. Hatred spewed out at me from his burning eyes, but he didn't move. "This isn't over," he spat.

"It is for you," I replied, feeling strangely calm.

Then I remembered Ricardo. "Cover him, Carib," I said, and then dashed back across the clearing. Ricardo was struggling into a sitting position. Sid and Chet approached, dragging Mendez between them. "Where's Gary?" he asked, sounding dazed.

"They got him," Chet answered, choking on the words.

"Are you okay?" I asked, leaning down towards Ricardo.

"I think so," Ricardo responded, still sounding disoriented. "The bullet caught me in the shoulder, and I fell back down the steps. Hit my head. Must have blacked out."

Just then two mounted policemen galloped up the path, guns drawn, and then eased their horses into the clearing. "What's going on?" one of them demanded.

"FBI," Ricardo identified himself. "Sid, show them your badge."

As Sid produced his ID, he said, "We called 911, but maybe you can bring help faster."

"San Francisco Medical Center is just up the road," said the cop. "I'll call them."

We moved back over to where Pat lay, and Carib began to minister to her. "You're through," I said to Wiley. "What's this all about?"

"It's a whole lot bigger than you are," Wiley said, glowering first at me and then at Marilyn. "You figure it out." He didn't respond to any further questions.

By the time the medical team arrived ten minutes later, Carib said, "The bleeding has slowed. She's going to be all right."

"Thank God," I said. "She knew this was going to happen, but she wound up saving our lives." I looked up at the heavens. "What's this all about?"

The answer didn't come right away. After the ambulances left with Pat and Ricardo, we began a slow jog back down to the beach. As the Beach Chalet came into view, Marilyn stopped. "I've got it!" she exclaimed. "The answer Bradshaw's riddle is Moby's dick."

I halted as well. "Moby's dick!" I exploded. "What's that supposed to mean?" I looked back towards Strawberry Hill as though the answer lay there. After staring up the hill for several moments, suddenly the meaning of Bradshaw's last words dawned on me. I looked around at the others and said, "I saw Susan going into the Beach Chalet. I've got to talk to her."

"I'm coming too," Marilyn asserted.

"We all are," Carib said, with a knowing look.

I broke into a run, heading for the Chalet. When I reached the steps, I scampered up to the second story, burst through the doorway, and jostled my way across the summertime-crowded room to the bar at the far end. People were standing three-deep at the bar and squeezed into the booths and chairs around the tables.

Melville and I spotted each other at the same time. A flicker of surprise flashed across his face, replaced a moment later with the squint-eyed expression of cunning. Until that moment, I hadn't been sure. Now I was. Susan sat to the left of Melville, and she stared wide-eyed as she caught sight of me approaching, then her eyes darted around the room as though looking for a place to hide. The chair to the left of Melville sat empty.

"What a surprise," Melville said, his voice lilting in mock merriment. He had removed his suit jacket and rolled up his sleeves, but I was sure he had a gun hidden somewhere. Melville took a long drink of his martini.

"I'm glad," I responded grimly, breathing heavily. "Does she know?" I continued, tilting my head towards Susan.

"No. Do they?" Melville asked, casting his eyes to Marilyn, Carib, and the FBI team who were rushing up behind me.

"No. Just you and me. And I guess Pat knew."

"Knew?"

"Wiley shot her."

"The casualties of war," Melville said.

"Know what?" Susan finally asked, her voice rising to be heard above the din of the room.

Melville glanced down at his Sprinter runner's watch, and then pressed one of the side buttons. Instinctively I stepped to the left just as the tiny missile whistled past my right ear and imbedded itself into the ceiling. I said a mental thank you to Hank as I dove across the table, and Melville, the chair. and I crashed to the floor.

I lay dazed for a moment, giving Melville the chance to spring up and dash past Marilyn, Carib, Sid, and Chet who stood transfixed, looking bewildered. I scrambled to my feet and rushed off in pursuit, shouting to Marilyn as I passed, "It's Melville!" Just then Rick Arnold appeared in the doorway and grabbed at me. Sidestepping the burly Arnold, I shouted back over my shoulder to Sid and Chet, "Grab this guy!"

By the time I reached the street, Melville was already across it and was disappearing into Golden Gate Park fog. I charged onto Kennedy, but my progress was slow, as I had to pick my way through the rush of oncoming cars and their blaring horns. Melville was wearing his street shoes, but he had a head start, and he was fast. He could easily lose me in the vast people, trees, rocks, hills, and fog that were Golden Gate Park.

When I reached the fork in the road, Melville was out of sight. Instinctively I took the path up the hill, between the two forks, towards the Equestrian and Polo Fields beyond. I reached the first summit, and peering through the thinning fog into the distance, I spied Melville cresting the next hill, and then dipping out of sight. I leaped ahead down into the next valley.

By the time I reached the spot where I had seen Melville last, Metson and Mallard Lakes lay before me. I spotted my quarry again and saw I was gaining. Melville shot a glance back over his shoulder and, seeing me, accelerated into the woods of Washington Memorial Bicentennial Grove, and disappeared.

With renewed energy, I sprinted down the hill. I swept across the field and into the woods, but Melville was out of sight. When I reached Transverse Drive, there was still no sign of him. I slowed, trying to decide if Melville had gone up Transverse Drive or continued straight on Martin Luther King. Again acting on instinct, I charged up the Transverse Drive hill.

I hesitated again when I got to path leading to the boathouse entrance. That would lead straight to Ricardo and the police, and I was certain Melville knew that. I swung onto the boathouse path anyway.

As I sprinted past the line of people and approached the boats on The Lake's edge, I sensed danger. I slowed, and then withdrew my gun from its holster underneath my zippered sweat top. By the time I reached the rock jutting out from the thick stand of trees, I was walking stealthily. Out of the corner of my eye I caught the glint of the late afternoon sun off metal, and I dove for protection of the rock just as Melville's bullet whizzed past my head and plunged into The Lake. Immediately a second bullet ricocheted off the top of the rock, skipped across The Lake like a flat stone, then sank.

I scurried to my left, then leaped up and fired three quick shots into the trees where the glint had been. Melville cried out as one of my bullets found its mark, but he responded with three quick shots of his own. I dove behind the rock again, but then heard the crashing of Melville's retreat through the woods. The shots would bring the police, and Melville had to escape before they arrived.

Melville was hit, but it hadn't slowed him down. He was headed in the direction of the Japanese Tea Garden, away from Strawberry Hill and Ricardo. I scrambled around the rock, up the bank, along the trail, and then plunged into the woods. Melville had another head start, and he was fleeing for his life.

A few minutes later, I broke free of the woods, but Melville had disappeared either over one of the many hummocks or into one of the clumps of trees surrounding the Tea Garden. I felt drawn to the path to the left and leaped onto it.

As I raced along, I heard a volley of shots ahead of me. Moments later I crested the next knoll, revealing a scene of two policemen, lying next to their horses. Melville shoved his left foot into the stirrup of one of the horses, mounted, and turned back in the saddle, aiming his gun at the remaining horse. Sensing the danger, the horse reared, and the bullet merely grazed his stomach. Melville dug the heels of his street shoes into his horse's flanks, and horse and rider bolted towards the Conservatory.

The other horse stood, waiting. Moments later I reached him, holstered my gun, and sprang into the saddle. Up ahead, Melville's blond hair blew back, and his left arm hung limp by his side. His gun and the reins he held in his right hand. His horse was bigger than mine, but the gap between us was shrinking rapidly as the smaller horse charged all out.

By the time Melville reached the bridal path, I was right behind him. Letting go of the reins, he turned in his saddle and aimed the gun at me as I lunged forward. I grabbed Melville's arm and unhorsed my quarry who fell heavily onto the horseshoe-pitted path, his gun skittering away. I reigned in my horse, dismounted, and dashed over to where Melville was desperately crawling to reach his gun. I whipped out my gun as fury raged up in me, but I caught myself as my arm snapped forward, Melville in my sights. The villain had just closed his hand around his gun in the dirt but froze as he looked up at my gun trained on him. "Do us both a favor," I spat.

Melville remained frozen on his knees for several seconds, staring up at me towering over him, his long, angular face contorted with hatred. Then he relaxed. "You're the luckiest—" Suddenly he flicked his right wrist upwards and fired, the bullet soaring over my head. At his movement I kicked at him instinctively, and his gun hurtled out of his hand and landed in a horse's hoof print on the bridal path. I ran over and picked it up, my eyes not leaving his kneeling figure.

I heard a distant thunder of horses' hooves and glanced back to see four mounted policemen bearing down on us. Just then Marilyn, Carib, and Sid burst out of the woods and raced over to us. Carib and Sid pulled Melville to his feet and Sid handcuffed him. Marilyn threw her arms around me and whispered, "Thank God," in my ear.

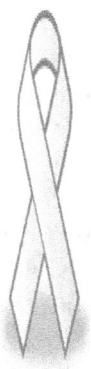

CHAPTER TWENTY-FIVE

We gradually fit the pieces of the puzzle together. Progress was made much more difficult because Bradshaw was dead, and Melville and Mendez weren't talking from their hospital beds at the Federal Penitentiary in Atwater. Wiley was silent as well. Ricardo had transferred Rick Arnold to Atwater and Pat to the Federal Pen in Dublin to facilitate the questioning.

Ricardo became satisfied that Susan had unwittingly given information to Melville, but she knew absolutely nothing of the conspiracy. She called me on Saturday, two days later. "I am so sorry, Nick," she said. "I've made a real mess of things."

"I haven't helped," I replied.

"You were really right about my drinking—it's totally out of control. I guess it took something like this for me to accept that I can't control it. Anyway, I'm heading back to Connecticut this morning to try to get my head on straight."

"Thanks for calling, Susan. I am sure you will beat this."

Ricardo finally got to Rick Arnold who had been involved in the plot only from a distance and had not actually known about the killings until after the fact. He filled in the details in exchange for immunity from prosecution.

I kept pushing Ricardo to find a string that would tie Sullivan into it, but each piece led only to Melville. Finally, the following Friday morning, Ricardo called me. "What are you doing for lunch?" he asked.

"I'm meeting Marilyn and Carib at Il Fornaio, but you're welcome to join us."

"Thank you, I will. I believe you will find it interesting, although probably not what you want to hear."

The maitre d' seated the four of us at a table outside, as I had requested. Once we were alone, Ricardo said, "Arnold is now telling all, and I have to conclude that Melville was trying to frame Sullivan for the bombing. He said that Sullivan's secretary, Hazel, was one of the many women in Melville's stable, and she planted those incriminating forged memos in the computer files. And Nick, Hazel told Melville that Sullivan had selected you to succeed him.

"But more importantly," he continued, "Sullivan was not a member of the inner circle of conspiracy which was spawned years ago in Melville's Green Beret unit."

"So that *was* the connection," I said.

"Yes, and Arnold was in the same outfit." He looked over at Marilyn. "And you know Wiley was as well."

Marilyn nodded. "And Bradshaw was also."

"I've been wondering about Mendez," Carib mused. "He wasn't part of the unit. Perhaps Bradshaw brought him in."

"Yes," Ricardo confirmed. "Bradshaw used both Mendez and Mundi in various CIA operations. He found them to be effective, so he brought them into this operation.

"It's still all so hard to believe," Marilyn said. "What were they trying to do?"

"Pure and simple, to rule the world, and they were deadly serious. All those years ago, they really got to know each other and discovered they had one thing in common; they wanted to change the world. They knew war was power, but the power behind the military was the politicians, and the power behind the politicians was money. So, they formulated a long-term plan to control all three."

"And Melville was the head," I postulated, but I said it as though it were a statement.

"Well, he thought that he was. He personally would control the world's largest company, the newly merged UNRC/Trans-Arabian consortium."

"How would he have pulled that off?" I asked. "Sullivan has more shares of UNRC stock than anyone."

"But he didn't have majority control. That's why Melville wanted to take Sullivan down on this anti-trust conspiracy. The value of the UNRC stock would drop, which it did, and he would buy all he could. He anonymously owned 80 percent of Trans-Arabian. With the UNRC stock being depreciated, Trans-Arabian could take them over. Melville would have had control of the combined company."

The waiter appeared and asked if we wanted a cocktail. "Now that the case is solved, Nick," Ricardo began, "Are you going to have a drink-drink?"

I smiled. "No, I don't think so. Not yet. I like being sober. But go ahead if you like."

All four of us ordered mineral water with lime.

"Where was Melville getting all the money for the takeover?" I resumed the questioning, bewildered by the scope of the conspiracy.

"That's another neat trick. Over the years he has been accumulating controlling interest in World Marine Bank, which is rapidly becoming number one. Melville was laundering Bellini's drug money through it, plus Arnold was arranging to funnel massive petrodollars from the Middle East into it. This would truly have become the *real* World Bank, not the one in Washington. Wiley was providing funds through Corporate Bank as well."

"And that would have funded the political arm," Marilyn guessed, her voice rising with the excitement of discovery. "With Wiley at its head as President of the United States. He told me that was his goal."

"Your right," Ricardo confirmed. "Arnold also told me Wiley had Senator Crock killed because Bradshaw's political dirty tricks weren't working fast enough. Bradshaw had Bellini, another Green Beret conspirator, order the hit. Wiley had to reach the Senate this year to run in the next Presidential election."

"Wiley wasn't very Presidential, laying in ambush for us in Golden Gate Park," I contended.

Ricardo shifted his gaze to Marilyn. "He wasn't. But it had become personal. He wanted to kill you himself for leaving him. You were right that morning at the Constitution Club. He would have killed you the night before if he had been able to get away with it."

The waiter returned with our drinks and took our lunch orders. When he had left, I said, "I never would have guessed Pat was involved. She despised Melville."

"But she also loved him; she loved him too much. Arnold believes she didn't know about it until the very end; she probably stumbled onto some piece of evidence which she confronted him with."

"And he probably admitted it," I suggested, "but I had de facto spurned her, so he was able to convince her he still loved her and to help him. Pat always said he could charm gold from misers."

"But at the last moment she couldn't go through with it," Carib said. "She saved our lives. How is Pat?"

"She's still in a coma, but the doctors think she'll be coming out of it soon," I replied.

"And Melville used Susan as well," I continued, knowing a hint of sadness crept into my voice.

"Yes," Ricardo agreed. "Arnold said she inadvertently gave him a great deal of information about you. Both of you were lucky to have survived that chase on the way to your Castle. But that shows you how truly ruthless he was; he would have sacrificed Susan to get you."

Ricardo shook his head. "Arnold also told me Melville got some sort of perverse satisfaction from sleeping with his arch-rival's wife. Yet he didn't care if she lived or died. Have you seen her?"

The conversation ceased while the waiter ambled up with our pasta specials and served them with great care. When he had left, I answered, "No, I haven't seen Susan, but she called me last Saturday to say she was sorry for everything. She called me again this morning to accept my property settlement proposal. She's started going to Alcoholic Anonymous meetings."

"Do you think you could put it back together with her?" Marilyn asked, with what was a tinge of fear in her voice.

"No," I said, shaking my head, "I couldn't. The good that we had was too little and over too soon. Nothing's left. And there's too much anger, hurt and betrayal on both our parts. She's strong; she'll beat the alcohol thing and get her life back together. Just not with me."

Marilyn smiled, a relieved expression on her face. She turned to Ricardo. "Bradshaw's the one who really fascinates me. I guess he appeals to my wild side. I mean here the man is dying and he gives us a riddle to lead us to Melville. It's as though the whole thing was a game to him."

"In many ways, it was just a game to him. He was brilliant, always at the top, including that Green Beret Unit. It appears he was just playing with Melville, letting him think he was in command, but if they had been able to carry the whole conspiracy off, Bradshaw would have wound up number one."

"But he was deadly serious," I contended. "I heard him tear Mundi apart at the Houston Airport. And you should have seen him in some of our meetings."

"He definitely had that side to him," Ricardo agreed, "but it was still part of the grand game he was playing. My friend in CIA records has provided me with unbelievable stories of the jokes he would play in many of those deadly situations. And he must have thought the funniest joke of all was that you shot him blind, with dust in your eyes. I'm sure that's why he was smiling."

"Maybe so…" I mused. "He always did like a good joke. He must have really gotten a kick out of Golden Green, knowing it would blow engines."

"I'm sure he did. He's the one who got it from Don Stanley in Iraq and gave it to Melville. Melville provided it to discredit you in Sullivan's eyes when it failed, as well as cause UNRC stock to drop.

"The P.P.I.P was also part of his game. He created the Puerto Rican terrorist group, had them carry out the amateurish bank robberies and kidnappings, but the real goal was the bombing."

Ricardo chuckled. "Probably his best private joke was what he called his plan. Remember the State Department's Operation Horseback to foster OPEC?"

Marilyn and I both nodded.

"And Slaves is the U.S. OPEC?"

We nodded again.

"Well, Slaves On Horseback was the computer name for his personal takeover plan. He was taking over OPEC, the UNRC industry, the world's largest bank, and the U.S Government itself. He was the king walking on the ground who would unhorse his slaves."

He chuckled again. "And you unhorsed him—and Melville as well."

I shivered. "I hate to think —" I didn't have to finish the sentence.

Months passed. Sullivan was found guilty of anti-trust violations and sentenced to three years in jail. Together with my new, larger block of stock, I led a successful stock proxy fight to oust him from UNRC. The Board of Directors installed me as Chairman. At once, I removed Flannery and Casey for their IRA activities. The FBI never could link Sullivan to them in those activities, but I remained convinced he was the main perpetrator. Stockton, the Company's corporate counsel, was found guilty of obstruction of justice for protecting UNRC during his tenure at the Justice Department and sentenced to 3 years in jail as well. I spearheaded his removal from the Board.

With the benefit of Rick Arnold's testimony, the jury found Melville, Wiley, and Mendez guilty of murder, and the judge sentenced them to execution.

Marilyn returned to Stanford to teach the fall quarter, and I commuted transcontinentally every weekend. On Sundays we attended services at Stanford Memorial Church. On the last Sunday in September Reverend Renaud announced he was deviating from the regular lectionary, as he had a while back. "You may remember," he said, "that the last time I took the liberty, I urged all of us to strive each day to become more God-like. Now I would like to look at what stands in our way, which needs to be overcome. We'll first look at Genesis 3, verses 2 through 6."

He slipped on his reading glasses and began, "The woman answered the serpent, 'We may eat of the fruit of the trees in the garden; it is only about the fruit in the middle of the garden that God said that we should not eat, or even touch it, or we will die. But the serpent said to the woman, 'You certainly will not die. God knows well that the moment you eat of it your eyes will be opened, and you will be as gods who know what is good and what is evil.'

'The woman saw that the tree was good for food, pleasing to the eyes, and desirable for gaining wisdom. So, she took some of its fruit and ate it, and she also gave some to her husband, who was with her; and he ate it.'"

With both hands Reverend Renaud carefully turned the thick sheaf of pages of his Bible from the beginning to near the end. "Now I'd like to look at what the First Epistle of John, Chapter 2, verses 14 through 17, says about overcoming Satan."

With his index finger he pushed the center of his glasses frame back up to the bridge of his nose. "I have written to you, fathers, because you have known him from the beginning. I have written to you, young men, because you are strong, and the word of God abides in you, and you have overcome the wicked one.

"Love not the world, nor the things that are in the world. If any man loves the world, the love of the Father is not in him.

"For all that is in the world, the lust of the flesh, and the lust of the eyes, and the pride of life, is not of the Father, but is of the world.

"And the world passes away, and the lust therein, but those that do the will of God abide forever."

The Reverend flipped a few pages to his final reading. "And now let's see what Revelation, chapter 20 promises us."

He resumed reading, "And I saw an angel come down from heaven, having the key of the bottomless pit and a great chain in his hand. And he laid hold on the dragon, the old serpent, which is the Devil and Satan, and bound him a thousand years, and cast him into the bottomless pit, and set a seal upon him, that he should deceive the nations no more, till the thousand years should be fulfilled: and after that he must be loosed a little season.

"And I saw thrones, and they sat upon them, and judgment was given unto them: and I saw the souls of them that were beheaded for the witness of Jesus, and for the word of God, and which had not worshiped the beast, neither his image, neither had received his mark upon their foreheads, or in their hands; and they lived a thousand years.

"But the rest of the dead lived not again until the thousand years were finished. This is the first resurrection."

The Reverend cleared his throat, and then continued, "Blessed and holy is he that has part in the first resurrection: on such the second death has no power, but they will be priests of God and of Christ and will reign with him a thousand years.

"And when the thousand years are expired, Satan will be released from his prison, and will go out to deceive the nations which are in the four quarters of the earth, Gog and Magog, to gather to them together to battle, the number is like the sand of the sea.

"And they invaded the breadth of the earth and surrounded the camp of the saints about and the beloved city: But the fire came down from God out of heaven and devoured them.

"The devil who deceived them was thrown into the lake of fire and sulfur, where the beast and the false prophet are. There they will be tormented day and night forever."

Reverend Renaud paused, and then he looked across the top of his reading glasses at Marilyn and me in the first pew.

"The concept of original sin in Eden is familiar to most of us."

I nodded as I remembered learning Adam and Eve eating the fruit from the forbidden Tree of Knowledge.

"So too is idea of redemption," he continued, "offered by Jesus who encourages us to resist Satan and follow him. John writes that fathers have done battle with the wicked one their whole lives, lost many of those struggles, but ultimately triumphed. The young people are strong and have won the first battle. But Satan is strong, and the young must remain vigilant as they age. As Jesus was tempted to turn stone into bread, we are tempted by the lust of the flesh. Similarly, Satan flashed all the riches of the world before Jesus to seduce Jesus with lust of the eyes. Finally, the Devil tempted Jesus with the sin of pride by encouraging him to leap from the temple pinnacle because he was the son of God. These are the sins of the world we are all confronted with. It is only by being sensitive to the will of God and having the willingness to follow His path that we can win the war against Satan."

Reverend Renaud paused, and then smiled as he looked around at all of us again. "What may not be as familiar to you is the passage from Revelation. This book is far out there and has been interpreted in any number of ways. To me what's fundamentally important is Satan's deception is a powerful force that we do, our forefathers did, and our progeny will have to deal with. Who knows when we will reach that first thousand years when Satan is chained and impotent? Who knows when he will break his bonds and return for his short but devastating seduction? Revelation does promise us that if we remain sensitive to and resolute against temptation, and we remain sensitive to and act upon God's will, we don't have to worry about this earthly time continuum."

Reverend Renaud lifted his hand from the podium, palms heavenward and shrugged his shoulders.

"Perhaps we all go through this scenario in this lifetime. Satan tempts us, we succumb, ask for forgiveness, receive it, and are strengthened the next time the evil specter rises in our lives. We resist, and Satan is imprisoned. Then in the 'mid-life crisis,' we choose the wrong path again. If we are lucky, strong, blessed, or whatever, we overcome Satan once again and we cast him out forever. Amen"

Reverend Renaud closed his Bible, retreated to his chair, and then bowed his head. The congregation followed suit. In the silence that ensued, I thought about my pursuit of the worldly. Reverend Renaud had called them sins of flesh, beauty, and pride. I knew they had been driving me my entire life. I had achieved the worldly, and it still wasn't enough. Now I felt hugely grateful that I was beginning to see past the worldly to what was beyond. I saw God's path opening before me. I had rediscovered love. I had seen death, and I had learned that life was a blessing, a gift to be lived the way God intended, not the way I intended. *And I knew I was ready to give new life at last.*

I was overwhelmed by Reverend Renaud's conjecture that we can go through the entire process of sin, redemption, succumbing again, and final deliverance, all in this lifetime. Then I remembered Carib's exhortation of long ago, "Life is to be lived one day at a time."

I felt Marilyn stir next to me, and I opened my eyes. She had the most serene look on her face, and then we both smiled and joined hands, fingers intertwining.

After the service, Reverend Renaud greeted us at the top of the steps leading down to the Quad. "Good morning, you two. You're becoming my best customers."

"We like what you're offering, Roger," I replied. "Although today's sermon was quite a mindful…or perhaps I should say a soulful."

"Ah, you did get one of the points," Roger replied. "But don't let it overwhelm you. Just stay open to seeing God's way every day, and He'll take care of the rest."

"Thanks, Roger. That's good advice. I was feeling overwhelmed. Marilyn's way ahead of me on this."

Marilyn grinned. "Maybe by a few steps right now. But you're catching up fast."

Susan's and my divorce was granted in early December. Susan called me to let me know was still going to AA meetings and that one day her writer, Robert Sand, showed up at a meeting as well. They started dating, and now they planned to marry and have children.

Marilyn and I decided to get married Christmas Eve in an intimate ceremony at Memorial Church. Carib and Ricardo flew in to share our joy. After the wedding, we drove down to Big Sur.

Later that night, as we lay together, quivering with excitement long suppressed, Marilyn gazed up at me. "Tonight's the night," she chuckled.

Much later that night, I snuggled up against Marilyn and murmured, just before I drifted off, "I wonder when we will be three."

www.ingramcontent.com/pod-product-compliance
Lightning Source LLC
Chambersburg PA
CBHW061551170626
46811CB00001B/162